The pursuit of perfection . . .

"I am executing the duty you assigned, Taercenn Nath," Rhys replied without making eye contact. "It appears I misunderstood your intent." He had expected criticism for hiring the giants, he even expected to be taken to task for allowing young Yelm to trigger the backup plan . . . but he never expected Nath to stand before him with real murder in his eyes.

"We will discuss your failings in more detail shortly," Nath said, dismissing Rhys's defense with a wave of his hand as he drew his sword with the other. The taercenn stepped back, raised his weapon, and drove it deep into Yelm's skull between the eyes, killing the youth instantly.

. . . is the survival of the fittest.

Rhys could not stop a short cough of surprise and objection. Yelm was of the Hemlock pack, and thus Yelm was Rhys's to kill if he decided killing was necessary. As he saw the spark of life abruptly go out of the young hunter's eyes, Rhys realized he'd already decided it wasn't.

Taercenn Nath withdrew his blade. He wiped it clean on Yelm's tunic before the youth's body could topple, and then Nath turned to Rhys.

"Taercenn, that was—"

"That was discipline, hunter," Nath said. "Pack discipline. Elf discipline. Gilt Leaf discipline. You should try it some time."

There can be no mercy.

Well-respected authors Cory J. Herndon and Scott McGough collaborate for the first time on an exciting new Magic: the Gathering® series.

EXPERIENCE THE MAGIC

ARTIFACTS CYCLE

The Brothers' War
Jeff Grubb

Planeswalker
Lynn Abby

Time Streams
J. Robert King

Bloodlines
Loren Coleman

INVASION CYCLE

The Thran (A Prequel)
J. Robert King

Invasion
J. Robert King

Planeshift
J. Robert King

Apocalypse
J. Robert King

MIRRODIN CYCLE

The Moons of Mirrodin
Will McDermott

The Darksteel Eye
Jess Lebow

The Fifth Dawn
Cory J. Herndon

KAMIGAWA CYCLE

Outlaw:
Champions of Kamigawa
Scott McGough

Heretic:
Betrayers of Kamigawa
Scott McGough

Guardian:
Saviors of Kamigawa
Scott McGough

RAVNICA CYCLE

Ravnica
Cory J. Herndon

Guildpact
Cory J. Herndon

Dissension
Cory J. Herndon

TIME SPIRAL CYCLE

Time Spiral
Scott McGough

Planar Chaos
*Scott McGough &
Timothy Sanders*

Future Sight
*Scott McGough &
John Delaney*

Lorwyn Cycle · Book I

Cory J. Herndon and Scott McGough

Lorwyn Cycle, Book I
LORWYN

©2007 Wizards of the Coast, Inc.

Cover art by Mark Zug
First Printing: September 2007

9 8 7 6 5 4 3 2 1

ISBN: 978-0-7869-4292-3
620-95958740-001-EN

U.S., CANADA,
ASIA, PACIFIC, & LATIN AMERICA
Wizards of the Coast, Inc.
P.O. Box 707
Renton, WA 98057-0707
+1-800-324-6496

EUROPEAN HEADQUARTERS
Hasbro UK Ltd
Caswell Way
Newport, Gwent NP9 0YH
GREAT BRITAIN
Save this address for your records.

Visit our web site at www.wizards.com

Dedication

The authors gratefully dedicate this book to the best writing teachers they ever had:

Steve Dixon of The Johns Hopkins University in Baltimore, MD and Sean Kidrick of Rose Valley Elementary in Kelso, WA

Acknowledgments

The authors wish to thank Editor Susan Morris, the *Magic: the Gathering®* Creative Team, and the legion of designers, writers, editors, and artists at Wizards of the Coast who help make these worlds exist.

The authors extend their gratitude to Boccherini, The Long Winters, They Might Be Giants, J.R. Cash, Bruce Dickinson, Simon Pegg, Nick Frost, Edgar Wright, Ricky Gervais, Vorenus, Pullo, Tony, Silvio, Paulie, Christopher, Carmella, and The D.

Cory special-thanks the brilliant, beautiful, and awesome S.P. Miskowski for inspiration, love, and support; and the razor-clawed Bayliss and Remo for the noisy, sometimes painful wake-up calls.

Scott also wishes to special-thank all those who helped him keep it together this winter: his friends in Seattle, his mad dingo girlie, the Kitten Brothers/Sons of Snowpea, a shopping mall filled with zombies (and power tools), and all the noble fighting men of the 13th legion. Thirteen!

CHAPTER 1

A small party of elves reached the road marker at the edge of the Gilt Leaf Wood an hour after sundown. As a signpost, the carved and sculpted trunk of the ancient, rust-colored oak stood in stark contrast to the lush and varied trees that made up the rest of the forest. The marker's carefully preserved bark was cut with the elegant, overlapping seals and symbols of every noble elf who had passed this way. Many of the seals still glowed with residual magic, for there had been much traffic through here recently, due in large part to the guests traveling to the upcoming wedding festivities.

Maralen eyed the glowing markers and fought back a sense of urgency that was not hers to voice. The wedding train should have arrived much sooner. It would have if only the bride had not lingered so long over her appearance. Peradala moved among the highest echelons of elf society. However, Maralen did not, so there was no argument to be made. Impatience from a subordinate like Maralen, no matter how justified, would earn only a rebuke— assuming the misdeed was even acknowledged.

Besides, a bride running late was a far cry from a catastrophe. Since Peradala had not yet met her intended husband in person, it was understandable that she took such drastic measures with her appearance to ensure a perfect first impression. By definition, Peradala was Perfect, an acknowledged member of one the most revered elf castes; elite and exalted even among the nobility. She was remarkably beautiful, her face and body, exquisite examples of delicate symmetry. Her eyes were wide and dark, her elegant features, sharp. Her hair was long and lush, and the top of her forehead was crowned with two short, gracefully curving horns. Yet as strikingly beautiful as she was without effort, it still took time and skillful effort to make her perfectly beautiful, to have her outward form match the sound of her flawless voice.

Elf castes were ancient, immutable things that superseded tribal boundaries, a universal hierarchy of merit that separated the elves according to their inner worth and their outer value. Perfect elves occupied the pinnacle of influence. Maralen was of the next highest caste, the Exquisites, who stood over the Immaculates, who in turn commanded the mere Faultless. Faultless was the lowest status an elf could have and still be an elf. To sink any lower was to lose Nature's Blessing entirely; such wretches had no status and deserved no name.

Tribes, on the other hand, were broken up along geographical and familial lines. No two tribes were equal in strength or number, but the elves of Lorwyn maintained relative peace through arranged marriages and rough diplomacy. The greatest of the tribes was the Gilt Leaf; guardians of the great forest whose name they shared and the masters of the lower species that infested so much of the world. There were none more perfect than the Perfects of Lys Alana, the Gilt Leaf tribe's shining capital, and soon Peradala of the Mornsong would join their number. Peradala's voice was acknowledged as the most beautiful in all of Lorwyn, most of all by her intended, the elf named Eidren. As Peradala's sweet singing had earned her a place among the most exalted of elves, so had Eidren's astounding ability to manipulate and sculpt the living trees of the Gilt Leaf earned him his place. They were an excellent pair, Perfect apart but so complementary to one another that they were even more glorious together.

Their respective tribes were not so well matched. Many things separated the Mornsong tribe from the larger, more powerful Gilt Leaf. Dialect, territory, wildlife, and hunting rituals were just a few differences that occurred to Maralen as she rode precisely ten steps behind and four steps to the right of her mistress. She was the only personal servant permitted to ride so close to Peradala. The rest of the party—the various admirers and courtiers and the Chorus that followed Peradala everywhere—were obliged to follow at a far more respectful distance.

Maralen's proximity was not simply an honor but a pragmatic necessity: it was her role to fulfill whatever whims or needs Peradala might require, however seemingly frivolous. Maralen had to anticipate Peradala's orders almost before they were given. As such, she had gained a special insight into the workings of the Perfect mind. Without thinking, Maralen knew Peradala was fixated on the same thing as everyone else: How Gilt Leaf standards of beauty differed from those of the Mornsong, if they differed at all.

Maralen did not need telepathy or mind powers to know the thoughts of the others. The matter on all their minds affected them directly and personally, as members of the Perfect's circle had to look the part and embody their mistress's glamorous aesthetic.

All minds except, perhaps, those of the Chorus. Maralen tended to overlook the dozen or so elves who marched in formation and wore the distinctive silvery robes of Immaculate vocalists. Peradala's Chorus continued their low, continuous, ever-changing melody, standing ready at all times to accompany their most splendid and Perfect mistress if she should burst into song. Even while Peradala slept, the Chorus continued to sing, rotating in six-member shifts like guards at a town gate.

Despite the Chorus's efforts, however, their most splendid and

Perfect mistress was not in a singing mood. Peradala did not sing without reason, and she had none at present.

It was a sign of how far from glory the Mornsong had fallen that any elf, let alone a Perfect's own entourage, would have to consider whether the Gilt Leaf would accept their mistress's beauty. None dwelt on the differing standards more than Peradala herself, Maralen knew, as her mistress tended to obsess over her appearance precisely because her voice's beauty set such a high standard. If Peradala allowed her vocal talent to completely outstrip her physical beauty, her status as a Perfect might be questioned. As a mere Exquisite, Maralen thought this rather foolish, but knew too well that her lot was not to give advice unless it was requested.

Peradala's impending nuptials would, in all likelihood, mean the end of the Mornsong as a distinct elf tribe. The Gilt Leaf would extend their influence, and in twenty or thirty years only the eldest of Lorwyn's short-lived elves would remember the Mornsong tribe. Yet the Mornsong ways would survive. If Peradala married as well as she planned, the songs themselves would echo across the woodlands for generations.

Peradala guided her long-legged cervin up to the marker tree. She could not pass by without leaving word that a Perfect elf had trodden this path. Strict elf laws directed her to leave her seal with the most potent magic she had to offer, and only a solution of pure riverwater and moonglove could permanently etch the aged bark of the way marker.

"Maralen," Peradala called from atop her cervin. The lithe, deerlike animal's pale fur glistened in the starlight that streamed past Peradala's elegantly curving horns. "I require fresh moonglove."

"Of course, most splendid and Perfect Peradala."

"Off with you, then." Peradala sniffed. "There have been

more than enough delays." As if the delays had been the maid-in-waiting's fault!

Fortunately, Maralen was no novice when it came to finding moonglove in the wild. Every elf, even Perfects, carried a small supply of the plant's extract somewhere on their persons for emergencies and for etching way markers. Maralen had already exhausted her store of moonglove on previous way markers. That Peradala had forgotten to bring her own supply was a sign of her anxiety.

The outer edge of the Gilt Leaf Wood was as likely a place as any to find good moonglove. In fact, it was probably better than most, if you wanted quality. Moonglove could not be cultivated, but the frighteningly poisonous flower could be encouraged to grow, especially in dense, unoccupied stretches of forest. The Gilt Leaf were masters of such encouragement, and Maralen didn't have to go far before she spotted the distinctive blue-white bells glowing softly beneath the boughs of a young bloodsap cedar. Moonglove grew on almost any tree, but the bloodsap made the effects of the flower's poison even more potent.

Maralen was still close enough to the party to call back, "Perfect, a good omen. I've found a most fine and uncommon bloom. I beg a moment to fetch it for you."

"I do not require frequent reports," Peradala replied. "I require moonglove—and river water with which I shall dilute the poison in the prescribed manner. Speak to me again when you possess it, Exquisite, and not before."

The Exquisite in question concealed a sigh. Peradala only called her "Exquisite" when she was displeased. Maralen nodded as pleasantly as possible before returning to the flowers and the problem of how best to retrieve the bloom of her choice. The spongy forest floor was a mat of mosses and ground-hugging vines of ivy, carpet oak, and intermittent brambles, covering who knew how many rodent holes. Maralen wondered how the Gilt Leaf got about in their famous homeland with these vines growing everywhere. She'd seen their likes back home in Arbor Morning but not this thick.

Leading the cervin to the side of the trunk and leaping from there to the lowest branch was out of the question—the risk of her mount's slender legs being caught in rodent holes and brambles was too great. Maralen paused to stretch her spine and neck, and then vaulted backward off her mount. In the process she turned a full somersault and landed on both booted feet. Carefully navigating the brambles that littered the forest floor, Maralen made her way to the base of the tree.

Moonglove flowers never grew less than ten feet from the ground, but this specimen was much higher. The Exquisite's silver dagger glittered in the scattered light of sunset as she placed the blade between her teeth and wrapped both arms as far as she could around the young cedar trunk. She dug into the bark with surprisingly sharp fingernails, braced a foot against the tree, and shimmied up the rough, cracked bark.

Maralen's fingers had just reached the tangled cluster of fibrous roots that held the moonglove fast to the tree when she felt a sharp and sudden pain on the back of her hand. She let out a short exclamation and jerked back her outstretched arm. She heard a chattering sound and craned her neck to see what had bitten her. Some kind of stinging insect, by the look and sound of it. She could hear its buzzing wings, but a direct look at the thing was impossible as it hovered just out of her field of vision, hidden in the shadows.

Tentatively, she extended her hand toward the moonglove again. She could still hear the buzzing, but it sounded as if it were coming from many places at once.

It was then Maralen noticed another change in the sounds

of the forest, beyond the buzzing of the mysterious insects. Something else was different in the aural landscape. The scattered birdsong and arboreal rodents' chirps hadn't changed in frequency or pitch, so whatever the stinging bugs were they didn't seem to be disturbing the rest of the local fauna. It took another moment for her to put her finger on it, as she flexed her long, slender ears to pick up the slightest variation in the background. And suddenly the difference was shockingly obvious.

The Chorus had stopped singing.

This was unheard of! It would fall to Máralen to discipline the singers, and she did not relish the idea of serving as the conduit for Peradala's most extreme ire. For the Chorus to cease creating their ever-present vocal backdrop was an unthinkable insult to their most splendid and Perfect mistress. The strange silence grew ominous, and Maralen placed thoughts of punishment aside. The Chorus willingly falling silent was unpardonable and unlikely, but the entire elf party doing so was a matter of far more serious concern.

Ominous silence or not, it would not do to return without the moonglove she'd been sent to collect when it was inches from her fingertips. Maralen reached up, stretching as far as she could, and plucked the moonglove from its home with far less delicacy than was normally prescribed. Whatever had stung her before left her alone, though she could feel the breeze in her hair from its tiny wings—it was watching her, and it was close by, hovering just out of sight. Its proximity sent an involuntary shiver down Maralen's spine, and the need to get both feet back on the ground overwhelmed her other senses. The maid-in-waiting jammed the flower into her belt as she released the tree trunk, spinning to land on both feet.

Maralen faced the road, gulping breath to replace what the fifteen-foot drop knocked out of her, but she saw nothing and nobody from Peradala's entourage. There was nothing where the cervins should have been peacefully nipping at low new growth and nothing where the Chorus should have been arranged to surround Peradala with tonally perfect song. Nothing. No admirers, sycophants, or bodyguards distributed respectfully along the open road. The entire Mornsong contingent awaiting Maralen's return was gone. Nothing but the marker, the road, and the forest remained—none of which could have been expected to depart in any case.

Maralen moved quickly but carefully back to the road. The sun had begun to set, and a stale breeze raised a dusty haze over the forest floor. Maralen felt real panic until she finally spotted a host of familiar faces and figures.

They were all there, arranged as they had been on the far edge of the road. Peradala sat in glorious repose atop her Blessed golden cervin. Maralen smiled briefly, raising a hand to hail her mistress, and received not even a nod in reply.

The Mornsong bridal party was as it had been, with one difference. The mounted nobles and marching chorus were upright but motionless. They stood rigid, frozen like topiary hedges cut into the shape of elves on a windless morning. Maralen stared, unable to formulate an explanation. She heard a crack and a slithering sound, and the road grew brighter as the uncanny glow from the dusty fog increased.

Maralen gasped as the newly illuminated scene presented itself. Thick vines, covered in blue flowers, wrapped tightly around the elves' throats. The Mornsong were choke-tethered like a pack of cuffhounds before the hunt. Their eyes were open, their mouths gaped, and the vines cinched tighter, doubling and redoubling around the elves' necks. The air above their heads was thick with dark, buzzing shapes that gestured with sharp-tipped limbs and sneered at Maralen, their eyes glittering in the light of the setting sun.

They were dead, all dead, that much was obvious from the frozen fear on their faces and the crushed windpipes beneath their chins. Only Peradala wore an expression of mild surprise rather than shock, as if her sudden and silent death was more inconvenient than painful.

She burst into a run the moment her heart resumed beating. "Perfect!" Maralen called, "Peradala!" She made it several feet before she caught one toe on a ropy vine whose other end wrapped around a Chorus member's neck and flew toward the writhing tendrils on the ground. She instinctively thrust her arms forward and splayed her fingers to make as little contact with the aggressive plant as possible. Those parts of her that did touch it—her palms and knees—tingled and grew numb.

Maralen tried to shout for her Perfect mistress once more, but she failed. Her limited contact with the vines appeared to have stolen her voice. This confirmed to her that the vines weren't a wild or natural phenomena of the Gilt Leaf Wood but dark magic that already had a hold on her.

The numbness spread as the vines curled up Maralen's spine and wrapped around her throat, pulling her off the ground. Other tendrils lashed at her like whips, slicing into her Exquisite skin, encircling her wrists and ankles. Strung up like a jester's marionette, almost lost in pain and panic, Maralen still felt the tiniest ray of hope. Whatever was happening to her, it was not elf magic, not one of the spells that the Gilt Leaf used to convert living things into vine-encrusted warriors. She might die, silenced as the rest of her tribe had been, but she would not become the joyless heart of a mindless wooden shell.

A cold stupor crept through her body, eclipsing all hopeful thoughts. Already Maralen could hardly move her arms and found her legs to be not much better. The vine noose tightened, and her head lolled to one side. Her breathing was ragged and labored. Swarms of indistinct, buzzing figures descended, not close enough for her to see them clearly or understand their words but close enough for her to hear their eerie, whispering voices.

A velvet half-darkness enveloped her mind as the vine continued to stretch and coil around itself and its victim. Yet she could still breathe and even move, to a certain extent. Perhaps the others were still alive!

After a short but painful struggle, Maralen twisted her upper body until her hand pressed against her belt. She carried a few simple and mostly ceremonial weapons on her person, like any elf of quality, but none of those could help her. Her dagger was far out of reach in the small of her back.

With another painful twist the Exquisite managed to pry the moonglove flower loose from her belt. With a grunt Maralen shifted her left leg forward and pressed the flower's glistening petals directly into the rough, writhing vines holding her right wrist. She heard something like a hiss of shock as the tendrils released her.

Maralen wasted no time in snatching the moonglove flower with her freed hand before it could drop and pressing it into the vine around her neck. When the vine recoiled and withdrew, the elf used the blue-petaled flower to free her other hand.

She was loose, and in the next instant she dropped hard onto the packed earth of the forest road. The numbing effect of the vine's stupefying magic saved her from pain upon landing, but the impact still knocked the wind out of her. She saw, but did not feel, the moonglove flower leave her fingers and flutter down to the dirt.

The grasping vines maintained their distance, but Maralen could barely move. Her eyes were completely free, however, and she saw things in the air—the thing that had stung her and its friends, looping and careening through the dark. She could see nothing else, nor could she hear any fauna in the trees.

The vines writhed violently. The insects' buzzing grew more frenzied. The shadows grew darker.

Unable to stand, Maralen pulled herself into a sitting position. Her chin dropped to her chest, and her eyes found the moonglove flower resting on the bare ground. It was the moonglove poison the vines feared, if plant fibers could be said to feel fear—and Maralen suspected these could. This conjecture was supported by a new shift in the tone of the buzzing insects. It seemed to rise in anticipation—or perhaps anxiety.

She let herself fall forward, landing atop the flower. This crushed the hundreds of tiny crystalline pollen inside it, which contained the most concentrated and deadly form of the moonglove's poison. Though elves were the only known species on Lorwyn largely immune to its effects, the raw moonglove could still burn skin with its acidity. Numb as she was, Maralen suspected she would hardly notice the inevitable rash that would result from the poison soaking into her clothing, but she was wrong. It was an irritating but hopeful discovery to learn that she did feel the burn of the poison, and her aggravated nerves helped reactivate sensation in her limbs.

The vines closed in again as Maralen's body shielded them from the blue flower. Maralen waited. Then she pushed herself to her knees, allowing the pungent tang of fresh, raw moonglove to waft into the air. The vines withdrew even farther, like wolves encircling a campfire but unwilling to venture into the firelight.

The stinging things continued their eerie buzzing. Maralen wished she could see one of them clearly, wished one would just come within reach so she could crush it in her palm.

Maralen's time was running out. Little more could be squeezed from the moonglove's pollen, though its petals were still shiny with a thin film of poison. Once that was gone, there was nothing between her and her tormentors.

Maralen clumsily forced the battered flower back into her belt and struggled to her feet. With hands that felt encased in thick, leather mittens, she smeared the moonglove extract over as much of her clothing and skin as she could manage, careful to keep it from her eyes and mouth. All the while the vines kept their distance, rustling without a breeze, waiting.

The rustling grew louder toward the center of the vine mass that had grown to enshroud the elf party. A familiar elf shape arose from the writhing mass, tendrils shaped into a ghastly parody of Peradala's lissome form, billowing like a merrow fishing net in a strong tide. The false Perfect was sallow and drawn, her woody skin taut and stretched, her body dry as old kindling and bizarrely lined with the seams of the vines from which it was formed. The copy's empty eye sockets opened sleepily, though thankfully not very much, and they turned toward Maralen with terrifyingly keen interest. The effigy spoke with a voice that would never be called the most beautiful in Lorwyn.

"Attend me," the parody of her mistress said. There was a wheezing, harmonic quality at the outer edges of the sound. "I need you."

Maralen had heard enough. This blasphemy brought on a surge of outrage that burned away the vines' poison in her veins. It was not her mistress, and its hollow call was a horrid mockery of the most beautiful voice in the world.

Without lowering her eyes, Maralen patted her belt until she felt the mild sting of the moonglove flower. She held the blossom before her like a lit taper in a darkened cave and turned deliberately from the emaciated mockery of the Perfect she'd served.

As she had hoped, the vines kept their distance, creating a bubble of protection that let Maralen walk slowly away from the

Peradala-thing. She could hear running water not far away—perhaps a quarter mile distant and down a steep slope was the river where she'd intended to draw water for the moonglove engraving solution.

Clutching the flower, Maralen picked up her pace. The vines continued to give her a wide berth, but they followed her every move. Whenever a few tendrils got too close, she'd wave the moonglove at them and they'd recede.

She reached the point where the forest floor met the top of a heavily wooded riverbank. The pursuing curtain of vines and insects retreated with something like a snarl. It was enough to give her a clear path to freedom. She willed her still-tingling legs into action and managed to lurch down the slope.

Maralen was lucky to have made it to the beginning of the drop before she tripped again—this time in some rodent hole—and tumbled down the incline like a tightly curled hedgehog. That way, at least she was still making progress. She suffered more cuts and bruises as she rolled toward the rushing water below. It was all she could do to maintain consciousness when her chaotic roll ended against a boulder overhanging the river itself.

The river was wide and fast and appeared devoid of murderous plants or stinging insects. Maralen pushed herself to her feet and leaned against the boulder, looking over it at the glassy black water, and at the dipping sun mirrored on its surface. The elf glanced back up the slope to see the writhing vines at last venturing over the edge.

She still held the moonglove flower, miraculously intact after her tumble, and her clothing was still soaked with the blue flower's poison. She wondered if it would keep the vines away for long.

"Damn it," she cursed under her breath. "Should have learned to swim." She could probably make it to the opposite shore if she could keep her head and remain afloat. She'd seen others do it; it couldn't be that hard. Holding the moonglove to her breast, she dived headfirst into open space, involuntarily closing her eyes and mouth in anticipation of the impact with the water's surface.

She'd deliberated a heartbeat too long. A thick vine lashed out like a whip and wrapped around her ankle, bringing her dive to an abrupt halt a few feet from the fast-running river. Maralen screamed in frustration as the taut vine held her dangling over the current. She managed to bend at the waist and wave the increasingly pathetic-looking moonglove flower, but the coil held her ankle fast even as the poison still on her skin caused its color to shift from dark green to brown. Perhaps, unfortunately for her, this vine had gotten over its aversion to moonglove and decided to sacrifice part of itself to prevent her from escaping.

Finally, deliberately, the living rope hauled her even farther out over the river's surface. Maralen managed to gulp a panicked breath before the vine dipped her headfirst into the icy current, letting her sink until only the sole of one foot remained dry. She flailed and screamed under the water, foolishly wasting what air she had left. Just as she thought she might black out, the vine pulled her back into the air, and water cascaded down her entire body, blinding her and choking her as it filled her nostrils.

She had been washed clean of the moonglove poison. From her upside-down vantage point, Maralen could see the flower bobbing away on the current. She hadn't even realized she'd let it go.

So that was it. No amount of kicking or cursing would make the vine release her. It slowly lifted Maralen and carried her back toward the riverbank and the rest of the ill-fated bridal party.

She couldn't reach the vine, but maybe she could reach the boulder. It was just beneath her, still bearing spatters of crimson blood from where her head had slammed into the side. She scratched at it with her fingertips, and after a moment she caught the edge of an inch-wide crack in the rock. Maralen forced her fingers into the crack, ignoring what sounded like a snapping tendon in her wrist, and soon found the whole of her body pulled taut by the vine.

"Not dead," she coughed. "Not yet."

With her free hand, Maralen reached the silver dagger in the small of her back. It wasn't easy to work the weapon loose, but once she did it fell easily from its sheath into her palm. She slashed wildly at the ropy vine, missing, striking only air, until she felt the blade catch against the tendril that held her prisoner. She sawed furiously, and with a *twang* and a *snap* the vine severed, and Maralen crashed onto the top of the boulder.

She blinked blood from her eyes. The air was abuzz with wings. Maralen yelped as one of the blurs stung her on the neck, and she slapped at it. Another sting in the small of her back and another against the side of her leg brought her to her knees.

A wooden rope lashed her neck and arrested her slow slide off the slick riverside boulder. Two more stings, three, and she could no longer feel the tiny jabs of pain. Or much of anything else. Not the wrenching agony of being lifted by the neck and rested against a rough, thick-rooted cedar. Not the scratches, cuts, and slivers. Not the tendrils that wrapped around her arms, legs, neck, and waist.

She could hear the questions though. Those came through loud and clear, as if the speaker stood within Maralen's skull. Despite herself, Maralen answered.

CHAPTER 2

The road that had, for a time, carried the Mornsong bridal party was connected to many others, branching across the countryside. Some were heavily trod arterials, smooth and wide. Others were narrow and overgrown paths that barely qualified as roads. It was one of the latter variety, an old trail out of favor with most travelers, that led a strange pilgrim to a grisly sight hanging from the side of a cracked, dead ash. The pilgrim wore a wide-brimmed metallic hat that mediated the flames on her head, but her skin was alight with pale orange flame that pulsed in time with her breathing. The pilgrim's steady pace slowed, caution lifting her pointed chin. She tossed her head back with a short jerk to widen her field of vision and stared silently at the morbid display.

At first the fiery traveler supposed the corpse was an eyeblight, executed at the stake—it was a punishment prescribed by many elf tribes. She'd never heard of the Gilt Leaf elves using such methods, but she hadn't been through their territory in years.

When she recognized the bound remains, living curls of flame flared around her shoulders. Her chest convulsed with a blunt, sickening jolt, and her eyes grew bright with shock. The grisly marker was one of her own: a flamekin. One of the burning folk from the crags had come here, just as she had. Only that distant cousin was dead, long dead.

The lifeless, extinguished body had been exposed for some time, perhaps years. The dead flamekin's face had degraded to brittle rock, and its torso had crumbled and cracked around the strong, thin coils of elven rope holding it fast to the dead, dry tree. One arm ended in a jagged stump inches below the shoulder, the other was intact but nearly skeletal and looked as if it might snap off in a strong breeze. The legs had worn away to tapered points that hung like stalactites over a patch of dead earth. Coal black skin that had once burned with living, breathing flame was blotchy and gray.

The pilgrim was shocked, but the shock didn't last long. Such displays and warnings were all too common in the elf nations. It made sense that the strongest of the elf nations would be the most strident, the most exacting and cruel. Elves didn't consider anyone but elves to be truly intelligent—not the towering giants; not the tiny, fluttering faeries; not anything in between. Elf territory was vast, and elves tended to enforce their harsh standards on all they encountered and subjugated. The elves were not at the top of the food chain; they were the top of the food chain.

The pilgrim automatically focused on the reason for her wanderings—her purpose—and with effort regained control. The shock of her murdered kin faded quickly, though the unsettled disgust did not. Her eager determination to continue remained unchanged. Dead flamekin or no, she was impelled in this direction by that which guided her.

Judging from the condition of the path and the fact that she'd seen no other such warning from the Gilt Leaf, she saw no reason to turn back. The flamekin fell in and out of favor with the Blessed Nation depending on who was in power—they mostly served as couriers, one of the few jobs for which the elves deemed the pilgrim's people worthy, and no pilgrim was foolish enough to refuse. It was likely that the dead flamekin dated from a period of disfavor.

The pilgrim paused only to draw an ancient glyph of farewell in the air before her face. The burning symbol hung there for a fraction of a second before dissolving into curling wisps of white smoke. The brief but compulsory observance was all she had time to perform.

The pilgrim was following her path, as pilgrims did, but that didn't mean she couldn't choose a fork every so often that would quicken her pace when it became urgent to reach the next stop on her long road. There wasn't far to go to her immediate destination—in the distance she could just make out the bells of the merrow ferrymen—and if she survived the short journey from here to there, she'd be closer than ever to her ultimate goal.

The pilgrim adjusted her hat, lowering the brim over her eyes. If she were lucky, she might even get a glimpse of what that ultimate goal was.

Her wry humor faded when she remembered something unusual about the vile but all-too-common warning sign, something that forced her to delay her progress a few moments more. She turned back to the dead flamekin to inspect it more carefully.

Elves that used these warnings invariably made them quite specific. If they wanted to keep flamekin out, they killed a flamekin and tied it up to a dead tree. If they wanted to say, "No boggarts allowed," a dead boggart would be hung every few miles along the road that bordered the boggart's warrens.

This warning sign, however, was not just a flamekin corpse. Beneath the dead thing's corroded legs were carefully stacked bones. The shapes were vaguely kithkinlike, but the skulls seemed deformed. The skeletal limbs ended in stubby black claws, even those that appeared to have belonged to juveniles and infants. Placed among the bones were bits of colored glass; greasy feathers of brown, blue, and green; and bent fragments of thick, nearly worthless copper thread. The bark of the dead ash had been adorned with simple pictograms drawn in charcoal and chalk, though none of the symbols reached higher than the pilgrim's chest.

"Boggarts," the pilgrim said, and her pulse visibly quickened in the flames at her neck.

That dead ash tree, the foundation of the shrine and the final resting place of her dead cousin, looked highly flammable. The boggarts needed to learn that no good would come of worshiping dead flamekin in this fashion, especially if it inspired them to try and make their own.

The pilgrim tossed back her hat. Flames swept from her, blindingly bright. A sound very much like thunder crossed with a giant stamping its foot boomed. The air stank of singed, filthy hair. The boggarts were still wailing in despair over their burning shrine when the pilgrim left the overgrown arterial behind and stepped onto the wider lane that led to the banks of the Wanderwine.

* * * * *

The merrow built their crannog towns amid the slow but steady currents of the low-country Wanderwine River. These structures of wood, stone, rope, and netting were split into dry upper sections, where merrow and landwalkers could interact easily, and the much larger, more open chambers beneath the river's surface for the merrow alone. There were crannogs for every purpose: permanent homes, piers, weigh stations, storm shelters, and even the odd kithkin-run tavern for river-goers looking to relax.

Merrow preferred to deal peacefully with the landwalkers and built crannogs adjoining landwalker docks that connected to landwalker roads. There, most two-legged folk (save boggarts, who hardly counted) were welcome. In one such crannog, a flamekin pilgrim had recently paid for passage with a particular merrow ferryman named Sygg—Captain Sygg, to be specific. He was singing, but broke into a hum when he reached the verse following the willowy merrow warrior-maiden's heroic rescue of the helpless, albeit dashing, merrow ferryman. He was trying to attract additional patrons, after all, as it was hardly cost-efficient to cross the Wanderwine with just a flamekin, and there was no point in driving away landwalker parents with landwalker young.

Sygg might as well have continued the song, he decided, and he would have if he hadn't already shifted into a different, thoroughly bawdy ballad he was now compelled to complete. Of late, the wharf was devoid of potential customers, and today appeared ready to follow suit. In fact, Sygg was the only ferryman operating this run at the moment, the others having already moved to busier routes, and there was still barely enough traffic to make it worth his while. The road to Kinsbaile had grown less popular thanks to the damned boggarts.

Even so, there was some big celebration coming up in that bustling kithkin town, and soon the wharf wasn't completely empty. In fact, the captain hoped he might just end up at half capacity. At least that would be a mild workout. Sygg believed he didn't get enough chances to stretch.

"And how many of you will be traveling with us today, ma'am?" asked Sygg's first mate, a relatively green—in every sense of the word—merrow named Dugah. The captain had taken the youth on as an apprentice as a favor to Dugah the elder. The apprentice's primary duty was to act as a steward, but he also collected fares, and on those rare occasions Sygg took a charter for a long run down the lanes to a distant port of call, Dugah was the cook—no mean task upon the running surface of a fast-moving river.

But skillfully preparing a delectably seared silverfin steak under improbable conditions didn't give young Dugah any skills with people whatsoever. The lad's waist barely even cleared the water, and Sygg knew he had reminded his apprentice that a ferryman had to have the dignity and respect to meet potential passengers in the eye. And it wasn't as if these passengers were giants either.

Sygg sighed and slowly let himself drift over to his apprentice while making a display of checking the wind with one thumb-claw.

"One, two, four? Four," the kithkin matron said, counting herself and her three small children off on her fingers.

"Four," Dugah said, then did some painstaking figures in his head for all of fifteen seconds. The figure he offered made the matron's eyes bulge in shock.

Dugah the younger had no business coming within ten miles of a paying passenger, and the lopsided deal he offered the kithkin made the captain's gills twitch. Sygg had let sentiment guide him in agreeing to teach Dugah what he knew, but it was clearly not sinking in. If Sygg ever met that sentiment again, he would drown it. Though it broke a promise he'd made himself only the day before, the ferryman cleared his throat, flared the spiny crest atop his head, and swam up to the deck to interrupt before the offended kithkin matron voiced her indignation beyond a stammering sputter.

"Mr. Dugah, it's clear she's with small fry, now, isn't it?" Sygg said graciously. "We can't charge a full fare for such wee kithlings." With a sly, slow wink at the trio of children behind the diminutive woman—an adult kithkin stood eye-to-chest with a short elf, which made it easy for the merrow to meet her eye to eye with a little effort of his tail that his apprentice could not, apparently, manage—he added, "At your service, missus."

The kithkin children—Sygg guessed from their clothes there were two females and a male—met his friendly banter with eyes as wide as saucers. Sygg had always had a knack for reading landwalker expressions, or so he told himself, more so than the average merrow. He cheerfully misread the kithlings' frightened faces and met their growing terror with a throaty chuckle that made his gills flap, eliciting squeals of alarm.

"Thank you," the kithkin woman said. Her pale, fuzzy landwalker skin was flushed pink with the effort of pulling her traveling trunk and herding three kithlings. "Don't mind them, this is their first river crossing. We took the airship to see my sister, you see, in Duinshyle, and—"

"Let's call it three," Sygg said before the kithkin could get too far. He extended a webbed, three-fingered hand toward the kithkin matron. She fumbled with one of the many woven bags she wore slung over her shoulders and produced a small beaded purse. She carefully counted out three short gold threads and draped them across one of Sygg's clawed digits. He wasted no time, smoothly twisting them around a silver loop on the inside of his eelskin belt, the captain's only article of clothing.

"Welcome," Sygg said. "Now, if you'd like to check any of your baggage, my apprentice is at your command." He fanned his barbels in a friendly manner and gestured along the pier, which hung over the racing water until it ended abruptly about thirty feet from shore. The only other paying passenger sat with her legs folded beneath her and her arms crossed at the pier's edge. The pilgrim's head was bowed beneath her wide-brimmed metallic hat.

After a few minutes in which no other passengers showed, Sygg turned on his tail and swam along the pier. He had five passengers—four, really. It was not half capacity, then, but a good third of what he would have liked. Not bad for a slow day in a slow season. Perhaps business was picking up. He continued past his apprentice and turned to round the end of the pier. The fact that Dugah had little to carry, combined with the light load, convinced Sygg to let his apprentice handle the bulk of the work on this trip, despite the captain's misgivings. He hadn't warned his steward, but then that was part of the training. If the youth couldn't ready the ferry magic on command, or if he couldn't sustain the shapewater to keep the passengers as comfortable as possible, he would never become a true ferryman like Sygg.

Before the captain had a chance to inform Dugah of his plan, the kithkin matron stopped short two-thirds of the way down the dock and threw out her hands on either side, stopping her brood short. The merrow ferryman noticed immediately and swam quickly to the side of the dock. Even he couldn't reach eye level with the kithkin here, so he cupped one webbed hand to the side of his mouth and called, "Missus, I'll need you at the end of the—"

"Captain!" the woman said in surprise. "What is going on here?"

"The meaning of what, missus?" Sygg replied with a shrug, shooting his steward a look that told the green youth to keep out of it.

The kithkin woman pointed at the solitary pilgrim. The pilgrim's skin burned ember red and wisps of smoke curled out from beneath her hat's edges.

"The flamekin," the kithkin whispered, stealing a glance at the burning creature. "How can it be safe to carry one of them across the river? Doesn't their fire hamper the . . . your . . ."

"Only if we let it." Sygg sighed and realized there was no chance this woman would allow him to have an apprentice take her brood across the water. "I'll be happy to refund your thread in the form of a voucher worth three round trips across the Wanderwine, and that is your choice, missus. But our policies are clearly posted at the gate. No thread refunds." He flashed a row of neat, pointed silver teeth in an unwittingly hideous grin and pointed at the rickety, wooden arch to which was nailed a wooden sign reading exactly that. "And really, missus," he added, taking another tactic, "haven't you ever received a message delivered by a flamekin from some distant friend or relative? Why, to refuse passage to flamekin would be uncivil."

This took the matron aback. "No, I have not received nor do I *want* to receive a message from one of those—"

"Now, missus, I understand your trepidation, I surely do," Sygg said. "But she paid her fare like anyone else—"

"Has she paid enough to guarantee the safety of my children? I think not, taer."

Sygg stifled another sigh and kept his barbels still. "Flamekin fire doesn't burn like that, ma'am—"

"I smell smoke," the flustered matron cried. "I feel heat. Fire is fire, Captain, and this isn't the first time I've been ferried, you know. Your ferry is made of water. She's made of fire. And I may just be a simple country kithkin, but I know that fire and water don't mix!"

"Missus," Sygg said, doing his best to keep the matron from slipping into hysteria. "She's not the first of her kind I've ferried, though to be sure we don't see many like her in these parts during the foggy season. Who knows what missives she carries or who needs them? Have a heart, missus." When the kithkin continued to sputter in protest, he continued, "Why, just look at her. She's hardly even glowing. This close to the river, why, I can't imagine she's too comfortable. I assure you, Captain Sygg's ferry is the safest way to travel in all of Lorwyn, for kithkin or flamekin. Or both."

The kithkin eyed the smoldering flamekin, who showed no sign of heeding the ongoing debate about her presence. It was doubtful the kithkin woman had never seen one of the flamekin in the flesh. Few kithkin villages went so much as a year without seeing a pilgrim pass through carrying a bag of messages from whatever towns the pilgrim had been through recently. But clearly the matron didn't ever have reason to interact with those pilgrims, so she presumably had no way of telling whether the flamekin was burning any more brightly than usual.

The wide-brimmed hat tilted up, allowing Sygg to see the flamekin's blazing eyes. She smiled at Sygg, waiting.

"If the flamekin lady has no objections," Sygg said, recognizing a fellow conspirator's smile, "we can take some extra precautions." The flamekin nodded. She must have seen this before and didn't seem to mind what would be significant inconvenience and discomfort—she'd already told the ferryman how eager she was to be across and done with the Wanderwine—and Sygg nodded in return. "I won't even charge extra." He twisted his long torso and called to his apprentice. "Mr. Dugah!"

"Aye!" the youth sputtered, swimming in alarm to his master's side only to feel Sygg's claws dig into his arm when he arrived.

"Follow my lead," Sygg whispered out of the side of his mouth. "Answer 'aye.' "

"What?" Dugah managed before another squeeze—one that drew just a bit of blood—shut him up. "Aye," he repeated at last and did his best to look confident.

"My associate is an accomplished ferryman in his own right visiting from the north lanes."

"Aye," Dugah said. "I mean, I am."

Sygg's barbels twitched. "With the flamekin's permission," he went on, "my mate will shape a comfortable sphere for our flamekin friend here, a sphere which will keep a protective skein of water between you and she. This magic, being independent of my own ferry, will not—and cannot—affect my own performance. Your children could not be in safer hands than these," he finished, spreading the webbed appendages in question palms up in a gesture of welcome.

"I'll expect a free ride the next time I pass through here, Captain," the flamekin said quietly.

"I suppose if anything goes wrong, she'll be doused," the matron said. "Very well," she continued, "but I hope that we can be seated well away from that menace. Whether she's flammable or not, news from far away never did any good for anybody. She's bad luck."

Sygg saw his apprentice cringe at the matron's words. To mention bad luck with your foot on the end of a pier . . . Well . . . , Sygg thought, the good fortune of carrying a flamekin would probably cancel it out.

"And now if you'll excuse me," Sygg said, "it's time we prepared the ferry for your voyage. Please step back at least three paces or I cannot guarantee your continued dryness."

"Wait!" cried a tiny, buzzing voice that was, in truth, three voices speaking in perfect unison. A trio of winged faeries, one male and two females, emerged from the brambles lining the shore. They made straight for the ramp of the ferryboat.

Each was no larger than a songbird, and they hovered on their iridescent wings in perfect formation. The faeries were spindly and sharp, bipedal but hornetlike: their bodies were striped and dotted with vivid bands of yellow, orange, and green. Their vibrating wings buzzed melodically, filling the air with a musical hum, and the trio left a glittering shower of rainbow color in their wake.

Their hard, laughing eyes sparkled with mischief and glee. One of the females was slightly larger than the other two, who appeared to be nearly identical in size. It was common for faerie cliques to consist of a pair of twins and one odd sibling out, and this trio appeared to fit the norm, though the gender diversity was unexpected—most cliques consisted of a single sex, and males were somewhat less common.

"Faeries!" cried the youngest kithling. "Look, Mummy, faeries!"

"They'll make us fly!" cried the boy.

"They most certainly will *not,*" the matron snapped. "They'd *better* not," she added under her breath. "If they even can."

Sygg sighed through his gills and let slip the threads of shapewater magic he'd only just begun gathering together. What did the faeries want? Passage? And why would agile flyers like them even need to book passage? Still, the ferryman could smell customers a mile away, and his gills were twitching again. No point in missing a fare on the off chance the tiny creatures even had a thread between them.

"Welcome aboard, my little friends," he said. "That is, if you're coming aboard. You'll have to decide quickly, I'm afraid. We're already running late."

"But Captain, they fly," Dugah said, voicing the obvious at precisely the wrong moment. "Why do they need us?"

"We like ferries," one of the two smaller faeries, the male, buzzed as the trio came to an abrupt, hovering stop in front of the kithkin matron's wide-eyed face.

"They're a real lark," the larger female added.

"Besides, it's snapping turtle season," the female twin finished, "and some stupid reptiles think we look like food."

27

Dugah's eyes shifted nervously from the faeries' feet and Sygg's impatient face.

"Just collect their fare, Mr. Dugah," Sygg said, "we're tardy enough as it is."

It *was* rather unusual for faerie to travel by water, Sygg thought, but not unheard of. This particular clique had quite possibly traveled with him before, on sheer whim. One could slowly go mad trying to figure out why faerie did what they did. When they bothered to interact with "big folk," they rarely explained why they were being interactive, and Sygg had learned long ago that it was better not to ask—not unless you wanted an hour-long session of word games and banter that left you exhausted but none the wiser.

"Welcome aboard, misses. And taer."

"Thank you, Captain," the relatively big female said. Possibly. They were not identical, but the trio flitted in their little orbits so quickly and constantly it was hard to tell one from the other, or which had just spoken.

"We don't weigh anything," the male said. One of the smaller pair was definitely male. "So we'll take your maximum discount."

At this, for some reason, the females burst into a laugh seemingly designed to bore a hole into Sygg's brain. Then the male faerie joined in, and, near as Sygg could tell, the sound did drill through his skull and on out the other side.

"Iliona," the smaller female said, "pay the merrow before we start getting on people's nerves."

"You're getting on *my* nerves, Veesa," the big faerie—Iliona, apparently—snapped. "You two do this every time we travel."

"Misses?" Sygg interrupted. "May I suggest we would be happy to carry you across the river for the price of a single kithkin?"

"Oh, that fare's fair."

"Fairly fair, that ferry fare."

"Agreed. We'll pay the fair faerie ferry fare."

Sygg let his steward accept the single thread of gold the one called Iliona finally unwound from her tiny waist. The Fae wore no clothing as such, but these faeries wore plenty of gold thread to make up for it.

The trio fell into a private conversation as they floated a few feet above the other passengers, speaking at a pitch audible only to faeries . . . and perhaps to kithkin hunting hounds. They no longer showed any interest in anything but each other. Very good, then, Sygg thought.

What most denizens of Lorwyn called "ferry magic" was indeed magical, a gift from ancient merrow who had mastered the art of manipulating water. These days, the magic was so much a part of the merrow as a people that its use felt as natural as breathing, even to a novice. It was the ability to shape water into functional and beautiful forms that separated the ferrymen from the fry, and Sygg would be the first to modestly admit he was one of the more talented ferrymen working the Wanderwine.

With practiced, sinuous strokes of his tail, he drew away from the end of the pier. He effortlessly maintained his balance with deft maneuvering through the dueling currents that met at this exact point in the river's tumultuous course. That alone was an art that most merrow never needed to perfect, but ferrymen were an exception. The current was key. He placed his palms atop the water's surface, using miniscule pressure against the surface tension. This pressure connected him instantly to the softer, slower currents of magic that drifted through the river and collected in something like a skin of vibrant mana where the Wanderwine met the sky.

At least, that's how Sygg had been taught to visualize it, and visualization was what really made the whole thing work. He heard the kithlings gasp as he called aloud to the river to offer up a small part of itself for one of its children to use. In his heart he wasn't certain the invocation was necessary, but Sygg liked to ask all the same.

He willed this skin of water to rise, and the water obliged with a concave shape some twenty feet long and fifteen feet across that took form between the captain and his passengers.

Sygg began to hum—a slow, melancholy tune he'd learned when he was younger than Dugah. The half-shell sharpened and smoothed, until it resembled swirling, but quite solid glass. The nadir of the shape flattened out until it was level with the rest of the river. Sygg's hum shifted in register and brought forth a shimmering rail that ringed the edges of the ferry. Another shift, and decorative water arches stretched to a height of twenty feet or more. It was also made entirely of water, perfectly contained in this shape, the currents continuing through the ferry without slowing—the key to getting them to move so efficiently at right angles to the river.

"Please step aboard, folks. We'll be getting underway," Sygg called. Once solidified, he could easily maintain the ferry's shape with a modest and mostly unconscious effort.

"The flamekin goes first," the matron said, pointing at the pilgrim. "I won't have my children atop a raging river when your ferry melts out from under us."

"I don't mind," the pilgrim said. She strode to the edge of the dock and extended a flaming hand. "Captain, will your apprentice seal me in before or after I step aboard?"

"After," Sygg replied.

Dugah's much smaller spell was still adequately shaped. A moment after the pilgrim set foot on the smooth, glassy surface of this very special portion of the Wanderwine, the edges of a sphere rose from the "floor" and enveloped her in a solid yet liquid prison. The sphere followed the flamekin wherever she moved. Dugah even remembered to leave large gaps in the top of the sphere to allow the flamekin's flames to get plenty of fresh air. If the kithkin matron noticed, she didn't mention it.

* * * * *

The three kithlings scampered about the mirrorlike surface of the shapewater saucer to the dismay of the hunched, exhausted kithkin matron, who had settled into the center of the magical ferry, as far from the unshaped water as possible. She looked as if she might drop to all fours if anything upset her balance, her digestion, or both.

"Mum," the oldest of the children—a girl of eight winters— asked when she grew tired of making freakish faces appear on the outside of the pilgrim's sphere, "Why did you make the lady stand in that bubble?"

"That's a silly question, Unice," her mother replied. "You don't want to learn how to swim, do you? Now hush, we'll be across soon. Can you not pass the time with your brother and sister? We've had a long journey, and there's a bit farther to go if we're to have those cakes ready for the tales."

"What will the tales be about, Mummy?" Unice's younger brother asked. "Will there be dragons?"

"I don't know, Irgil," the matron said. "There might well be."

"But *Mother*," Unice insisted, "how does the bubble of water keep the fire-lady from—"

"It wouldn't, if I focused on the task," the pilgrim said, adding wryly, "and if I moved very, very quickly." She stretched and popped her neck with a sound like two pieces of volcanic pumice grinding against each other. The pilgrim could see the kithlings were not about to let her be. She decided to spare the matron another round of unanswerable questions.

"I don't really plan to leave, though, so don't be afraid," she said, adding with a pointed look at the kithlings' mother, "any of you."

"Excuse me, fla—miss," the kithkin matron said with as much indignity as she could muster, "we shan't bother you, and I'd ask you kindly not to frighten my children."

"I'm not scared," Unice said. "She said not to be afraid."

"Yeah, Mum," Irgil agreed. "I'm not scared even more."

"Children—" the matron sputtered.

"Why isn't all of you on fire, fire-lady?" the younger girl asked.

The flamekin, her face still hidden by the steel brim of her hat, laughed, and the glow beneath the wide hat brightened for a moment. "I wear special fire-lady clothes," the pilgrim said, holding her long arms wide and turning slowly around. "And I do have some control over what parts of me are burning at any given time. And how hot they get." She thumbed the woven-steel fabric of her traveling garments. "But mostly, it's this stuff. Woven steel. We make it in the crags—my people, that is. We haven't much use for clothing in our homes, but when we wander, like I do, it helps keep you from setting anyone's furniture on fire."

Once the opening became apparent, the kithkin siblings stumbled over each other with their questions about the strange pilgrim.

"Why are you all alone?"

"Can you shoot fire out of your eyes?"

"Are you going to Kinsbaile? We're going to Kinsbaile."

"Are you going to listen to the tales?"

"Why are you wearing a hat? It looks like a platter."

"Your fingers! You can shoot fire from your fingers?"

"Do you really eat rocks?"

"What's your name?"

"Do *you* know any tales?"

"What about your bum? Can you shoot fire out of your bum?"

"Children!" the matron barked, and as this brought a sudden guilty hush to her audience, she was able to add with more restraint, "Will you leave her alone?"

"Are you made of stone?" Irgil asked, boldly ignoring his mother.

"Not exactly," the flamekin replied. "Have you ever seen a campfire?"

"Of course!" Ryleigh squealed, happy to contribute to the conversation.

"The things at the base of the fire—the coals," Ashling explained. "That's sort of what I'm made of."

"You're made out of coal?" Irgil asked, wide-eyed.

"Not coal, *coals,* nitwit," Unice said haughtily. "Like at the base of a campfire."

"A little of both, actually," Ashling said.

"You're funny." Irgil laughed.

"And you smell funny," Ryleigh added.

"Well, that's what happens when you eat nothing but rocks," Ashling said.

"I *knew* it!" Unice said. "You do eat—"

The kithkin girl's accusation was cut short when the smooth, concave shapewater ferry beneath them shattered like a pane of glass, splashing apart into heavy drops that moments later rejoined the rest of the river. The kithkin family plunged into the Wanderwine without even time to cry out.

Ashling instinctively reached out for the nearest of the kithlings, thrusting her arm through the silvery sphere that still held her, and her alone, above the surface of the river. She was able to wrap one gloved hand around Ryleigh's forearm and locked her hand in a death grip before the water cut off feeling below her elbow. She could only watch helplessly as the other two children and their mother bobbed up to the surface like corks, already several feet away. Ryleigh shrieked and called for her mother, but to no avail.

"Captain!" the flamekin heard Dugah cry, and suddenly the abrupt end of their crossing was explained. An arbomander had surfaced and collided with the master ferryman, who must have been caught unawares. Sygg floated facedown, apparently unconscious, as the adolescent—but still huge—amphibian gave the merrow a second smack with its flat tail. The blow knocked Sygg onto his back. Ashling could see no light in his glassy eyes.

Sygg's panicked apprentice struggled to keep Ashling, and with her the wailing kithling, aloft as he swam furiously to his fallen master. He appeared to have completely forgotten the other passengers.

"Dugah!" Ashling shouted. "Leave him! You're going to lose the kithkin!"

"Mumeeeee!" Ryleigh added.

"But—" the apprentice began. Then he saw the bobbing, wailing kithlings and their mother. Irgil and Unice had managed to snag their mother, who was doing her best to stay on the surface—she could swim, at least, but with the weight of the two kithlings dragging her down, there didn't seem to be much hope for them.

"Do something, fire-lady!" Ryleigh cried. "Make the fish-man do something!"

"Dugah, for bog's sake, do something," Ashling hissed as her floating shapewater prison buckled along with the apprentice's concentration. "Something that doesn't drop me in the water, please," she added.

Dugah didn't answer her, and most of the sphere's upper half disintegrated and splashed against her shins and feet, which fell numb, but at least her arm was no longer enveloped in the shapewater. Careful not to burn the kithling's forearm, she allowed her flame to dry everything up to her wrist, which brought back most of the feeling in her hand. With effort, she kept her footing and her grip on the terrified kithling, but she didn't know how long she could maintain either. Ryleigh's panicked flailing wasn't helping.

"Bog it, Dugah, get them before they drown!" Ashling called. "And, uh, don't drop us either, if you can help it."

"But I'm only a student," Dugah protested. "Captain Sygg is the one—"

"You've got to do it!" she called. "He's either dead or unconscious, and if it's the latter, he'll live. But those children can't swim, and you're the only ferryman in sight." Of course, *I* can't swim either, she added to herself, and I doubt this kithling can. For that matter, I can barely stand. It was more luck than balance that kept her on her two numbed feet as Dugah finally relented and headed downriver after his floundering passengers. He reached out with one hand, summoning power from the currents of the Wanderwine, keeping Ashling out of the river with the other. Even less of the sphere remained. She was essentially standing upon a flat disk of water at this point. Ryleigh yelped as her feet dipped into the cold current.

The arbomander struck so quickly Ashling didn't even have time to warn the apprentice of his mortal danger. One moment

Dugah was waving an affirmative hand sign at the flamekin and the shapewater was starting to grow more solid as the apprentice brought his emotions under control. The next moment there was an explosion of whitewater and the gigantic amphibian burst from the river, its mouth open wide to swallow Dugah in a single gulp. His last scream was over almost before it had the chance to begin.

"Oh, b—" Ashling managed before the disk beneath her dissolved. But to her surprise, immersion did not follow. In fact, she didn't lose an inch of elevation and was even able to lift Ryleigh's feet from the water.

"Settle down, we've got you," buzzed a tiny female voice from her right shoulder.

"Gyah!" Ryleigh cried. "Faeries!"

"You should really cut down on the sandstone, flamekin," said the male faerie from her left shoulder. "It's going straight to your hips."

"You too, kithling," the female added. "Less sweets, more meats."

The third faerie appeared before Ashling's eyes, hovering with her tiny arms crossed over her chest. "Well," the one called Iliona said, "don't you have anything to say?"

"You want my thanks? You have it," Ashling said. "But what about them?"

"They're just kithkin," Endry—the male faerie—said.

"That's my family!" Ryleigh cried.

"They're not important enough," Veesa agreed. "There are plenty of kithkin. No offense."

"Then why save me?" Ashling interjected.

"Because you're—"

"Shut up, Endry," Iliona said. "Why are you complaining, flamekin? You'd rather we dropped you in the water? And look on the bright side. You've still got one kithkin, there. How many do you need?"

"Mummy!" Ryleigh shouted. *"MUMMEEEE!"*

"You heard her. The girl wants Mummy," Ashling said. "Now help those people, or—"

"Or what?" Veesa buzzed. "You're not really in a position to make demands, brimstone-breath."

Without a word Ashling swatted at the sound of the voice with her free hand. She was rewarded with a squeal and the sudden, icy grip of the river water around her legs as a single faerie was left with the job of keeping her in the air. With an incredible effort the flamekin kept Ryleigh elevated, though the girl started crying again. Ashling could hardly blame her—if she herself had tear ducts she'd be right there with the kithling. Instead, she said weakly, "That . . . hurt. But I'll throw the kithling close to the shore and swat the other one of you unless you help that family. I don't know why you want to keep me alive, but if you're going to do it you're going to have to save them all."

"Can I kill her, Iliona?" Endry asked. "Or at least that kithling. My ears are bleeding."

"Yes, please do," Veesa said, floating down into Ashling's field of vision and rubbing her right antenna, which was bent. "We can find another one, can't we? And I know we don't need any spare kithkin."

"No!" Iliona ordered. "Keep quiet, both of you. Endry, get those two to shore, and don't drop the flamekin. She'll have to hold onto that kithling if she wants to keep her."

"As you say," Endry replied. He nodded, oddly businesslike and almost martial.

"Veesa, come with me," the larger faerie said to her smaller sister.

"You are *so* lucky," Veesa said to Ashling with a glare. The flamekin didn't feel particularly lucky with the river almost up to her waist, the arm holding Ryleigh screaming with pain that alternated with infuriating numbness brought on by little, unpreventable splashes from the terrified kithling she held aloft. Endry, it seemed, could not keep Ashling completely out of the water, so it was all she could do to keep her upper torso, limbs, and head alight. Still, they weren't far from the shore. When she was on shore with Ryleigh, she could burn away the residue of the Wanderwine.

"All right!" she heard Veesa shout. "I've got two of 'em. These kithkin weigh a lot less than flame-face."

"I have the mother," Iliona said. "Stop kicking, bog damn you!" she added, apparently to the matron, who was cursing a blue streak and kicking wildly. If the kithkin were kicking, they were still alive. So far, so good, Ashling thought. She felt oddly protective of the kithlings. It had been some time since she'd spoken with flesh-folk that were so accepting.

The shore was only a dozen feet away. Soon she could ask the faeries why they'd been intent on saving her in the first place. She wasn't sure she liked their protective attitude. She felt a few droplets spatter against the brim of her iron hat as a shadow fell over her, and she saw Ryleigh's waterlogged, awestruck siblings pass overhead. Unice clutched Irgil and vice versa as Veesa struggled mightily to keep the pair in the air.

A moment later Ashling felt her body rise from the river, and heard Ryleigh . . . cheer?

"Hooray!" Ryleigh cried. "We're saved!"

Yes, definitely a cheer. But for who, or what?

"Endry?" she croaked. The dull agony in her legs had her on the verge of blacking out. "Who . . . ?"

"Not me," the exhausted faerie buzzed, "but I'm not complaining."

"Steady, my flamekin friend," Sygg's familiar voice growled from upriver. "You too, faerie. Keep her on her feet, and I'll lift from below."

"Hello . . . " Ashling gasped, wearily turning her head to flash a lopsided orange smile at her rescuer, "Captain."

CHAPTER 3

The boggart emerged from the underbrush. It peered left, then right, then straight ahead, and all the while a silver arrow remained trained on the center of its bulbous, warty forehead. The dark little grotesque's goggling eyes didn't see the arrow, or the elf that held it taut against the string of a bow stained forest green.

Rhys, daen of the Hemlock Pack, saw the boggart clearly, of course. The well-hidden elf stared fixedly down the length of his greenwood arrow, beyond the razor-sharp arrowhead to the boggart's twisted, cunning leer. The vermin took a single careful step forward into the clearing. It sniffed the air through its broad, flapping nostrils.

Rhys's hand was steady, but his instinctual disgust of the boggarts hovered over him like a cloud of stinging flies. They were vile things—mockeries of elf perfection that dared to take roughly the same shape as Nature's Blessed. Boggarts shared with elves the same number of arms and legs, but where elves were tall and lean and elegant boggarts were squat, misshapen, and clumsy. Elves had skin that ranged from alabaster to polished bronze, each shade completely unique; boggarts only came in various shades of scab, from rusty red to dead, crusty black. Male and female elves alike proudly wore thick, curved horns that crowned their angular faces. The flat, squarish blockhead of the boggart was rarely crowned with anything but diseased fungi and slimy moss. A boggart's feet, each a unique, hideous deformity, were disgusting compared to the slim, cloven hooves of a noble elf.

And those, Rhys thought as he calmly drew another motionless breath, were only the physical differences. The general notion of what boggarts got up to in their dank, stinking, little hovels disgusted him beyond expression, and so he refused to consider the particulars.

Rhys continued to hold perfectly still, barely breathing, completely concealed by the foliage and a hint of glamer. The local boggarts had always been an ugly, unruly lot, but this particular band had inexplicably turned feral. They lived wild in the woods and of late had been waylaying any undefended travelers they could find. They were dangerous, behaving much like the boggarts' ancient forefathers had in the distant past, before elves like Rhys brought the peace and order of the forest to all Lorwyn.

Outrage simmered at the back of the daen's mind, threatening to distract his aim. Wild boggarts from the foothills once plundered bountiful kithkin caravans. Today, the average lowland boggart who found itself near a thriving, bustling town would do no worse than skulk around its edges and corners, creeping and crawling to avoid notice. The most brazen might steal a pie from a kitchen window or startle passing children by grabbing at their ankles from under a rock.

Rhys exhaled evenly and kept his arrow unwaveringly fixed on the boggart below. This vile thing and its fellows were not like most lowland boggarts. This ragged horde had actually attacked one of the kithkin's villages, Kinsbaile, weeks before. Kinsbaile was far from the river and several days' hike from the next kithkin town, but it was still elf territory, still subject to the authority of the Gilt Leaf elves.

When these boggarts went into Kinsbaile, they didn't skulk or grab at ankles. They charged straight to the center of town, where the richest shops and most expensive homes were, raging and rioting like beasts. When they left, two of those fine houses had been burned to the ground, and one kithkin family was missing, along with all of their belongings.

These boggarts had tasted both blood and battle in their attack on Kinsbaile and had developed a liking for it. They were now drifting toward Dundoolin, the largest Kithkin village in the region after Kinsbaile and one safely within the elves' reach. There was no telling what the boggarts would do when they reached Dundoolin. It fell to Rhys to ensure they never got the chance.

It did not matter one whit that Dundoolin had capable fighters and was, in fact, quite well defended. These boggarts were not simple vermin but bandit raiders brazenly operating in elf country, and they must be treated as such. They had shown no mercy to the nation's tenants in Kinsbaile, shown no fear or respect for the laws of the forest. Those laws had been set down by the elves, long ago and had been enforced for generations by dedicated packs of Gilt Leaf hunters and rangers.

These boggarts not only broke the Blessed Nation's law, they defiled the very ground beneath them. They were a living, breathing insult to the forest, to the nation itself, and it was Rhys's sacred duty to answer that insult with a stinging rebuke. Without the nation's strong, guiding hand, this bloodstained blighter and his feral cohorts would be the norm. Without the order and discipline that spread outward from the Gilt Leaf elves, Lorwyn's lesser tribes would quickly destroy each other, and then the land itself, before they finally destroyed themselves.

Rhys's eyes continued to bore into the oblivious boggart's skull. The sharp corners of his thin lips turned up, and his eyes narrowed. Chastising this lot was his sacred duty, yes, but it was also his passion and his pleasure. He had trained all his life for moments like this, mastering the sword and the bow and the trail so that when his nation demanded it, he could fight to preserve and expand its glory. Whenever he drew his sword, bent his bow, or worked his magic, he did so for his nation, for the Gilt Leaf. He was a functioning part of the tribe, shouldering his share of the elves' burden on their Blessed path to perfection.

Rhys quieted his rising joy, sobering himself with the renewed revulsion he felt as the first boggart turned and beckoned others out of the brush. Beyond the glory of the nation, beyond his sacred duty to make bloodied examples of these bandits, Rhys longed to simply banish the grubby, little creatures from sight. In every conceivable way, they disgusted him. The removal of these boggarts from the world would beautify Lorwyn in more ways than he could easily count.

This was the way of things. Elves ruled Lorwyn, and boggarts stayed out of sight. Rhys and his pack would remind the boggarts of that fact and in so doing remind every tribe why elves were their rightful masters.

The boggart below was carrying a mercifully unrecognizable hunk of flesh and bone as he scuttled into the clearing. Rhys followed his motion, confident that the dozen elf archers positioned around the clearing had already individually targeted the rest of the horde. He would wait until all the boggarts had emerged from the brush or until the clearing was full—his scouts had been unable to accurately gauge the size of the horde—and then Rhys would give the signal to fire. If his pack held to the standards he demanded, not a single boggart would survive the first volley. Any of the horde that managed to flee back into the woods or toward the river would be rounded up and driven back to the killing ground by his rangers. Any who managed to escape would quickly wish they hadn't.

Rhys had every intention of containing this rabble and ending the boggarts' rampages once and for all, right here. To that end, he had taken extraordinary steps to ensure the success of this mission. His pack's discipline had been strained lately with an influx of raw recruits. They lacked the experience and composure Rhys demanded, but Taercenn Nath himself, the Gilt Leaf's most feared and respected general, simply told Rhys that was why they'd been assigned to him: to gain much-needed experience and battle seasoning.

A mere daen like him could not object, but he was certainly not about to let these untried archer's rough edges jeopardize his reputation. He had retained the services of two non-elf specialists to back up his main force—an unorthodox move, but Rhys had learned first-hand that boggart hunts rarely go as planned even under ideal circumstances. On this hunt, on this punitive mission, thinking the unthinkable and preparing for it could mean the difference between victory and disgrace.

Rhys's ears twitched a moment before the boggart he'd targeted reacted to the tiniest cracking sound from the east. Rhys twisted his right ear toward the sound, but it was too late. The boggart started and dropped his grisly trophy. He craned his knobby neck and scanned the trees to the east.

The daen nearly swore out loud. The next few seconds would tell. When boggarts sensed they were being hunted, they shrieked to warn all nearby boggarts of the danger. Then they all fled or attacked together. The exact pitch of the shriek determined the outcome, and any elf that could not tell a shrieking charge from a screaming retreat would soon be a dead elf.

There had been no shriek yet. This boggart was wary, perhaps, but not ready to sound an alert. To Rhys's relief, the boggart moved again. Rhys did not, and his ears told him the rest of the hunting pack hadn't either. They might still pull this off.

Rhys followed the boggart, his fingers itching to loose the shot. Soon.

Below, the first boggart reached the middle of the clearing. There were at least a score of his kin crawling and hopping behind him in plain sight and thus in mortal danger from veteran elf archers—veterans he didn't have. He supposed amatures would have to do.

Another few seconds.

Rhys remained still, poised to let fly his envenomed arrow. His orders had been perfectly clear, and if his archers were up to snuff each one would know his or her target, no arrows would cross in midflight, and every last boggart would receive a single lethal bolt and be dead before they hit the ground. The best archers chose first, primary targets selected by position, size, and apparent age. Secondary targets were for the newer members of the pack, all within arrow-range of the primaries. Tertiary targets were near those. With mathematical precision, the elves would knock the boggarts over like individual stalks of threshed wheat. It was a more orderly death than the things deserved, but they would still serve as the example Rhys wanted after he left their bodies along the edges of the Gilt Leaf.

The first boggart relaxed slightly and dropped into a crouch. It had reclaimed its fleshy morsel and turned it around, making the torn flesh unfortunately more visible—and recognizable—to the waiting elves. Unable to restrain itself, the boggart snapped off a finger with a nearly full set of jagged yellow teeth.

Another boggart scrambled into Rhys's field of vision, an old war-horse whose leathery body bore dozens of jagged scars beneath its mossy growths. It seemed a secondary target wanted to move up in rank, which would have been fine by Rhys if the first boggart hadn't been so obviously the leader. For any other elf to take down the first boggart would be improper, even insulting. Rhys needed to make this kill. After that, so long as there was an arrow for every boggart, it did not matter in what order they were received.

Thinking too much again, Rhys told himself. He waited for the big, leathery boggart to hunker down and paw in the dirt. Then Rhys carefully settled the silver arrowtip so that it pointed between the ears of his original target.

The pack was in place. In a moment, Rhys would drop his chin and whistle the attack command, the first and only command he needed to give. Twin waves of moonglove-poisoned arrows would streak toward the scattered boggart tribe, and every one would find its target. In the time it took to blink, Rhys's projectile would slice through the air and strike the flesh-wielding boggart between the eyes.

A single silver arrow flashed across the pack leader's field of vision, knifing through the brambles to disappear into its yelping target. From his angle, Rhys suspected the early arrow had come from young Yelm, an apprentice huntsman promoted to Rhys's pack as a favor to the youth's mother.

As Rhys had feared, Yelm was not ready. The untested elf had lost his nerve, and with a single errant twitch the entire ambush had soured. It was understandable, explicable, yet utterly unacceptable. The other archers, thinking they had somehow missed the command to fire, rushed to catch up. The panicked boggarts commenced babbling and scrambling every which way once the first arrow hit, dissolving into a chaotic muddle that spoiled the aim and intent of the archers. Within seconds the carefully choreographed wave of arrows Rhys had seen in his mind's eye became a slipshod barrage of poorly timed shots that—judging from the sounds of impact—missed as many targets as they struck.

Rhys spat and dropped his chin, releasing his own shot

before the lead boggart could vanish into the chaos. His bolt hit home, and the boggart stumbled back, driving the arrowhead exposed from the back of his skull into the bark of a thick tree. Rhys felt a momentary twinge of sympathy—he had studied among Lorwyn's treefolk for almost a third of his life, and injuring the tree was painful to him, and harmful to his spirit. Yet Rhys brushed aside such concerns. It was hardly pressing, nor was it the first time an elf had done such a thing in the course of battle. It certainly wouldn't be the last, and few would have spared as much sympathy as Rhys. Later he would carefully clean the tree and wipe away the boggart's foul black blood. With the right spells and glamer, the tree would heal, and its bark would extend over the boggart's corpse like a shroud, securing the little monster in place and hiding its repugnant form from sight. Any who passed by would know the tree had been marred for a good cause without having to view the boggart's actual remains.

A duty for another day. Rhys bolted from his position and sprinted down to the increasingly loud melee, roaring for his archers and rangers to advance into the clearing. The ambush had failed, but the bloodshed had just begun. He was still determined that these boggarts would never leave the clearing.

The elf nocked another arrow, side stepping as a foam-flecked boggart charged him. He slammed his elbow into the brute's ear as it passed, driving it face-first into the loamy soil from where it sent up a wet cloud of moss and dirt. Rhys straddled the boggart, bent his bow, and then pinned the boggart's head to the spongy earth.

As he stooped to retrieve his arrow, a cacophony assaulted Rhys's sharp ears. The sound of boggarts shrieking was everywhere, a distinctive cry that meant, "Attack the intruders." Rhys was once more outraged at this horde's audacity. Faced with a full elf pack, he expected only the shriek that said, "Run for your lives!"

The boggarts had chosen to stay and fight, and that meant they would be at their most dangerous. If they had numbers on their side and could pack themselves tightly together, a boggart horde could give an elf pack real trouble. Boggart tactics like these were not meant to achieve victory but to make their opponent's victory as costly as possible. The boggarts would swarm over and over-whelm as many of their foes as they could through sheer weight of numbers. Boggarts bred like rats. Even well-disciplined elves could only hold off such a swarm for so long.

Rhys's pack materialized like ghosts from their camouflage among the trees. They fell upon the boggarts, gracefully slicing through them and slipping past them until the long, willowy bodies of the elves among the short, squat, forms of the boggarts struck Rhys as a stand of corn stalks in a mushroom patch.

The grisly sounds of close-quarters combat slowly over-whelmed the chaotic chorus of bowstrings. Rhys heard elves crying out in pain as well as boggarts' wails, and he smelled the blood of his Blessed pack members mingling with the noisome stench of boggart bile. He ought to let them fight it out. He ought to let the boggarts have their due. That wasn't the kind of experience Taercenn Nath had in mind, however, and Rhys knew it. He nodded grimly to himself. This was where his unthinkable backup plan came in.

First, he had to separate the elves from the boggarts. That would be simple enough, though his pack would be stung by the insult, perhaps rightfully so. Let them bear the insult, Rhys thought, rather than the scars of boggart teeth.

He shouted out the command to withdraw. There was shock and disbelief on the faces of his hunters, but they responded quickly enough. Those who lingered did so only briefly, as they could see the arrow Rhys had nocked.

It was another arrowgrass shaft, but the arrowhead was unique. Dull orange-brown in color, it was a translucent wedge of highly polished resin that glowed softly from within, like a dying lantern. Even the rawest new recruits recognized what it was, and they knew to get well clear before Rhys let this arrow fly.

Rhys aimed the hardened piece of yew sap at the center of the boggart's unruly formation. Yew poison was as rare as it was deadly, and Rhys had been fortunate enough to be apprenticed to the only yew treefolk still alive. Amplified by a yew sage's magic, yew poison was even more formidable.

The whispered words of a yew spell slipped past Rhys's tight lips as he let the arrow fly. All of his elves were out of harm's way, safely removed from the center of the clearing, so at the very moment the tip of the resin arrow touched the center of the boggart battle-mound, Rhys shouted the incantation's final sharp, percussive syllable.

The crystallized arrowhead shattered against its target, unleashing a cloud of glittering amber dust that surrounded the center of the boggart horde. Smoke wafted from the larger pieces, spreading over the boggarts' flesh like oil on water. As Rhys watched, every boggart that had glittering orange dust on its skin or in its lungs stopped breathing. As one they let out a ragged, mournful sigh and dropped where they stood, deader than stones.

The others fell into a renewed panic. Rhys heard the "Run for your life" shriek at last as the boggart formation disintegrated and they all broke and ran, fleeing from Rhys, howling and stumbling over themselves as they made for the river.

Rhys placed two fingers between his lips and whistled, the only signal that could cut through the din of the raging boggart retreat and carry across the forest to the cavernous ears of the elf's hired help. The reply to Rhys's signal was abrupt and impressive, if one valued strength over style, brute force over focused action, and the rock-solid durability of a club over the keenness and flexibility of a saber.

The nearest of his hirelings, Brion, erupted from beneath the soft loam of a nearby hillock, and the boggart mob skidded to a horrified stop. They backpedaled, scratching and clawing at the ground and each other to stay outside stomping range. Towering over them, Brion flexed his massive fists, each large enough to hold ten boggarts each. He positioned himself directly in the little brutes' path and planted his feet. The bulk of the hillock remained atop Brion's head and shoulders like an earthy crown and cape. The decidedly unregal figure opened his mouth so wide his jaw nearly touched his belt. Then Brion roared.

Rhys's sensitive ears tingled painfully, but the giant's bellow did far more damage than that. The sound bent all but the thickest trees and sent a horizontal shower of oak leaves and pine needles whizzing across the clearing. Some of the boggarts were blown completely off their feet, and others rolled like misshapen hedgehogs.

The hilltop crown crumbled, its thick, rich soil sliding away from its framework of tree roots and bramble thickets. It was still solid enough to lay hands on, however, and solid enough to throw, and Rhys's hired giant was not about to let that opportunity pass by.

Brion dug his thick fingers into the underside of his makeshift mulch regalia, shifted his hips and shoulders, and heaved upward, launching the crumbling remainder of the hilltop toward the boggarts. Those still standing scattered, and some of them even got clear. The rest, those who could not run or did not run quickly enough, let out a searing cacophony of wails and squeals as the giant's improvised avalanche descended.

The impact shook the ground. Brion's triumphant leap shook the ground twice more, once as his feet left the forest floor and again when they retuned. The sound of trees falling was almost lost against Brion's delighted whooping, but Rhys heard several topple in the woods behind the giants.

There was an eerie moment of calm as everyone recovered their balance or their hearing or assessed the state of their wounds. Rhys winced in distaste. Without the hilltop concealing his features, the giant's huge, lumpy face stood revealed. Where boggarts were obscenely ugly, giants were merely spectacularly repulsive. Fortunately giants weren't nearly as numerous or odious. Brion and his brother Kiel were the only giants Rhys had seen in the past five years, and it was his good fortune that they were looking for work.

A boggart's shriek rang out, one thick with the fear of being crushed underfoot. Rhys also heard murmurs of surprise and sullen whispers from the elves in his pack. He tucked this detail away for later, when he was attending to the pack's overall poor performance today.

There were still scores of boggarts loose about the clearing. In the wake of Brion's greeting, they scurried out from their hiding places and made once more for the river. A few even crawled out of the great mound of soil and rocks the giant had thrown at them, limping, staggering, yet somehow alive until they were trampled by their fellows swarming over the pile of bodies and dirt in a frenzied rush.

Brion lifted both of his hideously calloused fists into the air and roared again. He bounded forward, rotating his long arms in wide circles. The giant brought his knuckles and the soles of his feet down on the remains of the hillock, smashing flat those boggarts still moving underneath. Still whooping joyfully, the giant lumbered after the fleeing boggarts, sweeping his arms through the rapidly thinning crowd like twin mallets. He scooped up handfuls of the shrieking creatures and brought his palms together in loud, wet, booming claps over and over again. He scooped and clapped, scooped and clapped, until the rumbling echoed across the forest like thunder on a cloudless day.

Rhys saw a trio of boggarts disappear over a ridge to the west—where he had stationed Kiel, his second hired giant. Kiel was out of sight, which was something of a blessing, but Rhys could clearly hear him going to work with the same enthusiasm as his brother Brion.

Rhys listened to the sounds of carnage and shook his head angrily. This was not how things were meant to be. Killing boggarts en masse was supposed to be easy. There wasn't supposed to be a battle—the boggarts were supposed to be dead before they knew they were under attack. Melee with boggarts was degrading work, unfit for one of the Blessed . . . but totally appropriate for giants.

Gryffid might well have been correct, however. With the political situation being what it was, it would have been better if Rhys and his elves had accomplished this unpleasant task themselves. In hiring the giants, he had chosen success of the mission over protocol, and that gave Nath solid justification for whatever punishment the taercenn saw fit to impose. No one was allowed to question protocol—even if it meant the failure of the mission. In Nath's eyes, giants were not fit to work alongside the Blessed.

Rhys didn't see how he could have chosen otherwise. He wasn't sure of his pack, and if the pack had failed on its own, they all would have been punished—blighted, perhaps even killed. At least his way, Rhys alone bore responsibility. There was certainly honor in that, or so he told himself.

So focused on his thoughts was Rhys that he was nearly struck by a flying boggart that soared down from the west, where Kiel's lowing roars continued to underscore his increasingly violent rampage. At the last moment the elf deftly stepped aside and the boggart's flight ended with a thud at the base of a tree.

Rhys shook his head again. The sooner this messy business ends, he thought, the sooner I can atone for it.

CHAPTER 4

The cenn of Kinsbaile sat comfortably in tastefully appointed office, entertaining a visitor who filled most of the remaining space in the room. Gaddock Teeg was lean for a kithkin, and tall—it was often said outside his earshot that he must have had a little elf blood in his family tree. Cenn Teeg always wore a simple tunic and trousers, confident the large silver flower he wore was enough to tell anyone who didn't already know that he was the most important kithkin in town.

The cenn of Kinsbaile was seated, but he tilted his head up, peering over the edges of his spectacles at the red treefolk sage who towered over his head. "Sage Colfenor, I must beg your pardon and ask, is that wise? Surely you could contact your protégé and spare us the risks of sending this other away so soon after we've found her."

The treefolk sage answered with customary deliberation, his deep voice booming. "Did you just ask me whether my plan is wise?" Colfenor the Red Yew's sobriquet was easy to explain. He had a venomous temper as quick as any yew poison coupled with a remarkably sharp tongue for a creature of his age. Though he was certainly an ancient, revered sage and keeper of mystical lore, Colfenor was just as certainly something of a grump.

"I—Well, yes," Gaddock Teeg replied. He had been cenn long enough to know when one could maneuver around a direct question and when it was pointless to evade one. "Is it?"

"I think it is," Colfenor rumbled. "My apprentice has not been as . . . available as I require. He needs the most urgent summons I can send, a tangible, visceral message that he cannot ignore or put off. I want the flamekin to find him and bring him here. Why are you changing your mind now, Teeg?"

"I'm not. . . . I was just asking as to. . . ." Gaddock Teeg sighed and tried another tactic. "As you say, Sage Colfenor," he said, dropping into a more formal tone and nodding his head in an unconscious bow before the sentient tree. A drop of sweat ran down Teeg's forehead and hung off the end of his round nose. That nose twitched. The kithkin was clearly nervous.

One of his staff rescued Teeg by knocking gently and entering with his head bowed. Teeg straightened and summoned the young man to him with a crooked finger. The youth stood on tiptoe to whisper in Teeg's ear.

The cenn nodded. "Thank you." He dismissed the lad with a toss of his head and then turned to Colfenor. "They're here. Right outside Collemina's. It would appear our flamekin friend is quite punctual. Reliable."

"I never doubted it," the red yew rumbled with a nod. "Reliability is most important to me." He pointed a long finger at Teeg. "You will escort me to meet her. Now, please."

The great treefolk was crouched low in order to confer with Teeg, his long legs folded in a manner no kithkin or elf could ever emulate. With a series of creaks and pops, he straightened to his full twenty-foot height beneath the vaulted ceiling of the cenn's meeting chamber. The branches and foliage that covered his head, shoulders, and arms added another ten feet to that when he was in the open. They pressed against the skylights. He towered over the kithkin cenn, his upper boughs scratching Teeg's beloved ceiling frescoes without a thought, and the cenn could see the conversation was over. He filed away a mental reminder to have the frescoes restored as soon as possible. As it was, he led the giant treefolk outside to Collemina's.

* * * * *

"Ashling, isn't it?" Cenn Teeg extended his hand. The flamekin took it in hers—the kithkin, to his credit, never flinched, even as the cool flames licked his wrists—and shook it.

"At your service," the flamekin replied. "Cenn . . . ?"

"Gaddock Teeg," the cenn said. "I believe you met my predecessor Smitsmott, more than a decade ago."

"It has been a while since I've seen Kinsbaile, your honor," Ashling said graciously. "Cenn Smitsmott left the town in good hands, I can see. And it would appear, from the outside at least, that you haven't changed much about the cenn's mansion."

"No, indeed. Cenn Smitsmott made me promise not to. Swore if I ever tidied the place up too much, he'd stage a coup," Teeg said. "And I hope you are right about my good hands, though I do appreciate the compliment. Welcome back to Kinsbaile, Pilgrim."

"Thank you. I'm not often sent for—and not often found when I am. I was surprised you were able to get word directly to me. How did you know I would be on that crag at that particular time?"

"I did not," Teeg admitted. "I received help in finding you from another." Teeg's face lit up as he caught sight of a grim-faced kithkin approaching with a bow strapped across her back.

"Brigid Baeli, meet Ashling the flamekin," the cenn said. Teeg gracefully stepped aside to allow the Hero of Kinsbaile to bow deeply to the flamekin. Ashling returned the gesture in kind.

"Please, just call me Ashling," the flamekin said, bowing her head to the kithkin archer. "I doubt anyone will forget what I am, not in these parts."

"Brigid is my good right hand around town," the cenn said. "And she's the best ranger and tracker we have. No one knows the field like Brigid. That'll be a great help to you in delivering the message."

"I don't usually require a guide." Ashling spoke politely but firmly. "The path will lead me wherever this message needs to be delivered."

The cenn's eyes twinkled. "Ah, but will it lead you there in time? This missive has to find its recipient as quickly as possible. Who better to aid you than the hero of—"

"Trust me," Brigid Baeli said. Her eyes were as stern and inquisitive as the cenn's were open and bovine. Clearly this woman had not bought into the legend that had grown up around her. She was a tough-looking kithkin, hard and flinty, and her arms were thick and ropey from years of mastering the bow slung over her shoulder. "The paths around Kinsbaile are different from what they used to be."

"How so?" Ashling asked.

"Boggarts, for one," the archer said. She bit thoughtfully on a piece of long, mildly narcotic arrowgrass—the same stuff the elves used to make the shafts of their projectiles. "And the elves aren't much better, if they find you someplace they think you shouldn't be. You get along well with elves, do you?"

"Well enough," Ashling said. Baeli's seriousness might be normal for a kithkin archer, or it might be more of the same superstitious prejudice exhibited by the matron. But Ashling's instincts told her that it was neither, that Baeli had simply seen so much of life—hero or no—that she rarely joked about anything. Ashling decided to let the archer's question lie for the moment and turned to Teeg. "Begging your pardon, taer, but what exactly is this message that needs to be delivered?"

"If you and Archer Baeli," the cenn said, "would be so kind as to accompany Sage Colfenor and me back to my office, all will be made clear."

Ashling nodded and followed Gaddock Teeg as he turned on one heel and set off across the square and around to the back of the cenn's mansion to where Colfenor stood, majestic and aloof at his full height. "Sage Colfenor the Red Yew, may I introduce Ashling, a flamekin pilgrim who has agreed to help us ensure your message reaches its intended recipient."

"Wait, his message?" Ashling asked. "You were the one who summoned me, Cenn."

"You do not wish to carry a message for me?" the yew rumbled.

"It's not that," the flamekin objected. "I just like to know who I'm working for. The cenn led me to believe—"

"Teeg did as I asked," Colfenor said. "I am sorry this mild deception was necessary."

"It's no problem," Ashling said. "So who's the recipient?"

* * * * *

The faeries listened to every conversation they could. They were especially interested in what went on between the sage, the pilgrim, and the proud politician. Between the three of them, the clique could cover all of Kinsbaile without even straining, and there wasn't a single story they missed—not a tale, argument, insult, or sweet declaration of love that escaped their notice. From the window of Collemina's to Teeg's inner sanctum to Angus Gabble's general store, the kithkins' thoughtweft bound the inhabitants of Kinsbaile together and made the joyous job of collecting dream-stuff a breeze.

Ashling made arrangements with the cenn, the sage, and the archer. Endry, Veesa, and Iliona converged outside the cenn's mansion to make sure Ashling didn't get out of their sight, and they followed along behind when Teeg and the famous archer Brigid Baeli escorted the flamekin and the treefolk back to town square. The clique listened intently to Colfenor's words and the flamekin's response. They took careful note of everything that was said and remained unnoticed even by the towering treefolk. It wasn't difficult for them to draw on the kithkin thoughtweft, and it was an excellent source of information and control: two of the Vendilion clique's favorite things.

At last, the trio's eavesdropping produced something truly interesting: the target of the treefolk's missive. What Colfenor wanted was simple. There was an elf, the treefolk's student or apprentice or some such thing. The yew wanted to see this elf, this Rhys, but the elf had been hunting for some time and wasn't responding to Colfenor's summons. The flamekin was going to find the elf and bring him back here to meet with the sage, and the sour-faced archer was to accompany her.

The treefolk was very clear about the urgency of the summons, but the flamekin never asked the obvious question—why didn't the treefolk simply find the elf himself? She was a good messenger, obviously, experienced enough to know when not to be curious. Or maybe she just needed the thread and didn't want to risk losing the job for prying like a kithkin gossip-monger. Veesa nearly took it upon herself to ask Colfenor, but fortunately Iliona stopped her impetuous sister in time.

When the cenn and Ashling started discussing payment, the faeries drifted back away from the town square. They had gathered enough information to make sharing it worthwhile, especially the part about Colfenor and the elf. All they needed to do was find a place to pass it along to she who'd demanded the information.

Once they were outside the village, the trio broke into a shimmering storm of giggles and titters as they raced to their destination. Moments later, all three were gathering over a small ring of speckled white mushrooms growing along the western fringe of the village. They hovered, reverently closing their eyes as their happy trilling song died away.

The kithkin called them faerie rings, and believed faeries created the fungal circles when no one was looking. The Vendilion clique, and indeed all other cliques, also called them faerie rings, but not for the same reason as the kithkin. The faeries called such growths by that name because the faeries used them to travel to and from the glen that hid the being that was—to them—god, master, queen, and mother, all in the same package.

"Oona," they each thought silently, the name of their queen echoing in each of their heads. "Mother of Us All. Queen of the Fae."

It took Oona no time at all to notice them, and the trio leaned close together, touching their foreheads at the center of the faerie ring. Their wings buzzed excitedly, and scintillating powder swirled around them.

Within moments, they were gone.

CHAPTER 5

With the combined efforts of two giants devoted to the task of utter destruction, boggarts and disturbing bits of boggarts flew through the air with alarming and untidy regularity. Rhys dodged another wrinkled, leathery, screaming lump, slung his bow, and drew his sword. This boggart survived the impact, but its back was clearly broken. Rhys dispatched it with a swipe of his sword and moved on, resigned to the grisly, undignified mop-up job his carefully planned ambush had become.

Cleaning up after giants was appalling, but it was better than the alternatives, such as some of the boggarts escaping, or reaching Kinsbaile, or—worst of all—inflicting serious injury on the hunters. But it still wasn't going to look good. Rhys hoped that in the final weighing he would at least get credit for eliminating this dangerous mob of scavengers, even if it had been a sloppy, poorly executed affair.

Another boggart ran screaming through the clearing, its left arm a ragged stump. It tripped, and by the time its body struck the ground the creature no longer had the strength to rise. Rhys finished it off with a disgusted snarl. Fresh blood spattered upon his once-glorious hunter's mantle, already saturated with gore. The mantle would, of course, have to be burned and replaced at great personal expense. Another wretched bit of dishonor for any daen—doubly so for Rhys, currently wearing his third.

The dying screamer had only been the forefront of a stinking, panicked mob of its doomed kin. Down the same blood-soaked trail, a new, surprisingly intact boggart desperately charged Rhys from the woods, leading a small gang of his still-riled kin. Before the creature got within ten feet of the pack leader, a silver arrow appeared in the center of its chest. The arrow's momentum and a bit of mass-altering magic carried the shrieking little horror back into his followers, and the lot of them fell into a tangled heap—all but one rasping boggart at the rear. It barreled wildly over its prone friends like a punch-drunk kithkin and leaped at Rhys's throat, trailing blood from an open chest wound that had probably collapsed one lung, judging from the choking sounds that interrupted its gasping cries of fury.

A second arrow just cleared the pack leader's shoulder and struck deep into the howling boggart's neck, immediately freeing the boggart of the need to draw breath ever again.

Rhys quickly set upon the stunned survivors of the boggarts' desperate charge with his sword and dagger. They were little trouble, though a burly female in unusual robes (unusual for a boggart, at least) attempted some boggart swamp magic. The burgeoning red glow in the female's eyes was easily doused with the swipe of a blade. And with that, anything resembling a boggart counterattack was over.

This victory filled Rhys with disgust: with himself, his situation, and his hunters. It was, briefly, almost overwhelming, but a moment later his training reasserted itself and demanded that discipline in the pack be maintained. Rhys knew exactly who had fired those wasteful and inelegant shots into the boggart mob, and he whirled upon the pair of elves approaching from the south.

These two were newcomers to Rhys's pack. Each wore expressions of relief that Rhys was safe mixed with lingering pleasure and pride over their bloody work, but their faces fell under his sharp, stern glare. "Well?" He spoke calmly, but specifically addressed neither one nor the other.

"Well what?" parroted Tiristan. The female hunter nocked another arrow and scanned the tree line as she spoke. "We just saved your life. Taer."

Her silent male counterpart Grath nodded in agreement as he, too, slipped another arrow into place.

"One of you made a shot barely worthy of a kithkin child, let alone a hunter. Your arrow buried itself in its breastbone and punched it back. You might as well have thrown a rock. Your bolt should have gone straight through its rib cage and on through every boggart behind him.

"And you," Rhys snarled at Grath, "took a needless chance for the sake of drama. If I had tried to dodge or draw my weapon . . . if I had moved at all, your arrow would have hit me instead of the target. Unacceptable. Track your target, or don't target anything. There can be no cracks in the face of perfection."

The pair visibly sulked but held their tongues. Rhys let his glare slip into a scowl, and he spoke with a touch of true menace. "We will speak of this further upon our return. Now get busy. Help the giants finish this mess. Until you master discipline with your bow, this is the only duty for which either of you is fit." He straightened and nodded. Tiristan and Grath did the same, almost simultaneously, though they did not straighten quite as much, nor nod quite as sharply.

As the two sullen archers went across the clearing toward the sound of the giants' mayhem, another elf emerged from the tree line. He was tall and handsome, a study in elegant elf beauty, and he wore a confident smile.

"They weren't the ones that fired early, and now they're mopping up. An orderly end to a fight like this is unlikely," the new arrival said. At a scowl from the daen, Gryffid saluted stiffly and added, "Taer!" He was Rhys's second-in-command and no fool. He was also a friend, though one who wouldn't have been spared his superior's wrath had he not snapped to attention.

"They fired badly in the middle of an ambush gone bad," Rhys replied. "And they smiled at me like I ought to have thanked them for it."

Gryffid sidled up to him and glanced over at the smashed trail of corpses Brion had left in his wake. "Shall I discipline them further, taer?"

"You call that discipline? I barely scolded them."

With his eyes down, Gryffid said, "Permission to speak freely? Taer?" He smiled guiltily. "Rhys?"

"Granted," Rhys said with growing irritation. "But Gryff, for bog's sake keep it brief. I have a fiasco to clean up and I'm not—"

"That's what I wanted to say, my friend. Bringing giants into this was a mistake. Pulling back the pack to let the giants work was a mistake. Using yew poison? Big mistake. Nath won't like it." Gryffid leaned slightly as another boggart flew past them and landed with a crunch against a tree trunk. "Even if it was effective."

"I am a Gilt Leaf pack leader," Rhys replied. "Taercenn Nath commands many packs at once, but this one is mine. For as long as I hold my rank and my pack's respect, it is mine."

"You are Faultless," Gryffid agreed. "But Nath is Exquisite. Don't delude yourself: He alone commands your sword. The pack may be yours, but it's also his. The mistakes . . . those are yours, I'm afraid."

"It is not something I am proud of, but it was necessary," Rhys said. "You know as well as I that something's gotten into the boggarts of late. I chose to ensure the success of this effort, and I've done what Nath wanted done. What he ordered done."

"But not as Nath wanted it done."

"Nath was not here." Rhys shook his head angrily. "And he is my superior in the pack, not my master. I had a master for many years, but now I am my own."

Gryffid scowled. "Your treefolk sage isn't Nath, Rhys. I worry when you talk like this. Every treefolk you cite and giant you hire tells Nath you're not fit for his service. When Nath sees this . . . when we all see this, we wonder why you hunt with us at all. Why one so privileged and elite deigns to chase boggarts in the blood and the mud alongside lowly soldiers."

Rhys glared at his friend. "Are you finished?"

"Almost. Someone has to say this, my friend, and say it plainly. You may not call Nath master, but you are a member of his pack. He has the power of life and death over you. You must follow his orders . . . and honor his intentions."

"While following my own initiative," Rhys replied. "Always."

"More treefolk blather," Gryffid said dryly. "Even a sage's teachings are subordinate to pack discipline, my daen."

Rhys abruptly turned back on his second. "Is this a friendly warning or a friendly threat?"

Gryffid dropped his eyes and said nothing.

"Thank you for your opinion and your advice," Rhys said, "but I will continue to lead my pack my way. Let Nath raise his objections. I will answer them." Rhys dusted off his hands. "Now then. I have order to enforce, discipline to mete out, and perfection to preserve. Unless you feel a need to undermine me further, I'd like to get on with it."

Gryffid straightened his lean body and drove both hoofed feet into the earth. "My daen," he said soberly, and this time he sounded like he meant it.

"Very good," Rhys said. "Now, your orders. Pick three

hunters. Take one with you. Send the other pair in the opposite direction. You're marching the perimeter of this hunting ground. Any stragglers or survivors the giants missed are to be exterminated. If you see young Yelm, do nothing but send him to me. I will deal with him."

Gryffid touched two fingers to his right horn by way of salute, turned on one hoof, and stalked off to carry out his orders without another word.

Rhys allowed a small sigh to crack his stern façade. He and Gryffid had been comrades for a long time, and it could just as easily have been Gryffid in command of the fourth hunting pack. But the rivalry between the elf nation's military and spiritual factions seemed to have finally trickled down to the individual hunting packs. Gryffid had not been chosen for apprenticeship with a treefolk mentor, and he was becoming increasingly vocal about the need for elf and treefolk to keep their distance. Rhys lamented that Gryffid's opinion, whether motivated by resentment, politics, or true concern for the future of the Blessed Nation, would inevitably ruin their ability to function in the same pack.

Gryffid's bitterness was unfortunate, but Rhys found that which really troubled him crouched in fear atop a thick knotbole branch, twenty feet off the ground and roughly seventy yards to the east of the daen's initial position in the ambush—the exact location from which that first arrow had flown before the signal was given, triggering the unnecessarily chaotic slaughter.

"My daen," Yelm managed. Rhys was slightly impressed. From the look on the pale youth's face, it was remarkable Yelm could speak at all. It was a disciplined testament to whatever scant training the young hunter had been able to grab before earning a place within the pack, perhaps, or a hint of the youth's future potential. Right now, neither of those positives were enough to forestall Rhys's anger.

"Hunter Yelm," Rhys said, stopping and nodding to the youth. "Come down here."

"Yes, taer," Yelm replied immediately with the appropriate honorific. He leaped from his perch and gracefully reached the carnage-strewn forest floor with a few nimble hops. With another quick step, he stood before Rhys at attention. Only a mild twitch in his fingers and a cocking of the right horn betrayed the young hunter's nervousness, but in a pack hunter it was a glaring sign of fear.

"You fired before the signal was given," the daen said. "Why?"

"I heard a sound," Yelm said, "a crack, and I saw movement. I—I thought I had missed the signal somehow. We had to time things so precisely, taer, and I wanted to follow your orders as you had given them. And so I fired." Honest, to the point, and a touch defensive. Young Yelm was a natural. Again Rhys felt his anger tempered by a sense of pride in this subordinate who, though clearly anxious, did not try to dance around his own culpability.

But this didn't temper his anger much.

"And because you fired," Rhys said with forced calm, "we went from an organized extermination to this—"

"Daen Rhys of the Fourth Gilt Leaf Pack!" bellowed a strong, sharp voice. It was the last voice Rhys expected or wanted to hear at that moment. The daen jumped a little bit, an embarrassing loss of composure before a subordinate—or rather it would have been if the voice of the Gilt Leaf supreme commander, Taercenn Nath, had not caused young Yelm to whimper aloud.

"What is the meaning of this?" Taercenn Nath stomped through the boggart-ridden battlefield with his fierce eyes fixed on the daen. From the sound of it, Taercenn Nath had been watching and listening for some time. Nath was taller than Rhys—taller than any elf Rhys knew—and he wore armor of gleaming mesh woven from rare silverwood bark. His horns were full and magnificent, thick and strong and sharp, and he walked with the authority of one who could order the death of any creature he happened upon with a single word and without regret.

"I am executing the duty you assigned, my taercenn," Rhys replied without making eye contact. "It appears I misunderstood your intent." He had expected criticism for hiring the giants, he even expected to be taken to task for allowing young Yelm to trigger the backup plan . . . but he never expected Nath to stand before him with real murder in his eyes.

"We will discuss your failings in more detail shortly," Nath said, dismissing Rhys's defense with a wave of his hand as he drew his sword with the other. The taercenn stepped back, raised his weapon, and drove it deep into Yelm's skull between the eyes, killing the youth instantly.

Rhys could not stop a short cough of surprise and objection. Yelm was of the Hemlock pack, and thus Yelm was Rhys's to kill if he decided killing was necessary. As he saw the spark of life abruptly go out of the young hunter's eyes, Rhys realized he'd already decided it wasn't.

Taercenn Nath withdrew his blade. He wiped it clean on Yelm's tunic before the youth's body could topple, and then Nath turned to Rhys.

"Taercenn, that was—"

"That was discipline, hunter," Nath said. "Pack discipline. Elf discipline. Gilt Leaf discipline. You should try it some time." He jerked his head roughly. "Conclude any business you have with your hired thugs and send them as far from here as fast as they can go. I do not wish to see them again. After you've done that, return to my camp and wait for me there." Nath drew himself up, and his voice boomed.

"I'm taking charge here. As of this moment you are formally and officially relieved of command."

* * * * *

Brion stood next to a rocky hill, up to his calves in a mound of broken boggarts. His brother Kiel sat nearby, his dull features fixed and his eyes unfocused as he absently sifted dirt and stones through his massive fingers.

In this relative state of calm, Rhys steeled himself before taking a good look at his hirelings, if such a diminutive-sounding word could be applied to such oversized creatures. They claimed to be brothers, but beyond their enormous size they appeared to have very little in common.

Brion was at least forty feet tall, but he was built broad and round like some great shambling hillock. His head was as bald as an egg, and his crown sloped down to a huge, curved brow that cast shadows over his deep-set eyes. Brion's nose was wide and bulbous. His thick, lantern jaw was twisted by an underbite that forced a row of tusklike fangs over his upper lip like a poorly laid fence. Brion's earlobes were long and drooping, and they wagged every time he moved his head, their ends flapping below his chin. His torso was round and fat as a baby's, but his arms and legs were thick with knotty muscles. He wore a rough-stitched shirt made from some greenish animal hide, and he bore a distinctive scar across his throat where—he had told Rhys by way of introduction—his brother Kiel had tried to tear it out when the two were no taller than cervins.

Kiel's height equaled his brother's, but his shape was entirely different. He was broad-shouldered, even more so than Brion, but his muscle-swollen upper body tapered down to a narrow waist on top of a stunted pair of legs that seemed better suited to a kithkin than a giant. Where Brion was almost proportional from head to toe, at least two-thirds of Kiel's body length was his torso. Kiel's long arms hung straight to the ground, and the calluses on the backs of his knuckles had been hardened and polished smooth from years of being dragging along behind their owner.

Kiel's head was long, almost oblong, and it came to a rounded point at both crown and chin. His face was narrow, the features crowded together near its center, and his tiny, round ears stood out almost perpendicular to his skull. Kiel was bald, but he sported a set of long white chin whiskers that stretched down to the ground. The end of his beard was a tangled mass of dirt, rocks, blood, and tree limbs.

Rhys strode up to Brion, who handled all of the negotiations. Brion could string words into sentences fairly reliably, but Kiel had so far not said anything more coherent than a grunt. The elf whistled loudly as he approached, and the forty-foot brute looked down with a sneer. Then he saw Rhys and grinned through a mouthful of crooked, broken teeth.

Rhys extended twin coils of gold thread. "The job's done. Here's your payment."

Brion peered at the elf's relatively tiny hand. "Not done, boss," the giant said. "Not yet."

Rhys spoke as calmly as he could. "The job is done," he said again. The proximity of the giant's bloody fists as Brion crouched on one knee to speak to him was concerning, but the giant-sized cloud of halitosis coming from Brion and his silent brother was downright painful.

"Still boggarts left, boss," Brion said. He scratched the back of his domed skull thoughtfully. "Won't take more than a few days to stomp 'em all out, though."

"That won't be necessary. The Gilt Leaf will handle things from here."

Brion shook his head. "No good. We had a deal."

"And I am honoring it." Rhys extended the thread once more. "Take this and go. I don't have time to argue, and you have to move along. Now."

Brion leaned back and sat, his heavy body sinking into the soil. "If we don't do the work, we don't get the thread. That's the deal."

"I'm releasing you from the deal."

"You can't. Deal's a deal, boss, make no mistake, and the deal's not done. Still more boggarts."

"Listen to me." Rhys's voice was cold and level. "I hired you. I'm the boss. I define the—I tell you what to do, you hear me? The boss is telling you to take your money and go. There's no more work for you here."

"Can't take the thread if we didn't do the work," the giant objected. "We don't need elf charity. We have pride."

"Fine." Rhys tucked the gold thread back into his pack. "Don't take it. You still have to move along."

"But you owe us," Brion said. "We helped fight the boggarts."

"And you won't let me pay you for it. How is that my problem?"

"Let's forget the money," Brion said. The giant had a thoughtful gleam in his huge eyes that Rhys didn't like at all. "Let's call it a favor we did for you."

"A favor."

"Not a job."

"Right," Rhys said, nodding impatiently.

"And in return . . . instead of money, which we can't take because we didn't do the job, which was really a favor anyway . . . you can do a favor for us."

Rhys blinked and nodded. "I . . . Sure. That works. Did you have something in mind?"

"Message," Kiel said, speaking at last.

"In a minute, Kiel," Brion said, and then he replied to the elf. "We like it here. We might be staying in Kinsbaile. Good cooks, the kithkin. Good ale. Good stories. Kiel and I, we do a few jobs, make a few threads, hear a few stories. Then we bring them home to our sister.

"That's all very interesting. You were telling me about the favor you want."

"I am telling you, yes. Hush and let me tell." Brion paused, visibly trying to remember where he left off. Then his face brightened. "We collect thread for us and stories for our sister. Her birthday is coming up. We can't keep collecting stories and deliver the stories in time. You make the delivery for us, eh?"

"Message," Kiel said again. His huge chest expanded, and he exhaled hard.

"Kiel has a birthday message for our sister too. You deliver that as part of the new deal, all right?"

"I don't deliver messages, my friend." Rhys said.

"You get messenger for us. We're busy, you know. You get messenger to bring stories and message to our sister." He wiped his hands on the filthy rag stretched across his chest. "Then we are all even, favors repaid."

"I can arrange to deliver your message," Rhys said slowly, with a growing certainty he'd been duped somehow, but not in any way he could yet comprehend. The sensation was unsettling. "But not right away. I have other business."

"We just want it done before the big sky-show," Brion said. "Otherwise, we miss her birthday. And that would be bad." Brion shivered, and Kiel nodded so vigorously his beard swept up a cloud of dust.

"Very, very bad," Kiel said.

Brion held out his thumb and peeled off a single, grimy thread. Rhys saw a speck of gold underneath the patina of filth. Brion gingerly held the thread out and said, "Here. For paying the messenger."

Rhys shook his head. Brion shrugged. He squinted one eye and carefully wound the thread back around his finger.

"Tales," said Rhys.

"Aye, tales," Brion rumbled with a nod toward his brother. "Kiel wants tales, tales for our sister. So we'll stay near Kinsbaile a while. Maybe we can hear stories from their festival. "

Kiel spoke again. "Tales. Message. Elf."

"Tales, and a message," Rhys said. "Fine. What is the message? What is your sister's name? And where will I find her?"

"Kiel is *giving* you the message, elf," Brion said with a touch of menace, or perhaps he had a boggart leg stuck in his throat.

"I understand," Rhys said, but he honestly did not.

After a moment Kiel stood with a grunt and a cascade of pops and creaks that pinged through his oversized bones. "Message," Kiel said, and raised a fist in the air. The giant's giant hand blotted out the sun and cast a shadow over Rhys, but he didn't move an inch.

Kiel crossed his other arm across his chest and plucked a small scroll of dried leather from the mosslike fur that lined his armpit. He held out the scroll delicately, between his blood-caked finger and thumb, and dropped it into Rhys's open hands. "Message," Kiel repeated. "Tales. Rosheen."

"Message," Rhys muttered with a nod, tucking the foul-smelling roll of leather into the cuff of his boot. "Rosheen." The scroll tingled with magic against his fingertips—Brion or perhaps Kiel apparently knew a shrinking spell. That made sense for any giant who ever planned to do business with someone Rhys's size. Unfortunately, the once-enormous hide had been poorly cured. He supposed there were worse things than smelling of a giant's armpit. Combining that smell with half-rotten arbomander hide certainly meant you were headed into lethal territory. Few predators would feel compelled to pick up his trail on the way back to camp, that was for certain. Any who tried would probably go blind.

Perhaps this Rosheen would find him, following the invisible pungent trail.

Rosheen. The elf cocked one horn in curiosity. "Wait . . . Are you telling me your sister is Rosheen Meanderer?"

Brion nodded, and Kiel thumped the ground.

"She talks," Kiel said.

"All the time," Brion added. "Won't be hard to find her, just do this." He cupped a filthy paw around his elongated ear. "Follow the sound of Rosheen talking."

"I'll pass that along to the messenger," Rhys said dryly. "Can you also tell me where to start? Rosheen hasn't been seen around here in a very long time. Where am I supposed to find her?"

"No," Brion said cheerfully. "You just find her. Always works for us."

"Then how can you be sure I've repaid the favor? If I can't find her, I can't—"

"You'll find her. Kiel said you are delivering this message, so that means you are."

"Really," Rhys said with an arched eyebrow. "Is that a threat, Brion, or is Kiel is some kind of ogre oracle?"

"I don't know what you just said, but then elves are always too smart for their own good," Brion said. "It is simple. Kiel said you are doing it, so you are doing it. He knows. Like you elves know the leaves are about to turn. He knows a lot, but he doesn't say as much as he knows. He did say that little elf would trigger your attack too soon. Probably should have told you about that, I suppose, but we were getting so bored."

"What?" Rhys said but forced his temper to remain in check. Even if Brion had informed him of Kiel's prediction, the then-daen would have laughed it off as madness.

Brion soldiered on, ignoring the elf. "He also predicted I would be wearing a hill-hat. I know you didn't miss that beauty. And he said you'd go back to your big boss in shame."

"If he knew all that. . . ." Rhys said, unable to contain himself any further but unwilling to get into an argument with the giants. Such arguments turned violent quickly, and Rhys was far too pragmatic to think he had a chance against two giants. "Bog it all," he finished. "He just—he just should have mentioned something sooner," Rhys said.

"Oh, no," Brion said earnestly. "He's good that way. The best thing about Kiel knowing stuff is that he doesn't go around crowing about it." Brion thumped his brother and Kiel issued another unintelligible grunt. "We'll be around Kinsbaile, elf. You go do us this favor, and we'll be even."

With that, Brion placed a calloused hand on his brother's shoulder and steered Kiel in the right direction, and then the two lumbered off to the road that ran along the riverbank all the way to Kinsbaile.

Rhys's path led in the opposite direction, around the smoldering remains of the twice-stained battlefield. Nath must have ordered his pack to put the clearing to the torch on their way back to camp, and the whole area was becoming a blackened swath of charred bone and smoking earth. Rhys went on, walking along an oft-used game trail into a typical stand of silverwood pines and up an unmarked path through the canopy of the forest to a temporary shelter that housed the taercenn of the Gilt Leaf and his staff.

On top of his failure and dismissal, twin dishonors he could hardly conceive but which had already happened, Rhys was going to be late. Negotiating with the giants had taken far too long. Late, and smelling of. . . . He reached for the scroll in the back of his belt, intending to discard it, but something stopped him.

Rosheen Meanderer was said to have foreknowledge, and if Brion and Kiel were her brothers, maybe it ran in the family. Kiel's talent might be legitimate. Colfenor regularly made predictions that came true—they were always cryptic and opaque until it was too late for them to do any good, but they were accurate predictions nonetheless.

Rhys squared his shoulders, avoiding eye contact with the last few straggling elves walking through the bloody bodies. They ignored him in return as they mechanically marched through the woods, swords drawn, ready to finish any boggarts that had survived the poison and the giants.

They wouldn't find any, Rhys expected, but the formality was necessary. As was the far more painful formality of whatever punishment Taercenn Nath had in store for him.

CHAPTER 6

Rhys lifted clear of the saddle as his mount effortlessly bounded over a mossy boulder. In that moment of weightless unfettered flight, the disgraced elf forgot demotion and failure. He was simply a hunter, and this was the chase. As far as punishments go, he thought, this one is not so bad. Yet.

On the far side of the age-worn rock the cervin shattered a rotten log and a thriving, unsuspecting anthill into mulch beneath her hooves. Rhys felt no noticeable impact and needed to lean only slightly forward to urge his steed on at a full gallop. Of all the treasures the Blessed Nation had wrung from the wilds of Lorwyn, the cervins were the most magnificent. They were sleek and elegant, with overlong limbs that placed the cervin's back anywhere from ten to fifteen feet off the ground on a typical ride. Their limber, stiltlike legs allowed them to negotiate the most treacherous woodland terrain without slowing their remarkable pace. These legs were improbably long, but this apparent awkwardness belied a flexible set of limbs far stronger than they appeared. Cervins could quickly lift their bodies from the ground to full height and back again without breaking a sweat. To an onlooker, a sprinting cervin navigating a large obstacle often resembled some strange insect or snake, not so much hurdling or climbing the impediment as flowing over it. Smooth foreheads gave way to the soft fuzzy antlers both male and female cervins sported. A cervin's silky coat was a pale tapestry of woody brown and sunrise orange, and mature cervins sported white, catlike whiskers on their muzzles, lending their faces a noble air of wisdom and experience.

Cervins were highly prized among elf nobles and had been for as long as anyone could remember. The Gilt Leaf elves had hunted them for their beauty and for the considerable challenge they posed; it was said that a cervin was the only thing in the living world that could outrun an elf. In their wisdom, Rhys's Blessed ancestors could not bring themselves to simply destroy something so beautiful, or so useful. They began to capture cervins not for their coats, but to domesticate them, to breed and tame them as mounts and draft animals.

Rhys's steed crouched down and pounded the soil with its hooves. The trees blurred along his peripheral vision and Rhys's joy cooled. The cervin he rode was a fine specimen, a direct descendent of that original breeding stock, but it was at least a dozen generations removed from the wild. He surmised it had been bred in one of Nath's kennels in the east, which the taercenn had maintained for as long as Rhys could remember.

Fifty paces ahead and to the north, Nath himself rode a great smoke gray cervin whose bloodline was clearly only a sire or two removed from the wild chargers of the deep wood. Gryffid was mounted on a similarly robust steed, riding twenty-five paces back in the position of honor to Nath's right. As newly demoted third in command, Rhys was relegated to the left, twice as far from Nath as Gryffid, as he led the reserve segment of the taercenn's assembled force. Rhys's cervin straightened its legs to ascend a slight rise, and the improved vantage gave Rhys a full view of the prospective battleground as the elf legions surged forward. The taercenn, Gryffid, and Rhys were positioned at the head of their respective troops, composed of the combined might of the Gilt Leaf's Nightshade, Hemlock, and Deathcap hunting packs. Only the officers were mounted. The rest of the scouts, archers, and rangers moved through the forest on their own two feet in a deceptively chaotic pattern carefully choreographed to cover every last scrap of ground, to root out the vermin they'd been ordered to harass.

Nath's army was bearing down on the Porringer Valley, a broad lowland trough cut at its base by the Wanderwine River. Porringer was the ancestral home of the ash treefolk, who counted among their number some of the largest warriors and oldest sages in all Lorwyn. Even though Porringer hosted far more of the latter, it was still one of the ashfolk's most secure strongholds. The trees were so numerous it was impossible for any kind of sizeable force to advance quickly by land or sky. Once an invader's slow progress roused the ash to action, it would be a fight for every inch against a thousand angry treefolk and their less mobile relatives.

Indeed Porringer had formidable defenses when the treefolk were roused to action, but those times were rare, and though he'd never personally seen the ash in action it sounded nothing like the orderly defense Rhys usually associated with the word "defense." In fact, the valley was really not "defended" at all: the philosophical ashfolk allowed anyone to come and go through Porringer at any time so long as the denizens of the valley itself were left more or less alone. The outer edges of Porringer's thick, endless groves were rife with criminals and vermin, outlaws from every tribe, yet the treefolk never raised a complaint, much less their fists. So long as the visitors made no mischief and did no harm to anything of interest to the ash, they were welcome to roam the valley for as long as they liked. Perhaps the community's surfeit of scholars and philosophers was behind this attitude.

The valley's role as sanctuary caused nothing but strife for the Gilt Leaf. Bandits weren't the only fugitives hiding within Porringer, the place was also a last refuge for eyeblights and other disgraced elves (the valley was the only place Rhys had ever heard of where elves who had been merely disgraced did not slaughter eyeblights on sight, as was the custom). Boggarts lived here by the score, entire colonies squatting like rodents among the roots. Random gangs of the vicious little things would run and hide here whenever they had cause to run and hide. The only thing they all had in common was respect for the ashfolk, which kept conflict within the valley to a minimum. Sanctuary for one was sanctuary for all, but anyone who started a fight that resulted in injury to a tree tended to disappear.

Rhys heard a mournful birdsong and recognized the trail-talk signal he'd been expecting. He squeezed the cervin's rope-muscled neck, and the mount responded instantly, coming to a gentle stop.

The Gilt Leaf's quarry had come to Porringer, driven and herded here by the assembled might of three full hunting packs. Nath's army could have overtaken the wild, bloodstained band in a matter of hours and overwhelmed them in the woods long before they ever reached the valley, but Nath had other ideas.

The taercenn's plan (which he outlined to Gryffid while pointedly ignoring Rhys, whom he kept waiting like a servant outside his command tent) was to drive the boggart raiders all the way to the supposed safe haven of Porringer. To Gryffid, Nath declared his determination to clean out the valley once and for all, to remove every last boggart and villain infesting the place. It was a task that no Exquisite had yet managed, indeed, one that many would never attempt for fear of antagonizing the treefolk who lived there.

Nath was dismissive, almost disdainful of this attitude, which he raised himself rhetorically only to tear down and immediately dismiss. Since the ash did not object to the boggarts' presence, he reasoned, they could not object to the boggarts' removal, so long as the ashfolk weren't directly affected.

Gryffid properly asked the question Rhys would have asked before leading warriors into such a battle. "To where shall we remove them, Taercenn?"

Nath brushed the query aside with a mysterious dry chuckle. "Once we have succeeded," he said, "I will enact a new initiative in which you shall play a central part. You see, I believe it's long past time the Gilt Leaf established a permanent outpost near here." The taercenn lowered his horns and fixed his cold, gray eyes on Gryffid. "Which, unless one is far dimmer than one has appeared thus far, is all the answer one needs." Nath raised his head and turned his back. "Sufficient?"

"More than sufficient, Taercenn." Gryffid's voice was sharp and hungry. "Excellent, in fact, if I may speak freely."

"You may."

Rhys was not so sanguine. If Nath intended to encroach on Porringer, not only the ash, but all the treefolk on the high council would surely protest. Porringer's warrior ashfolk contingent might even be roused from the heart of their sacred grove to defend their home.

But Nath had not risen to the highest ranks of the elves' ruthless hierarchy by thinking small or shrinking from a challenge. If he cleaned out Porringer, he would be in an extremely strong position to establish and defend an outpost here. He would add a large, valuable piece of unclaimed territory to his holdings. Taercenn Nath would also control all traffic and commerce between the Gilt Leaf Wood and western Lorwyn.

Rhys shook such thoughts from his head as Gryffid approached. Gryffid's huge brindle cervin trotted as silently as sunlight, and though its eyes were fixed on Rhys, Gryffid kept his face turned away from his old friend and comrade.

Rhys noted with satisfaction that the troops of the combined packs elegantly altered their maneuvers without altering their tactics as his fellow commander drew up next to him.

"Taercenn Nath wanted me to make sure you understand your role here," Gryffid said, his eyes carefully locked on the foliage above his own right shoulder.

"I do," Rhys answered. "I am to hold the reserve force ready until he signals me."

Gryffid turned and glared. "And you will comply without delay."

"Of course."

"Of course what?"

"Of course, taer," Rhys said.

Gryffid turned away once more and stared ahead, his position in the saddle indicating his subordinate was dismissed.

Rhys hesitated. What he was about to do was still frowned upon by most elves. Sudden empathic intrusion was rude, and in practical terms, could sometimes get the intruder stabbed, shot, or dropped from a great height. But he needed to communicate his unease to Gryffid—Rhys felt with growing certainty that this raid was a very bad idea.

Gryffid. I must speak with you.

Rhys saw Gryffid slap a hand to the side of his head with a start, almost losing his balance. The proximity of the mighty silverwoods made the Rhys's thoughts reverberate inside both their skulls like a crannog's bell tower in a thunderstorm. The message traveled along a one-way channel, to one who had not learned the techniques Rhys had mastered with Colfenor. Gryffid could not respond in the same way—another factor that had made the intrusion risky. Gryffid scowled, silent but furious at Rhys's terrible and intrusive breach of etiquette.

Rhys chose his next words as carefully as he could. "This attack . . . it's bad strategy. We don't know why those boggarts went mad, we don't know if they even came from here; they might have been passing through. Attacking may make the problem worse. It may drive more desperate boggarts out into the woods. Not to mention the uproar from the treefolk—"

"Only you give a leaf for the treefolk's opinion," Gryffid snarled. "Which I count as more evidence of your unfitness, even for your current position. As for the boggarts . . ." Gryffid grinned knowingly, with a predatory sneer that had never disquieted Rhys until this moment. It did now. "When this is over, it won't matter how those vermin react. They can't go mad when they're all dead."

"All—" Rhys barely managed to bite out the word when a call from ahead snapped his mouth shut.

"Maintain your positions." Nath's voice came through the trees, clear and strong. It was remarkable that he was not using trail-talk. His voice was loud though he was not shouting, and Rhys knew the words hardly carried beyond his own ears—a rhetorical skill that served the taercenn well on the battlefield or on the hunt. Nath's verbal proclamation gave the proceedings a grander, more formal air that Rhys found more disquieting than any empathic contact.

"If you must prattle like kithkin, do so when our duty is complete," the taercenn called, "and do it far from my ears."

Gryffid's face flushed with embarrassment, and without a word he dug his heels into the cervin's side and cantered back to his place at the head of the right flank. Rhys was sorry to see him go, but even sorrier at Gryffid's reaction. His friend's promotion, though probably temporary, was clearly of utmost importance to him. With Gryffid technically being Rhys's superior, Nath's continued approval became the lifeline to greater prominence within the packs, perhaps even to the distinctive taercenn's tattoo that all hunters hoped to wear. Stacked against such a weight, the idea of continuing their long friendship was woefully inadequate.

While these thoughts raced through his head, another section of his mind—the hunter—continued to search the trees for prey or large predators. As Rhys's contemplative thoughts turned to the well-known fact that Nath, like most powerful elves, was one to hold a grudge, he saw movement in the trees—movement that should not have been there . . .

Quickly and silently, he double-checked. The overlook teams were in the canopy where they belonged. The combined forces moved forward, dozens of stealthy elf hunters slipping silently through the trees. Gryffid was once more leading the right flank with Nath at the tip of the lead formation. They were both focused forward, alert and on the attack, ready to fall on the enemy before them.

So they did not see what Rhys saw: a lone boggart emerging from a hole it had dug for itself. It was the color of wet ashes and unarmed, its body clad in a filthy black loincloth, a layer of mud, and nothing more. It rubbed its dirt-encrusted eyes sleepily until it noticed the elves moving away from it, toward the valley. The boggart reacted like a frightened hare when it saw Rhys looking at him, freezing in place, and hoping a lack of further movement would give the hunter no reason to look again. Perhaps it hoped to blend back in with the shadows, but Rhys easily kept it in sight.

For a moment he considered calling to Gryffid. He did not, instead reminding himself that he could still expect the rank and file hunters in his flank to follow his orders. Using only hand signals, he sent word through the pack, with instructions to pass the information up to Nath and Gryffid. Then Rhys sent a pair of hunters around the silverwood to capture the boggart for interrogation before it could raise an alarm.

His hunters were up to the challenge. They doubled back and crept around the silverwood, flanking the boggart on each side. It didn't even notice them as they drew their swords and struck as one, twice skewering the grubby little beast where it stood.

Rhys muffled a warning cry. Fools, he thought. We needed him alive.

Nath's whisper, sharp as wind shear, cut through Rhys's head.

"Rhys!" The mounted taercenn had materialized in front of Rhys, his eyes wide and angry. "What is the meaning of this?"

"My taercenn," Rhys said, lowering his head. He spoke quickly, pointing at the dead boggart. "That creature was buried here for a reason—I think to spy on us. We sought to trap the boggarts here, but they may in turn be laying a trap for us."

"And I am to fear the defenses of vermin? Should I also fear to kick an anthill, Rhys, lest the insects bite my tender feet?" Nath snorted, then thoughtfully pinched the end of one horn between his thumb and forefinger. "That rotting hunk of flesh was obviously a stray. We're here to put such strays down."

"Honored Taercenn," Rhys said, "I speak a little of what these things call a language. Let us take one alive. Let me interrogate the creature. If we are being led into a trap—"

The taercenn drove a fist into the center of Rhys's chest, knocking him backward off his mount. Rhys landed heavily and rolled, mindful that he should not rise until Nath gave him permission to do so, or risk another blow. Breathing heavily, Rhys noted that Nath could have easily landed the blow on his face, but hadn't—even the taercenn was not angry enough to mar Rhys's features and make an eyeblight of him. Not yet.

"Do you question me?" Nath said, his eyes closing to slits, his hand dangling near the hilt of his silver long sword. "Do you, Rhys?"

Though he could still barely breathe, Rhys forced himself to straighten and respond. "Reconnaissance, then, taer," he managed. "Knowledge is the sheathed claw that strikes the unwary and unworthy."

Nath grimaced at having his own words—words he'd used more than once with raw, inexperienced hunters—thrown back at him, but after a few seconds he nodded. "You speak well when you quote your betters. Very good. You have three minutes to scout ahead. Address your concerns in that time, for in three minutes we are moving into the valley."

"Yes, Taercenn," Rhys said. He climbed up onto the cervin's back.

"You now have two minutes and fifty-five seconds," Nath replied, and without another word, turned his cervin and guided it back to the head of the pack.

"Two minutes fifty." Gryffid said.

"I heard him, Gryff," Rhys muttered to himself. He tapped his heels into the cervin's ribs and the lithe creature sprang forward. The elf scanned the ground as he rode, searching for other buried boggarts, for the signs that other holes had been dug and refilled with sleeping sentries inside.

He saw nothing. Either the boggarts had learned to hide their efforts, or there were no more hidden guards. Rhys rode within view of the ash tree line below. He had to turn away before he was spotted, but he could not go back to Nath without something. . . .

Rhys pulled his cervin up short and urged it to move slowly. The elf's sharp eyes saw hundreds of figures moving in the haze. He counted his remaining time to himself, each second an agonizing eternity as he struggled to make sense of what he saw.

The boggarts of Porringer were bustling, but they were not preparing defenses . . . nor were they massing for an attack. They were standing in clusters, building small bonfires, setting up tables. Most were talking, and some were even singing. Rhys actually heard sour harmonies lilting up from the valley. Wandering around the middle of the group of boggarts, Rhys recognized an older boggart matron—Auntie Thumb.

Realization dawned, and Rhys felt a surge of purpose. These boggarts were from Auntie Thumb's warren . . . and that was all the proof he needed. The cervin responded to his gentle nudge and spun about. Together they raced back to the approaching elf army, silent but for the wind in Rhys's ears.

Nath waited like a statue, not even deigning to acknowledge Rhys's approach. Rhys exhaled sharply, relief flooding his mind. He had made it with thirty seconds to spare.

"Time's up," the taercenn said, daring Rhys to point out it was, in fact, not. When Rhys didn't, Nath nodded. "Your report."

"Taer, the boggarts aren't behaving as they should be," Rhys began.

"That much is clear," Nath said.

"Taer," Rhys said with all the patience he could muster. "They belong to Auntie Thumb. The Thumb warren, alone among boggart tribes, has never given the nation cause to chastise it. They have farms. They trade with the kithkin and the merrow. The raiders we hunted were not from this tribe."

"So you say. But they could be. Suppose for a moment that you are mistaken. Would not that prove the depths of boggart treachery, to abuse the protection Porringer provides?"

"Treachery?" Rhys blurted. "These are boggarts, I hardly think they have a master plan."

"Your thoughts mean little to me. All you've proven is the necessity of the lesson we are about to dispense." Nath swept an arm ahead of him. "Pack, hold. Prepare to strike on my command." The taercenn scowled at Rhys. "Close to me, both of you. The reserve force can mind itself for now, Rhys. I want you near. I will personally see you fulfill your duty. You will relearn what it is to lead, or I will see you dead."

Nath kicked his cervin's haunches, and the gangly steed dropped into a crouching gallop. Rhys and Gryffid quickly followed suit. They broke through the edge of the grove a half-minute later, and Nath reined his mount to a halt. Rhys and Gryffid flanked him on the edge of the rocky cliff overlooking the busy boggart gathering below.

"Taer, look at them," Rhys said as his eyes took in the crowds of babbling, cackling, buzzing boggarts. "These boggarts are not a threat."

The boggarts milled around in groups of two or three, scrabbling through tents, hovels, and shacks as they continued to sing their horribly off-key songs. At least fifty boggarts had stripped away all totems and scraps of clothing that marked their tribal affiliation, and they danced in noisy circles around a trio of large fires. As Rhys watched, a boggart several feet away from the fire heaved a jawbone into the air. It was at least as big as the boggart that threw it, and appeared to have been wrenched from a river croc—even at this distance, Rhys spotted a patch of green scales still affixed to the bone. Boggarts closer to the fire caught it and heaved it again. This time it landed in the fire with a noisy sizzle and snakes of black smoke.

"Look at them?" Nath sneered. "I see them clearly. Roiling like a swarm of insects, readying to spread death and plague."

"You don't understand," Rhys said. "Usually there are only a few boggarts among the ash."

"So?" Nath shrugged. "Today we enjoy a much wider range of targets."

"Taer!" Rhys said, losing his temper for a split-second. "Between what you see now and what I saw earlier, I estimate there are at least three to five hundred boggarts down there. I would stake my reputation as a hunter—"

The indignant taercenn snorted, but let Rhys continue.

"The boggarts in the valley are *not* planning murder, or anything else."

"Why is that?" Nath asked.

"They are in the middle of their most important festival, the Feast of . . ." Rhys had to think for a moment, the boggart word was a rare compound form.

"Yes?" Nath said impatiently.

"Footbottom. The Feast of Footbottom."

"Really."

"Yes, taer. Auntie Thumb's followers always participate. It's an annual warren reunion of sorts." Rhys pointed to the fires. "Boggarts from all over the region come here, to Porringer, where they know they'll be safe. They've done it for generations. Most of the boggarts here aren't bandits but celebrants. They are not a threat."

"Boggarts in large numbers are always a threat." Nath's angry expression turned exasperated, with a touch of disgust. "I know all about this Thumb's ridiculous little festival. Why else did you imagine we're here if not to take advantage of the largest gathering of boggarts in the entire region?"

Rhys remembered Gryffid's hungry sneer. His chest went numb, and he stammered, "We can't attack them, taer. Not now, not here."

"That is not your decision."

"These aren't the boggarts we've been hunting," Rhys said,

struggling to maintain control. It was the only argument he had left. "There's no sense to it, and if the fight spreads to the ashfolk—"

"You are a coward, and you insult hunters of the finest packs in the Gilt Leaf with your insinuation. Even if you are correct," Nath said. "The raiding boggarts must be punished, even if we have to kill every boggart in this forest to get to them." Without turning from Rhys, he bellowed, "Packs, take strike positions!"

"Taer!" Rhys shouted as the assembled pack formed up along the cliffside, assembling in the perfect formation to sweep down the wide path leading to the camp. "This is a—"

"You will remember your place!" Nath bellowed. "Now, get back to your command and prepare to engage the enemy on my signal."

The boggarts still danced around their blazing fires and sang their songs. They babbled with their kinfolk beside crude tables mounded with more food than the average boggart got in a month.

Rhys's jaw locked. There was nothing he could do. "Yes, taer." he said.

He prodded his cervin and sprinted back to his position at the head of the reserves, but he craned his head to watch the taercenn behind him. When he arrived, Rhys signaled his troops to stand ready.

Nath's voice echoed loudly through the woods. "Archers," the taercenn said, and a line of arrows snapped into place, "ignite!" On Nath's command, the arrowheads combusted in a flash. "Gilt Leaf hunters," he called. "*My* hunters. There are to be no survivors. We have an infestation here, and it must be cleansed. The boggart raiders and their cretinous progeny are below. And I say none shall leave this valley alive. I know you brave sons and daughters of the Blessed Nation will allow nothing less."

The taercenn produced a glittering coil of polished gold and held it in his upraised fist. "That said," he shouted with a wicked smile, "if the boggart matriarch herself is present . . . a thousand threads of gold to the hunter who brings me her head!"

It was to the elves' credit that they stifled their cheers, issuing only impressed murmurs. Nath maintained his predatory sneer. "No survivors," he repeated, sounding like one waking from a beautiful dream. He turned to his lieutenants with a bloodthirsty glare. "No mercy. Now, execute!"

"Fire!" Gryffid ordered, and dozens of boggarts died without ever realizing they were in danger. Their siblings and cousins within ten feet quickly caught on, however, when the flame-tipped arrows exploded in a shower of boiling boggart blood and burning boggart flesh. This sizzling shower of gore in turn ignited a fire that quickly spread to every tent, shack, hovel, and lean-to nearby. The flames fed off the arrowgrass projectiles and the moonglove in which they'd been dipped, adding enough poison to the oily black smoke that curled into the air to cause several more boggarts to drop to their knees and tear at their own eyes in agony.

Gryffid turned to Rhys as Gryffid rode into the newly born battle. It was up to Rhys to deliver the final blow, to sweep in at Nath's bidding and launch the final prong of the attack against whatever hapless survivors endured the initial charge.

If nothing else, Rhys could ensure that those boggarts who fell to his hunters would die quickly and cleanly, not choking on their own noxious blood as they fled the horror around them. The boggarts as a species did not deserve mercy, but Nath's planned massacre was beneath the dignity of the nation, let alone Rhys's own. Nothing could convince Rhys he was wrong, and Nath's willingness, even eagerness, to launch this attack on these creatures, at this time, went against Rhys's every instinct. And so Rhys buried instinct. Another second of delay would only bring further rebuke.

Rhys drew his sword and raised it overhead. "Hemlock, Nightshade, and Deathcap! Strike now, hunters of the Gilt Leaf! *Strike!*"

CHAPTER 7

Rhys killed boggarts. They died swiftly, each receiving a single, lethal blow before Rhys moved on. There was no joy in him as he carried out his orders, no enthusiasm . . . only cold, ruthless efficiency. This was no hunt, and today Rhys was no hunter. He was a butcher. He felt none of the usual pride that came from exercising his skills because they were being wasted here in Porringer. There was no real threat in the valley among the ash, no real challenge, and so there was no glory for Rhys or the Blessed Nation.

Rhys gave himself to the battle, surrendering himself to instinct as much as he could without abandoning the clean, sudden kill. He cut his way into the tangle of boggarts as the war cries of his hunters mingled with the terrified shrieks of their prey. His sword flashed as it reflected the firelight, the blade moving so swiftly and ceaselessly that it left gentle, swooping arcs of glittering yellow in the shadows.

As the fires danced tall and broad, consuming the boggarts along with the outer rim of their formerly safe haven, Rhys saw himself and his fellow elves as equal to the flames. They were all component pieces of the same primal force, scouring the boggarts from Porringer. He was no longer an elf, he was killing itself, a relentless, inexhaustible bringer of death.

Barely aware of the battleground beyond his next target and

his next strike, Rhys waded deeper into the ash grove. *Slash.* A boggart was beheaded in a spray of black gore. *Hack.* A small boggart fleeing headlong from the slaughter was cleaved in two at the waist, its gnarled legs staggering an extra five steps without their upper half. *Slice.* An old boggart let out a sad, wet wheeze before he fell to the blood-slick moss.

Rhys's nose twitched as the smell of burning corpses wafted over him. Perhaps the elves were adding corpses to the bonfires like fresh kindling, or perhaps some of the boggarts were being cooked alive as the fires swept through the outermost rows of dry ash saplings.

Then Rhys's mind twitched as a familiar presence slipped easily inside.

Student.

"Colfenor—?" Rhys reflexively scanned the sky as his mentor's voice rumbled in his mind. At least, that was his intent, but a flailing boggart head wreathed in bubbling flames slammed into the back of his right knee before he could manage the final syllable.

The elf fell forward as a screaming boggart scrambled over him. Rhys rolled onto his left shoulder and swung his blade wildly at the screeching, half-immolated creature. The sword slid neatly across the boggart's throat, and a red waterfall splashed down its chest. Rhys rolled on to extinguish any remaining flames then tumbled back to his feet, near-covered in grime, black blood, and ash.

Rhys.

This time he was ready. He resumed his part in the merciless slaughter, but the deeper part of his mind stayed focused on the presence of his mentor. *Sage.*

You must stop this, Colfenor told him.

You are still too presumptuous, Sage. I am Gilt Leaf, and I am on the hunt.

This . . . is not a hunt.

Of course it is, Rhys thought reflexively, despite what he'd told himself when the fighting began. The old log had said far too much against the hunting packs over the years. It was one thing for Rhys to doubt Nath, but he would not allow Colfenor to use this nightmare as fodder for his endless tirade against Rhys's duty to the Blessed Nation.

Kick. A crunch of bone and a snapped neck ended another scream of futile boggart terror. *The taercenn declared it a hunt,* Rhys thought, *and so it is.*

I am not some petty taercenn. I am your mentor. You will heed me.

In a moment.

Parry, riposte. Another boggart struck the ground dead and in several pieces.

Every moment this atrocity goes on is a moment—

Another flaming boggart of undeterminable sex interrupted him with its screams, charging toward him from a blazing tent. Rhys knocked it to the ground with a fist and crushed the pitiable thing's skull with the sole of his boot. It twitched once and fell still. Within seconds, flames covered it.

This is not the time for debates, Sage. This fight is what it is, and I am duty-bound to see it through.

At last, the treefolk relented. *Very well.* And with that, Rhys felt the connection between them sever. He could still feel Colfenor's presence—ever since he'd become the treefolk's student, the old yew's vast and noble soul was always there at the outer edge of his mind. At the risk of offending the treefolk, Rhys felt a wave of relief. It wasn't easy to carry on a mental argument while fending off shrieking boggarts driven mad by pain and death . . . especially when he was on the argument's losing side.

Part of the relief may also have had a little to do with what Colfenor had told him and how it dovetailed with Rhys's feelings on this brutal raid. He concentrated, to make sure Colfenor was not still lingering nearby, and then Rhys stopped for a moment, squeezing his eyes shut tight. It didn't matter what the taercenn said. This was not a hunt.

Rhys opened his eyes. Everywhere he looked, the slaughter continued, a blight on the honor of the Gilt Leaf far worse than anything Rhys had done. He could not bring himself to sympathize with the filthy boggarts, but, unbelievably, Colfenor did. Rhys added this to the long list of things he would never understand about his mentor.

Rhys was leaning forward to stab another boggart when he felt a jarring impact from the side. Whatever had hit him was much heavier than a boggart. He went tumbling to the ground, entangled with the snarling elf that had collided with him so violently.

Gryffid, still snarling, raised his bloody sword overhead to strike blindly, and Rhys managed to catch his wrist before the blade could find home.

"Gryff!" he bellowed. "It's me!"

The elf looked at him with confused eyes. "Rhys," he gasped, "something's gone wrong."

"You just noticed?" Rhys said, as they helped each other get to their feet. "It's been going wrong for some time now."

"No, the boggarts," Gryffid said.

"What about them?"

"They're fighting back," Gryffid said.

"Of course they're fighting back. We're attacking them," Rhys said. "We—"

"No, damn it!" Gryffid said, suddenly angry. "This is different." He pointed with his blood-caked sword at the center of the boggart's festival preparations. The brutes were clustered four and five deep here, and many of the fires nearby were already starting to burn out.

Rhys wiped sweat and smoke from his eyes and focused on the assembly. Individuals were difficult to discern, but as a whole they seemed more feral and frenzied, larger, wilder, and angrier. What had been a crowd of placid Porringer festival-goers seemed to have far more in common with the bloodthirsty raiders Rhys had ambushed back in the deep woods.

Was Nath correct? Was the seemingly innocent festival a ruse, a mask to hide the snarling faces of violent brigands? Or were these boggarts simply responding to the danger Rhys and the other elves clearly posed?

A trio of boggarts lurched away from the larger mob and fell upon an elf hunter, tearing his flesh with their black teeth and broken fingernails. Before either Rhys or Gryffid had time to charge to the rescue, the boggarts had ripped the elf apart, pulling the hunter in twain like a wishbone. A sickening snap and a spray of blood ended the elf's screams.

"They're doing it again," Rhys said in quiet horror. "It's just like before. They're going berserk."

"Pull yourself together," Gryffid said. "They've just killed an elf is what they did."

Despite his bravado, Gryffid recoiled when a boggart raised one of the dead elf's legs overhead and tore off a hunk of warm, bloody flesh with its jagged teeth. Nearby, another small mob of boggarts had turned on another hunter, who ran, shamefully weaponless, in a blind panic for a few feet before the babbling boggarts bit through the tendons of his left leg and brought him down. Another fountain of blood erupted into the air from the elf's leg until the boggarts tore open the elf's chest and pulled out the hunter's still-steaming heart.

Elsewhere, the elves—but only a few—were having a better time of it. Many were still ceaselessly slaughtering boggarts, unaware that the creatures had exchanged their terror for fury. But the boggarts' sudden and unaccountably stiff resistance disrupted the elves' delicately balanced advance, and some of the pack officers roared for order as their formations fell apart.

"They've gone mad," Gryffid said. "This is simple panic, that's what it is. They know we're going to burn this place to the ground." With a swipe of his sword, he bifurcated one of the still-terrified boggarts that came within reach as Gryffid and Rhys surveyed the scene.

"I don't know," Rhys said. "They're not . . . Damn it, they're not fighting like boggarts, not even like desperate, furious boggarts. They're moving in packs, small packs, and they're not even pretending to use weapons of any kind. When's the last time you saw a boggart stand and fight without something heavy or sharp to flail around?"

"No, they're just terrified. Terrified of us and—"

"Gryff, they're *eating* us. They're not terrified."

"Enough talk." Gryffid waved his sword, hollering for all nearby elves to rally behind him.

No one heard Gryffid over the melee, so Rhys was the only one to fall in behind him. They carefully made their way toward the largest mob of the strange, deadly boggarts, which were huddled over the corpse of a fallen elf, tearing at it like jackals.

Rhys scanned the area and despaired. The elf formations had almost completely fallen apart. The elves had become scattered, caught up in their killing frenzies and individual battles. Rhys had never once in his life thought of his own people as lacking in discipline in any way. It wasn't that there were too many boggarts for three full elf packs to neutralize, but there were too many of this braver, more violent tribe.

The elves had not anticipated such a battle or such a foe. They perhaps could not have anticipated it.

"Where the hell is Nath?" Rhys asked aloud, but more to himself than to Gryffid. Like Gryffid and Rhys, the taercenn had abandoned his cervin outside the camp—the graceful steeds were near-useless in the close-quartered chaos erupting all over the valley.

"Gilt Leaf, to me!" Rhys turned to the sound of the taercenn's voice and saw Nath's apparently not-so-useless cervin rear up on its hind legs in the distance. The taercenn's commanding voice boomed over the melee again as Nath brought his steed's fore-hooves down upon a pair of charging boggarts, crushing them both.

"To me!" Nath roared again. "Rally to me!"

Without giving the boggarts the chance to land a crippling blow upon the cervin's ankles—by the Wood, Rhys thought, where are all these damnable boggarts *coming* from?—Nath kicked the cervin into a charge that knocked the swarming boggarts aside like ninepins. As he emerged from the encroaching mob, he reigned the cervin around sharply, crushing yet more of the maddened vermin, and then he drew his sword. The taercenn's silver blade was the aspiration of every hunter, and, despite growing suspicion among their number that not even the Gilt Leaf elves could overcome this horde, the blade—if not the man—inspired even Rhys. With shouts of furious savagery, every elf in the vicinity charged into the horrid mass of ghastly corpses and bloodthirsty carnivores.

Rhys rode a surge of power beneath his feet as he ran, hacking at every screaming, mad-eyed shape that lunged at him. The taercenn was calling on the magic of the forest, the vital force that was strong here at the edge of ash territory. Nath channeled the arcane energy into a wave of courage, ferocity, and loyalty that surged through the elf packs. Rhys grabbed onto this wave and felt a flood of raw power blast through his body. He drew the power to him, contained it, and held it within him until he could shape it to his own purposes.

Rhys whipped his left arm up in a sweeping gesture, and a wave of magic rolled across the grass and moss straight toward the boggarts, widening as it went. Every blade of grass that the spell touched became a three-foot length of tempered arrow-grass, razor-sharp and ready to be plucked and nocked on the nearest elf's bow. Nath's archers let out cheers as they crouched and loaded their weapons. No longer limited in the number of shafts they could fire, the archers sent up a thick stream of arrow-grass bolts that ripped the boggart mob into a quivering mass of bleeding, dying flesh.

"Many thanks, Colfenor," Rhys said under his breath, "you old log." This spell was merely one example of the magic Colfenor had shown him, just the sort that Rhys had turned to his own purposes. Rhys veered along the edge of the killing ground and saw no boggarts clinging to life within range of his spell-grown arrows. He noted with satisfaction how he'd allowed the archers to kill at least half of the largest mob of boggarts, maybe more, and that all had gone down quickly and efficiently. Colfenor would appreciate that, he hoped, even if the yew sage considered this entire enterprise to be a ghastly, bloody error.

Rhys drew close to Nath at the center of a slowly growing circle of elves. He saw Gryffid approach from the other side of the circle. Then Rhys whirled on the mad boggarts hissing and howling from his unprotected flank. He crouched to scoop up a handful of soil as half a dozen boggarts charged. The power of both Porringer and the surrounding forest cut cleanly through the carnage, clearing his mind and sharpening his focus.

He wanted the charging boggarts dead, and the spell obliged.

He closed a fist over the dirt in his hand and raised it to his mouth. With a puff of exhaled breath, the soil took flight. It accreted into thin, weblike strands that lashed the air in an ever-expanding outward radius. The strands continued to gain length and definition even after Rhys's hand was empty.

The thick tangle of gritty threads leaped forward into the boggart mob, shredding those that led the charge. Their bodies exploded into nebulae of bone and gore that spattered against the ground with a sound like someone tossing out a bucket of rotten milk. Those behind them almost had it worse, for they had time to feel the pain of death by a billion cuts before they were reduced to broken skeletons by the diamond rain. The boggarts behind them died even more slowly, but still they died, until the grasping, undulating mass of strands finally ran its course.

To the elf's relief, he saw that he and Nath had been joined by at least two-thirds of the assembled elf packs. Rhys guessed that of the remaining third, half were probably dead and half had been forced to fall back or were otherwise unable to reach the circle around the taercenn. For a moment Rhys felt hopeful. The Gilt Leaf packs might yet turn this into a victory. That didn't mean they all wouldn't be soundly disciplined after this fiasco, assuming there was an after. If only the seemingly endless stream of the damned things would slow.

Rhys could feel his connection to the forest's magic dwindling against the aura of the boggart mobs. He hadn't even realized such a thing was possible, though he doubted the boggarts were doing it on purpose. There was definitely strong magic at work here, magic not of the Gilt Leaf or Porringer, but magic that stood in opposition to the spells of elf and treefolk.

A pair of boggarts wielding rough, bloody stone axes led a sudden charge, which—like the rest—consisted of a large clump of boggarts breaking off from the surrounding mob to run full bore at the ring of determined elves. As Rhys tried to pull the magical energy he needed to him, the lead boggart hurled one of its axes with all its might. It tumbled end over end, landing with surprising accuracy between the eyes of the hunter to Rhys's immediate right. Spatters of blood rained upon Rhys before the stricken elf flopped over onto his back, twitching with sickening finality.

His concentration broken, Rhys took his sword in hand and joined the other elves as they met the rest of the charge head-on. Boggarts died by the score, but one by one so did the elves. Every time the defenders beat back a clutch of the ravenous creatures, another group stepped in. The boggarts attacked this side of the ring and that at random, sometimes charging in from several directions at once, at other times sending just a single gang to wear a gap in the hunters' line.

When Nath's cervin succumbed to the boggarts, Rhys entertained the frankly horrifying thought that the boggarts—the peaceful, celebrating boggarts they'd come to slay in cold blood—were in fact going to wipe out the entirety of all three Gilt Leaf packs. It was almost as if the dying boggarts had called their more formidable cousins here . . . or become them.

The cervin's death wails rang in his ears but ended when Nath, who had leaped clear of the dying mount, mercifully cut its throat.

"Gilt Leaf!" Nath bellowed. "For Gilt Leaf! Fight them to the last, hunters!"

Rhys had almost forgotten about Gryffid until he saw his friend stagger into his field of view, one arm hanging limp and useless, the other swinging wildly with a long-handled stone axe he'd acquired. Gryffid stumbled into Rhys, who caught Gryffid before he could collapse.

"Stay up," Rhys said. "You're not dead yet."

"Do something, you cur," Gryffid said, his loss of blood making him speak slowly and with a slur. "What good is your damned treefolk magic if you don't use it? If you can't do something to help, I'm going to kill you where you stand." Gryffid's eyes rolled. His expression was blank. Rhys wondered if Gryffid even knew what he was saying . . . or if Rhys was supposed to hear it.

Gryffid's voice rose, but he could not maintain a consistent volume or cadence. "Do something, damn you! Can't you do . . . something?" The last word trailed off as Gryffid collapsed against him, unconscious and fading fast.

Rhys dropped his sword and supported his friend's limp form with his sword arm while he stretched his left arm out before him. Forcing himself to ignore the boggarts drawing ever closer, he said, "Yes, Gryff. I can do something. And it might even work."

He closed his eyes and focused on the recent presence of Colfenor, on the air of infinite wisdom the old log exuded, on the profound knowledge that had rumbled just on the edge of Rhys's dreams since the day the treefolk had taken him as a student. Rhys grasped at the threadbare power left in the ground, in the grass, in the scorched brush around him, and in the still-healthy ash in the deep recesses of the valley. Individually, none of these sources would be enough for Rhys to call on Colfenor's power, let alone enough to fuel a spell that could save the packs from utter defeat. But taken all together, Rhys weaved these threads of vital, eldritch force into a fabric that was more formidable than the sum of its parts.

Colfenor, I need you.

He wondered how long he would have to wait for Colfenor to respond. Then, in a blinding flash of amber light and withering force, came the yew sage's reply.

* * * * *

When Nath awoke, he thought at first he must have been camping in the crags, buried as he was within folds of cervin fur. That dreamlike memory faded instantly as his nostrils were flooded with the smells of blackened flesh, withered hair, and stifling death.

He blinked and tried to focus on the brown shadow before him. He gasped and tried to draw a deep breath. He saw the brown shadow was a bloody mass of cervin fur, rotting cervin innards, and what appeared to be a boggart's leg burned off at the knee. The noble steed seemed to have shielded Nath from the force of the blast—there had been a blast, hadn't there?—but now the dead cervin was in danger of compressing Nath's broken ribs to the point where the taercenn could no longer breathe.

With every ounce of his considerable strength, Nath shoved against the smoldering corpse. Inch by inch, the dead cervin slid off his chest. Nath had wriggled free of the debris within a minute, and pushed himself unsteadily to his feet.

He blinked again. He could not summon up the memories of what had actually happened, but he could see the shadows around him and the setting sun. It must have been hours since the battle, perhaps even a day or more. There was choking gray-brown smoke everywhere, but other than that Nath could make out little but a twisted field of immolated bodies and denuded trees that seemed to stretch infinitely in all directions.

"Bastards," Nath said, and his voice was little more than a dry, parched croak. "Takes more than that to kill . . ." He coughed painfully and felt two of his ribs scraping against each other. "To kill me," the taercenn finished before he was wracked with another bout of hacking that drove broken rib against broken rib.

Nath forced himself to concentrate on the last moments before he lost consciousness. He remembered the hordes of boggarts and the battle gone hopelessly awry. He remembered his cervin falling out from under him, dead. And then . . .

"Rhys," the taercenn spat. Rhys had closed his eyes and raised his arm. Even though it had nearly blinded him, Nath had seen the explosion begin. Just before the body of the cervin had slammed into him and saved his life, Nath saw the burst of dull yellow energy erupt across the battleground, with Rhys at its center.

Nath heard another painful cough, and this time it wasn't rattling in his own chest. The short, gravelly hack came from not far away, and when Nath staggered toward the sound, his sharp ears told him the coughing came from overhead. His eyes adjusted to the strange half light among the shadows, and then Nath spotted the coughing survivor, twenty or so feet up the side of a scorched knotbole tree.

The hunter's left leg was impaled upon a bare, jagged branch—but that was the only thing keeping him aloft. Judging from the blood, he had severed no major arteries.

The impaled figure groaned and forced his face to rise. "Taer," Gryffid managed between coughing fits, "what happened?"

Nath popped his knuckles in reply and began climbing the tree, branch by charred branch. Soon he reached Gryffid, and Gryffid's eyelids fluttered. He tried to salute, but his broken arm would not respond.

"Hold still," Nath muttered. He paused only briefly to ponder the wisdom of saving Gryffid's life. His wounds were extensive and wholly visible. He was marred, scarred, imperfect . . . no longer fit to call himself a member of the Blessed Nation. Even if Gryffid could survive, he might not wish to.

Gryffid turned his head. "Taercenn," he started, but as Gryffid's glassy eyes focused on Nath's face, they widened in shock and horror.

"What is it, Gryffid?"

Gryffid let his face fall, unable or unwilling to maintain eye contact. "Your face, Taercenn."

Nath gingerly reached up and ran his fingers along his horns, forehead, nose, both cheeks, and his chin.

"Yes," he said without surprise, only stern reproach. "We shall speak of this later. Right now we are faced with far more pressing concerns." Gryffid nodded weakly, and with little ceremony and an exhausted pull Nath helped Gryffid yank his leg free. The residents of a merrow crannog a mile away heard the ensuing scream.

There was not another word exchanged until the elves were back on the ground. Nath performed the necessary healing magic to stop Gryffid's bleeding and begin mending his broken arm. As the ritual did its work, Gryffid sat tearing strips of the ragged remains of his left sleeve. With one hand he wrapped the strips around the wound in his leg as it closed over. Nath could have assisted him, but Gryffid did not ask for his help.

His injury seen to for the moment, Gryffid broke the long silence. "What happened, taer?" he repeated. "Where is Rhys?".

"It matters not where he is," Nath said. "I am going to find him. And he is going to suffer for what he has wrought."

CHAPTER 8

Rhys felt pain creep into his skull, and it pushed him over the foggy line into consciousness. He had been adrift in an endless black cloud, buried alive but floating freely. Then the sting hit, like the twinge of a pulled muscle. It quickly spread until he could feel the bones in his head buzzing.

His nose and lips were sealed shut by the clinging darkness, but there was fire yet in his lungs that demanded release. A wave of nausea rushed up his throat, and for a moment he saw Colfenor, glaring in disapproval that was also tinged with . . . sadness? Gruesome pride? The yew's splendid needles shivered and fell as Rhys gaped, unable to tell whether the image was behind his eyelids or in front of them.

Rhys lungs convulsed explosively, but he sucked in as much dirt and grit as he coughed out. He smelled seared flesh and burning wood as his fingers scratched deep into the lush forest soil. Blinded by tears and a fine dust that still hung in the air, Rhys coughed again as all the muscles in his torso cramped.

The boggarts, he thought. The pack. The *packs*. Rhys's vision was blurry, and his legs were unsteady, but he forced himself to his feet. He tried to call out Gryffid's name, but the words never cleared his throat. Rhys staggered against a greasy, black-trunked tree and weathered another surge of dry, wracking coughs. At least everything that was supposed to be inside his chest still was, much of it was even intact, and those were things to be thankful for.

Rhys's vision cleared with a few splashes from his water skin. He drank what remained, tossed the skin aside, then slowly stood and wiped the smoke and grit from his eyes with the back of his hand. Though awake, he found himself surrounded by a nightmare.

He was still within sight of the ash forest of Porringer, standing at the center of a one-hundred-foot diameter circle of foul, blackened trees. Nothing green or growing had survived, and if the caustic, magical film of poison continued to spread, the entire area would be nothing more than a pit of slime and bones.

Bodies were everywhere. Hundreds of them, elf and boggart corpses alike, some intact, some unrecognizable. The alignment of the bodies and the bending of the trees showed Rhys the center of the explosion was directly under his feet. The conclusion was inescapable, and as he slowly remembered what he'd been doing, Rhys knew that it was true, however impossible it seemed. He had done this, and he did not know how. If it was yew magic, it was more powerful than anything Colfenor had ever described.

His ears still ringing, Rhys took a stumbling step forward and thought better of a second. Slowly, painfully, he filled his lungs and let out a sharp, strong whistle, the trail-talk signal for any nearby hunters to regroup on Rhys's mark. He stood for many minutes among the choking death-haze, but the only sounds he heard were his own rasping breaths. There was nothing alive, nothing moving of its own volition for as far as Rhys could hear—and elf ears could hear a long way indeed.

Rhys risked another step and then another. He was not yet sure which way to go, but his duty was clear. He had to search for survivors. Everyone around him was definitely beyond help, but there was perhaps an elf or two to save.

Rhys's heart grew stronger, and his mind grew sharper as he staggered on. He heard the welcome and familiar sounds of forest life as the local birds and bugs returned to the scene of the explosion.

He also heard footsteps. Rhys contemplated calling out, but was unwilling to give away his position until he recognized friend or foe. His bow gone, he slid a sharp, angular dagger from its sheath and held it ready by his side.

Whoever approached was not making much of an attempt to be stealthy. Rhys was sure it was not the careless stumbling of a boggart, nor was it the light, graceful tread of an elf. It sounded like something in between, perhaps a long-legged boggart walking on tender feet, or a wounded elf, forced to limp.

An elf woman emerged from the smoky haze. Rhys's fingers tightened around his dagger.

"Hold there," he said.

The elf froze in place. She was definitely not native to the Gilt Leaf Wood. She was taller than any female he'd ever met, taller even than the Perfects of Lys Alana. The newcomer's porcelain skin was shaded with flushes of rose on her cheeks. Her hair was jet black and cropped to shoulder length, glossy and luxurious beneath a pair of smooth, sleek horns that curved back along the top of her head. Her eyes were dark and deep, and her intense expression marked her as someone who took in far more than most before she spoke.

The odd female was dressed in typical elven threads, but in hues of amethyst, sapphire, jet, and silver instead of the Gilt Leaf green and gold. She was unarmed but she wore a small, serviceable pack on her back. The newcomer was lean and athletic, but her rich yet practical attire was more suited for court than for the hunt—perhaps she was an all-purpose troubleshooter for a higher-ranking elf of whatever nation she called home.

She looked at Rhys without fear, only curiosity. She tilted her head to one side, fixed her penetrating eyes on the elf, and said, "I'm holding here, friend, like you said. What happens next?"

"Who are you? What are you doing here?"

"Who are you?" she shot back.

"I am Daen Rhys of the Hemlock pack," Rhys said, deciding not to burden the newcomer with the recent change in his rank and status. "This is Gilt Leaf territory. Identify yourself and your tribe."

"I am a traveler from the forest of Mornsong. My name is Maralen."

"What are you doing here, Mornsong?"

Maralen smiled, slightly flushed. "I am lost," she said. "I've been lost for days . . . maybe weeks. I was part of a wedding party, you see, and we were attacked. I barely escaped with my life." Her face grew sad and introspective. "I saw a Perfect die, Daen Rhys. It was horrible."

Rhys realized Maralen must be of a much higher status than her desperate appearance indicated. He moderated his tone, addressing her as if she were his peer. "It's no safer here, lady. We've had . . . boggart trouble."

"I gathered," Maralen replied, suddenly animated. "Yes, it was boggarts that attacked us, I remember now. They were mad, not like any boggarts I've ever seen. When the Perfect was killed, I . . . I fled. I ran away into the woods." She cast her eyes to her feet at the admission, though Rhys, having seen the mad boggarts in action, could not bring himself to blame her for running. "By the time they stopped chasing me I had no idea where I was. I managed all right for a while, but . . . well. To make a long story short, I saw a flash and heard a roar so I came here to see what had happened." She glanced around at the killing ground. "So . . . what happened?"

"First you must answer my questions. What is your purpose in the Gilt Leaf, traveler? Should you not have returned to your people after your wedding party was attacked? You're a long way from home."

The woman's head straightened, and her face lost its quizzical air. Her voice was soft, almost mournful, and tinged with a Mornsong burr. "I am," she agreed. "My home feels as if it is beyond the far end of the world. My mistress was the Perfect Peradala, the most beautiful voice in all the Mornsong, perhaps in the whole world. I was her attendant, her maid-in-waiting, her strong right hand when one was needed." She held her arms up and framed her face with her hands. "I am here due to sad fate or, if you prefer, unfortunate circumstance. Faerie lights twinkled in the eaves on the day I was born and the spiders in the nursery cast webs of pure-spun gold. Or so I was told. I carry a curse, perhaps not one that you can see but a curse all the same. I should never have agreed to serve Peradala. If . . . I had not, she might well still live." Maralen lowered her hands and cocked her head once more.

"As you say," Rhys said. He thought for a moment, relieved that the ringing in his head was almost completely gone. There was still pain, but he was able to think clearly. This woman was unusual in appearance and accent, and there was something else . . . She didn't smell quite right. Her scent was close to what he would have expected, but there was an undercurrent of something strange to his sensitive nose. Her story also stunk of convenience and coincidence. On a hunch, he sprang forward, drawing his dagger as he moved, and pricked Maralen's upper arm with the tip of his blade before she could blink.

"Hey!" The dark-haired elf clapped a hand to her bicep and backed away, eyeing Rhys warily. "What was that for?"

Rhys paused. There was a small drop of red between

Maralen's fingers and another on the dagger. She followed his eyes to the blood trickling across her knuckles.

"You've laid me open, Daen Rhys," she said. "What's wrong with you?"

"My apologies," Rhys said. He sheathed the dagger and drew a leafy bandage from his belt. "I had to make sure you weren't wearing a glamer." He offered her the leaf. "It's just a pinprick. Don't overreact."

"You Gilt Leaf must employ some pretty big pins." Maralen did not seem angry, exactly, but her eyes had an outraged intensity that Rhys felt he deserved.

"One apology is more than anyone should expect. I had to startle you to see if you'd reveal your true form."

Maralen grunted dismissively. She muttered, "He thinks I'm wearing a glamer."

Rhys gestured with the leaf. "I have offered my apology. I am offering redress."

Maralen reached out for the leaf. As her fingers took hold of it she said, "And how are you, Daen Rhys? Is there any medicine in your pack for serious head wounds?" She took in his confused expression and tapped one of her own horns. "Not my head—yours. It would seem I'm not the only one who's been cursed, I'm afraid. And I'm not the one who needs a glamer."

Rhys ignored her rambling talk of curses—the Mornsong were famed for their heavenly voices and infamous for superstitions that would make a kithkin blush—and waited until Maralen took the leaf from his hand. "Hold it over the wound," he said. "Press tight. It wasn't deep." She obliged, and a look of relief passed over her face as the healing magic went to work.

Rhys let her recover for a few seconds and said, "Did you see any other elves or boggarts on your way here?"

"Hmm? Oh, no. There was a rush of activity in the opposite

direction, right before the flash . . . rodents and birds . . . but after that"—she nodded down at the forest floor—"only this. Only you. Did the boggarts do this?"

Rhys fell silent. Maralen peeked at the skin under the leaf on her arm, smiled, and then folded it up. She offered it back to him. He shook his head, and she slipped it into the sash around her waist. She said, "Please, taer. What happened here, and how did you survive?"

"I don't know. But I mean to find out."

She lowered her head respectfully. "May I join you? As I said, I am lost, and somehow I must get word back to my people about Peradala's fate. I had hoped to reach the spires of Lys Alana. I am sure they are distant, but they are not nearly as distant as my home."

"You're right about that," Rhys agreed, and he considered her request. His first responsibility was to find whatever remained of the pack. He had no real idea how long he'd been unconscious, however, and given that he now had a civilian on his hands he decided a return to the taercenn's fortress in the deep woods was the first order of business. Any other elf survivors would surely head there, and he could unload this beautiful stranger on the next patrol heading back to Lys Alana.

All that aside, he was alone and injured. He could use company, even unusual company such as this Mornsong woman. Rhys nodded.

"I can take you to safety. There's an elf stronghold not far from here. You'll be able to find your way to the capital from there, I'm sure."

Maralen raised her head and arched one sharp brow. "Will I be welcome there?"

"Not entirely," Rhys admitted.

"Fair enough," she said. "And thank you, Daen Rhys. But if I may be so bold . . . will *you* be welcome there?"

"What do you mean?"

"I mean . . . Well, as I said, you have a serious wound. I was not merely speaking in jest when I said you are cursed." The dark-eyed woman suddenly sounded hesitant. "Have you seen yourself? I suspect your Gilt Leaf friends would find you a bit more disturbing than me, at the moment. We Mornsong aren't quite as obsessive about appearances, and since I too am cursed I cannot bring myself to disdain you, but your people. . . ." she trailed off into a shrug of sympathy.

Rhys had put aside the pain in his limbs and his head, but a new, dreadfully cold sensation squirmed in his guts. He stared blankly as Maralen reached into her pack and pulled out a thin metal box with an ornate clasp on its lid. She exhaled on the box's underside and polished it with her sleeve. With a last anxious glance, she offered him the box.

Rhys watched his own numb fingers close around the metal box and raise it to his face. The reflective surface was not large enough to contain all of his features, so he centered on his eyes, nose, and mouth. Apart from a layer of soot, an angry red welt on his cheek, and a spattering of blood in his brows, he saw nothing out of the ordinary.

"Higher," Maralen said nervously. "Your forehead."

Rhys tilted the box. The cold in his stomach exploded, and an icy numbness shot up his spine and settled in his brain.

His horns were gone. The left had broken off two inches above his forehead, leaving a jagged, irregular spike where once there were smooth, regal curves and a fine tapered tip. The right was charred and blackened, ending in a rough stub of crumbling dust halfway up its length.

Rhys's knees buckled, and he dropped to the ashy ground. The box tumbled from his fingers, but Rhys still cradled the awful memory of his reflection as tears streamed down his face.

"I am eyeblight," he said in a hollow monotone. "I am nothing."

"Calm down, taer, please." Maralen said. "In the Mornsong—"

"Damn the Mornsong!" he cried. "I'm a monster. I am less than nothing. The scarblades couldn't have done a better job of disgracing me." He clenched his fists and stared at the strange traveler, her face twisted with concern, and he said, "I am not fit to lead . . . nor to hunt . . . nor even to call myself an elf. I am no longer Blessed. How can you even look at me?"

Maralen stood quietly as Rhys's breath rasped in and out. "Eyeblights are treated with perhaps a little more compassion by my people," she said. "And again, we are more or less in the same accursed straits. Losing my mistress, failing her as I did will shame me as much as any blighting. You have another option though."

"Mornsong," Rhys said hotly, "if I were still among the Faultless I would kill you where you stand."

"I only meant—"

"You meant I should hide myself behind glamer. A lie. I would cut my own throat before doing what you suggest. Perhaps your backward tribe accepts eyeblights, but you are in the Gilt Leaf Wood now. We are the perfection of perfection. I would rather die in disgrace before . . ." His voice fell. "Glamers are for tricks. Diversions and frippery. They can fail in the heat of battle."

Maralen bowed her head again. "I only meant you might put on the glamer long enough to get me into this stronghold of yours." Without lifting her chin, she added, "Perhaps the Gilt Leaf way is not the only way, taer."

Rhys sputtered, unable to articulate the furious rush of emotions overwhelming him.

"It's selfish, I know," Maralen said, ignoring Rhys's outrage. She looked at Rhys pleadingly. "But I've been lost for a long time. I've had to do what was necessary to stay alive. I am capable for a courtier, but I'm no hunter."

The tumult inside him suddenly fell silent. Rhys nodded to Maralen, not in agreement but in acknowledgment, in recognition of her presence. He felt his mind growing still, and he wouldn't have her thinking he had just abandoned her.

"Please wait here," he said.

"Where are you going?"

Rhys didn't answer. He settled onto the ground, cross-legged, eyes closed, with his palms pressed into the soil beside his hips. His horns were gone, and no matter what the mad elves of the Mornsong thought, he was an outcast forever barred from the nation. For that matter, he doubted he'd be accepted in Maralen's tribe either, even if he wanted to find refuge there. She was, as she said, in need, and was clearly overlooking his hideous deformity for pragmatic reasons.

Rhys pushed thoughts of tribes and disgrace aside with great effort and drew on the arcane force of the deep woods, on the potent currents of power that sustained the elves and drove their magic. He shaped that power and sent it out into the ruined ground around him, feeling the blast zone as if it were a wound upon his own body.

He wanted to reach out to Colfenor himself, but at the moment he was impossibly removed from the necessary state of mind. So Rhys prepared to do the best he could on his own. As much as he had avoided the old red log these days, his mentor had given him the tools he needed to heal the damage he had done. He just had to do as he'd been trained, clear his mind, and take considered action. Colfenor had taught him to think before he acted, and while Rhys had never faced circumstances this dire before, he was still dedicated to living up to the best parts of Colfenor's teachings in the service of the elf nation.

He felt the death all around him. What had he done? It was no rhetorical question. Rhys truly could not conceive how this had happened. He could find a trail or rally a pack or heal a battlefield wound well enough, and his poison magic was unmatched, but destruction on this scale was far beyond his skill. He wouldn't know where to begin casting such a spell, or where to find the magic to fuel it. The ground was lifeless, cracked in some spots and bubbling in others. He had done this to the forest, to himself. Every fallen limb, tree, and corpse pointed inward, at him, with silent accusation. He would ask the forest for guidance, gauge its reaction to what he had done and his continued presence here. If it forgave him, he would rise and lead Maralen to the camp. If it cursed him, he would simply sit here until he died.

Rhys felt the vibrant life force at his command seeping through the blasted ground, but there was no interaction between the two. Whatever he had done here, it seemed it would have long-lasting effects. Whatever he had killed would stay dead.

Behind closed eyes, he imagined the forest around him as it had been at dawn, before the ill-advised attack on the boggart festival in Porringer: full and green and teeming with life. Rich browns and deep greens flooded the scene as far as his mind's eye could see. He held this image for a moment, trying to savor it, to capture it in his memory forever. Then a liquid, tingling sensation flushed through him, and his vision of the forest changed.

The leaves on the trees shone with a reddish light that sparkled and danced like rain at sunset, spreading down the leaves to the stems, to the branches, then to the thicker boughs and limbs, and on to the stout trunks themselves. Then the glow spread to the forest, the rich verdant colors slowly melting into a soft haze of scintillating shapes, shrubs, and vines of yellow and white light, flowing silver trunk-shapes that drifted broke apart, and then merged again, like oil in water.

The dreamy sensation sharpened into painful clarity. Rhys opened his eyes and saw that the changes were not just in his mind—the forest around him was a swirling kaleidoscope of shapes and colors that only vaguely resembled the forest in which he sat.

"Daen Rhys?" Maralen's voice was tight and anxious, but she did not sound afraid. "Something's happening," she said. "Is this your doing? Is this Gilt Leaf magic?"

"No," Rhys said. "But I think I know what it is." The wound he had inflicted on this place must have been even more severe than he had thought, and he would be called to account for it by the highest, most august authority.

High overhead, among the blackened skeletons of the trees, a proud, magnificent animal form gained definition and substance within the chaos. It glowed eerie green as it emerged from the miasma of colors and shapes.

"Rhys? What is that?"

Rhys had no answer, at least not one that would help Maralen understand. It most resembled a mountain elk, but much larger. A pair of glorious white eagle's wings spread from the figure's back and grew until they spread improbably over the scene of destruction, filling the sky. Despite his fresh deformities, Rhys could not find it in himself to be ashamed—his shame would have sullied this rare, perfect thing.

"Taer, please," Maralen said. "Should I be frightened?"

"No. This is something few have ever seen, and even fewer elves have ever seen," Rhys said at last. "An elemental. A manifestation of the highest form of magic, power so strong it becomes a living, immortal thing."

Maralen stepped beside the elf, slightly behind him. "What does it want?"

"I cannot say. I think it is angry."

She considered this. "Can we run?"

Rhys shook his head.

"Why not?"

"You see the wings, yes? How will you escape its reach?" Rhys said. "Whatever its purpose, we will have little say in the matter."

"Then we're doomed?"

The great elk spirit's aura had filled the forest with unearthly green light. It snorted through its huge black nostrils and fixed its glowing yellow pupils on the pair. "I do not think so."

"Can't you do something? Reason with it? Scare it off? Appease it? Your kind do so love to tell others what to do, surely this is no different."

Rhys shook his head, not even bothering to defend the honor of the Gilt Leaf.

"Well, can you do anything?" Maralen asked, fear edging into her voice for the first time since he'd met the strange elf.

"I can fall to my knees and wait for the spirit's judgment. You should do the same."

"Don't be asinine. You have to try. I'm a stranger here." She waved her hands, her voice rising in panic. "You're the local hero. You killed the forest, you went into a trance and summoned that thing here. So just . . . I don't know, send it back."

"I can't."

"Then do something! Anything!"

An ethereal chorus of droning voices rose up as the elemental snorted again. Its wings expanded, folding over themselves until Rhys and Maralen were completely sealed under a dome of ghostly greenish white.

The elk's face grew distorted and the spirit bellowed angrily. It drew back and opened its jaws as if to bite. Rhys reflexively drew his dagger and said a silent prayer to his mentor. He was honestly unsure whether he meant the dagger for the elemental or himself.

Colfenor, he thought. My path has led me here, and here is where it will end. Forgive me.

Rhys called once more upon the vital force of the forest, gathering its strength and its healing power. Maralen was right. He was ready to die, but not for this beautiful stranger to die along with him. He would stand against the spirit for as long as he dared, and then he would use the last of his strength to protect Maralen. It was a far nobler death than an eyeblight like him deserved, but the Mornsong had endured the sight of him, and perhaps she would speak well of him someday.

The elemental stopped, its hot breath forming clouds of sparkling steam around its muzzle. The elk spirit made no further hostile move toward them but simply loomed there, gazing down on them as its gleaming white throat rippled and its teeth clicked together.

"It's trying to talk," Maralen said.

"No it isn't. They are beyond words, beyond our understanding," Rhys said. "They do not talk, they . . . wait. By the Wood, you might be—I can hear it!"

"You can? What's it saying?"

"It's . . . difficult." Rhys marveled at the glorious spirit despite the danger it posed and the guilt he felt. "It's like remembering the details of a picture you've long forgotten."

"Well, then, what are the details?"

Rhys emptied his mind. He thought of nothing but the great elk before him and the sentient power that flowed from it.

"It has begun," Rhys said, though he knew the thoughts were not his own. The words came out of his mouth with a haunting echo that vibrated along his entire spine. "The mountains will move. The river will reverse its course. The sky will burn and scream. It cannot be stopped."

"What?" Maralen roughly nudged his shoulder. "What are you saying?"

"Leave here," Rhys said, still not in control of his tongue. "Harm follows wherever you go. Return to your own, creature. Begone, and let me heal the damage you have done."

Maralen prodded Rhys. "But what does it all—"

Rhys whirled on her then, his eyes flashing with energy. *"Leave,"* he said sharply and with forceful intent, and a moment later he pitched forward, landing on his hands and knees. He blinked and coughed, suddenly in control of his own voice once more, and spat up something like moss. The presence of the great elemental spirit withdrew, and he longed to follow, to stay in that exalted state of communion. It fled from him, however, leaving him empty and hollow.

"We have to go," he said simply. "It does not want you here. Or me."

Maralen paused, watching as the great spirit pulled back its wings. The phantasmal lights faded slowly as the setting sun reasserted itself through the smoke and the haze.

"What did I do?" asked the Mornsong.

"I only heard as much as you did," Rhys said. "It wants you gone. It wants me gone."

"I'll go anywhere that isn't here," she agreed, "provided you're still going with me."

"Of course." Rhys shook his head sadly, trying to dispel the last of the crushing emptiness the elemental had left behind. "Though I don't see why you'd feel any safer in my company." He gestured up at the rapidly fading spirit. "I am twice-cursed: once by my own hand and now by the elementals themselves."

"I've no doubt I'm better off with you." Maralen pointed to

the last vestiges of the elk's horns that were still visible in the trees. "That thing was ready to devour us, but you made it back it down."

Rhys laughed harshly from the back of his throat. "Hardly. That was a divine, primal force of life. It could have destroyed you and me both with less than a thought if it cared to."

"But it didn't care to," Maralen said, "not once you stood up to it."

The spirit had wholly gone, and the forest was fully restored to its blasted, blackened state. The wind whistled sadly through the ruined trees.

Rhys listened to the mournful sound, his fists clenching tight.

"Is it safe to leave?" Maralen asked.

"You Mornsong really don't know much about your own world, do you?" Rhys said. "It's safer to leave than it is to stay. And the sooner we begin . . ." The elf trailed off, his ears orienting to the west.

"What now?"

"A party," Rhys said, "coming this way. Fast." He motioned for Maralen to get behind him, and the dark-haired woman quickly complied. He sniffed the air experimentally and thanked the ancient gods of Gilt Leaf that his sense of smell, at least, was unchanged. "Two . . . maybe three people on foot: a kithkin or a boggart, and something bigger. They're on foot and traveling light, but at least one of them is armed. More than three scents, though. Strange. Not enough footsteps."

Maralen smirked. "Can you tell what they're wearing?"

"Quiet," Rhys hissed. He thought but didn't add: *And you still don't smell right, either, but I can't tell why.*

"All right then, can you tell if they're friendly?" Maralen ventured.

"Not from listening," Rhys said. "Which I can't do if you

keep talking." He straightened up and took a deep breath. "Never mind. We'll find out momentarily in any case."

Maralen muttered something Rhys didn't catch. Then, louder, she said, "Forgive me, taer. Your secret will be safe with me."

Rhys cocked his head but didn't turn away from the approaching sounds. "What?" he asked. His vision blurred, and he felt the light, smoky skin of a glamer settling around his head. He tilted his neck, and the familiar but impossible shadow of his intact left horn fell across his eyes.

Hot rage surged up his throat, and he whirled, snarling, "What have you done?"

Maralen's face was concerned, almost pleading. "Shh," she said. "They're almost here. It's only temporary, to prevent impertinent questions. We . . . You shouldn't have to answer to the likes of them."

Rhys clenched his teeth tightly. Maralen's glamer was strong and subtle, expertly cast. It would take time to dispel . . . and once it was gone, he'd have to face whomever was approaching and endure their pitying stares.

"We will discuss this later, lady." Rhys planted his feet in the ash and sheathed his dagger, though he kept his hand on its hilt. His shoulders square and head high, Rhys waited as two women broke through the underbrush.

He had been right. The two runners were a kithkin archer and a flamekin. They were careful as they entered the scoured-out clearing, but the flamekin could not keep her eyes from widening when she saw the elf and his unusual companion.

"Are you Rhys?" the flamekin called. "Daen Rhys of the Hemlock pack?"

Rhys nodded.

"I am Ashling, a pilgrim. This is Brigid Baeli, an archer of Kinsbaile. We bring an urgent message from Colfenor."

* * * * *

Ashling would have been lying if she said she had enjoyed the company that had been forced upon her. A flamekin pilgrim's path was meant to be a solitary one, a journey that shaped and was in turn shaped by an individual. As travelers and wanderers, the pilgrims touched the lives of many others, but only briefly. As messengers, they bore news to others—the dire and the wonderful, items trivial and profound—yet they themselves were unaffected by it. Flamekin did not typically read the missives they carried, and if they did they felt the words as keenly as the sender or recipient.

Like all pilgrims, it was Ashling's custom and her preference to travel alone whenever possible. She had learned and accepted long ago that it was not possible as often as she'd like it to be. On those occasions, when wisdom or necessity dictated against her natural inclinations, Ashling did her best not to trouble or be troubled by her companions.

Yet this Brigid Baeli troubled her. In fact, the archer's formidable aura of ego had already pushed Ashling beyond troubled and on into genuine annoyance. Brigid clearly knew the terrain. She hiked with all the confidence of an experienced ranger. She even hummed cheery tunes as she forged ahead of Ashling through the woods, finding and following hidden paths before the flamekin had a chance to see or a chance to choose for herself. Brigid laughed off all of Ashling's milder objections, and when the flamekin had pressed the point, Brigid had grown sullen . . . and had pressed on ahead all the more forcefully.

At least the kithkin stopped humming songs about herself after a while. The last thing Brigid had said before she started to sulk was that she knew the shortest route to Rhys's territory, and that Ashling should follow her if she wanted to complete

Colfenor's mission quickly. Ashling did not argue but kept close behind Brigid, watching and waiting for the chance to honestly disagree with the archer's trailblazing so she could strike off on her own. The path presented itself to the pilgrim, it was true, but the kithkin archer seemed intent on taking the path by the neck and taming it like a wild springjack. Colfenor himself had admitted he didn't know exactly where his student was, so Brigid's best guess was no better than Ashling's, despite the archer's superior knowledge of the region.

As the pair moved deeper into the woods, Ashling was sure she heard faint, familiar titters on the path behind them and had little doubt the Vendilion clique was, for whatever reason, shadowing them. It wasn't uncommon for a clique to do such things, for a trio to find someone or something interesting for a day or two, just long enough to become nuisances. But this trio was starting to get on the flamekin's nerves. She lost sight of Brigid for a moment, but as soon as the flamekin broke through a particularly thick holly hedge she saw the kithkin standing silently on a large rock, shading her eyes with her hand as she peered into the dense forest ahead.

Ashling walked up alongside the rock so that she was shoulder-to-shoulder with Brigid and tipped back the wide steel brim of her traveling hat.

"We're being followed," the archer said. Brigid did not lower her hand and did not look at Ashling.

"I know," Ashling said. "I think it's the faeries I met on the river."

Brigid shifted her feet but kept her eyes fixed on the terrain. "Are they playing with us, or is there some sort of grudge between you?"

"Playing. Almost certainly." The flamekin smirked. "What, you've never picked up a clique on a long journey?"

"Maybe they seem harmless to you, but faeries can make real trouble in the deep woods. They'll stir up the wildlife with their tricks and their magic, then flit away, leaving us to sort out the trouble they've caused."

"That's a terrible thing to say." The happy, airy voice floated down from above them.

"We only ever try to help," said a similar but slightly deeper voice from behind Ashling.

"Though sometimes we do get carried away. . . ."

"Quiet, Veesa."

"Or distracted."

"You're not helping, Endry."

"Children of Oona," Ashling said. "Show yourselves so we can discuss terms."

Brigid's brow creased, and the kithkin sighed. She lowered her hand and hopped down from the rock as all three faeries flitted into view, hovering in the brightly colored circle of light from their glittering wings.

"Terms?" the big one, Iliona, asked with a laugh. "Are you looking to make a deal?"

"We don't work cheap, flamekin."

"You don't work at all, Veesa."

"Shows what you know, Endry." Veesa batted her huge, glittering eyes. "We're doing terms."

Iliona shrugged, unconcerned. "Please ignore the twins."

"Way ahead of you. Now. The kithkin and I are on a mission," Ashling said. "What will it take for you to leave us to it?"

"Oh, no, no." Iliona shook her head. "We came all this way. We're not going back."

"We want to watch."

"We want to help. And you can't stop us."

Brigid looked up at Ashling. Her voice was low, barely above a whisper. "They're right. They will do as they please no matter what bargain you strike."

"Do tell," Ashling said with a spark of irritation.

The trio flew in faster circles. "That one's mean for a kithkin."

"She's mean for a boggart."

"But she's famous."

"Oh, very famous. The Zero of Kinsbaile."

Ashling addressed Brigid in a quieter tone. "Ignore them. What do you suggest?"

The archer let her hand fall so that it rested on the lower tip of her bow. Ashling's flames flared brightly in surprise, distorting the air around her head. She hesitated. Together, she and Brigid might be able to chase the faeries away, or at least discourage them for a time. It would not be a pleasant chore. Would it be worth the effort? Would another irritating clique appear to take their place? And really, shooting arrows at faeries? A waste of ammunition.

"We don't want to fight," the trio said together as if reading her mind.

Endry smiled sharply and added with an un-faerielike hint of real menace, "But we will."

Iliona broke off and flitted down to Ashling's eye level. "You shouldn't fight us anyway," she said. "We saved you from the river."

Ashling's flames cooled. The only thing more wasteful than a skirmish with these tiny flying irritants would be to try to recount the tale of that incident.

"They're right," Ashling said to Brigid. "I'd be another stone at the bottom of the Wanderwine if not for them." She looked back to Iliona and nodded. "All right. You can come along."

"Like you could stop us."

"But you have to keep quiet and stay out of our way," Ashling said. The kithkin nodded slowly, agreeing though she was clearly no more enthused about Ashling's suggestion than Ashling. "Or else we'll see how hot those wings of your can get before they burst into flame. Agreed?"

Iliona buzzed happily around Ashling's head. "Deal! Twins, listen up! We just came to *terms!*" She hovered, her expression colored by a momentary flash of confusion. "Wait, what are we doing again?"

"I'm looking for someone, and Brigid is helping me. You need to leave us alone and let me look."

"We can do more than that."

"We can help!"

"It's better if you just watch," Ashling said. She glanced down at Brigid and added, "I'm the pilgrim, after all, and this is my path."

To Ashling's surprise, the surly kithkin smiled, her lips stretching across her wide, round face. "All right, flamekin," she muttered. "Point taken."

Ashling nodded gratefully as the faeries' voices poured down on them in a fresh deluge of enthusiasm.

"Which way are we going?" The smaller female, Veesa, squealed as she rose over her siblings and swooped between the low-hanging branches of a knotbole. "I'll scout ahead!"

"No," Ashling said. "Just stay behind and follow me. All right?"

"Veesa," Iliona said firmly.

Crestfallen, the lone twin buzzed lazily back down to the others.

"How much farther to elf territory?" Ashling asked Brigid.

"Not far, if we keep up our pace," she said with a meaningful glance at the faeries. "If nothing else slows us down, it'll be less than an hour."

Ashling was about to answer, but a strange sound stopped her.

She felt a flush of heat rise to her face as the air itself shifted away from her, as if a giant were preparing to sneeze. Ashling smelled ozone, and felt the presence of something she could not name. A presence that disappeared as quickly as it had appeared, leaving the flamekin feeling not unlike a rabbit fortunate enough to meet a predator that had already eaten its fill.

There was a brief flash in the sky like a sheet of lightning. A moment later, a blinding crescent of light rose up over the tops of the trees. The shape intensified, and Ashling saw the rest of the sphere take shape, a massive ball of crackling energy. The sphere was too distant for Ashling to tell how truly large it was, but she saw it expanding outward, and she could feel its terrible force even from here.

The ground shook violently as something like thunder rolled across the forest. Ashling winced at the sound. Brigid clapped her hands over her ears. Even the faeries were buffeted back by the shock wave.

Seconds later, a dazed Ashling jumped up on the large rock. The energy ball was gone, leaving a black and smoking hole in the dense green canopy. The ground continued to shake, violently enough to shift the boulder under Ashling's feet. If the tremors were this strong here, they must have been strong enough to rip trees up by their roots closer to the center of the blast.

The rumbling died away. Ashling stared at the site of the explosion as she spoke to Brigid.

"Less than an hour if we maintain our pace?"

"That's right."

Ashling faced the kithkin. She smiled. "And if we run like stuck springjacks?"

Brigid smiled back. "Only one way to find out." She slung her bow up and across her shoulders so that she could extend her legs to their full stride. It would have been comical to Ashling if she hadn't seen Brigid on the trail. The archer's legs were little, but she was swift and nimble when she chose to be.

"What was that?" Iliona said. "You know, that thing. That thing that just happened."

"It hurt my ears."

"It hurt my feelings."

"I think I broke an antenna."

"I'll break your antenna."

"I don't know what that was," Ashling said before the twins came to blows. She took off her hat and tied it to a thin strap on her belt. Her flaming hair and eyes blazed brightly. "Who wants to go find out?"

"Race you!"

"One-two-three-go!"

"Last one there is a stinky boggart!"

With a flurry of sparkling light and high-pitched giggling, the faerie trio streaked on ahead. Ashling turned to Brigid and said, "Shall we join them?"

"You go on," the Hero of Kinsbaile said. "I could probably keep up with you for a while, but we kithkin weren't built for long-distance sprints. Just go. I'll be right behind you."

Ashling nodded, feeling more respect for the archer than she had on the entire journey thus far—it took self-knowledge to admit such a thing, even more when one was a living legend. The flamekin touched her fingers to the brim of her hat in a half-salute, turned, and plunged into the forest, her long legs driving her toward the site of the explosion. The fire in her body surged, making her limbs loose and light. Her boots dug into the turf as she weaved between trees and hurdled thickets.

As Ashling entered into the blast zone, the ground cracked beneath her feet, and she missed a step. She half-stumbled and righted herself, slowing to a brisk jog.

The signs of elf skirmishes littered Lorwyn, dozens of sacred copses planted as memorials to the fallen. Ashling had been to many—she had carried messages and prayers to such sites dozens of times—but she never seen one so fresh after the slaughter. She glanced left and right as she ran along at her reduced pace, overwhelmed by the scene. The trees, the rocks, the ground itself had been stripped bare and covered with a greasy black film. Countless smoldering bodies still lay face-down in the ruins, unrecognizable as members of any particular species.

Flamekin were creatures of fire, so Ashling knew none of her tribe's flames had caused this destruction. It didn't even smell of fire as much as it reeked of incendiary energy—the distinction was fine, but a flamekin could recognize the difference between simple combustion and the raw power of fire magic. The wisest and most experienced mages among her kind had the ability to unleash such pure, infinite combustion, but they also had complete control over their flames and were trained specifically *not* to cause such utter destruction. She had seen one tribal elder demonstrate his heat and precision by conjuring a perfect faerie-sized cage of flame that fit its occupant like a second skin. So long as the faerie didn't move, he was unharmed. If he touched the flames, they'd burn his bones to ash. The tiny creature had volunteered for the demonstration, and though he was completely unharmed Ashling never forgot the frozen, awe-struck look on the faerie's face when the flames flickered out.

This was not fire damage at all. At least, the fire had been a secondary effect of the energy she'd seen—some kind of caustic, withering force, more like a potent acid than a crackling flame. It was as if the life-force of everything in the area had burned its way out and through whatever it had inhabited. The devastation grew the nearer Ashling got to the epicenter. If she allowed herself to be distracted much more, she'd lose all momentum and wind up wandering, dazed, and weeping. Her path was calling her, urging her on, but for a change she almost dreaded what lay ahead.

She leaped over a narrow stream and her boots sank into the mud on the far side with a chilly sizzle. Before she could extract herself, the faeries were there, buzzing in circles around her face.

"Better wait here," Endry said.

"There's no room ahead."

"Something big is taking up all the space."

Ashling paused, concentrating, but she felt nothing. "What do you mean?"

"We decided to wait here a moment."

"You should wait, too."

"It's bad luck to intrude on such things."

"What things?" Ashling craned up on her toes to see over the next ridge. "What did you see?"

"Silly pilgrim," Veesa said. "Didn't you hear? We didn't see anything. It wouldn't let us near."

"What wouldn't?"

Endry's eyes suddenly glittered like small blue stars. "All clear," he said. The azure sparkle spread to his sisters' eyes and all three faeries buzzed toward the ridge with a merry giggle.

Ashling heard something small and fast moving toward her, and she waited. Brigid splashed across the narrow stream and dropped to one knee beside Ashling, panting lightly.

"What's happening?"

"Whatever it is," Ashling said, "it's over. Come on." She started toward the ridge. "You were never that far behind, were you?"

"I didn't want to miss anything. Not with the faeries about."

The two women broke in to a run until they cleared the ridge. Ashling planted the sole of her boot in the center of a thick bramble thatch and Brigid clambered over the bramble. Ashling rocked forward on one leg, keeping the stinging vines safely pinned below her foot, and hopped into a clearing that was shrouded in a foul-smelling haze.

An elf warrior stood beside a strange-looking woman at the far side of the clearing. They both looked like they had seen better days, but the elf was especially dour. Ashling ignored the prattling faeries.

"Are you Rhys?" the flamekin called. "Daen Rhys of the Hemlock pack?"

The solemn elf nodded.

"I am Ashling, a pilgrim. This is Brigid Baeli, an archer of Kinsbaile," Ashling said. "We bring an urgent message from Colfenor."

CHAPTER 9

Brigid Baeli instinctively moved to fill the conversational void, as any kithkin hero worth her salt would. The archer stepped forward and bowed deeply before the stunned elves.

"Cenn Gaddock Teeg sends his highest regards."

A trio of tiny voices added, "And we are the Vendilion clique. I am Iliona, this is Veesa, and—oh, my."

"What?" Maralen interjected, defensive.

"Nothing," the faerie said.

"She certainly wasn't going to point out that you're the ugliest elf we've ever seen," the male faerie said, indignant at being left out.

"Mind your tone!" Rhys said. He seemed to have no patience for their frippery. "How do you know me, flamekin?"

Iliona's sharp, playful voice echoed down from above. "And *your* companion, Mr. Big Elf?"

"She looks funny to me."

"I'll say. Not from around here, is she?"

"Hey," the woman said, her dark eyes narrowing in annoyance and something else Ashling couldn't quite place. Whatever it was, it shut the faeries up immediately.

Rhys's jaw tightened. "You travel with faeries?"

"Not by choice," Ashling said.

"And we saved her from the river."

"Yes, she'd be a rock if not for us."

"And does she thank us? Of course not."

Rhys had already ceased to listen to the faeries chatter and seemed to slump, but then the moment passed and he stood perfectly straight with his shoulders squared. "This is Maralen, a traveler from the nation of Mornsong. She is under my protection. Deliver your message, flamekin."

Ashling went across the clearing, surprised to find herself nervous. There was something about this elf . . . no, something that was on him, the scent of a power Ashling had spent her life searching for. This elf was awash in the intoxicating aura of a pure wild elemental. But it was only a whiff—did the elf even realize he'd been in contact with something so spectacular? How had he found what Ashling had sought her entire existence?

She had a thousand questions, but she also had a job to do. She believed this was why her path had led her here, but Ashling had learned long ago to distrust the completely open path. Such a road was often cleared only to lure unsuspecting travelers into danger.

The heat rose in Ashling's chest, causing the flames that licked up from her collarbone to flare bright and hot. She drew a thin, leather parcel from her pack and handed it to Rhys. The elf broke the seal and produced a single, huge leaf.

Fascinated, Ashling watched as Rhys pressed the leaf between his hands and shut his eyes. The flamekin used meditation to attain greater levels of control over their inner flames, to produce stronger, more colorful, and more profound magic. She knew treefolk practiced something similar, but she had never seen an elf wield magic for anything but tactile, pragmatic results. Ashling found it surprisingly unsettling.

Rhys opened his eyes. "You know what this message contains?"

She nodded. "I have not read it, taer, but I was given instructions that revealed some of its contents. I am to accompany you back to Kinsbaile, if you will go."

Rhys folded the leaf and put it inside his tunic. "I did not know Colfenor was in Kinsbaile."

"The Red Yew has been waiting for you there for some time now, or so I gathered," Brigid called. She came closer, slowly. "The storytelling festival is only a short time away. Cenn Teeg and Colfenor both hoped to speak with you in person before then."

Rhys did not reply and Ashling felt the mood growing uncomfortable. Before the faeries could pipe up and make things worse—she was quite surprised they hadn't already—she said, "Will you come with us, taer?"

"I need no guide to Kinsbaile, nor an escort."

"Then allow us to accompany you," Ashling said. "I have been retained and paid to do this. Brigid is also duty-bound." Swallowing a bit of her pride, Ashling bowed low and said, "Please. We are at your service."

"We'll help," Iliona said.

"We know lots of stories," Veesa interjected.

"Especially stories about faeries," Endry added. "The best kind."

Rhys interjected, addressing the faeries directly. "Hail to you, children of Oona. I am honored by your presence, but surely there is something more . . . festive . . . to occupy your time? Somewhere else?"

"You won't get around us like that," Iliona said. "We're on duty with the Zero of Kinsbaile and the . . . the flamekin," she finished with a shrug.

"The flamekin already tried to make us go away, but we were too clever."

"Yeah, we're coming along whether you or the flamekin or the Zero like it or not."

Ashling saw Rhys reach the same conclusion that she and Brigid had: until they actually started making trouble, it would be far better in the short run to simply endure the faeries' company.

"Very well. But none of your games." Rhys looked to Ashling and Brigid. "We are in a hurry."

Both women nodded. Ashling felt her flames dim, but the heat inside her did not diminish. The job was already half done, maybe even more so, but there were plenty of complications. The elf was hiding something, and it was more than just a brush with an elemental. There was the field of fresh corpses and the ruined landscape to consider, not to mention this strange elf woman Maralen. Ashling was more in touch with the elemental forces than most other beings, and the elemental forces around Maralen were fogged, yet bore the faintest whiff of the same power in which Rhys seemed to have been immersed. She resolved to keep one eye on this Mornsong traveler.

"She can't come with us," Iliona said, as if reading Ashling's mind. The pilgrim wondered absently whether the faerie had. "We don't like her," the largest of the trio continued.

"Who?" Maralen said. "Me?"

"Yes, you."

"That's right, fat weird elf, you can't come."

"Fat?" Maralen objected with a show of amusement. "Why do people keep saying that? I hardly think it accurate."

"Stop that at once," Rhys said. "I told you the Mornsong is with me." He turned to Maralen and said, "Kinsbaile is closer than the Gilt Leaf camp. You'll be safe there."

The elf woman hesitated. "Is it a busy place?" she said. "That is, will I be able to leave quickly—promptly—if need be?"

"It's not far from Wanderwine River," Rhys said. "Ferries come and go all day long."

"So long as you keep an eye out for arbomanders," Veesa said.

"Yes, those arbomanders aren't to be trusted," Endry agreed.

"Sometimes they eat people," Iliona added. "The fatter, the better."

Maralen nodded, bemused. "All right. And thank you."

"Maybe you didn't hear us." Iliona's voice was sharp and dangerously playful. "The fat elf can't come."

"Tall, too, for an elf. And really pale. Stay behind, big fat elf."

"Children of Oona," Rhys said, and Ashling heard a real edge of menace in his rich voice. "I won't explain this to you again. Maralen is part of my party until we reach Kinsbaile. Whoever wishes to travel with me must accept that, or accept the consequences."

The faeries buzzed angrily, but their tone and volume was muted. Two of them spun down in ever-contracting circles, mirroring each other's flight until they were only a few feet overhead.

"Back to Kinsbaile then," Iliona said.

"But once we're there, things change."

"You said a mouthful, Endry."

"I say we put her on the first ferry down the river."

"What have I ever done to you?" Maralen said. Endry zipped off in a cloud of glittering dust and resumed circling with his twin sister.

"Please, miss," Ashling stepped up to Maralen. "The three of them are as fickle and unpredictable as any faerie you've ever seen. And just as powerful. They may insult you, but I don't think they'll harm you."

Maralen sniffed. "You don't think so, eh?"

"No." Ashling smiled. "But that's not to say you shouldn't keep an eye on them on the way. I'll do the same. Between the three of us"—she nodded to Rhys—"I don't think they'll try anything."

"The four of us," Brigid said. "Counting Lady Maralen." She eyed the tiny siblings, and Ashling could almost feel the archer mentally planning where to put her first arrow if the faeries misbehaved.

Ashling turned back to Maralen. "You'll be safe. Just don't antagonize them, whatever you do. It's not worth the trouble."

Maralen fixed her dark eyes on Ashling. Slowly, the odd woman nodded. "All right. I'm going to hold you to that, by the way."

"Of course."

Maralen looked up. "Wait just a moment. I only see two faeries," she said. "Where's the third? What happened to the big one?"

Ashling blinked. It was true. Only two of the trio currently traced perfect circles in the smoky air.

"I honestly don't know," Ashling said. She cupped her hands around her mouth and shouted up to the faeries. "Hey, Endry and . . . the other one! Where's your sister?"

The duo did not reply but instead flew in faster and tighter circles, whistling and moaning like the wind.

"Does it really matter?" Brigid said. "She probably got distracted by a pretty flower or a bright sunbeam. Let's count our blessings that we only have two of them to deal with for the moment."

Ashling agreed, but she didn't like the idea of a missing faerie flitting about unsupervised.

"I'm sure you're right," Ashling said. "Wherever she is, she'll find her way back to us sooner or later."

* * * * *

Iliona zoomed through the forest, little more than a blurred streak of light and color. She had every reason to hurry. She had to find the nearest faerie ring right away . . . and besides, she didn't like being away from her siblings for too long. The twins tended to gossip about her behind her back, and, by Oona's blessed pistils, if they were going to do that she wanted to be there to hear it. Still, she was clique-prime, and she had a responsibility, even if she wasn't entirely sure exactly what was going on.

Oona would want to know about the strange elf creature traveling with Rhys, and such a juicy tidbit was worth a little loneliness. She shot past a band of elf hunters who looked very serious indeed, but Iliona was too fast and too high up for them to notice.

The tiny, winged creature broke through to a large, silent clearing. Huge-boled trees lined the enclosure, and thick moss covered the ground. Iliona skirted the edge of the tree line, her sharp eyes scanning the forest floor.

There. A tiny circle of purple and blue honeysuckle blossomed, and Iliona veered toward it. Not just a faerie ring, this, but a direct connection to the Great Mother—a ring of her own flowers, awaiting the touch of a faerie before blooming to full maturity. Such connections could only be used once, then the petals fluttered to the ground and somewhere nearby, a new ring of flowers would break through the same ground to await the next faerie with a dire need to speak with Oona.

The air was full of the sweet perfume of opening blossoms by the time she daintily alit on one of the expanding petals. Her wings hummed softly as she closed her eyes and reached out to the Great Mother, Oona, Queen of all the Fae.

* * * * *

The trip to Kinsbaile could have been much worse. The kith-kin and the flamekin seemed capable and professional enough to focus on the job at hand and not waste Rhys's time with impertinent questions he would never answer.

The faerie continued to abuse Maralen, of course, but so far they were satisfied to mock her unusual appearance rather than doing her actual harm. For her part, the dark-haired elf kept pace easily and without complaint, though she did swat at the faeries whenever they came close.

Rhys navigated a wide deadfall and checked his bearings. They were already halfway to their goal. If nothing else went extraordinarily wrong, he'd be with Colfenor by sunrise and seeing what the old log had to say. Rhys scowled. Colfenor would see through the glamer Rhys now shamefully wore. He would call out the folly of Rhys's decision to return to the nation as a blight beneath a false warrior's mantle. He would seize the opportunity to press Rhys to return to the ways of a sage, if the Gilt Leaf didn't kill him first.

They were arguments Rhys had listened to and rejected count-less times. He would reject them again, in spite of the additional weight and sting lent them by his current predicament. Rhys marched down a slight incline, planting his hoofed feet in the soil with every resolute step. Too many questions and decisions stood before him. He would deal with each individually, in succession, starting with discharging his obligations to Colfenor. Whatever his former mentor had to say, whatever Rhys himself decided as a result, this was the last time the yew sage would summon him like a footman.

Veesa flitted up in front of Rhys. "Wait, wait," she said.

"No," Rhys replied. He strode on, directly under the hover-ing faerie.

"It's important," Veesa said.

"Iliona's coming," said the other, hovering beside Rhys's head on the opposite side.

"We're not stopping," Rhys said. "We've already settled this. She'll just have to catch up."

The female faerie floated closer to Rhys. "We should get ready."

"Veesa's right."

"And Endry's right about me being right. It won't be long now."

"What are they nattering about?" Maralen asked. She hiked behind Rhys, with Ashling and Brigid close behind. Neither the flamekin nor the kithkin spoke, but they both cast nervous glances at the path behind.

"Something's back there," Brigid said. "Closing fast."

Rhys listened. He cursed himself for not paying closer attention. "What is that? It sounds like a storm of arrows."

"I've never heard an arrow buzz like that," Brigid said.

Maralen stepped closer to Rhys. "Another elemental?"

The flamekin started as if slapped. "I knew it," Ashling said as she half-lunged forward and grabbed Maralen by the shoulder. "What did you say about an elemental?"

"Get off me." Maralen twisted away from the flamekin's cool, blazing grip.

"You saw an elemental?" Ashling persisted. "A real elemental?"

"That's what he says." Maralen pointed at Rhys. "Me, I saw a big, glowing, winged elk. You tell me what it was because I have no idea. I've never seen anything like that in the Mornsong. He is the one who communed with it. Ask him."

The fire in Ashling's eyes smoldered, and she stared off into space over Maralen's head.

"I have nothing to say about it, and I suggest you do not press the matter. Wake up, flamekin," Rhys snapped. The woman's fiery mantle flared, and Ashling nodded, though she was still clearly lost in thought.

A sudden change in the pitch of the constant buzzing accompanying their faerie companions heralded the arrival of Iliona. The tiny faerie streaked over Brigid, Ashling, and Maralen, dipped down to zip past Rhys's eyes, and then shot back up to bowl into Veesa and Endry.

The wild-eyed faerie could not hold still, darting and flitting around her siblings as they righted themselves. Iliona's words poured out in one long, fluid stream of Faerie, without any pauses.

"What the bog are they talking about?" said Maralen.

"We're expected in Kinsbaile," Rhys said. "I have important business there. You may stay and chat with each other to your heart's content, but the rest of us are moving on."

"Oh, you're no fun."

"Elves never are."

"No." Rhys turned to Ashling. "Now, if you're ready, flamekin. . . ."

"More than ready," she said. "And call me Ashling."

* * * * *

"Taer," Ashling said as soon as an opening presented itself, "I would hear of the elemental you summoned."

"I didn't summon anything," Rhys said angrily. His eyes were on the trail ahead, and he spoke through clenched teeth.

"But you saw an elemental?"

"I did." Rhys did not turn or stop walking. "But it was not the glorious, rapturous encounter you seem to expect. The spirit came to punish me."

"Are you sure?" Ashling shook her head. "That doesn't sound right."

"I'm not sure of anything anymore," Rhys said. Together, he and Maralen quickly recounted their experience. They described the great, winged elk, the terrible feeling of judgment, of how it had changed the landscape for a time and then warned them—without speech—that they had to leave. Ashling hung on every word, struggling to imagine what it must have been like. They were omitting something, an unspoken but firmly agreed-upon conspiracy . . . either that, or their minds were too consumed with their trek through the forest. Ashling was wise enough not to press for more until she had a better idea of what they were leaving out. Elves were not known for verbosity when interacting with Lorwyn's other tribes, and Rhys would certainly take offense if she challenged the completeness of his account. It was a mystery that could wait until Kinsbaile.

Ashling resolved to simply listen and observe the strange pair along the way. If there was something about Rhys or Maralen that warranted the direct attentions of an elemental, she would root it out. Anything that helped advance her understanding of the great spirits would justify this leg of the path.

They moved on silently for another hour or so until they were close enough to hear the river. Ashling and Rhys both heard the approaching footsteps at the same time, and they turned to face the path behind them with Maralen safely sequestered behind a thick berry bush.

Brigid appeared on the path, her bow slung over her shoulders. "The Vendilion clique seems to have wandered off."

"No matter," Rhys snapped. "Archer, do you know a direct but concealed way into town from here?"

"She does," Ashling said. Brigid smiled thinly at the flamekin and nodded to Rhys.

"Then lead on. Go as fast as you can. If you go at full speed, the faeries may have trouble catching up with us."

"Sounds good," Brigid said. Without another word, Brigid smirked and sprinted past Rhys. The archer veered into a thick stand of trees to the north. Rhys and Maralen followed, with Ashling bringing up the rear.

Brigid's remarkable pace was undiminished. Even Rhys seemed to have trouble keeping up with her, mostly because of Maralen, and Ashling had to strain to keep the kithkin archer in sight. She led the party under hollow logs and through stands of trees so densely packed together that there was barely room to squeeze between them. It was an unfamiliar route to Ashling, completely different from the path they took away from the village, but they were moving so fast the flamekin did not have time to feel lost.

The party broke through the trees and emerged on a grassy hill overlooking Kinsbaile. The bustling kithkin village seemed small in the distance, but it was a cozy, welcome sight. Ashling felt a rush of excitement—her mission was nearly complete, but it had opened up a whole new avenue for her to pursue. The thread she'd earn for delivering Colfenor's message had become an afterthought. Ashling's true reward would be the information she gathered from Rhys and Maralen.

Brigid smiled at Ashling, clearly proud of her progress through the last leg of this trek. Rhys stood nearby, gazing down on the town. Kinsbaile marked the end of his current journey as well, but the elf did not seem comforted. If anything, he seemed to view Kinsbaile with equal parts weariness and dread.

Only Maralen's expression was opaque to Ashling. Her face displayed none of the satisfaction, anxiety, or expectation that the others held. The dark-haired elf simply seemed thoughtful, almost contemplative, as if her honest reaction to arriving safely in Kinsbaile would have to wait until she was done thinking it over.

Ashling believed she understood why. Kithkin were genial and excellent hosts, but they were also suspicious of strangers. The flamekin had not seen a Mornsong elf in all her long life, and even she wondered how the little people would receive the strange, pale woman.

A joyful buzzing and trilling sound rose up behind them as the faeries swooped into view.

"Found you!" Iliona said happily.

"Faeries rule the skies!" Veesa squealed.

"If I had thought to bring my glider along," Brigid said, "I'd have loved to test that claim."

"Any time, lumpy."

"Borrowed wings are never as good as the real thing."

"The only way you'd win is if we couldn't stop laughing at the sight of a flying thumbhead like you."

"You three," Rhys said, "go on ahead and announce me. We're sure to attract attention in town, and I don't want anything to slow me down between here and Colfenor."

"What, we're heralds now?"

"Can I have a trumpet?"

"I want some drums."

"Shush." Iliona turned to Rhys and bowed, her wings a blur as she bent at the waist. "Of course we'll do as you ask, Mr. Big Elf." The siblings shared a glance, nodded, and zipped down the hill toward the village.

"Told you," Iliona called back. "Told you that you couldn't get rid of us!"

"You shouldn't even have tried."

"You should be nicer to us next time."

The prattling continued as the faeries flew out of earshot.

Rhys waited, allowing the trio enough time to reach the village gates. Ashling, Brigid, and Maralen waited silently beside him. Then the dark-haired woman spoke.

"Before we go any farther," she said, "I want to thank you. All of you. I don't know what would have happened if I hadn't met you."

"You'd have died," Brigid said.

"It was my duty," Rhys said. "The Mornsong are strangers here, but you're still an elf, and that's what's important."

Ashling's lip curled slightly at the unintentional flash of casual bigotry intrinsic to Rhys's compliment. "You're welcome," she muttered.

A soft roar not unlike a cheer floated up the hill from Kinsbaile. Rhys nodded to himself and gestured to Maralen. Together, the two started down the hill with Ashling and Brigid close behind.

CHAPTER 10

Rhys could feel Colfenor's presence in Kinsbaile, looming over the village like the fragrance of burning leaves. Rhys ignored it . . . in fact, he tried to ignore everything as he entered the town: the curious kithkin onlookers, the serious-faced sentries, the occasional greetings, even the members of his own party.

Brigid, Ashling, and Maralen silently accompanied him through the Kinsbaile gates and on into the town center. The faerie trio had flitted off somewhere, capering and chatting.

Rhys stopped outside Cenn Teeg's large wooden door. He waited for Ashling and Brigid to catch up, and then he said, "Your mission ends here, if I'm not mistaken. I thank you both for your trouble."

"My job is to escort you to Colfenor," Ashling said.

"And I report to the cenn," Brigid added.

"I will speak privately with Colfenor," Rhys said, "or not at all."

"Of course, taer. But I intend to see my duties fully discharged."

"And compensated," Brigid said with a smile. "Eh, flamekin?"

"Aye," Ashling said, but she was looking at Maralen when she said it. Clearly the pilgrim still had questions about the spirit Rhys and the stranger had encountered in the forest.

Rhys called out. "Maralen," he said, "I have been honored to escort you. You will be safe here. The Mornsong tribe is far away, but you can easily send word to them up the river."

"Thank you, taer," Maralen said. "But I trust this is not the last time I will see you?"

"That I cannot say," Rhys replied. "Though I can offer a bit of practical advice: If you travel from here, choose your conveyance and your company wisely. There is something . . . strange in the air." He thought about adding a warning not to mention she'd traveled with an eyeblight, but found the words wouldn't form on his lips. He cursed his own cowardice.

Maralen bowed. Rhys nodded and turned back to the cenn's door. Before he could knock or announce himself, the painted wood swung open and Gaddock Teeg stood beaming in the doorway.

"Excellent!" the ruddy-faced kithkin said. His eyes danced over Rhys. "You've arrived! And well in advance of our self-imposed deadline."

"Mind your manners, kithkin," Rhys replied.

"My pardon, taer. Hail to you, Daen Rhys of the Hemlock Gilt Leaf hunting pack. You honor us with your presence."

"I am here to see Colfenor."

"By all means. Your mentor awaits you inside. May I accompany you to my office?"

"You may." Rhys glanced back at Brigid and Ashling. "You may also dismiss these two excellent retainers with congratulations on a job well done."

"Of course, of course. Archer Baeli, your special duty has concluded. And you, flamekin . . . please wait here. I shall settle our account once I've shown my noble guest in." Teeg's face clouded as he noticed Maralen. "And who is this? A lady of the Blessed. On behalf of all Kinsbaile, great lady, let me welcome you. It is an honor we do not deserve."

"Thank you, your honor," Maralen replied with a moderately respectful nod.

Teeg waited for an awkward moment. When he spoke his voice was impatient, nervous. "Splendid, splendid. Shall we away to your mentor, then?"

"With haste." Rhys turned to his party and said, "Good-bye to you all. If we meet again, I shall greet you kindly." After the briefest and curtest of bows he dismissed them, steeled himself, and followed Teeg inside.

The building's interior was deserted and dark. Rhys stepped lightly across the wooden floor and stood rigidly outside the closed door of Teeg's interior office. Colfenor was on the other side. He could feel the old log's thoughts like a cold wind, inscrutable but undeniably present. When the cenn made as if to open the door for him, Rhys flashed him an angry glare.

"Excuse me," Teeg said, sweating slightly. "I will leave you two alone and see to the flamekin's fee." Mopping his brow, he bowed low and backed away from Rhys until his ample posterior bumped up against the far wall.

Rhys waited until he heard the outer door open and shut, relishing this last moment of solitude. He knocked on the cenn's door, and Colfenor's deep, stentorian voice instantly boomed out in reply.

"Come in, my child."

Rhys opened the door and entered. The cenn's office was even gloomier than the rest of the building, its thick, wooden shutters completely blocking out the morning sun. In the darkness Rhys saw Colfenor hunched behind Teeg's broad-topped desk, the yew's upper branches scraping gently against the ceiling. The ancient tree simply stared at Rhys without the slightest hint of a recognizable expression on his broad, columnar face. Of all Lorwyn's diverse denizens, treefolk were the least like elves, and of all the treefolk, the rare and deadly yew were the strangest of all. Faeries, kithkin, giants, and even merrow shared the same basic bipedal design, though only the elves realized its full potential for grace and beauty.

In contrast, Colfenor was, well, a tree, and like trees would have, he appeared out of place within the cavernous office. He had limbs like an elf—that is, strong, rigid boles for arms that ended in surprisingly dexterous branching wooden fingers, and thick, rootlike legs—but the trunk that made up most of the treefolk's body was also crowned by hundreds of boughs and branches that had no analog on the bodies of elves or kithkin. The ancient yew was glorious in his crimson-tinged needles, and his gnarled bark skin was pure, perfect brown. He moved slowly, eyes, lips, and fingers almost glacial in their progress, but Colfenor had long ago proven that what he had to say was worth waiting for. And if he raised a mossy brow at something Rhys said, it was in Rhys's best interests to wait for his mentor's reaction before saying anything else.

If he had seen through the glamer, Colfenor had not yet reacted to Rhys's injury. The great tree simply stood and stared and mused as his broad, rough lips pursed and unpursed.

"You have called, Colfenor," Rhys said at last. "And I have answered."

The red yew chuckled, but his face remained stern. "For the first time in months," he said. "Most students would apologize to their masters for 'diligence' such as this. Most students would call me 'master' when addressing me in such circumstances."

"I am not 'most students.'"

"No. You are not even the student I expected." He raised a woody finger and pointed to Rhys's forehead. "What happened to you, my child?"

"That is why I came," Rhys said. Colfenor had seen through the glamer without apparent effort, and Rhys's words poured out in a strange rush of relief and anxiety. "I was in battle. I was in danger. We all were. The boggarts . . . they're different. Organized mobs, eating the flesh of—never mind. The point is, I felt a powerful surge of—of something. Magic, yew magic . . . poison magic like nothing I've ever seen. When I awoke, the enemy *and* my pack had been utterly destroyed." He swallowed hard. "And I, too, am destroyed. I am eyeblight, Colfenor. I am of no use anymore. Whatever you had in mind, you should find another student who won't cast shame upon you."

"So," Colfenor said, "you came not because I called, but because you were in crisis. A crisis of your own making."

"What does it matter, old log? You called and I came. I needed you, and you were here. We've both gotten what we wanted."

"Not yet, my student. I have a special favor to ask." Colfenor settled back against the wall in a symphony of creaking wood. "One that I could not rely on you to hear except with your own ears."

"I have been busy. Bearing my share of toil on behalf of the nation."

"Consider the rewards of such toil," Colfenor said, with a careless wave at Rhys's forehead. "Seek you answers here, or absolution?"

"I seek the meaning of it all." Rhys threw back his head, met Colfenor's cold, appraising eye, fully aware that his broken, blackened horns stood exposed before his mentor's studied attention.

"I am no longer fit to call myself one of the Blessed." Rhys gestured at his horns. "And so I must know, Colfenor. Did you set this in motion? Did you bring this about? I've never seen anything like what happened, let alone caused such death and destruction."

Colfenor sniffed. His melodious voice dripped with outrage.

"I had gathered from your own account," he said, "that you did it to yourself. Unless that was the mewling of a self-pitying child?"

Rhys scowled at the old yew's attempt to chide him into a better state of mind. "Yes . . . It was me. I can feel it. So tell me this: Did you know I was capable of such a thing? Did you withhold that information from me, knowing that I would one day destroy my future with the Gilt Leaf and have no choice but to follow your teachings?"

Colfenor's eyes blazed. He was slow to anger, but once his temper reached a boil it remained searing hot for days. "I would never have allowed you into a situation that would cost you your horns, and you insult me with the insinuation. I want you to choose to obey me because your heart and your mind are so inclined. The option I offer is superior to all others. I have no need to hobble your other options in the race to win your devotion." His words came strong and sharp, stabbing into Rhys's brain like a blade. *I have never harmed you, Rhys, not by action or inaction. And I have never delighted when you have come to harm.*

Rhys unclenched his teeth. He bowed, his legs trembling, his voice choking against the unbidden lump forming in his throat. By the infernal bogs, he was so tired. "Thank you, Colfenor."

The sage closed his eyes. "So we'll have no more baseless accusations? And you will honor the request I have yet to make?"

"I will listen, Colfenor. If it is within my power, I will consider it."

Colfenor opened his eyes. The great yew sighed, his branches and needles rustling.

Finally, Rhys added, "Master."

"That's more like it," Colfenor said. His broad face softened.

"The future, Rhys, is more important than the past. The petty squabbles between master and pupil should not transcend the value of the wisdom we exchange. You do not know it yet, but you are the last of my students. I will take no more apprentices. If you do not do this thing that I ask, if my past does not help create my future, all of the oldest yew teachings will wither away as if they had never been."

"Are you ill? Injured?" Rhys felt his face twist in confusion and concern, his own injuries immediately forgotten. "Surely you're not so old that—"

"I have important business here in Kinsbaile," Colfenor said. "And though I pulled up my roots long ago, I am not free to move about the countryside as I wish. There is a chance I will never again see the Murmuring Bosk, never anchor myself to the sacred soil that nurtured me. I cannot risk losing all that I am, all that I have been. I cannot risk leaving this world without passing along my knowledge." The yew's eyes warmed, and a smile turned up the corners of his mouth. "And for once that is not a veiled aspersion of your value as a student. There is only one way for a sage to ensure his teachings survive him, and that way is impossible for anyone but the sage himself."

"Then how am I to help?"

"You will be the means," Colfenor said. "I will provide the method." The old yew grinned widely and triumphantly. "I must ask you to put aside the ways of the hunter and become the gardener I always wanted you to be." Rhys bristled. "I am not suggesting you commit to the life of a seedguide, not permanently. But you must understand: No one but me knows yew lore better than you do. You are the only one who can do this for me, and once it's done you need never do it again.

"And before I expound and you consider, let me hold forth for a moment. You have endured my lectures in the past, but this is more important than scholarship. I wish to apologize to you, Rhys."

Rhys choked on confusion and was momentarily unable to answer.

"I diverted you from the path you wanted, as well as the one you were meant to walk. No, you were not meant to be a hunter, but a seedguide, my boy. The oak sage on the council was keenly interested in having you shepherd his sapling warriors. You would have been a great mentor to the next generation of oaks, my pupil, but I could not allow that to be. As much as the oaks needed you, I needed you more.

"Now, as when we met, I am the oldest of my kind. I was very old then, and I am older today, older by far. Long ago, I received the whole of my tribe's arcane lore and wisdom, magic and traditional rites from ancient days. Before I die, it is my responsibility to pass that on. My own memories and experiences must join with those of my ancestors. We must endure."

Rhys spoke quietly, his voice low and strained. He had known Colfenor most of his life, and he could sense the red yew wasn't being entirely honest with him. "So that was the whole of your interest in me? To make me a vessel for your knowledge?"

"Only in part. You proved ill suited to that particular discipline. You showed only the slightest regard for the honor I had bestowed in choosing you—there were times you seemed to regard it as a burden rather than a boon. I could see you only ever wanted to be a hunter, and you proved it when I gave you the most powerful poison spells in all Lorwyn, the deepest foundations of yew magic . . . and you bent them to a hunter's needs. In your hands the subtle, indirect influence of the seedguide was fashioned into a focused, lethal, offensive tool. Only a strong mind and a stronger will could change the fundamental nature of our ancient lore. Only an elf could take a blade of grass and use it as a weapon.

"That quality in you, the unyielding stubbornness of character that seeks to make the world conform to its own desires . . . to me, that was an acceptable alternative to true spiritual dedication. I taught you all I could, knowing that you would only ever use it for the benefit of the elves. But I did not begrudge you for it. When you declared your intent to leave and return to Gilt Leaf, I did not argue."

"Of course you did."

Colfenor scowled, his wooden skin creaking loudly. "I may have . . . expressed my disappointment, which was heartfelt and genuine, but I did not argue to exhaustion a point which I had already conceded. I let you go. I let you choose your own path. Now I must ask you to step off that path for a time. A short time, and inalterably the last."

Rhys bowed his head, showing Colfenor his horns. "That path is closed to me."

"Your injury changes nothing. If you were the Perfect king of the entire elf nation, I would still ask this of you. I chose you all those years ago because you have many gifts, Rhys . . . You were always possessed of a great deal of potential and a will strong enough to develop it. All I am asking is that you harken back to our time together, to the secret wisdom we shared. Be my pupil one last time. Have I earned at least that much consideration from a Blessed hunter?"

Before Rhys could reply, Colfenor plunged his hand deep into the tangle of branches atop his own head. The yew rummaged around, his face screwed up in concentration, until he latched on to something deep in the middle of his crown. He gently withdrew his cupped hand and extended it to Rhys.

The elf stepped forward. Colfenor opened his hand to reveal a compact, segmented, wooden cone, freshly plucked. The seedbody filled Rhys's cupped hands—from this would sprout the next generation of yew sage, the offspring of the great, solitary Colfenor, possessed of all his knowledge but unburdened by his long lifetime of habits, opinions, and quirks. Already the cone's casing had cracked, revealing tantalizing slivers of green within.

"This is ready to sprout," Rhys said.

"You see?" Colfenor beamed. "It's already coming back to you. I taught you well, I must say." The yew's smile faded. "Take this to the sacred grove," Colfenor said, "to the place you and I spent so much time together. The Murmuring Bosk . . . Ah, such happy times there, eh, my boy?"

"Happy," Rhys agreed, half-mesmerized by the seed cone, "between liberal dashes of abuse and condescension." He looked up at the old yew, and they both shared a quick, almost inadvertent smile.

"Why?" Rhys asked. "Why me? Why now?"

Colfenor gestured impatiently. "And still you question me. Go now," he said. "Plant this tree in my name, in the same sacred soil that nourished me. Follow the rites and rituals I drummed into your head for ten years. Do that, and return, and I will answer any question you ask. If I am able. In the meantime"—Colfenor's upper branches rustled and scratched the ceiling—"accept this final gift from your old mentor, who knows how dangerous your pride can be."

The ancient yew's needles shifted from red to yellow to green. Rhys felt the familiar touch of glamer settling over his head. He felt the protest forming in his throat, but as he had done with Maralen, Rhys choked it back down.

"I accept your gift." Rhys bowed his head, and then stood tall. "But Colf—*Master*—what do I do about—"

"Go." Colfenor's needles faded back to a dull, dusty red. The old yew sagged and slumped back against the wall behind him. "I have much to do. Your questions tire me. Do this thing for me, or do not. If your deep love and respect for me as your mentor does not prompt you to accept, perhaps the common law of the marketplace will: I gave you strong magic. In return, I ask of you this favor. Settle this debt, my former student, and we will be quit of each other."

Rhys paused. "I still—"

"Go, you contrary little shrub. The longer you tarry here, the less likely it is you'll succeed."

Rhys bowed. "As you wish. Master." He straightened and said, "But when I return, you and I will commune. I will understand how my use of your magic destroyed everything I held dear. I will do this for you, Colfenor, but then you will do as I ask."

"Agreed." Colfenor settled deeper into Cenn Teeg's creaking wall. "When you return, I will help you make sense of it all."

"If you can."

"To the best of my ability. Now hurry," Colfenor said. "Each grain in the hourglass that falls brings strange and unforeseen dangers a step closer."

"Farewell, Master. We shall meet again."

"Farewell, my pupil."

Rhys cradled the seed cone between his hands, bowed to Colfenor, and then left the darkened room without another word.

* * * * *

Taercenn Nath stood at the center of his command tent with his sword clenched tight in both hands. The weapon was heavy, but he hefted it easily, holding it before him with his arms extended. The wide, single-edged blade—almost a cutlass—gleamed in the light. He'd recovered his weapon from the battlefield not long after he had found Gryffid impaled in the boughs of the tree. After an hour of attention the weapon had gleamed, with a day's worth of caked bloodstains wiped away.

He examined the blade's razor edge and planned his next move. The disgraced elf's continued existence was an ongoing insult to the entire elf nation and to Nath himself. Hiring the giants was enough to warrant Rhys's ouster alone, perhaps his permanent banishment. But Rhys's wholesale slaughter of his fellow elves by use of his damnable and uncontrolled treefolk magic demanded the ultimate punishment. It seemed the outlaw had fled to Kinsbaile, which enabled Nath to pursue two of his immediate goals at once. Kinsbaile had a value all its own, but with Rhys there it was too tempting a target to overlook.

Already, the few survivors of the Gilt Leaf packs, along with fresh recruits, were dismantling the camp and preparing to march. Nath had sent for additional forces and as soon as they arrived he would lead the packs to Kinsbaile. He would have Rhys's head on a pike before the next day's end, and then he would have a long talk with Cenn Teeg about Kinsbaile's future service to the Blessed Nation of Gilt Leaf. If Teeg protested, Nath would take great pleasure in beheading the kithkin toad with his new sword.

Nath lowered his blade and took cold comfort in another fact. Rhys's potential role in the elf nation was moot, and his preferred status no longer applied. Not even the oldest and most respected treefolk could save the former daen from the nation's vengeance.

Gryffid appeared outside Nath's tent. "The vinebred are ready for review, taer," Gryffid said. "And the cuffhounds are howling to be let loose."

Nath's eyes darkened. "You're keeping them separate, of course?"

"Of course, taer. Also, the warriors you sent for have arrived. I wasn't quite sure what to make of them . . . the vinebred, I mean."

"They aren't damaged?" Nath rose angrily, slinging his armored chest plate over his torso. "They're unblemished and ready to fight?"

"Yes, taer. They're in excellent shape. In fact, they're . . . they're. . . ."

"What are they?"

"They're magnificent," Gryffid said. "The most perfect I've ever seen. All proud and noble elves. I am honored to serve alongside them, taer, but. . . ."

"But what?"

Gryffid lowered his eyes. "They put the vinebred we've cobbled together to shame, taer."

"There is no shame in adapting to the terrain when on the hunt, Gryffid."

"No, taer. But we've been enchanting whatever low creatures we could find. The vinebred you sent for might well be insulted if we field them alongside such rabble."

"The honor of serving me directly will counterbalance any shame they might experience," Nath said. "Is that all you came to say, Gryffid?"

"No, taer." Gryffid looked miserable, frightened, and anxious at the words he was preparing to say. "Some of them . . . the elves you sent for, even some of the vinebred . . . they aren't just hunters, taer. They carry fearsome weapons. They have the air of serious, dangerous men. I believe there are winnowers among them."

"There are," Nath said, "because I sent for them." Gryffid shifted uncomfortably. Nath said, "It's time for you and I to have a serious talk about your future."

Gryffid hesitated. The fear left his eyes, and his voice was clear, strong. "I agree, taer."

"Right now, you're thinking about what you saw in the tree. When Rhys left you hanging like a trophy fish and I came to pull you down."

"I saw nothing, taer. I was half-blinded by pain and feverish. Anything I might remember is completely unreliable."

"Well said. But we both know that isn't true. We both know what I look like when something breaks my concentration. When the glamer fades." Nath planted the tip of his sword in the dirt and allowed the magical façade around him to dissipate. Gryffid stood at perfect attention, emotionless as a stone.

"I have been in service to the Blessed Nation for thirty years," Nath said. "I am the oldest Exquisite on the council and the oldest living elf. But I am far from past my prime, no matter how scarred and callused my features. The journey toward perfection is too important for me to abandon. While there is strength in my body, I will continue to serve the Gilt Leaf. If I have to mask myself, then that is what I will do.

"I am not the only one. There are many of us positioned throughout the nation. Years ago we saw that the council was too influenced by the treefolk, and our Perfect monarch too influenced by the council. We, who would be drummed out of the nation because of the toll our service took upon us . . . the scars and burns and broken bodies. . . . we saw that we were more fit than they. Those winnowers you saw work for us. They exist to hunt blighted elves, to kill them and remove their stain from the nation. But under our direction, they also recruit their prey. Many of the eyeblights gladly give their lives to serve the nation one last time. They consent to becoming vinebred, to end their lives as strong and perfect servants of the tribe."

Nath strode forward and lowered his horns, thrusting his face into Gryffid's. "Not all of those magnificent vinebred out there are willing eyeblights. Some are unwilling conscripts taken from the ranks—elves who could aid us in our work . . . Or who pose a threat to it.

"You have an important choice to make, Gryffid. Swear loyalty to me, and to my peers. Serve us willingly, see yourself revenged on the traitor Rhys, and advance to the highest ranks of the pack . . . Or serve me as a vinebred winnower, see yourself revenged on the traitor Rhys, and die when the vines burn through your life-force."

Gryffid held Nath's penetrating stare. "I am yours to command, Taercenn Nath. Test my loyalty if you must. You will not find it wanting."

"Excellent." Nath stepped back and resumed his full, robust veneer. "Bow your head."

Gryffid bowed, and Nath touched him lightly on the top of his skull, between the horns.

"Now rise, Gryffid, Daen and Commander of the Hemlock Pack."

Gryffid straightened. "Taercenn."

"Come with me now as I review the pack," Nath said. He picked up his long-handled sword and sheathed it. "We leave immediately thereafter."

Gryffid saluted and backed away from the tent flap. Nath carefully positioned his battle headdress around his horns and strode out into the cold evening air.

A hundred Faultless hunters stood in precise formation, backs straight and eyes hungry. As Nath strode past, each in turn bowed his head and sank to one knee, remaining this way until the taercenn reached the end of the ranks.

Gryffid remained two steps behind Nath as the taercenn strode past the cuffhound pens. Though full of energy and enthusiasm for the coming hunt, the huge, agile canines fell silent and still as Nath approached. The sleek, beautiful animals had been trained to recognize their superiors and show proper respect. Over the years Nath had learned he could easily gauge a pack of hunters by the quality of its cuffhounds and its cervins.

The officers then entered a dense thicket of brush and brambles. They moved easily through the tangle of thorns and ivy, barely disturbing a single leaf, until they broke through to an artificial clearing the elves had cut from the forest.

Under the direction of the Exquisite leadership, elf druids spent months or sometimes years rearing and tending the vinebred. Virtually any living thing could be controlled by the special magic nettlevines that were the key to the process, taking root in the spine and spreading across their host's entire body until the original creature was completely encased in tough, flexible braids. Tiny thorns along the vines pierced the skin of the host, feeding on its blood even as the vines returned nutrients and powerful, strength-enhancing magic back into the host body. Once enshrouded, the vinebred creature was magically bound to obey the commands of all elves. The higher that elf ranked, the stronger his control over his puppet warriors.

Vinebred creatures were not mindless, and they were not the product of necromancy. They were alive, and the most useful were intelligent and aware of their abilities and place in the order of Lorwyn. They were also perfect slaves. When given an order they would carry it out to the best of their ability, sparing no effort, and if something went astray they would adapt, also to the best of their abilities. It was this threadbare autonomy that made the vinebred so effective and valuable—they were not just willing to follow orders, they actively wanted to and often made extraordinary efforts to achieve the goals set for them.

The vinebred Nath had cobbled together locally were

extremely distasteful to his sight, but he knew they were worth having. They had been enchanted quickly, even hastily, and they were rough and misshapen compared to the exalted creatures that had just arrived. All vinebred were undeniably effective in battle, however, their natural strengths enhanced and their ferocity unmatched.

Nath approached the silent line of vine- and leaf-encrusted warriors. There were ten in all: six boggarts (one of the only ways the vile, little brutes could ever be made useful), three kithkin, and a cast-out female elf who had been blighted in one of the frequent conflicts that broke out between the noble clans.

"Gryffid," Nath said.

Gryffid replied immediately. "Yes, taer."

"How quickly can you march this lot to Kinsbaile?"

"An hour or two, taer. No more than that."

"Very well. I want you to take this group and one-third of the pack to Kinsbaile now. Wait outside the village. I will take the rest of our hunters and the cervin and follow."

"Very good, taer."

"Let the kithkin see you, but do not engage them. Do not even speak to them. Hold your position until we arrive, and then fall in behind us. I do not intend to stop or even slow, but to march straight into the town center. The kithkin village will become our new base of operations until the traitor Rhys is captured and publicly executed." He paused, looking down the line of vine-encrusted warriors. "Or hunted for sport. With Rhys's death, it will be decades before another Faultless is permitted to apprentice with the treefolk."

"As it should be."

"Very good. You are dismissed, Daen Gryffid. We shall meet again on the edge of Kinsbaile."

Gryffid moved off, organizing the vinebred as he walked.

Nath turned and marched toward the newly arrived contingent of hunters. Rhys would die, Kinsbaile would shake, and the Blessed Nation would continue on toward perfection.

Soon all would be as it should be.

* * * * *

Cenn Teeg found Ashling in the town square, just outside Angus Gabble's General Store. Ashling watched the round figure bob through the crowd, and she nudged Brigid.

"Cenn's here," she said.

"It's about time," the archer replied. Brigid had gone away, but had returned a short time later. The townsfolk were gearing up for the annual story festival and it seemed there wasn't much for warriors to do inside the village. Brigid said she'd have to wait for her commanding officer to return from patrol before she'd get her next assignment . . . which, she thought wearily, would probably involve scouting out the surrounding forest on foot or in a glider to keep an eye out for boggarts. It wasn't easy being the most celebrated archer in Kinsbaile, she admitted, especially when everyone wanted the folk hero's time . . . And when part of the appeal of this hero was that she was not the commander, not the general, but just a damned talented kithkin with a knack for being in the right place at the wrong time.

"Hello, hello," the cenn called. "So glad to find you two together. I trust the wait was not overlong?"

"Not at all," Ashling said, with a barely perceptible wink to Brigid.

Cenn Teeg presented her with a small coil of gold thread—easily enough to keep the flamekin solvent for the next leg of her path, wherever it might lead. "The remainder of your fee," he said. "And, as our honored guest suggested, it comes with my thanks and congratulations."

"You are welcome, taer. A pleasure doing business with Kinsbaile, as always."

"But now that your initial task is complete," Teeg said, "I wonder if you might be persuaded to accept another?"

"I'm not sure I'm available," Ashling said. She thought of Rhys in the cenn's office and Maralen at the inn. The elf would be harder to approach, but Ashling was relatively sure a meal and a flagon of kithkin ale would loosen Maralen's tongue about the elemental.

"Oh, but I must insist. Colfenor himself has requested that you attend our storytelling festival. You would be his honored guest, and mine."

Ashling smiled. "Thank you, Cenn. I am glad to accept." And, she thought, gladder to have an excuse to linger in Kinsbaile.

"Splendid. Do come see me if you have any interesting stories to tell." Cenn Teeg turned to the Brigid. "Brigid, if you are not occupied at present . . ."

"I am not."

"Then I have something for you, as well. We've had reports of a pair of giants lurking outside the village. They have done no harm as of yet, but with the festival approaching . . . well, we can't have any disruptions during the storytelling, now can we?"

"No, Cenn."

"Would you head out and ascertain what these giants intend? I don't want to make trouble, but if you could find some way of . . . encouraging them to camp elsewhere, I would consider it a personal favor."

"As you wish, Cenn."

"No violence," the cenn said. "Just talk to them. If they

give you any trouble, come back here and we'll try a different approach."

"I understand."

"Good, good. Well, I'll leave you to it. I look forward to seeing you at the festival," he said to Ashling. "And do drop by my office if you need anything. Anything at all." Cenn Teeg bobbed off and disappeared into the bustling square.

Brigid positioned her bow across her shoulder and said, "So, flamekin, care to join me in bracing a pair of giants?"

"Not right now," Ashling said. "But thanks just the same."

"Suit yourself. I'm sure I'll see you around town."

Before Brigid could leave, a familiar voice said, "Excuse me?"

Ashling turned and saw Maralen. The dark-haired woman's spirits seemed low.

"Hello again," Ashling said.

"I hate to trouble you any further," Maralen said, "but have you seen Rhys come out of the cenn's office yet?"

"No, not yet."

"Well, I had something I wanted to ask him. May I wait with you?"

"We're not waiting for Rhys."

"Oh?" Maralen smiled knowingly at Ashling.

The flamekin shrugged. "I admit I hoped to speak with him. What of it?"

"Maybe I'll wait with you two," Brigid said. "You've got my interest peaked."

But Maralen was barely listening. Her dark eyes were fixed on the cenn's office across the square. Ashling watched her stare for a moment. From Maralen's intense look of concentration, the flamekin calculated that the Mornsong elf would be more likely to talk to her after they had both spoken to Rhys.

Sometimes a pilgrim's progress was slow and deliberate, and waiting was often as much of a test as traveling. Ashling pulled the wide brim of her hat down over her face, leaned up against the shop wall beside Maralen, and settled in.

* * * * *

Rhys emerged from the cenn's office and started across the town square with Colfenor's seed cone held gingerly in both hands. The reinforced glamer hid his broken horns, and while Rhys was grateful for that respite he couldn't help noticing how Colfenor's parting gift also made it simpler for Rhys to do the old tree's bidding without the distraction of facing up to his ruination within the Blessed Nation. Rhys took both as a comfort and proof that the meddling, old log would never change.

"We know something you don't know," three faerie voices sang out in perfect harmony, and Iliona, Endry, and Veesa buzzed into view over his head.

"Hello, children of Oona," Rhys said.

"Hello, Mr. Big Elf." Iliona said. "Do you want to hear a secret?"

"Do I have a choice?" he asked.

"Not really."

Rhys continued to walk, he and his plant towering over the diminutive kithkin crowd.

Iliona and her siblings kept pace. "Crowded here in town, isn't it?" she said.

Rhys slowed down. "Please get to the point," he said.

"Seems like everyone and their brother has come to Kinsbaile for the festival."

"A fat elf. A flamekin. Lots of elves." Rhys felt a familiar, unpleasant knot form in his gut. He had thought to leave the elf nation behind for a time, but he should have realized the nation would not let him go. Not if Nath was still leading the Gilt Leaf.

"And two brothers. Two big brothers," Iliona continued.

Rhys slowed down. A creeping suspicion formed in the back of his mind.

"Giants," Iliona concluded. "Two giants camped right outside the gates."

Rhys nodded as he kept walking. "Have they been causing trouble?"

"Not at all. But trouble will soon find them anyway."

"The cenn doesn't like the giants so close."

"He sent the archer to shoo them away."

"What?" Rhys asked. "When?"

"Moments ago."

"She's on her way there now."

"You can catch her before she gets there if you run."

Rhys paused just long enough to imagine the nightmare that would ensue if the kithkin tried to drive the giants away by force. "Thank you," he said. "For once I am grateful you see so much and talk so often."

Rhys moved swiftly through the crowds, his progress facilitated by the fact that every kithkin hurried to get out of his way. Giggling merrily, the trio buzzed and flitted overhead, keeping pace with Rhys as he picked his way through the square.

"Rhys." The elf turned toward the sound of his name and saw Ashling, Brigid, and Maralen waving to him from in front of the general store. He continued heading directly to the gates as the three moved to intercept him.

"How did the meeting with your mentor go?" Ashling asked.

Rhys said, "It was brief. I've been given a task to perform. My best chance of success is to go and do it right now."

"But the mean elves are coming!" Veesa said.

"And there are a lot of them."

Maralen's face darkened. "Your former pack, taer?"

Rhys nodded.

"I'd like to come with you, please."

"What? Of course not. Absolutely not."

"These elves that are coming," Maralen mused. "They're coming in force?"

"Big force," Iliona said.

"Big, big, force!"

"The biggest!"

"So they'll have rangers and archers," Maralen confirmed.

"Yes," Rhys said.

"And cervin. And cuffhounds, too, I suppose?"

"Yes, yes," Rhys snapped. "What is the point—"

"Cuffhounds that have been following your scent for days. And mine along with it. Cuffhounds that will lead whomever is after you straight to me when they can't find you in Kinsbaile. I would prefer not to be here when that happens. They'll find us one way or the other . . . I think our chances are better if we are together, don't you?"

Rhys opened his mouth. He was unable to come up with a suitable rejoinder, so he closed it again.

"Very well," he said. "But you must understand: You are no longer under my protection. I cannot see to your safety as I did before."

"I expect it won't be necessary. Not to the degree it was."

"You'll change your mind when the faeries start in."

"Oh, I'm not worried about them. I think I'm getting the hang of dealing with their kind."

"If you need to get out quickly," Ashling said, "I know a merrow who can ferry you."

Rhys nodded. "Thank you."

Brigid glanced back at Kinsbaile for a moment. "I have to move some giants first, but my scent follows your trail almost as much as Maralen's," she said. "If elves are coming, I should leave as well."

"We can discuss the giants later; we must go now."

As the group moved out of the square, the faeries spun in happy circles over their heads.

"Together again!" Iliona cried.

"Friends forever!"

"Except for that fat elf. She's fat."

The dark-haired woman smiled patiently. "Is it bad luck," she said to no one in particular, "to drown a faerie in the river?"

"Yes," Iliona said.

"Especially helpful faeries like us."

"But only if you actually do it." Veesa flexed her sharp fingers. "Which you never will. Just try it, fatty."

CHAPTER 11

Gryffid crossed his arms and scowled. He sat in a folding, canvas chair, at a folding, canvas desk, inside the largest tent in the Gilt Leaf camp. A glowing blue lantern hung over his head, casting his dusky features into strange light. The elf looked the spitting image of the statue of his revered ancestor, the long-dead Taercenn Grieve of the Oak Fall elves. The statue occupied most of the town square in the distant kithkin port of Fen Grieve. Gryffid had never felt any need to visit that distant town, but he'd been told of the resemblance. Aeloch—the young scout who had just made his initial report on the Kinsbaile situation—was from Fen Grieve, and did notice the resemblance, but he was far too nervous to mention it. Newly promoted from the Cascara pack after the disaster at the boggart village, Aeloch was only concerned with two things at the moment—making an accurate report to the new daen and leaving the presence of the new daen's bodyguards as quickly as possible.

The bodyguards, a pair of silent scarblades, flanked the tent's entrance. The silent assassins of perfection stood ready to deform—and, pending a nominal fee, kill—anyone who entered Gryffid's Immaculate domain or threatened his Immaculate person without permission. They were wrapped from neck to toe in scaled black leather that faded in and out of view with a persistent camouflage glamer, while their faces were concealed by wrappings of fine widow's silk harvested at great risk from the distant Funnelwood Forest. Each carried the traditional weapons of the scarblade: the dant, a long, curved dagger shaped like a carving knife and slung over the left hip; and the ewynn, a flat, hooked, flesh-ripping blade hanging over the other. The weapons were more commonly known as the tooth and the claw, respectively. Gryffid had seen both in action in the hands of other scarblades and believed the names to be more than apt. There was little chance of anything or anyone getting close to Immaculate Daen Gryffid.

Immaculate. At Nath's discretion, Gryffid had become a member of that most exalted class to which he had hardly hoped to reach. And why should he have? A daen was only Flawless, by rights. Nath had granted him the honor, however, because the taercenn could. It was an act clearly meant to ensure utter loyalty on the part of the new daen. And it had worked all too well, Gryffid knew. He now had the right to petition for an audience before the Perfects of the Sublime Court, and the petition would have to be honored according to the most ancient elf laws. It was something he'd aspired to his entire life, but, having acquired such status, he found that it was a burden. He didn't have anything to say to the Perfects, in all honesty, and now he had to consider the entire pack. Gryffid felt he should be doing one and only one thing: finding the outlaw Rhys and bringing him to justice.

Added to that was the burden of secret knowledge with which he'd been saddled: the knowledge of his own, glamer-hidden injuries; and the more alarming knowledge that Nath himself was using the same trick, and had indeed been doing so for years. This secret society of the taercenn's made Gryffid extremely uncomfortable, for it seemed to go against everything he'd ever been taught about perfection. Then again, he could see the logic behind such a group, and could accept that he might well become a part of it.

The Gilt Leaf daen and his pack—the new Hemlock pack, culled from the brightest survivors of Nath's amalgamated command—had been here through most of sunset. Soon the sun would stop setting and begin to rise again, piercing the low clouds on the eastern horizon. Gryffid knew this instinctively despite the fact he could not see the sky. Any hunter worth a tent in the hierarchy of the Gilt Leaf elves didn't need to see the sky to feel the morning drawing near and the forest slowly flickering to life. If Rhys hadn't run yet—Gryffid had to assume his former commander would not be doing the honorable thing and giving himself up—he would soon.

That traitor was not Rhys anymore. Maybe he never had been an elf in the first place. How could an elf have done what the traitor did? How did one summon power like that?

The explosion, the energy wave, the poison cloud—whatever it had been—had been bright—so bright Gryffid's eyes still hadn't quite recovered. The daen had no idea how or why he had been spared, especially since he had been touching the source of the destruction at the time.

Perhaps that was it—Rhys had survived, after all. Not that it mattered. Rhys had to be punished, and he had to die. There was no room for mercy or questions. And no effort was to be spent trying to understand how Rhys had done this thing.

It was that last part that stuck in Gryffid's craw more than it should. If Rhys was an elf, he'd tapped into a great power that could benefit the Gilt Leaf. If he was something different—some freakish spawn of treefolk magic, perhaps, long insinuated within the Gilt Leaf—then the elves needed to understand the potential threat he and any like him posed.

Gryffid had never had a firm grasp of what others called

"irony," but he found it supremely ironic that this traitor would be hunted down and destroyed by elves who were themselves secret eyeblights, and thus traitors. Perhaps it wasn't ironic, but it was a difficult thing to wrap his head around.

As Gryffid thought these highly inappropriate thoughts, he noticed one of his bodyguards appeared to be staring directly at him. Had his glamer fallen? No, that wasn't it. Probably just taking in his new charge, Gryffid reasoned.

The scarblade guards were Nath's. "On loan," the taercenn had said, but their presence irritated the new daen considerably. He also had the feeling they followed him when he left this cramped command tent, but did so behind one of their scarblade glamers. And it was almost a certainty that when push came to shove, Gryffid's bodyguards answered not to the daen but to Nath. Were the scarblades in on Nath's secret? Was that why this one stared at him so?

Scout Aeloch had brought unwelcome news, but the slightly winded elf standing before him was a welcome reprieve from waiting silently, studying maps and trying—pointlessly—to strike up conversations with the scarblades. Gryffid shifted in his seat and considered leaning his elbows forward on the flimsy-looking field desk, but chose to place both palms atop it instead. That seemed stable enough.

"You're certain?" Gryffid asked quietly. "He's gone?"

"Yes, taer," the scout said hurriedly. "Rhys—"

"The target," Gryffid corrected irritably. "The target that was Daen Rhys."

"Taer," the scout said, averting eye contact with his commander. "The *target* is leaving Kinsbaile, on a 'mission' of some kind for the red yew. The treefolk, taer, the one called Colfenor."

"I know who the red yew is," Gryffid said. "He's the only red yew, Aeloch."

"Of course, taer," the scout said. "That was all I could make out from what was said. We were not to reveal ourselves, otherwise I might have—well"—the young elf looked embarrassed, but Gryffid prompted him to go on with a look—"he had companions. A kithkin warrior, a flamekin, some faeries—I think—and . . . and . . ."

"And?"

"Another elf, from some tribe I didn't recognize. She's very tall, and her horns are unusual—something like an antelope's. Thin, and pale."

" 'She,' eh?" Gryffid asked. He had heard, along with the rest of the camp, that the Perfect Eidren's Mornsong bride never arrived. "There was a party of Mornsong that disappeared en route to Lys Alana a while back . . . perhaps there was a survivor. I can't imagine why she would have taken up with the traitor, however."

"Yes, taer," the scout agreed. "In fact, taer, most of his companions are female, now that you mention it. You don't suppose—?"

"No," Gryffid said, "I do not suppose, because I have a job to do. Leave gossip to the kithkin." He crossed his arms again and intently considered the roof of the tent. "A Mornsong female, a famous kithkin archer, and a flamekin pilgrim. What are you about, Rhys? Why don't you just give yourself up and die like an elf? Why degrade yourself with companions like these?"

"Taer?"

"Scout, do not interrupt me again," Gryffid said, and as he heard his own voice, he was suddenly reminded of Nath. He didn't like the sound. "Forgive me, Aeloch," he said, standing and stepping out from the accursed folding desk. "We will catch up to the traitor. If we do not catch up to him, Lorwyn will."

He moved toward the tent's opening, ordering the scarblades

to stay put and gesturing for Aeloch to follow. Gryffid told himself they might even obey him, as he stepped outside, into the temporary camp he'd occupied since Nath dispatched him on this duty. It was a small encampment by yesterday's standards—standards that had fallen by the wayside in the short time since Rhys had become a kin-slayer. A few tents, much smaller than Gryffid's, surrounded the tiny mess and a small stockade that held a pair of badly burned boggart prisoners. The two had wandered into the camp, raving and babbling about an explosion, and it had taken all of Gryffid's newfound authority to keep his hunters from slaying the boggarts on the spot. The foul things had information in their heads that might be useful later.

Gryffid walked to the edge of the firelight and gazed into the darkened forest. There were so many things out there that could solve the Rhys problem entirely, but the certainty of the deed was up to the new daen. Even if Gryffid got lucky and wasn't forced to kill someone he had once called friend, he had to confirm the issue was resolved.

The fresh air helped his mood. He still wondered how long it would be before Nath showed up—and wondered more at why the taercenn hadn't given him the authority to pursue Rhys on his own. Something to do with his secret peers, no doubt. Gryffid sensed Nath was being less than fully truthful with him. But the cool, early morning, before sun stopped setting and still a few hours from sunrise, helped him ignore this near certainty.

And then there was that stranger. He hadn't spent the entire day inside his tent. He knew the hunters were abuzz with talk and rumors about this apparent survivor of the lost wedding party, which had been big news when the Most Glorious and Perfect Eidren had revealed his intended bride's disappearance. Gryffid could read it on Scout Aeloch's face like an open book—he was even more eager to track down the traitor if it meant the mystery might be solved.

"Whoever she is, she won't get far," the taercenn said, slapping a hand onto the scout's shoulder. Aeloch stifled a yelp Gryffid chose to ignore. "When the taercenn arrives—"

"Yes?" came a louder, familiarly authoritative voice floating down the long road that lead back to elf country. "What, pray tell, will happen when the taercenn arrives?"

As Nath said the word "arrives," he dropped the powerful glamer that hid his person from casual view and strode forward from the darkness. Of course, Gryffid knew that he'd merely replaced one glamer with another, but the difference was undetectable even when one looked for it. As the taercenn's personal glamer fell, or shifted, as it were, a ripple of magic revealed the translucent shadows behind him to be some of the vinebred the daen had seen back at Nath's camp. Gryffid could make out their distinctive shadows among the normal Gilt Leaf hunters.

Not that this was much of the daen's concern. Or so he hoped.

"I meant to tell Scout Aeloch that when you arrived, taer, I planned to seek your approval for a punitive mission against the traitor who disgraced the name Hemlock," Gryffid said. "He has just departed the Kinsbaile gate, and as you said, he must pay for his crimes."

"You presume to give yourself orders, Daen Gryffid?" Nath asked, with a touch of menace. "Shall I await your commands?"

"Taercenn, I merely seek to exact a measure of justice for the losses our nation has suffered today," Gryffid said. "And I am eager to begin."

"Well said." The taercenn nodded. "But you should know I had every intention of dispatching you and your new Hemlock pack to hunt down this traitor. But you must also know, Daen Gryffid, that your taercenn has reasons for the orders he gives, and they are not to be cast aside lightly." He waved Gryffid to him with a gesture and a knowing look. The daen dismissed Aeloch with a nod and joined Nath. The taercenn accepted Gryffid's own report, the daen pointing out first that Rhys was on the way out of town and headed to the river. Nath asked him more than once for additional details about the treefolk Colfenor's activities in Kinsbaile.

When he had received and digested Gryffid's report, Nath wasted no time in giving Gryffid his marching orders.

Minutes later, the pack was on the move, the camp abandoned. Nath's forces, no doubt, would reuse the tents and other equipment since supplies and rations were already pitiably low.

The hunt was on. As far as Gryffid was concerned it was about time.

* * * * *

Sygg was nowhere to be found, and Rhys decided to take cover at the edge of the woods until the captain returned to the docks. They hardly had time to get comfortable before a familiar scent reached Rhys's nose. He looked at Ashling.

"I was just had an idea. Ashling, if you'd follow me, I might have a job for you. It won't take long," he said. "Brigid, you might want to come along. I think we can combine our two tasks." Rhys strode away, expecting all of his recent acquaintances to do the natural thing and follow his lead. Which, in their own time and their own fashion, they all did.

The party stole through the wilds outside Kinsbaile until Rhys brought them to a silent halt. He motioned for silence and stepped aside, presenting the rolling valley below.

The giant brothers' camp covered roughly the same area as Gryffid's temporary base of operations, though the camp population density was, of course, much thinner. It was dangerous enough having Brion and Kiel so close to Kinsbaile, but if Nath's army was also on the way, there was sure to be violence. Rhys wanted to spare the town if he could . . . And put the giants to good use if he could not.

As soft blue light delicately played along the horizon, marking the onset of another day, Brion and Kiel slept. The former was curled up in an almost—no, Rhys corrected, a *very*—fetal position before the still-roaring fire. Brion, who resembled a small hillock even more as he slumbered, snored with surprising delicacy.

His brother Kiel was seated, upright, his back rigid. He snored too: long, rumbling roars interrupted by abrupt choking sounds at random intervals. Rhys wondered if Kiel's sleep was troubled, and momentarily tried to estimate exactly how far the giant's foot would reach if, for example, Kiel kicked while in the throes of some giant's nightmare.

"Rhys," Ashling said in a quiet but clear tone that cut through the faeries' chatter. "They're sleeping giants. I think I've heard somewhere that sleeping giants should be left to their slumber."

"These giants," Rhys whispered, "are the job for which I need your help. Just play along."

"So how do you intend to wake them?" Maralen said.

"I could stick an arrow in the sole of this one's foot," Brigid volunteered. "Wouldn't do him any harm, I'd think. They might wake up angry, but, by the bog, it would make a fine ballad, eh?"

"Let's play it safe. These giants are friends of mine. Or at least, they've helped me out in the past," Rhys said, stifling the memory of the chaotic slaughter that had ended his tenure as a daen. "I owe them a service. I'm to deliver a message—a collection of stories—to their sister Rosheen for her birthday before the aurora. Obviously, I can't do that at the moment, but if I guarantee them that *you* will deliver the message—"

"That's the only reason I'm here?" Ashling said. "I'm a—I'm a prop for your argument?"

"That's what it sounds like," Maralen said.

"And how are you planning on getting them to move?" Brigid asked.

"We'll deliver your message!" Iliona interjected.

"We can go anywhere."

"And we're fast. When we want to be."

"I'm hoping that hiring this flamekin will help sweeten the deal when we try to get them to move," Rhys said to Brigid. He turned to the faeries. "And keep it down, would you? I'm still not sure how we're going to wake them, but squeaking in their ear won't exactly put them in the best of moods."

The air overhead sparkled with color, and the clique said as one, "Leave that to us." And with that, they flew straight at Kiel's face.

"No!" Rhys had time to shout before Endry flew into one of Kiel's ears, Veesa into the other, and Iliona perched upon the end of the snoring giant's nose. "Don't wake up *that*—"

"Wake up!" The faeries cried simultaneously. The giant's eyes flickered open for a moment, and Rhys steeled himself to run, since there was little even he could do against Brion or Kiel. Then the giant's eyes closed again, and the deafening snores resumed.

"One," Rhys finished, and exhaled. "Good thing that didn't work. Faeries, get down here, would you?"

"Hey, knob-nose!" Iliona shouted with surprising volume for such a tiny creature, ignoring Rhys entirely. "We said"—the faerie drove one foot into the giant's nose—"wake"—*kick*—"up!"

The giant's eyes blinked open again, and this time stayed more or less that way. With surprising speed, Kiel lifted one hand and swatted at the faerie, who only just dodged away in time to avoid becoming a smear on the end of the huge creature's warty proboscis. Kiel's eyes narrowed and crossed as they focused on the minute, buzzing thing in his field of vision, and he raised a hand to swat at Iliona again.

"Wait!" the other two faeries cried out. They bolted from the horrendous confines of Kiel's ears and flew to their sister's side. "We are the children of—"

This time, the giant did not try to swat the annoying gnats. Fortunately for the faeries, he chose to bat them away with the back of his hand. With a chorus of shrieks the faeries were carried aloft like arrows, disappearing into the morning sky. Rhys only watched their arc long enough to see they would probably land safely in the forest canopy, assuming they didn't regain flight control first.

"Kiel," he said quickly, "it's me. Daen Rhys of the—"

"Eyeblight," the giant said, pointing at Rhys with a finger the size of a bog-ox.

That was the last thing Rhys had expected to hear from the giant, and it took him momentarily aback. Had the giant seen through his glamer as easily as Colfenor?

Ashling took advantage of the pause to step forward. "Kiel," she said, "we must awaken your brother. I am a messenger. Rhys is hiring me to deliver your message. My name is Ashling of the flamekin."

"His brother is awake now," rumbled Brion. With creaks and pops that sounded like falling timber, the giant pushed himself up like reclining nobility and gazed sharply at Rhys over the dying fire. "He's not happy about it." Squinting—giants were famously far-sighted, and had trouble focusing on things that were close—he finally got a good look at Rhys. His expression didn't change much upon recognizing the elf, but the side of Brion's mouth did curl into a slight smirk.

It was a start.

"You have been taking the message to Rosheen?" the giant asked. "We are awaiting tales, and wonder why you are here."

"About that," the elf said. "The kithkin—well, they're expecting a full—that is, there's going to be—"

"Messages, messages," Maralen said. "Doesn't anyone just talk anymore?"

"What?" Rhys asked.

"Nothing," the strange elf said with a smile. "Perhaps I can handle this."

"Who," Brion inquired of the Mornsong female, "are you?"

"I am Maralen. I am a traveler from a distant land." Brion pushed himself out of the crouch and rose to his full height to get a better look at the elf. Despite the giant's proximity, and the fact that the face she was addressing was now some thirty feet overhead, she maintained her composure.

"Rhys is trying to help you. There will be more tales," Maralen said, glancing at Brigid for confirmation. The kithkin gave a slight, but encouraging nod. "There will be tales for many days. And songs. This is the famous Hero of Kinsbaile here, you know. There will be ballads and tales sung of this day." There was another nod from the kithkin, and a shrug. "So you will be able to hear many of them."

"Kiel is collecting tales," Brion said. "Kiel needs tales."

"But this first day is special. All the kithkin will be there, and many others. You are magnificent, Brion, so strong and powerful and noble, but you and your brother are so—well—giant. It just wouldn't be safe. Not for the kithkin, because with so many of them running around, there's a good chance one would get stepped on. And not safe for you, Brion, or your brother. Kithkin can carry infections—"

"Hey!" Brigid objected, forcing the Mornsong elf onto another tack.

"Kithkin can carry sharp things that can cause injuries to giants, injuries you might not notice right away. And if you were to stumble and fall against one of their buildings—why, think of the splinters you'd have to endure." As she spoke, Maralen's voice became smoother, richer, like a balladeer heading into the third verse of a four-verse tune. "It's better in the wilds. That way." She pointed as she took a few steps toward Brion, and then she kept going past him to address Kiel, who still sat where he'd been sleeping.

"Tales," Maralen said, and pressed her hand against the giant's boulderlike big toe. "Soon, Kiel."

Rhys could not believe the stranger was negotiating with the giants on the basis of public safety and personal injury. Giants were more or less the antithesis of public safety, which was why they generally stayed away from anything the "small folk" called public. His plan had been to use the flamekin's reputation as a reliable messenger to sweeten the request that the giants clear out of the area, but Maralen had barely allowed Ashling a chance to speak. He caught the flamekin's glowing orange eyes, and she simply raised her hands, palms up, and shrugged. Her stony expression was difficult to read, but her gesture indicated she thought Maralen's tactics were working.

"Tiny elf," Kiel said. He pulled himself to his feet, and Rhys noticed for the first time just how much taller he was than his brother—easily forty feet to Brion's thirty. "Strange elf. Or are you?"

"I assure you I am," Maralen said, "strange to these parts, anyway."

Rhys wondered if Brion, too, would lose his loquacity in a decade or two. The truly old giants never seemed to speak at all, or if they did, they never bothered to do so with beings that—to them—were less than insects were to elves. When you reached your second or third century, you could become a bit solitary and set in your ways. The elder giants ended up living hermit-like existences in the crags. Elder giants slept for decades at a time and lived on a different scale than the elves and kithkin. The elders left things like travel, tale collection, and the like to the young, and despite their size, Brion and Kiel were youths by giant standards.

That's when Maralen's simple plan suddenly made sense to him. Brion and Kiel, though separated by decades, were both adolescents. Maralen, strange though she was to Rhys's eyes, was friendly, pretty, and female. He tried to picture her through the eyes of a giant, and then tried to think of anything else.

Brion was clearly thinking along the same lines. "Pretty," he said, and without ceremony crouched again and scooped the stranger up with one hand.

"Hey!" Rhys and Maralen said almost simultaneously, though Rhys was the only one to add, "Put her down!" Maralen, for her part, didn't make another sound, though Rhys wasn't sure if this was because she didn't want to, or because she wasn't able to. Giants were not known for their delicacy when it came to handling, well, anything.

Brigid already had an arrow nocked and ready to fire, while Ashling had dropped into a defensive crouch, her iron hat pushed back off her crown and one hand burning brightly, collecting energy for the most powerful fireball she could muster in such a short time. Rhys, armed only with a dagger, a kithkin short bow, and a dozen stubby kithkin arrows in a quiver so small he wore it on his hip, placed his hand on the dagger hilt but did not draw it. The giant had to have tendons like any other creature, and if he could hack his way through that leathery ankle, he might be able to free Maralen, if she still lived.

"Damned giants," he heard Brigid say. "Damned unpredictable giants."

The elf raised his dagger overhead and caught the eyes of his companions. He set his feet and prepared to charge into what was by definition a hopeless fight.

Then the entire forest, giants and all, disappeared in an ear-splitting cry and an explosion of blinding magical sparks that filled the air.

"Haiiiiikeeebaaaa!" The faerie clique yelled as one. As Rhys's vision returned, he could just make out the tiny, flitting creatures, moving together like a living comet. They slammed into Brion's right eye, knocking the giant off balance, and he stumbled against the dead trunk of an ancient oak. The rotten column crumbled, showering the ground with a rain of spongy wood chips and several thousand surprised insects. Before the giant could regain his balance, the faeries split up, one continuing to poke and peck at Brion's face while the other two—it was impossible for Rhys to tell which faerie was which—moved over to Kiel, who for his part was still staring at Maralen.

And for her part, the stranger finally regained her voice.

"Stop!"

Maralen's shouted command froze even the faeries in mid-flight. Rhys, Ashling, and Brigid remained ready to attack, but the elf kept his blade in the air. Only Brion continued to move until he steadied himself against his brother's shoulder.

"Why?" one of the faerie asked.

"They started it," another added.

"Think they can shove people around, just because they're so big."

"I'm going to pop this one's eye out!"

"No," Maralen said, "in fact, I think that's the worst idea I've heard all day."

If nothing else, Rhys thought, this settled the question of whether the Mornsong stranger was still alive.

"Please, everyone," Maralen continued, bringing up the one hand she'd been able to free while clutched in Brion's fist—the other was still pinned against her side, "there's no need for this fighting."

Brigid and Ashling shot Rhys a look, waiting for the command to attack. He slowly shook his head in response. Brigid scowled, but lowered her bow. The flamekin lowered her hand, though she kept it wreathed in flames, and tipped her wide-brimmed iron hat back atop her head. Finally, Rhys lowered his dagger, certain the move could not be misinterpreted.

"Maralen," he said, "are you all right?"

"I'm fine," the Mornsong said without taking her eyes off the somewhat confused giant. "Brion, after the kithkin have their opening ceremonies, you and I, and your brother are going to listen to some tales. That's what the two of you do, isn't it? Collect tales? Tales are what you want Rhys to deliver to your sister?"

"You are collecting tales?" Brion said, mildly awestruck. "You are a tiny giant, you think?"

"I'm a lost elf, that's all, my friend, but I do love tales," Maralen said, and whether this was true or not, she said it with such conviction even Rhys believed it. "But Brion—and Kiel, you too—listen to me. We'll collect tales soon. Just not today. You and Kiel can move your camp into the forest, just for a day or two. We'll find a place for you, don't you worry. We'll find the perfect place. You don't want to deal with all those babbling crowds of kithkin." Brigid harrumphed, but left it at that.

"And you can rest assured," Maralen continued, "Rosheen will get the tales you're sending to her. We may even be able to add a few more to the message before the flamekin departs. Agreed, Brion? Agreed, Kiel?"

Brion peered at the small thing in his hand, holding the tall, pale elf away from his face to better focus on her. But it was Kiel, the older of the two, who spoke first.

"Agreed," he said.

The indignant faerie trio responded all at once.

"Oh, this is just—"

"*Hit* me! That son of a bog-ox hit me! *Me!*"

"Can't I just puncture his eye a little bit?"

Fortunately, no one paid attention to them. Unfortunately, this was because everyone was paying attention to the shouted command coming from the north, just beyond the tree line. Rhys recognized the voice, and it made his blood run cold. He had almost forgotten his status—outcast, eyeblight, pariah. The voice brought all that back in a rush.

"Strike!" bellowed Daen Gryffid of the reassembled Hemlock pack.

CHAPTER 12

All at once the sky was filled with deadly, poison-tipped arrows, every one of them on a trajectory that would end with Rhys, his companions, or one of the giants. Ashling, one hand still engulfed in flame, did the only thing she could do—rather than release the elemental fire as a weapon directed at the giants, she whirled in place and sent as much energy as she dared into a wide sheet of burning plasma that ignited the very air over the heads of her companions—or rather, most of her companions.

The plasma sheet incinerated the arrows headed toward the elf, the faeries, the kithkin, and Ashling herself, but there was nothing she could do about the projectiles headed for the giants. Out of the corner of her eye, she saw Brion shield Maralen with one hand just before the barrage struck home. Dozens of arrows tipped with potent moonglove poison punctured their thick hides. Within seconds the poison's effect was visible—and audible. Brion roared in pain as the venom coursed into his veins, and soon Kiel joined in the chorus of deafening agony. Brion was the first to stumble, when he tried to take a step toward the source of the arrows and caught his foot on the remains of the rotten tree trunk. Rhys, Ashling, and Brigid barely escaped being crushed by several hundred tons of toppling giant. Rhys shouted a warning and then scooped up the archer and charged out of the impact zone. Ashling was already moving. She didn't have the strength for another display like the sheet of plasma, and wouldn't have for hours. They had to be out of the target area before the next volley of arrows came flying from the woods.

Brion's face-first collision with the ground shook the earth and knocked the flamekin off her feet. She flew sprawling to the ground just she as heard the chorus of whooshing sounds marking the imminent arrival of another volley.

She may not have had the energy to shield them all, but Ashling could at least protect herself and survive to help the others. As projectiles landed all around her, she concentrated on the living flame that wreathed her body, willing it to burn with the heat of a thousand suns, drawing on reserves she'd never had to tap before. A rush of heat and light enveloped her, and she boldly stood to face the attack. The blazing flamekin strode purposefully toward the fallen giant's hand, resting slightly open, and every arrow that came within two feet of Ashling was reduced to ash. Maralen was not moving and appeared unconscious or even dead, but the shelter of Brion's curled fingers shielded her from the second rain of death.

The giant definitely *was* unconscious, and from what Ashling had heard of moonglove he would be lucky to ever wake up.

Another thunderous crash shook the ground, but this time Ashling managed to keep her feet. She could not see Rhys or the kithkin, so she could not tell what effect Kiel's collapse had wrought on them, but, as the giant fell first to his knees, and then onto his side with an anguished groan, Maralen was shaken loose from Brion's palm and slid onto the ground like a rag doll.

You could run, Ashling told herself. Save yourself. They can't touch you. The path does not have to end here. But was this a path she really wanted to walk? A selfish path?

No, she decided. And then, to bolster her convictions, the

flamekin said aloud, "It's not the end, but I think it's going to be a substantial fork in the road."

Keeping her flame has hot as she could, she finally reached Maralen, and just in time. The third volley was slightly more ragged than the second, which told Ashling the elves were beginning to split off and close in, but she was able to place herself between the Mornsong traveler and the attackers to incinerate the third volley, though Maralen would probably require some burn ointment when she woke up. The third round of arrows would most likely be the last, and soon the hunters would close in for the kill. Ashling had spent much of her time on the path avoiding encounters with elves—her people and theirs had never been allies, and these days they were at best mildly antagonistic neighbors who stayed out of each other's business. But the flamekin had been witness to elf attacks before. When a pilgrim wandered Lorwyn long enough it was bound to happen, and more than once. The new daen, whoever he was, seemed to be sticking with traditional tactics.

Ashling grimaced as the third volley of arrows petered out. Rhys and the kithkin could be dead, the faeries could take care of themselves, and there was nothing she could do for the giants. Perhaps the brothers' size would save them, but it also meant there was no way a flamekin and the unconscious stranger could do anything for them. With a thought, she pulled the heat of the living flames back within her stony flesh and cooled herself enough to sling Maralen over one shoulder without causing the stranger any additional injury.

Before she turned to flee, Ashling spared a glance over one shoulder at the forces in pursuit. The fact she could see them at all was a sign the attackers were fairly certain they'd already won. Like most pack predators, elves showed their true numbers only when the kill was assured. A daen adorned with gleaming silver pauldrons of high rank stood at the edge of the tree line, a silver sword flashing in the first rays of dawn held high over his noble head.

"Vinebred! *March!*" the elf ordered, dropping his sword and pointing the tip directly at Ashling. On his command, what had appeared to be wild undergrowth moved. Ashling had seen elves in combat before, but her experience with the vinebred amounted to a few distant battlefields sighted from the hilltops of Taenskarper, where the elves employed them against the savage boggart tribes of that forsaken place. She'd heard about them, of course. The elves considered them living works of functional art. They were slaves, they were protectors, and above all they served as shock troops. But beautiful as they were, at their heart they were prisoners in a living hell Ashling could not even imagine. The threat that those who opposed the elves risked becoming vinebred was one of the reasons—perhaps the main reason—that the elves ruled most of Lorwyn.

"Hey, flame-face," a lilting voice said, and Ashling saw sparkling lights. She looked up to see one of the faeries hovering overhead—Iliona, she guessed, but it was hard to say without the other two present to compare. The faerie's tiny face wore a mask of extreme irritation. "Do you suppose bloodvines can get their roots into one of your kind? I can see from here you've got plenty of blood."

"Not mine," Ashling said. "It's Brion's."

"Tragic, I'm sure," the faerie replied. "Now follow me if you want to live. And I want you to know that the *only* reason I'm doing this is because Rhys asked me too."

"I don't doubt it for a second," Ashling said, shifting her burden slightly for the run ahead of her. The elves' hand-grown shock troops did not move quickly, but they would pick up speed over the open meadowland and wouldn't lose much of it in the scattered trees that lined the road. Still, with any luck, Ashling could make it into the deep forests she had seen on the walk into Kinsbaile. Even if they were mostly plants themselves, the lumbering vinebred wouldn't be as agile—she hoped—as she could be. And if the worst came to the worst, Ashling still wasn't completely powerless. Surely she had more reserves somewhere.

"Was there something about 'come with me' that was unclear?"

Ashling resisted the urge to swat at the faerie. "Lead the way."

Now the trick was to get where the vinebred couldn't reach them, and the elves wouldn't find it much easier.

"The forest," Ashling called after Iliona as the faerie led her into the sparse stands of alder. "We've got to get into the deep forest."

"No, we've got to get to Rhys," the faerie said. "He and the kithkin are waiting at the river."

"Of course," Ashling said. "I stand corrected."

"I wouldn't be standing around at all, corrected or otherwise," the faerie called back. "Good way to get yourself dead."

* * * * *

Cenn Teeg paused a moment in his pacing to take another long look down the road that—just around the bend and a few miles through the woods—ended at the Kinsbaile Dock. The finest kithkin landscapers had carefully manicured the road. Its cobblestone surface was swept and polished up to the point where it became packed earth, and the packed earth was swept smooth for half a mile beyond the town gate. Persistent potholes had been filled in, and someone had planted two new rows of dazzling, deep green topiaries that Teeg though were a fitting and noble honor guard for the town's most distinguished visitor: the treefolk Colfenor. Behind him, the entire town was abuzz with anticipation for the day's tales. The entire population of Kinsbaile had turned out in their finest attire, of course, and with the many visitors from the surrounding villages, a huge crowd had assembled by dawn. Most milled about in the town square, speaking with Colfenor, who amiably held conversations with several people at once. Others bought sweetmeats and cra-bapple pies, tried their luck with the games of chance that always seemed to spring up at any large kithkin gathering, or joined in one of the many rousing renditions of "Hero of Kinsbaile" that always seemed to spontaneously arise whenever kithkin came together in this town.

Overhead, hundreds of faeries filled the air, their wings lend-ing an ever-present hum to the bustle of activity. The faeries didn't buy sweetmeats or attempt to hurl pinecones at stacks of ale bottles for money, but they did light up the dawn sky with hundreds of twinkling lights that lent the entire town the appear-ance of an enchanted village from the oldest tales—stories with origins in Lorwyn's deep, distant past.

So much was going right. But there was trouble in the air. Loud trouble.

The trouble had driven Teeg to pace back and forth in front of the open town gate for the last fifteen minutes. He nodded and smiled to the occasional passerby, but most gave him a wide berth, and he cursed himself for being unable to mask his con-cern that this day could be in jeopardy.

To his dismay, those hundreds of kithkin and hundreds of faeries gathered to hear the tales that Colfenor would spin were also engaged in agitated, nervous conversation about the terrible sounds they had heard for the last half hour. Teeg had dispatched a few scouts to report on what sounded like a giant trying to uproot the entire forest, but they had not returned. Whatever the giants were doing, they didn't seem to be getting any closer, and sometimes giants just made noise—it was a fact of life. But there was too much at stake, too much pre-festival organization that stood to collapse in ruins, and Teeg forced himself to consider sending out the city's armed militia to restore order in the forest.

Teeg's nerves were shot. So it was understandable, he would tell himself later, for him to scream like a kithling girl when a nearby piece of shrubbery he'd assumed was a new decorative addition pulled its roots from the ground and stepped into the street.

After that initial outburst, Teeg was able to keep his mouth shut, and wished he could do the same with his eyes. Especially when another ten . . . no, twenty . . . By the Bubbling Bog, every *one* of the new topiaries was moving. They were glorious, and they were frightening.

The vinebred stepped slowly but precisely into a formation, three abreast, that filled the street and blocked any hope of making out what was happening with those distant giants. Teeg had not seen vinebred in action, but there was no mistaking what the new arrivals were. They had the same rough shapes as the creatures they once had been. Now that they were in motion, it was easier to spot the host body within the tendrils, moss, and flexible wooden musculature. The three in front were once elves—eyeblights, no doubt. The one on the left displayed two dark patches of bare bone, long since stained green with moss, on its forehead where its horns ought to have been; The other two had similar injuries. All three were covered with a mass of green vines. Teeg blamed the vine's deep emerald coloration for the fact that he'd failed to notice a small army of deadly, remorseless, beautiful killing machines taking up position on the main road into his town. He intended to make that fact quite clear at the next meeting of the town elders, should such a meeting take place, and should the town still have any elders at the end of this day. "When the vinebred appeared, living things died, or they became vinebred," he would say. "Yes, good citizens, that is true. And no one—*no one*—else noticed that they were on our doorstep." Let them talk their way out of that.

Other than that clever dodge of responsibility, Cenn Teeg had no idea what to do. Where were the elves? There would have to be elves somewhere controlling these things. Surely they couldn't have wandered into town on their own. He wondered at the wisdom of allowing the outlaw Rhys to visit Colfenor here. Perhaps it had been a mistake to invite the red yew at all.

"Cenn!" said the young kithkin clerk who chose that moment to appear, sparing him the need to find a course of action. Gaevin clutched a scroll in one hand. "This floor plan is completely unworkable, Cenn. There must have been a miscalculation early on. It appears someone mistakenly annotated this sketch with inches instead of—vinebred! Cenn, they're—"

"Silence," Teeg said, grateful for the opportunity to show his boundless courage by denigrating that of his inferior. "Yes, of course they're vinebred, Mr. Gaevin. Just noticed, did you?" He meant the words to sound friendly and light, but they came out filled with recrimination.

"Now, now, Cenn Teeg, the creature cannot have been expected to notice them any more than you did," came a commanding voice from somewhere just off the road ahead and to Teeg's right . . . no, above the road. Was that a shadow in the boughs of the Kinswood copse? Yes, it clearly was, and as Teeg stared at the shadow it took on the shape of a tall, noble elf in the golden attire of a taercenn—as Teeg understood it, the highest rank a hunter could hope to achieve without becoming Perfect.

Worse, the cenn recognized this particular taercenn.

"Nath," Teeg said aloud.

"Nath?" the confused and terrified clerk stammered. Even the green bureaucrat knew the name. "What does he want?"

The next words the Gilt Leaf taercenn spoke were not directed at the cenn. "Chevor," Nath said in an almost conversational tone that still somehow carried all the authority a voice could contain, "establish your perimeter."

"Yes, taer," came another voice, a younger female voice, also from the trees. But the voice's owner didn't stay there for long. With the hum of dozens of leather gloves sliding along dozens of hangman vines, the vanguard of the Gilt Leaf pack entered Kinsbaile. They seemed to drop from every direction, upsetting small flocks of faeries forced to dodge their descent. Meanwhile, at a gesture from Nath, the vinebred marched into position.

"Kithkin of Kinsbaile," Nath said as he strolled through the crowd flanked by a pair of honor guards, the kithkin obediently parting to make room. "For those of you who were unaware, I am Taercenn Nath, supreme huntmaster of the Gilt Leaf nation. You kithkin are here at our discretion, but we mean you no harm. You will be allowed to go about your business, so long as it does not interfere with mine. You may listen to your tales, and share your stories, but know this: Your town has the honor of being the headquarters from which I shall strike down the enemies of the Blessed Nation."

Teeg felt his feet moving to intercept the taercenn before he even realized he was moving. Well, in for a farthing . . . .

"Honored Taercenn," the cenn said, and he genuflected before the elf. "You are welcome, as always. The Blessed cast their blessings upon their kithkin brothers and sisters. This time of tales is for all to share."

"Yes," Nath said without bothering to look at Teeg, "I'm sure it is." The red yew that filled most of the greensward in the town square occupied the taercenn's attention. Colfenor had said nothing since the elves and their vinebred servants had appeared, but then the treefolk supposedly had a very different kind of relationship with the elves than the kithkin did. Teeg could not even be certain that Nath wasn't here at Colfenor's request. Though the yew had shared many secrets with the cenn of late, he could certainly be keeping more within his noble boughs.

Colfenor's first words with the taercenn did little to assuage Teeg's suspicions, but neither did they confirm any complicity on the treefolk's part.

"Nath," the treefolk said, "you have come to hear the tales." It was not a question.

"Among other things, Sage Colfenor," the taercenn replied. "Among other things."

* * * * *

"What other things do you have?" Sygg asked. "Because if this is all you have to offer, you're wasting my time. I lost an apprentice recently, and one doesn't lure new apprentices when one is unsuccessful."

"But that's everything I earned from the cenn," Ashling protested. "We don't have any more thread." She looked sideways at Rhys—carrying the still-unconscious Maralen over one shoulder—and Brigid. "Do we?"

The elf shrugged and shook his head. The kithkin was engaged in an intensive study of the toe of her boot.

"Captain, you just ferried me across the river. And you still owe me two passages from that journey. I sympathize with your loss, as unexpected as it was tragic," Ashling said, trying to keep the exasperation out of her voice. The elves would be on them at any minute; the giants could not keep them occupied forever. She was surprised, in fact, that it was taking so long—the giants had hit the ground before they'd made their hasty retreat to the river. Whatever they were doing to those giants, she didn't want to think about it. She was already wracked with guilt over leaving them behind, and she'd barely known them. Brion and Kiel had fallen without a fight, and that rankled Ashling.

"You're not telling me anything I don't know, pilgrim," the merrow said groggily. He had been sleeping when they'd arrived at the dock, floating in slumber and tethered to the dock by a slender vine-rope. It was the usual way for merrow ferrymen to rest, for it meant they never had to be away from the docks that provided their livelihood. True, some slept in the crannogs, but Sygg was clearly a traditionalist. "And I never said when you could collect."

"This coil of gold is a hundred times what I paid you for that ride!" Ashling protested. "Now, I can promise you more, but I can't tell you when you'll get it or how much you'll get. But we have got to get out of here. You hear those footsteps? Those are vinebred."

"Yeah, fish face," Endry said, "*big* vinebred."

"They're going to turn you into walking kelp," Veesa added.

"You know, Mr. Big-Elf," Iliona said to Rhys, "we could always carry you all. For a few minutes at least."

Before Rhys could reply, Ashling said, "Nobody is carrying anyone. Captain, forgive them, they're—"

"They're faeries," Sygg said. "That's beside the point. You woke me from my nap. I have no first mate, and you of all people should know that. And you want me to ferry you to where? The Bosk? And all the while under fire from bog knows what, into waters I haven't navigated in thirty years, and you want me to bring an suspicious-looking elf—no offense, taer—and a shifty kithkin, and these buzzing, nattering faeries, to say nothing of that unconscious lady, there. Flamekin, you're lucky I haven't doused you for making me such an insulting offer."

Ashling cast about in frustration, looking for something—anything—she could offer the merrow captain, when her eyes fell upon a flash of gold at Rhys's belt. Without a word, she marched to his side and pulled free the coil of thread meant for the giant brothers. The flamekin ran a thumb over the frayed end of the coil. "I can double the offer," she said.

"Flamekin, you shouldn't—"

"If the giants live, elf, I'll pay them back out of my own pocket," Ashling said. "Now Captain Sygg, is this going to get you to see reason, or—"

"Strike!"

For the fourth time that day, Ashling heard the telltale sound of hundreds of poisoned arrows flying her way. Their time was up. She glanced up and saw a cloud of tiny black lines arcing upward against the pink dawn sky. In another second they would begin their descent.

She glanced at the road, where that other hunter—Rhys had called him Gryffid, and he was clearly the daen of this pack—stood flanked by lieutenants with drawn silver blades. There were no vinebred in sight as of yet. This new daen had realized at last that the creature's plodding steps would only give the pack away. He'd approached in stealth, and had probably been waiting to open fire until all of his hunters were in position. It was a common elf tactic: the sudden, precise, and decisive ambush.

Sygg reacted with alarming speed for someone who had been in a deep state of unconsciousness only minutes ago. "You've got a deal!" He raised his arms and with supreme effort summoned a simple concave disk of shapewater, not bothering to add the usual flourishes—this ferry was functional, and that was it. Without breaking his focus, the ferryman shouted, "Get aboard, everyone! All aboard, now!"

The small party made it onto the shapewater ferry just as a torrent of deadly silver rained down uselessly upon the dock, but the rest of Gryffid's hunters were already charging, blades in hand. Ashling felt the chill soaking into her boots, and willed flame into her skin to keep her dry. It would work for a while, but once they were away she'd need to figure out something better.

"You want to take the long way around, or the short way, flamekin?" the captain barked.

"What?" Ashling said. "But I don't know anything about—"

"Short way it is!" Sygg called, bobbing slightly in the water to avoid an arrow that slipped silently into the current. "Make sure everyone's secure. I don't have time to worry about people falling off!"

"Yes," Ashling said. "Er, aye."

As the merrow dropped back into the water, his long, powerful tail kicked furiously. Sygg thrust his splayed, webbed hands into the air. He called out a few bubbling, unpronounceable words of an ancient merrow tongue, and moments later a soft blue glow formed around the shapewater saucer. The glow spread, became cohesive, like a sheet of blue water, until it formed a thin bubble of energy.

With a jolt that almost knocked Ashling onto her flaming charcoal posterior, Captain Sygg set off, he and his passengers safe—Ashling hoped—within the bubble.

CHAPTER 13

As Sygg launched his charges downriver, Rhys tumbled to the smooth, glassy surface of the shapewater ferry and became entangled in Maralen's arms and legs before the two of them—one awake, the other still blissfully out of it—came to rest against the lip of the concave saucer. He checked the Mornsong's pulse, and it was steady. She had not been struck with any arrows. She simply refused to regain consciousness.

Brigid, the only one of them to keep her footing when the cruise had begun with a jolt, sidled over to him and offered the elf a hand up. "Hasn't she been out a long time?" the kithkin asked.

"Maybe," Rhys said, allowing the stocky archer to pull him to his feet. He immediately had to grasp the cool, spongy lip of the ferry as they entered a patch of tiny whitecaps kicked up by the winds coming down off the Tanfell Plateau. "I don't—ow—know how long she can be out safely. She's the first Mornsong I've had much to do with. This might be a healing trance among her people."

To his surprise, Ashling was standing. The reason became obvious—if she sat down like they did, she'd be that much closer to the water. It must have taken tremendous courage for her to set foot upon the glasslike ferry. He shot her a wave, and she glanced over one flaming shoulder as she dropped into a crouch. "Hold on!" she called.

"Has it occurred to you," Brigid continued, "your Mornsong here might be injured on the inside? She was in a giant's fist when the fist hit the ground. Could be bleeding out on the inside. Would explain her pallor."

"She was already pale. But I think you might be right," Rhys agreed. The elf stood and set his feet apart a few more inches to stabilize himself as he peered at Maralen's unmoving face. It was the color of the merrow-spun porcelain. "Bog it," he said as their shapewater ride hit a rough patch. Rhys dropped into a crouch like the one Ashling had assumed and still held, doing her best to avoid any contact with moisture. The tips of Rhys's fingers could still detect the pulse of blood through Maralen's veins, but it was definitely running at a slower pace than just a few moments earlier.

"She's an elf," Brigid said confidently. "What's so strange about her? No offense, but one elf looks a lot like any other to me."

"Besides the ears?" Rhys asked. "Or the horns, or the fact she's a half-head taller than even me?"

"She dresses differently than you," the kithkin said. "Classier. That counts for something among elves, doesn't it?"

"Do not mock me, 'Hero of Kinsbaile,' " Rhys said. "And that is beside the point."

"No offense intended." The kithkin eyed the unconscious woman clinically. "Ask me, she looks like mountain stock. Thick and hearty."

"Really thick," Iliona piped up.

"If by 'thick' you mean 'fat,' " Veesa agreed.

"This isn't getting us anywhere," Rhys retorted.

"What's going on back there?" Ashling called, all of her attention and concentration required to keep her on two feet. "Is everyone all right?"

"Is she dying?" asked Iliona hopefully. The clique had long since given up trying to find a way through the blue bubble that enclosed them. Veesa and Endry joined her, and all three crowded around Maralen's pale face.

"Sure looks like she's dying," Veesa said.

"Well, I guess we won't learn any more about that mystery," Endry said. "Let's toss her over the side."

"Nobody is tossing anyone anywhere," Rhys leaned forward to wave the trio away as Ashling gingerly stepped forward.

"I'd like to try something," she said. "I might be able to help."

Rhys felt his brow furrow. "Might?"

"I'm not trained as a healer," Ashling said. "But I've got plenty of experience when it comes to seeking out the elementals. Maralen here was recently touched by one, and if the elk spirit left behind even a small trace of its power . . ." Her voice trailed off and she shrugged. "I might be able to learn what's wrong with her so we know what kind of healing magic to seek out."

"You're not fooling anyone, pilgrim," Brigid chided playfully. "You just want to pick her brain about the elk."

"That too," Ashling said. "But I think doing so will help us help her. With your permission, Rhys, I would like to try."

"Do it," Iliona chirped. "She's full of secrets, that one. Poking around in her brain can't help and it might hurt."

"You got it backwards, Iliona."

"No I didn't." The largest faerie smiled sharply.

Rhys sighed. "We have no other good options. Proceed, pilgrim, but tread lightly."

Ashling half stumbled and half walked to the rear of the shapewater disk, fighting the disorienting effect of the watery blue bubble enveloping them and ending her short attempt at lateral movement by colliding with Rhys. The elf clutched the lip of the saucer with one hand and wrapped the other around Ashling's arm. The flames on her bare coal-like skin engulfed his arm up to the elbow, but there was no heat.

"I'm all right," Ashling said, pulling her arm gently away from Rhys's grip and shifting onto one knee. She let out a soft hiss when her knee made contact with the wet surface of the ferry, but the pain appeared only momentary.

There was a second hiss as the flamekin dropped onto her other knee so she could remain upright while holding both of her hands over Maralen's torso. Rhys placed an arm around the unconscious woman's shoulders to keep her from rocking around as the shapewater ferry thumped and bounced. He was certain Sygg could have given them a smoother ride if he'd had time to prepare, but at the moment speed was much more important than comfort.

The flames around Ashling's hands changed color, slightly at first, but soon more intensely as the flamekin's eyes grew bright. The flames settled into a light, scintillating blue that spread from Ashling's palms to envelop Maralen's torso, just as it had engulfed the end of Rhys's arm. This flame flickered differently, however, almost as if it were burning down instead of up. At certain points—as Rhys had suspected, those points were along the ribs—the flames glowed more brightly than others.

A flash of a different sort caught his attention then—the blue of the merrow's magic, protective bubble reflected in Maralen's dark eyes as they blinked open. Her eyes immediately locked with his, and Rhys felt an exhilarating wave of relief.

The wave lasted long enough to crash against the sharp and unforgiving walls of reality. In a flash of blue and a sudden shower of icy raindrops, the shapewater energy bubble surrounding the ferry burst. Ashling winced and swore as thousands of droplets sizzled against her skin and the strange fire she manipulated, but neither flamekin nor blue flame was in danger of being extinguished.

* * * * *

The flamekin felt her body melt away from her mind as she plunged deep into Maralen's trancelike state. The strange elf had indeed been brushed by powerful, ancient magic, but it was not like any Ashling was familiar with—barely recognizable as the presence of the primal spirits, if indeed that's what it was. The great elk spirit had been somber, its presence a huge, pressing weight, but Maralen did not seem burdened by it. It was quite unlike the aura Ashling got from her own elemental, which was lighter, faster, and sharper.

Ashling's perceptions had descended—or ascended, depending on one's point of view—beyond the rigid structures of language, shapes, and structures. Instead, the pilgrim saw colors, energy, and light—little fractal pieces of living soul within the strange elf whose life rested in Ashling's hands.

She'd never seen a life-force like Maralen's. The elemental energies that glittered across her mindscape were strange, and stranger still was the manner in which they interacted with Maralen. The elf woman's strangely muted aura was brightest around her ribs, lungs, and heart. Perhaps Maralen was healing herself as she slept?

Frustrated, Ashling pressed harder, trying to catch a glimpse of the stranger's inner mind. She felt herself being pushed away as Maralen's mind asserted control. Rhys needn't have worried about treading lightly—Maralen's secrets were entirely safe from the pilgrim.

Then the strange elf's eyes snapped open. "Hello," the patient croaked as she regained consciousness and intruded on Ashling's thoughts. "I'm fine now. And you're making me uncomfortably warm."

"Shh," the flamekin replied. She rushed to gather as much from the elf woman's mind as she could before Maralen's waking thoughts grew clear enough to break their connection. "Conserve your strength and don't break my concentration."

Maralen's aura grew stronger and brighter as Ashling spoke. The elf woman's black eyes widened a bit, and she scowled in frustration but finally let her head loll back against the smooth shapewater.

"Rhys," the Mornsong said weakly. "Is he here?"

"Yes," Ashling said. "And that's your last question, please. You will be all right but only if you let me concentrate."

"Thank you, no," Maralen said. "I am feeling much better now." She sat up, the form-fitting sheath of fire around her torso moving with her. With a definite, hard blink of her eyes, Maralen severed her connection with Ashling.

"She's alive," Brigid said.

"Oh, pooh," said Iliona.

"It's not too late to chuck her overboard, is it?"

"Let's tie her to a rock and use her as an anchor."

Rhys turned toward the front of the shapewater craft and shouted, "Captain! We're all present and accounted for."

"Great news!" the merrow captain replied. "Because we just got to the shortcut."

Rhys shot a weary glance at Ashling, and saw the blue flame enveloping Maralen glowing brighter, brighter still, until it slowly subsided. The flamekin sighed in exhaustion, and the Mornsong elf pulled her feet under her and rose on unsteady legs.

Rhys heard a whoop of strange, terrified glee from Captain

Sygg. A moment later, he felt the shapewater saucer tip forward, slowly at first, but gradually the incline grew steeper and more problematic.

"What—" Rhys said again. Ashling's eyes, aimed directly forward, glowed orange—with fear or with fury the elf could not tell. But as the ferry continued to roll over the lip of the waterfall, it quickly became apparent that the feeling was fear.

Rhys could imagine little that would terrify a being of living flame more than a sudden drop over a waterfall, plummeting nose-first into a dank, dark, underground river, protected only by the sudden appearance of a shapewater bubble, riding along on a ferry made of that same shapewater and held in place solely by the willpower of an eccentric merrow.

CHAPTER 14

Captain Sygg's secret tributary of the Wanderwine was distractingly tranquil. The dark, wet air gave the cavern a dreamlike quality as the flamekin's flames cast flickering shadows upon the smooth, eroded cave walls and the other people aboard the merrow's shapewater ferry. In fact, the only light here issued from living sources: thin lines of glowing moss and patchy mats of luminescent fungus on the cavern walls; Ashling's living flame; and the faerie trio's own cascading ribbons of sparkling color.

Iliona, yet unnoticed, took stock. The tributary's currents were gentle, and there was even a breeze, cool and soothing despite its brackish, sour scent. The sound of the waves lapping against the semisolid craft's outer edges was like a lullaby to the party, whose ears had been too full lately with the sounds of strife and conflict.

Sygg was also a calming influence. His cheerful patter was familiar and reassuring, and he steered the shapewater craft with such confidence that it was easy to relax—easy to imagine that no one could ever disturb the surety of this placid journey. Kinsbaile was far away, along with all of the dangers and mysteries it contained. As the town fell farther and farther behind, it was easy for the others to imagine their troubles growing more distant right along with it.

Ashling asked Sygg why the merrow was sure this shortcut

made them safe from pursuit by the elves. His answer, delivered in the same cheerful tone he used to deliver a bawdy limerick, seemed to unsettle the flamekin: "Because the merrow call these the 'Dark Tributaries.' "

"Why do they call them that?" Ashling pressed.

"Because they're dark," Sygg replied. "And dark water can hide terrible things. Many of these caves are connected, and even a merrow can get lost. That fungus doesn't grow everywhere. Most merrow who enter the Tributaries without proper preparation are never seen again. And if they are, they're . . . different." He had flattened his fore-crest and lifted his shoulderfins in a merrow shrug. "I was lost down here once, and was lucky enough to find a way out before I was—before anything too horrid happened along. Later, I came back and worked out a few safe routes, ones with enough illumination to get a ferry through to the other side."

"Do these horrid things you mentioned stay away from the light?" Maralen asked.

"Oh, no," Sygg laughed. "But they're slow, and can be avoided if you see 'em coming." He flashed a toothy smile. "My shapewater doesn't run into things unless I tell it to."

Their doubt lingered, but as time passed and the lazy passage continued, Iliona felt the group's doubt shrink. The group was too tired to take on another challenge, even if it was the simple question of how Sygg did what he did.

The shapewater craft was large enough for everyone to have some privacy if they all faced outward—a small measure of time and space away from the others. Brigid, Rhys, and Ashling each took this opportunity in different ways. As the hours ticked by everyone on board managed to perform certain small yet significant actions that none of the others could see or would ever understand. Or so they thought, Iliona giggled to herself.

Brigid busied herself with inspecting her equipment, checking each arrow tip for keenness and each shaft for balance. Once that was complete, she set about organizing them so the sharpest and straightest were within easiest reach. While Ashling and Rhys were on the opposite side of the craft and Maralen was absorbed in the view of the glittering cavern, Brigid also performed several small ritual castings. All kithkin were adept at augury. Some simply forecasted tomorrow's wind and weather, but others practiced a grander, more sweeping kind of prognostication that involved the great spirit elementals themselves. Brigid's totems and fetishes were basic and unspectacular—perhaps she was trying to gauge the river's flow and speed? Maybe she was seeking guidance, or reassurance regarding the fate of Kinsbaile under Nath?

The archer had been dour—even prickly—since the Gilt Leaf elves had descended on her village. She muttered something about how she ought to have stayed to help her fellow kithkin, but then she loudly claimed helping Rhys fell under her original duty to the cenn, in furtherance of Teeg's lifelong awe and respect for Colfenor. She also allowed that helping Rhys escape might draw Nath and his pack away from Kinsbaile entirely, but of those few passengers who had a spare thought for the kithkin's reasoning, none of them fully believed her . . . not even Brigid herself.

Maralen was almost fully recovered from her injuries, but she was no more outgoing than the archer. The stranger claimed to be exhausted and overwhelmed. Her oddly shaped face went slack as her eyes fluttered closed. If she was telling the whole truth about her time spent lost in the forest, this was the first time she had not slept wild in quite some time.

But after her eyes had been closed long enough for everyone to stop paying attention, Maralen's fingers tapped out an almost-inaudible tattoo on the shapewater's smooth surface. It was no more than a nervous habit, perhaps absent-minded fidgeting, but there was something calculated and measured about her movements, especially for one who seemed to be fast asleep.

Rhys eventually sequestered himself and sat cross-legged in deep meditation for over an hour. The words that formed soundlessly on his lips were not recognizably Elvish, but he was a pupil of a treefolk sage, and who knew what languages he spoke to himself? Likewise, Ashling crouched with her eyes closed in silent contemplation. If not for the constant fluctuation in the color and intensity of her flames, one might have assumed that she was simply resting.

Iliona floated up near the cavern's ceiling. Veesa and Endry joined her, and the siblings spoke in gentle whispers.

"Time for a treasure hunt," Iliona said. The twins nodded, for once holding their tongues. "Veesa, you take the archer. Endry, you get the stranger. I'll see what the elf and the flamekin have to offer. If Sygg pokes his nose up, push him back under." She gestured down at the others on the craft. "They're all quiet now, lost in their own thoughts. It should be easy to find out what they're really thinking."

Veesa smiled and beat her wings, releasing a small shower of colorful dust. "Let's make a game of it."

"Last one to harvest a bit of dreamstuff is the loser."

"You're on!"

Iliona smiled. "Count me in. But to make it completely fair, let's put everyone to sleep at the same time."

The three nodded in unison, and then Iliona said, "Off you go, now." The twins quietly fluttered down to the water's edge and circled around to the rear of the shapewater craft, Veesa toward the archer and Iliona toward the stranger. There was nothing stealthier than a faerie looking to avoid notice, and soon each of the trio was close enough to weave their sleeping spells without alerting the others at all.

The slumber song emerged from Iliona's mind as a soft, echoing sound that was quickly picked up and enriched by her siblings. Like a swarm of liquid bees, magic swirled from the siblings, flowing and eddying between them before stretching out on each side of the moving shapewater craft, creeping toward its passengers. The smoky essence caught and reflected the dim bluish light from the cave walls, casting an azure sheen over the entire deck.

No audible voice could ever match the silent song's fragile beauty. To the ears and minds of all non-faeries, it was an irresistible push toward unconsciousness, much the same as a waking person's desperate urge to remain within their favorite dream rather than abandon it and see what that awful noise outside was. The world of dreams was so warm and safe and comforting—who could resist its call?

With the spell complete and actively affecting the party, Endry, Veesa, and Iliona hovered over their slumbering targets. One by one, the trio each drew gleaming knives that glinted silver-white in the strange light of the cavern. They alit on the sleeping others, on shoulders and breastbones, their wings keeping them all but weightless. The faeries held knives to the throats of their companions, turned their faces to each other, and nodded. A galvanic crackle sizzled through the air, and the siblings' minds connected through a skein of dreamstuff and faerie magic.

Iliona knew they'd have to harvest quickly now that the game was on. She could count on the twins to play quietly for a while, but Veesa and Endry would quickly grow bored. Iliona sighed under the awful burden of responsibility. It was not her fault she had been the first to awaken when the trio was born. Only a few seconds had passed before Veesa had emerged, but in those seconds Oona, the Great Mother, had spoken to Iliona.

"Welcome to the world," Oona's voice had intoned, nowhere and everywhere. "You don't have long. None of us do. Be sure to make the most of it. Your name is Iliona, little one. Stretch your wings now. I must greet your siblings and give them their names."

The hard distinctions between the siblings shattered once Endry woke, received his name, and rose into the sky. Three faerie bodies and three faerie minds slipped into perfect coordination, parts of a unified whole, and they drank deeply of the love and magic that Oona offered. In less than a day they were ready to leave the Great Mother and venture out into Lorwyn to do her will and enjoy life to its fullest.

As the sleeping spell thickened over the shapewater craft, Iliona felt her own conscious mind vanishing, trickling away like the melting snow in the crags. This void quickly filled to bursting with the combined perspective of her, her siblings, and the other passengers. It was a heady, fulsome rush of thoughts and sensations as broad and strong as the Wanderwine after a ten-day rain.

Brigid's sleep was like that of a big forest cat or a soldier on maneuvers: light, fragile, and easily disrupted. Veesa did herself proud, holding the dagger steady without breaking the skin as their magic wormed its way into the kithkin's mind. Brigid hadn't been casting for augury or divination earlier, she had been sending a message to . . . whom? Cenn Teeg? The treefolk? It would take more digging to find out.

In the meantime, Brigid's mind had a clear picture of what she had done. Brigid's body had hidden her work from the others. The archer had combined a rusty arrowhead, a scrap of paper, and a lock of yellow hair in a small wooden box. She had whispered a word and, after a jagged slash of light singed the bottom of the box, a tiny, glittering moth had fluttered up. It was gray-white and luminous, but its pale glow vanished against the soft light from the cave walls. Brigid had watched the moth flutter away from the ship, back up the cavern the way they'd come until it was no more than another glittering reflection from the walls and water.

Veesa would be hard to beat in this game, Iliona realized. Secrets were always the most highly prized bit of dreamstuff, and Brigid's actions were tantalizing in their simplicity. It was a minor spell, capable of delivering a minor message, but what was that message? To whom was it addressed? If Veesa teased that information from the archer, she'd flog her siblings with the victory for weeks.

Nettled by the strength of Veesa's find, Iliona focused harder on Rhys and Ashling. It would do no good to complain about having twice as many people to sift through—her siblings would simply see that as twice as many chances to glean something good. Iliona would have to work quickly and hope for the best.

Ashling's intensity about the elemental was not just due to her growing interest in Rhys. Lately she had been feeling the elemental's presence with increasing force, but always just ahead, always just out of sight and out of reach.

Even in Ashling's deepest thoughts she did not dare to imagine what shape it had, what powers it could confer upon her—but she longed to find out so strongly that it almost eclipsed every other thought in her head. She dreamed and daydreamed about it, seeing herself and her path clearly, but only the spot she was on and a few clear feet beyond. Something was just beyond her vision, known to her only as a shapeless, indistinct thing. Whatever it was, it beckoned to her via all her senses: sound, taste, smell, sight, and touch. It drew her to it, calling her on. But just as someone trapped in a glass maze can see the torch that marks the exit; Ashling knew where she wanted to go but not how to get there.

Rhys's dreamstuff was similarly focused, but nowhere near as interesting. His body had the tinge of glamer around it, but his mind was a tightly organized thing, a stack of leaves arranged so that each tip and each stem stood in perfect alignment with those above and below. Iliona knew she could flip through these leaves, rifle through them in the hopes of spotting something juicy, but she did not have the time . . . not if she wanted to do so without alerting Rhys.

Annoyed, Iliona withdrew from the pair and cast her hopes on Endry. She didn't want the youngest of the twins to win the game, either—but Endry was easily distracted and too in love with the new and the novel—he was half as likely to boast as Veesa, half as much and for half as long.

To Iliona's surprise, Endry had acquired none of Maralen's dreamstuff. Was the stranger's secret so fabulous that Endry had abandoned the game to keep it for himself? That would be most unfair of him. Iliona was about to tweak Endry for an answer when her youngest sibling's voice stabbed out, calm but cold and deadly serious.

"The game's over," Endry said, sounding more urgent and focused than Iliona could remember. It was an unfamiliar, even uncomfortable sensation to have the youngest and most frivolous of their clique sound so dire. "You both need to see this right away."

"What is it?" Veesa's voice whispered.

"Shh," Endry replied.

"You just don't want to lose."

"I said, 'shh.' Now follow me."

Iliona focused on Endry's point of view, made the sights and sounds and thoughts in her brother's head foremost in her own. Endry had indeed infiltrated Maralen's sleeping mind . . . but what she found there was impossible, unacceptable, and inconceivable to one of Oona's many children.

Maralen's thoughts were like a great dark sphere, featureless and impenetrable. It was not the absence of a dreamscape, but rather a very large and very well-protected fortress, a round, dense monolith that had so far proven impervious to faerie magic.

"What is that?" Veesa said, her voice soft with wonder.

"Told you," Endry said.

Iliona started to answer. "We must inform the—"

Even in dreams, you can't stop babbling. Maralen's voice was calm and even, but it was so loud it drowned out the slumber song and the faeries' shared thoughts. *I can't say I'm surprised or disappointed. Only amazed. How do you ever accomplish anything, the way you distract each other?*

So . . . you're spying on me, little bugs? Crawling around my thoughts like wasps on a windowpane? I was willing to tolerate your behavior in the world, but in my head is another matter entirely. This is rudeness I can't overlook.

"What are you going to do about it?" Endry said, his voice rising.

"Yeah," Veesa echoed. "You can't get mad at us for snooping. We're faeries."

Iliona fought back the reflexive urge to add her voice to the discussion. Gently, so as not to disturb the others, she unmade the larger part of the sleeping spell, calling the magic that powered it back into the bodies of her clique. She left enough of the song in place to make sure Rhys and the others remained unconscious, because she didn't want them demanding an explanation before she had time to think one up. But the largest share of the magic they had woven was hers to reshape any way she liked.

Iliona's vision shimmered, and she found herself hovering near the front of the shapewater saucer. She buzzed along its edge, homing in on Endry and the stranger, knowing that Veesa was doing the same.

Endry had backed away from Maralen, who stood wide-awake, her arms casually crossed over her chest. She was not smiling, but there was an amused quality to her posture. Her dark eyes were fixed on Endry as Iliona and Veesa joined their sibling.

"What are you?" Iliona said.

"You really don't know," Maralen said, amused, and cocked her head to one side. "I am what I said I am. A lost and lonely traveler."

"And I'm a giant's codpiece," Veesa replied.

Iliona hovered closer. "What magic are you using?" She lashed the air with her sharp, tubular tongue. "It tastes familiar."

"Magic?" Maralen dramatically placed the tips of her fingers over her mouth. "Surely no magic is greater than the dream spells of the fae."

"I think it's time for you to . . . what's the word, Veesa?"

"Drown?"

"Die?"

"Disembark," Iliona said. She spread her wings wide and buzzed them menacingly as she drifted toward the stranger. Her siblings instantly joined in on either side. "Hope you can swim."

"You were only ever dead weight to begin with."

"All ashore that's goin' ashore."

"You're going to kill me?" Maralen propped a clenched fist on her hip. "Throw me overboard before you've gotten any answers? I thought the fae were curious folk."

"Curious," Iliona said, "not stupid." Maralen only appeared to be standing still and smirking, but Iliona recognized real danger behind that careless demeanor. The stranger was waiting for them to cast a spell on her . . . eager for it, in fact.

Iliona decided to change tactics. Everyone assumed faeries

were insubstantial creatures, mischievous tricksters who trafficked in games and glamers . . . little more than colorful pests, really. Iliona smiled. Endry especially loved shattering that particular illusion, and in that respect, like so many others, the three siblings were of one mind.

"Get her!" Iliona shouted, and they rushed forward in perfect coordination. Iliona went toward Maralen's face while Veesa and Endry each curved around behind. They left dusty trails of color in their wake, trails that bent and swung into a triangle that completely surrounded Maralen. The boundary thickened and hardened into solid bars of smoke and light.

"Up," Iliona said. The faerie siblings rose higher into the air, towing the triangular shape up with them. At its center, Maralen's feet rose off the deck. The stranger was suspended and held fast within her magical enclosure. She did not seem troubled at all by her predicament, but rather continued to smile sharply with her head cocked to one side. Her dark eyes darted back and forth between the siblings, but otherwise Maralen was utterly still and placid.

"Well," she said, "you've got me. Though I daresay you don't know what you've got. Now what are you going to do?"

The twins giggled and chattered. "Oona! Bring her to Oona!"

The mention of the Great Mother's name drew a flicker of . . . concern? Recognition? Both? Emboldened, Iliona cried out, "Hold on tight! If we don't mess this up, we'll be the first in a hundred generations to show the Great Mother something she hasn't ever seen before."

"And then we'll be rewarded!"

"Oona doesn't know it yet, oddball, but she can't wait to meet you."

Maralen's head straightened, but her smile remained

unchanged. "I'm looking forward to seeing her, too."

Faerie wings sent a waft of dank air against the cavern walls as Iliona, Veesa, and Endry guided their strange cargo away from the shapewater craft, moving against the river's flow as they disappeared in the dim, flickering lights of the cavern.

* * * * *

Ashling awoke disoriented and confused. She grappled with foggy memories. When had she drifted off? *How* had she drifted off?

She heard angry voices from the rear of the shapewater, and she noticed that they were drifting, floating along no faster than the river's lazy current. She isolated Sygg's voice from the others and knew that something had gone wrong.

Ashling rose to her feet, privately swearing that she would never travel by water again—at least not with Sygg, who seemed to be a magnet for maritime disasters. She moved quickly toward the angry voices and found Rhys, Brigid, and Sygg firing hard looks and sharp words at each other.

"I couldn't do anything," Sygg was saying. The merrow's upper body bobbed on the water alongside the shapewater craft, and he thrashed his tail to keep his face level with the others'. "One minute I'm piloting along, no problem, with everyone onboard and accounted for. The next minute I turn around and see the faeries absconding with your companion. I tried to slow down and call after them, but I . . . couldn't. It was like watching a mural move."

"I've never seen a merrow lose control of his shapewater passangers," Rhys said. "What happened?"

"I'm not sure I take your meaning," Sygg said sullenly. "But I don't think I like it. Are you saying I'm at fault? That I let this happen? Or that I profited from it?"

"You tell me, Captain. If you blacked out somehow, why didn't we all drop into the river?"

"I don't know!" Sygg objected, clearly frustrated. "I'll tell you, I've had dealings with those three before. I don't know how many faerie clients you've had to deal with, out there in the woods, but let me tell you something, my son: Only a fool thinks he's in control when faeries are involved."

"Do we really need them?" Brigid said. "Any of them? I mean we're better off without them. Aren't we?"

Ashling did not like the uncomfortable silence that followed the archer's words. It was too much like agreement by default.

"We can't leave Maralen to them," the flamekin said. "They've made their opinions of her clear."

"So they don't like her," Brigid said. "So what? They're not likely to kill her. They'll probably just strand her somewhere. Leave her in the woods with no memory of the past few days, naked but for a pair of funny shoes. Wherever she turns up, Maralen's arrival will be the stuff of story festivals in that village for years."

"We should go after her," Ashling said. "We should turn around."

"Not a good idea." Sygg shook his head. "Maybe not even possible. It's certainly not desirable, not from where I'm swimming. We're almost at the end of the Dark Tributaries, miss. The grove isn't far from there."

Ashling turned to Rhys. "You want to go after her," she said. "I know you do. You can't rescue her from the woods, and then save her from the elves, only to let the faeries have her." She recalled what Rhys had told her about the great elk spirit, how it had seemed to stand in judgment on Rhys for what he'd done. "Your path is nobler than that."

Rhys bared his clenched teeth. "Don't lecture me," he said. He looked back down the cavern, then to Ashling, then to the river ahead. "How hard would it be to track them?"

"Considering they can fly? Impossible," Brigid said.

"Harder than I care to work, and for less reward," agreed Sygg.

Rhys nodded. "I agree. And I have been charged with a sacred duty. The sooner I discharge that duty, the sooner we can take up the search for the—for Maralen."

Ashling felt deflated, in part by Rhys's words and in part by the satisfied reactions they drew from Brigid and Sygg. Then the gloom inside the cavern grew thicker and more oppressive. Ashling thought for a moment that she was falling asleep once more, but as the world around her dissolved into darkness, she felt a yearning, a powerful hunger that called from every direction. She heard the distant thunder of massive hooves pounding the soil, smelled the scent of burning applewood and cedar, felt the world shift below her—not as shapewater shifts with the current, but more as a saddle shifts between rider and steed at full gallop.

Against the endless darkness, Ashling saw a flash of fiery mane and a glimmer of ghostly white. It was coming toward them, racing down the cavern from the direction they'd come. She stared, wide-eyed, though she was unable to hold any details about the presence for more than a fleeting second. She felt it sweep by the ferry and surge on, down the river toward the approaching end of the cavern.

"Sail on," Rhys said to Sygg. Neither he nor the others had reacted to the fiery apparition. "As fast as you can, Captain." He faced Ashling and said, "This is turning out to be an especially busy stretch of your path, pilgrim. If you accompany me to the grove now and help me see my mission through . . . I will retain your services again in the search for Maralen."

Ashling's mind cleared. The cavern returned to her sight, along with the shapewater disk, its captain, and all the remaining passengers. She almost wept with joy. She had her sign at last.

The flamekin's light flared and she hid her triumphant smile under the broad brim of her iron hat. "Very well," she said solemnly. "But I will hold you to that."

Sygg nodded and slipped below the surface of the water. Brigid slung her bow over her shoulder and followed Rhys to the front of the craft—both warriors were intent on spotting the cavern exit as soon as it appeared.

Ashling stood for a moment, trembling with excitement as the sound and the sensation of those thundering hooves still resonated inside her. Then she followed the others, and stood beside them. Each was alone and silent, thinking their private thoughts.

CHAPTER 15

Iliona and her siblings streaked through the night sky, one at each tip of the glowing prison with Maralen suspended at its center. They had crossed almost half of Lorwyn already by way of the faerie circles, and after passing through that particular piece of magic, the stranger was far less confident.

Iliona giggled slightly. Perhaps Maralen didn't expect to be taken so far so quickly, or perhaps she was worried now about how she was going to get back. Silly stranger, she thought, and she was instantly rewarded by her siblings' musical laughter. Endry and Veesa's voices tinkled like bells on the wind.

"You shouldn't be so quick to judge on appearances."

"We're tiny. But we're tenacious."

Iliona buzzed her wings faster, guiding the forward point of the triangle up toward the clouds. If anything, she and her siblings were growing stronger and livelier as they came closer to the Great Mother's hidden home.

Iliona felt (and felt her siblings feel) that Maralen had done herself a favor by settling down. And in doing so, she had done the siblings a disservice. All three were downright eager to employ some of the special magics they had if the stranger couldn't remember her place, spells to render a person silent or stupefied for the duration of the journey.

And that was only the beginning. Veesa was prepared to give

Maralen the head of an ass just to keep her from talking, and on top of that, Endry planned to visit her with an unquenchable thirst so that she'd be both silent and miserable. Iliona privately wished Maralen would tilt her head cockily as she had back on Sygg's shapewater ferry, just so she could watch her siblings compete for the right to blight her.

Without the Gilt Leaf hunter to protect her, however, the stranger's sass seemed to have drained away. By the time the strange procession crested the last big hill before their destination of Glen Elendra, Maralen was silent, possibly anxious.

"I'd even say docile," Endry said.

"But not awestruck." Veesa laughed sharply. "Not yet."

The clouds overhead broke, and bright sunlight shone down on Glen Elendra. It was not a large place, barely a hundred acres of gently curving hills covered in a thick blanket of trees, shrubs, and grasses. In the daylight the glen was rife with blooms and blossoms of every size and color and the air was filled with birdsongs.

At sunset, the glen's beauty was quieter, but perhaps more breathtaking. Jasmine flowers bloomed, catching and reflecting the light, as silver-white moths fluttered between the vines. Sparkleflies and will-o'-the-wisps flickered everywhere—from the forest floor all the way up to the canopy—wreathing the misty grounds and the towering greenery in a festival of light.

Iliona angled their course downward, guiding the procession toward the glen. Elendra's obvious exterior beauty was all any non-fae would ever see of the place. Countless layers of the most powerful glamers ever cast by the fae—and therefore the strongest magic in the world—concealed it. Thousands of faeries were hard at work all across Lorwyn, finding and harvesting dreamstuff that the Great Mother used however she pleased. And it pleased her to use a large portion of it to keep unwelcome visitors away.

Anyone who happened by or sought the glen out instantly forgot about it as soon as they drew near. Even an experienced ranger with a map, two cuffhounds, and a guide could not hope to enter the Great Mother's sacred home. His map would change to confound the trails, or vice versa; his dogs would bolt off in separate directions, baying after tantalizing hares; and his guide would lose his memory and all sense of direction—and if that was all he lost he was luckier than he deserved.

For Glen Elendra was not only concealed, it was also vigilantly protected. The sharpest and fastest faerie cliques patrolled its gentle rolling hills, and woe betide the traveler who met them. Eyes that beheld Oona's glen were destined to be plucked out, throats that sang its praises were invariably cut, and hearts that gladdened at its splendor were often found transfixed upon the branches of the tallest trees. No strangers were welcome in the glen. Particularly determined or stupid ones were not allowed the chance to return.

The glen was not a complete mystery, however, nor was it a forbidden subject among the professional storytellers and tavern-going blowhards of Lorwyn. There were folktales, of course, lore and legend about the secret faerie birthing place. But these were tales designed to discourage, ones that always ended with some variant of the stark homily which the Great Mother and her children had made sure to spread: You can't get into Oona's sacred glen—and you couldn't get out if you did.

Iliona plunged through the outermost glamer that protected the glen. As always, she felt a shiver of awe as she was received into the Great Mother's presence, a shiver she shared with Endry and Veesa before they, in turn, shared theirs. Maralen stirred, but she was still subdued and sluggish. If Iliona read the stranger's expression aright, Maralen was more roused by the notion of getting back on the ground than by the awesome presence inside Glen Elendra.

This was where the fae began—the source and origin of the entire tribe. No one knew how long the Great Mother had been here, but she was believed to have lived as long as Lorwyn itself. Individual faeries didn't live long, but Oona endured. Oona was the ever-blooming flower; the tiny, flighty faeries were the pollinating bees. They preened, played, and filled the world with a bit more life and light, and then they withered away in a few short years to be replaced by the next generation of fae.

Iliona shuddered, reveling in the majesty of her connection to the queen. She shared a mind with her siblings on a daily basis, and had since the day they had emerged. But she also shared with the Great Mother, her voice added to an uncountable multitude, joined together in a joyous cacophony of everyone speaking at once. In Lorwyn, there was no secret that was safe from the fae. They saw and heard everything. In turn, Oona the Great Mother saw and heard everything her children did, and what was more, she understood it all—every single confused, overlapping syllable. Only a mind like hers could process the deluge of facts, lies, half-truths, and rumors that the faeries brought her in a steady stream. She never tired of it, and was always hungering for more, in fact, so her children never hesitated to bring her the latest news and freshest gossip, which was only ever a faerie ring away.

Less than a hundred feet from the forest floor, Iliona noted with pride how the view inside the glamer was identical to that from without—with the all-important exception of the Great Mother herself. She was here, as she always was, looking as she always did: a constantly shifting woman floating in midair, her body woven of flowers in a rainbow of blue, purple, magenta, and white. Two long spires of clean white wood stood proudly behind her, giving the impression of a throne. Between these spires swayed a gigantic female shape, a woman from the waist up, but all glorious flora from there down. Oona's long, petal-shrouded arms trailed against the surrounding vegetation as she drifted back and forth like a willow in the wind. The whisper of the wind through her flowery form was as soft and as soothing as a mother cat's purr.

Yet Maralen is not soothed, Iliona thought. She fluttered near the ground, twenty paces from the outer edge of the Great Mother herself. If anything, I think our new friend is downright agitated.

"I agree," Endry said.

"Let's agitate her some more," Veesa added.

"No, no," Iliona said. She turned in the air and hovered at eye level with Maralen. "Slow, calm, and respectful. That's what you want to be, missy."

Maralen dropped her head, her dark hair completely hiding her face.

"I'm sorry." The stranger spoke without lifting her face. "I realize now that I've made a mistake. I was so very wrong."

Veesa moved away from her position on the cage, but the spell was not diminished. "Is she begging?"

"Not quite," Iliona said.

"More like lickspittling," Endry said.

"Lickspittling? What's that?"

"That's what a lickspittle does. Really, Veesa, you should read more."

Maralen raised her head, her dark eyes wide and pleading. "I'm just a stranger here. I didn't know what I was getting myself into."

Iliona's wings buzzed hungrily and she smiled. "Glen Elendra is hard on strangers," she said. "And even if we wanted to turn you loose—"

"Which we don't."

"So we won't."

"Even if we wanted to release you, you're too interesting. Not to us, you understand. *We* three think you're an utter bore. But we don't really know what you are, which means the Great Mother doesn't know, either, and that's no good," Iliona continued. "Not at all. The fae know all, you see, so Oona has to meet you right away."

"And she'll decide what to do with you."

Maralen's eyes darted from sibling to sibling. Quietly, her voice shaking, she said, "What will she do to me?"

"Whatever she wants," Iliona said. Her siblings laughed. "Hush now, weird elf. Keep your eyes and your voice down."

"It won't help."

"But it won't hurt, either."

Maralen's glassy eyes and slack expression made it hard to tell if she had heard and understood. Iliona shrugged, and the gesture spread to her siblings. It was way past time for preparations. The Great Mother was ready to receive her children and their new toy.

The great mound of blossoms shuddered, and the woman's figure stretched her arms out to each side. She grew longer and taller, rising up and out. Oona's head bloomed to life, with dark green leaves and snow white flowers unfolding across its surface. A cloud of faeries buzzed up from her shoulders and circled around her head like a crown, their voices sweet and pure.

Oona opened her eyes, each pupil a five-petaled bloom that rotated in its socket like a pinwheel in a gentle wind. The Great Mother smiled.

What have you brought me this time, my children? Oona's voice raised a thrill in Iliona that was ten times more intense than the one she had felt upon entering the grove. Endry and Veesa echoed it back to her, enriching and magnifying Iliona's rapturous awe with their own.

"We don't rightly know, Great Mother," Iliona said. "So we brought her to you."

You did well. Oona listed and swayed for a moment before leaning forward. *Now then, my children . . . bring her closer.*

Iliona and her siblings returned to the points of the triangle and together they moved Maralen's enclosure to the center of the glen, where the mother of them all waited with open, loving arms.

* * * * *

Captain Sygg brought the shapewater ferry up from the cavern via a side channel, heroically fighting the current until they emerged onto a main stretch of the familiar Wanderwine. Rhys was grateful for the daylight, even if it was a few weak rays of sunshine through a cold, clinging fog. There were troubles behind them and the unknown ahead, but a new day had dawned. Today they would reach Colfenor's sacred grove. Rhys sighed. It wasn't much. Calling this dawn a good omen was a bit of a stretch, but he resolved to make the best of what he had.

Rhys made his way forward to where Brigid had spent all sunset, steadfastly refusing to eat, sleep, or do anything else that might compete for her attention. She looked haggard, but the fierce resolve in her eyes was undiminished. Rhys and Sygg both attempted to reassure her that such vigilance was unnecessary, but the archer was as stubborn as stone. She and her arrows were ready for any foolish elf or bounty hunter who may have tried to follow them through the Dark Tributaries.

Ashling roused herself from a sitting position and followed Rhys to the front of the craft. To her credit, she had not persisted in arguing with Rhys's decision to press on. Her stoic acceptance of the situation came without reservation or complaint, even though it was clear she felt that honor demanded otherwise. Rhys valued this sort of determination in his compatriots, and he appreciated the quiet discipline Ashling showed. Elf packs stood or fell based on the strength of their discipline, which in turn hung on the quality of their leadership.

He knew this group was far removed from the effortless unity of an elf hunting pack, especially one under tight command . . . but he was also far removed from a position of Faultless leadership. So far, in fact, that he would probably never know it again, which only improved his opinion of the flamekin's elf-like determination. She stood ready in word and deed to follow Rhys, to work without reservation for the greater good of the party, even though it was clear she felt her own goals remained unfulfilled.

Ashling joined Rhys and Brigid on the foredeck. With Sygg swimming nearby, the entire group was within earshot of each other.

"How long?" Ashling asked.

"Not long at all," Rhys replied, scanning the banks for a familiar landmark. "I've only come this way a few times, and the forest has changed. But we're very close. I can feel it."

"How does it feel?" Ashling asked. She kept her voice low and steady, but Rhys heard the longing behind the calm.

"I don't understand your question."

"Is it familiar? Is it anything like what you felt when the elemental appeared?"

"Are you still on about that?" Brigid muttered.

Ashling stiffened. "Mind your own business."

"Flamekin don't have a monopoly on deeper magic," Brigid replied. "Look, all I'm saying is that you're making too much of one chance encounter. I watch the elementals for signs all the time. It doesn't always work."

"You augur to inform your daily life." Ashling said hotly. "I've got more on my mind than the weather for an upcoming festival week or whether some expectant mother is going to have a boy or a girl."

"And boggarts pray to a pile of mud," Brigid muttered, voicing a familiar kithkin aphorism about the inadvisability of arguing inter-tribal religions.

Ashling's flame darkened and Rhys decided to end their pointless argument. "Keep to your watch, archer," he said sternly. "Or get some rest."

"I'll rest when the job is done," she said. "I've got a reputation to protect."

The shapewater ferry lurched slightly as Captain Sygg stopped impelling it forward. The solidified water settled on top of its own wake, slowing as the merrow swam back to its edge. Sygg's silver face broke the surface of the river, and he rose up through the waves to tread water with what appeared to be only a mild effort.

"You won't have long to wait," Sygg said. "The Murmuring Bosk is just around the next bend." Sygg winked, sank back into the river, and the shapewater vessel picked up speed.

Rhys's ears quivered, and his hand fell to his belt. He felt the reassuring weight of Colfenor's seed cone and forced himself to breathe normally. He had not seen the Murmuring Bosk in many years, but he knew it well. The great, sprawling grove served as a kind of parliament for all the great treefolk varieties—oak and ash and poplar were all represented, along with the rare and mysterious varieties of treefolk that were hardly ever encountered outside the deepest, wildest woods. Many of the oldest and wisest treefolk that ever lived had found their way here to commune with one another, to pool their knowledge, apply it to the present, and preserve it for the future.

If Rhys had chosen the path of a seedguide, this was most likely where he would have ended up. Elves were the only tribe that had ever been admitted to the Murmuring Bosk, and generations of seedguides had served here, tending the treefolk sages, petitioning them for their wisdom and serving as ambassadors between the great trees and the Blessed Nation. He was still thinking of his last visit, lost in the memory, when he felt the saucer bump against the edge of a short, sandy beach and come to rest there.

He opened his eyes, and immediately wished he'd stayed within the memory.

"Ye gods," Sygg said.

"Damn," Brigid whispered.

Ashling pushed her hat back, showing Rhys a face of confusion and concern. "What happened here?"

Rhys said nothing. After all he had endured over the past few days, the sight of the Murmuring Bosk hit him like a hammer blow. His lungs deflated, his heart stopped beating, and his eyes burned all the way back to his brain.

The Murmuring Bosk had been leveled. Huge, gaping holes in the soil marked where the parliament of elders once stood. Carelessly stacked mounds of half-burned wood smoked and smoldered all along the grove's perimeter. Giant boulders that had been buried for centuries lay sundered and broken, dredged up from their silent slumber to be shattered into pieces and added to the ugly, heaping piles of ash, mulch, and moist, black soil.

As nauseating as the sight was, the smell was even worse. The floral scents and woodsy perfume were gone, replaced by a noxious haze of greasy smoke, boiling pitch, and rotting timber. Rhys didn't think it possible, but he found this devastation even more obscene than the site of his battle with the boggarts. In that case, the destruction had been magical, and his own fault. Here, it was clearly a case of a physical force and a brute frenzy capable of overpowering some of the most powerful beings in the world. This was not some inexplicable case of powerful magic gone awry, or a spell beyond the control of its caster. Magic may well have been involved here, but this was no freak occurrence. Someone had set out to do this with a careful plan and a sustained will. Someone had worked long hours to see it done. And if Rhys had anything to say about it, someone would pay.

Rhys shook his head and once more fought back rage and regret, though this time a backdrop of crushing personal guilt did not frame those emotions. He was grateful for that, at least. If he had been personally responsible for this horror as he had been with the other, he would have killed himself on the spot. Better to die than endure another moment of its gruesome spectacle. Better to sleep forever than to risk seeing this sight every sunset when he dreamed and know that he had created it. As had become his habit when his thoughts drifted to that dreadful event, he pressed two fingers to his forehead, through the glamer to the jagged edge of what remained of his left horn.

"What happened here?" Ashling said again.

"I don't know." Rhys's voice rasped in his own ears like the hiss of a dying snake.

"It had to be giants," Brigid said. "Who else could pull out centuries-old trees by their roots?"

"No," Rhys said. "Giants and treefolk sometimes fight, but only in single combat . . . or at worst, in small groups." He paused, thinking of Brion and Kiel. "This is too wide-scale for giants—too calculated and too complete. Giants might have torn up the trees, but they wouldn't have uprooted them all. Giants wouldn't have burned every last one." He peered sharply at the numerous bonfires. "They wouldn't have used axes to split the boughs. They wouldn't have bothered to made individual piles and set each one alight." He clenched his teeth. "They wouldn't have been so organized or so efficient. Giants didn't do this."

Brigid scowled, uncertain. "Then who did?"

"I don't know, but I will find them and make them suffer," Rhys said. "It's time we went ashore."

"Aye." Sygg's face was dour, but he did not hesitate despite the gross breach of river protocol Rhys had committed by giving an order to the captain. Gingerly, as if their steps might somehow increase the destruction they saw, the small party walked from the shapewater and onto the shore of the Murmuring Bosk.

Rhys turned to Brigid and Ashling. "I swore to honor Colfenor's wishes," he said. Not that the old log had allowed for the state of the place when Rhys arrived. He must have had some inkling, some sense of the danger. Perhaps that was why he was so desperate to put Rhys to work. "Now that we are here, it is the least I can do." He somberly withdrew the seed cone and clutched it tightly in one hand. It felt warm to the touch, as if eager to get on with it. "Wait here," Rhys said.

Brigid's thick fingers traced along the surface of her bow. "Not on your life," she said.

With nowhere else to put his rising ire, Rhys vented some of it onto Brigid. "This doesn't concern you," he said.

"It concerns us all," Ashling said. "We came to assist you. You can't expect us to just sit here and watch."

Rhys shot Ashling an angry look. He should have known she would not be able to maintain her elflike demeanor.

"It is not permitted," he said. "No one but treefolk and elves have ever been allowed inside the Murmuring Bosk."

"The Murmuring Bosk is no more," Brigid pointed out. "There's no one left to object."

"Rhys," Ashling said. "You can't do this alone. You don't

know what caused it. You don't know if the danger still remains. Let us help you."

The former daen wrestled with his emotions, weighing them against the purely pragmatic streak that all elves shared. Would the time he spent convincing the others, breaking their determination to accompany him, be worth the effort?

"Follow behind me," he said to the flamekin and kithkin. "And say nothing."

There was a splash as Sygg allowed the shapewater to revert to its natural state with a great sigh of relief. "I imagine that's something like what it feels to lay a clutch of eggs," he said to no one in particular. "You all go on, I'll be here when you get back."

Rhys barely heard a word the merrow said. The elf strode forward with the seed cone cradled before him in both hands. He did not rush. He did not tarry. But Rhys maintained a deliberate, solemn pace as if he bore the body of a Perfect to a funeral pyre.

Brigid and Ashling followed behind, mercifully silent as he had requested. They stayed several paces back, never allowing him to get too far ahead. They were content to be ignored, and he was content to ignore them.

Up close, the horror was even more pronounced. There was not a single living adult tree for as far as Rhys could see. Virtually the only intact plants were a thin line of black poplar saplings along the edges of the mud flats. Black poplars were the most resilient and durable of Lorwyn's treefolk and were famous for their weedlike ability to recover from devastating injuries. Things grew quickly in the Murmuring Bosk, and Rhys had no idea when the grove had been sacked, so he could not gauge how long it had taken these nascent poplars to achieve their current growth. The fact that there was yet life in the place gave him something to pin his hopes on, even if it was in the form of sinewy swamp trees.

Rhys reached the spot he'd been searching for, the large patch of soil that had once sustained the root system of Colfenor himself, long before the great red yew had pulled his roots from the earth and taken his first steps. Reverently, Rhys kneeled. He hollowed out a small depression in the dark soil, gently placed the seed cone inside, and then covered the cone over with dirt. Then Rhys bowed his head and said a silent prayer, infusing the seed cone and the ground with some of the oldest and most powerful yew spells. He finished with an ancient blessing for whatever new life sprang from the seed—if anything but an anemic horsetail or a black poplar could spring from this blasted place, he thought bitterly.

"Rhys," Ashling said, "what happens now?"

The elf stood but did not turn to face his companions. "Now we wait," he said.

"Wait?" the archer replied. "For what?"

"For a sign," Rhys said. He spun on his heels and fixed the pair with a steely gaze. "I must wait to see if the seed will survive. I must make sure my mission is complete."

"And if your mission cannot be completed?" Brigid said. "If the seed cannot sprout and take root?

"Then I must take it back to Colfenor and seek the yew's guidance." His thoughts hardened as Rhys realized another meeting with Colfenor was unavoidable. He would have to confront his mentor with what he had seen in the Murmuring Bosk . . . and with the question of how much Colfenor had known when he sent Rhys here.

"How long?" Ashling said. "How long until you know?"

"A day," Rhys said, "at the most. I will know then if Colfenor's teachings have been passed down to the next generation."

Brigid considered. "We should make camp on the bank," she said. "I'd like to keep an eye on our fishy friend. It's a long walk back if he decides to take a long swim without us."

Rhys nodded. "Good idea."

"I should collect some—" Brigid stopped herself before she said "firewood." Instead the archer bowed awkwardly and hiked back across the grove.

Ashling remained, silent, patiently watching Rhys.

"May I wait with you, taer?"

"You may. But do not speak. I must try to help this new life emerge. I have a connection to it, and I owe it to Colfenor." He did not mention that if he returned to Colfenor without doing everything he could to ensure the seed cone had sprouted, he might as well not return at all, for his mentor would know why he'd failed. But if he remained, and tried, and the cone remained in the scorched earth, Colfenor would know that too.

Ashling nodded, but said nothing. Thankful once more for her circumspection, Rhys brushed the dirt from his hands, crossed his arms, and stared fixedly at the fresh mound of soft soil.

It occurred to the elf that had absolutely no idea how long it might take for a yew to sprout.

CHAPTER 16

Brigid Baeli could not sleep. She wanted to. The archer was one exhausted kithkin, but duty prevented so much as nodding off. The others hadn't questioned her when she'd volunteered to keep watch during sunset, and Brigid took full advantage of the widespread, but somewhat inaccurate myth that kithkin only slept once a week. True, a kithkin could easily go forty-eight, even sixty hours without tiring too much, but the archer was going on her seventh day. The myth was putting Brigid to the test, and the weariness in her bones and the steady allure of blissful slumber were the twin demons palpably willing her to fail. If not for the distant connection to the powerful thoughtweft of Kinsbaile's citizens, she might have collapsed days ago. But the kithkin of Kinsbaile believed in their hero, and so their hero believed in herself just as much.

She could not fail. She could not fail Kinsbaile, nor Gaddock Teeg, and certainly not the ancient and distinguished name of Baeli. None of those were on her mind at the moment, however. All Brigid could concentrate on was the fact that every sunset, when the opportunity allowed, she had pulled away from the others and spent the long, dark hours preparing her offering, calling on the elements, and staring upward. She was waiting for a message that had, as yet, stubbornly refused to arrive. It wouldn't have been so bad if she hadn't spent days before readying for this mission, again working round the clock to prepare. Preparation was literally in the Baeli family crest, and she'd be bogged if she didn't devote proper attention to the many possible outcomes of her limited possible actions once the message arrived.

As luck would have it, on the very sunset Brigid began to doubt even her duty—if only it would buy her an hour of uninterrupted slumber—the message arrived.

It arrived by moth, which told Brigid how desperate Teeg must have become. A bird would have been faster, better able to defend itself, and might have returned to the cenn with Brigid's reply. A moth from Teeg meant no reply was expected. A moth could reach her undetected, but the cenn—whose skills in this particular arena were far behind even a novice archer's, let alone one of Brigid's stature—must have had to send at least three dozen of the insects to ensure at least one reached her in time. Brigid did not need to send extra messages for insurance.

She wondered if this moth were the last one to reach her and make contact, enduring bats, birds, reptiles, and rodents that slaughtered its dust-winged kin. Perhaps the moth was merely the first of the survivors to reach her, and more were incoming. Either way, it meant she could stop staring at the cloudy, starless sky at last and find out which course of action the cenn—and the yew, no doubt—had settled upon.

The moth alit upon the back of her hand and folded its glittering silver wings. It bore the pattern that matched Gaddock Teeg's official seal. The seal was blood red, and that told Brigid everything she needed to know.

It told her which of the two—the outlaw elf or the meddling flamekin—she would have to kill. The thought shocked her a bit. She'd known it was coming but she had been able to keep it from overwhelming her by concentrating on the present. The shock, however, gave way to the certainty that this must be done. The thoughtweft reached her more strongly than ever, as if Kinsbaile were just on the other side of the river—which it was, of course, but it was also many miles away. This was a united effort, and she could not resist it if she'd wanted to. It was the price one paid for being a kithkin folk hero. The kithkin expected their heroes to fulfill the stories they wanted to hear, and this story ended in the death of someone Brigid had foolishly begun to consider a friend.

* * * * *

Rhys stared at the freshly packed earth in the center of the sacred grove known as the Murmuring Bosk, as he had stared and stared at it for the last several hours. Or he stared at what was left of the Murmuring Bosk, at least. The similarity to the devastation that surrounded him after the last boggart raid was not lost on him, but he knew—knew without a doubt—that he had not done this. He had not set foot in this grove for months. Was it someone else who could do . . . whatever it was Rhys had done? Had he mistakenly blamed himself for the deeds of another back in the Porringer Valley? He didn't know. And no matter how long he sat cross-legged, hands on knees, meditating and contemplating to fight the specter of inactivity, he could not find an answer. How could he, when he couldn't even fathom what had happened in the first place?

And there was the inescapable thought that whatever he was doing, it wasn't enough. He hadn't planted the seed cone quickly enough. It wouldn't be strong enough to break through.

For bog's sake, the entire Bosk was gone. How was a young yew sapling supposed to survive here?

Have I followed the letter of Colfenor's wishes so closely that I have already failed? Rhys asked himself. Should he have just returned to Colfenor immediately when they found this devastation had struck the Bosk?

Did watched seeds *ever* sprout?

And then, from a few hundred yards away, where they'd established a camp on the muddy banks of the inlet, there came a piercing, painful scream. It was either the kithkin or the flamekin, but at this distance, he could not be certain. Not even when the scream morphed and turned into his name.

Whoever it was, she was in agony. Any answers to his introspective questions, however enlightening, would have to wait. Rhys vaulted and dashed over the broken, smoldering ruins and wreckage of the devastated grove. He took no care to find a level path through the destruction, but simply made a beeline for the camp and scrambled across anything that got in the way.

When the campfire came into view, Rhys momentarily thought he must be losing his mind. Sygg was nowhere to be seen, and the sandy beach was bloody and empty—very bloody and very empty.

"Damn," he murmured.

The elf ran from the crest of the path to the deserted encampment. Blood was everywhere. Here and there were heavy scorch marks where Ashling had apparently been fighting with someone. The gore on the ground was definitely of two different types. Rhys could smell and see the stone rivulets of cooled flamekin flesh, and the bright red color and vivid iron tang of kithkin blood.

Only the kithkin was still here. It took Rhys a few seconds to pick up the labored breathing that came from the low foliage at the north end of the small beach, but once he did he spotted Brigid immediately. She was in bad shape—burned, cut, and clawed, with one arm shattered above the elbow, swollen, purple, and twisted at a sickening angle.

Brigid sounded horrified and confused when she looked up at Rhys and weakly asked, "Why? Why did she do it?"

"Who?" Rhys asked. "Ashling?"

"She went mad, screamed something about her path, and—and some kind of flying elk? Does that make sense?"

"A little," Rhys said.

"When Sygg refused to leave you behind, she killed him, Rhys," Brigid said, waving away the elf's offered hand. "No, my arm—I don't want to move if I can help it. I don't think we're going anywhere anyway."

"Sygg is dead? This doesn't make any bogged sense," Rhys said. "Why would she? She's a pilgrim, they don't—" He paused. "Wait, where is Ashling?"

The kithkin jerked a thumb toward the river. Brigid had lost the entire sleeve of her remaining unbroken arm, and the skin was laced with deep cuts and scratches that looked like they came from an animal. "I figure if what I've heard about her kind is true," the kithkin said, "your flamekin's got a few hours before there's no chance to revive her. Could be six, if someone were to get her out of the water soon. Don't know why you'd want to. I didn't have an easy time getting her in there in the first place, but I suppose she should face justice. I've got some rope in my pack, if you could—"

"I will pull her out to . . . face justice," Rhys said, struggling to remain calm. Nothing about this was right. "And she's not 'my' flamekin. So, tell me again—the pilgrim—she just snapped and killed the only person capable of getting us back to Kinsbaile."

"She was raving," the kithkin said quickly. "I think it was the moisture. She said she was going to go out, going to—what was it—'gutter out like a candle' if she didn't get going. Then it was 'like a candle in a light breeze, not even in a hurricane,' and she laughed." Brigid smiled and pointed wearily at her arm, which was turning black and needed serious attention. It had swollen to twice the size of the other. "I think her kind call it 'water poisoning.'"

The kithkin might have fooled Rhys if he wasn't always listening for the telltale sounds of a lie, the altered breathing and the change in tenor and rhythm, the hiccups between words and the movements of the eye.

Elves did not lie casually, but when they lied, they lied well, and could always spot when others did so, as easily as they tracked their prey. Brigid was a very good liar for a kithkin, but she *was* lying, of that there was no doubt. The lacerations on her arm only confirmed what Rhys's ears told him was true. He entertained the thought of killing her as he smiled at the kithkin, but fought the urge for a quick end to the problem she represented. She clearly knew things the elf needed to know.

It was best to leave her in place and retrieve Ashling. Then, he would somehow get them all to a flamekin village by himself. It would take a day, maybe a few hours past that if he hurried. All right, it wasn't a great plan, but none of his options were particularly good. If he attacked the kithkin, Ashling wouldn't have a chance. What was more, he had a sneaking suspicion Brigid was not as incapacitated as she appeared. The arm was certainly broken, but she had somehow taken out both Sygg and Ashling on her own. A move to attack her could cause an unpredictable move on her part that could, if he was not careful, bring an end to his own life as well. He continued to play along, determined to make the kithkin make the first move.

"I'm going to drag her out of there," Rhys told Brigid as casually as he could. "If the red yew can ignite her again, we can confirm your hypothesis about water poisoning is right." He smiled and placed a reassuring hand on her good shoulder. "The important thing is you made it. Wait here. As soon as I haul the flamekin out of the water, I'll see if I can do something for that arm. I may be no good with internal injuries, but I can set broken arm."

Internal injuries? Why had he said that? When had he dealt with any internal injuries lately? From the confused look that passed across Brigid's features, he could see she thought it was an odd statement as well. Then the moment passed and was forgotten. As forgotten as Maralen and the faeries, as it happened, though Rhys would not reflect upon that until later.

As Rhys turned toward the river, he paused. "Sygg. You said she dumped him in the water. Before you dumped . . . ?"

"Yes," Brigid said with the wan smile of the good soldier. "He floated away, before she came after me."

"Too bad," Rhys continued, fighting to keep his voice level. "She's probably not going to make it. I certainly can't summon any flaming elementals, and I sure can't fly. Not without help." He raised his eyebrows. "Unless you . . . ?"

"No," the kithkin said with what Rhys knew was mock sadness. "I watch the elementals, as do all kithkin, but they do not appear at my command. It just doesn't work that way." She smirked. "And I may be good with a glider, but I couldn't fly one now if I wanted to."

"So much for that idea," Rhys said, forcing joviality into his voice. "Well. Just in case, eh?"

Rhys gave Brigid a nod, then pulled off his boots and prepared to dive into the river, scanning the murky water for some sign of Ashling. So focused was he on his search that he almost dived directly atop Sygg. He caught himself before his feet could leave the ground but grabbed at the merrow's shoulderfin to steady himself.

The merrow, who bore several fresh-looking scars but appeared little the worse for wear, had silently emerged from the water, carrying a familiar but horrifying burden. Ashling hung limp over Sygg's shoulder, her flame extinguished, her skin like wet, igneous rock, her head and shoulders resembling an unfinished statue without her flaming corona. The flamekin's body emitted no heat or light whatsoever.

Rhys had to make a snap decision, and he made it instantly. Sygg was alive, which changed everything. There really was a chance for Ashling's life. There was no need to maintain the charade.

The flush of victory only lasted as long as it took Rhys to turn around, just in time to receive a mightily swung stone against the side of his head. The elf staggered and collapsed to his knees as Sygg shoved Ashling's body unceremoniously onto the sandy bank and pushed himself out of the water. The merrow coiled his tail to stand, which Rhys knew was a painful thing for the fish-man to do for too long.

Had the kithkin had use of her broken arm, she might have downed him immediately. As it was, Brigid was seated, holding the grip of her bow in place with her boot and pulled the arrow back with her good hand. Rhys, dazed and bloody, hadn't even seen her retrieve the weapon, let along nock an arrow and aim it with just one hand and one foot. There was no doubt her aim was as good as ever.

"Back. Up. Fish-man." The kithkin drew the arrow back another quarter of an inch to add emphasis to each word.

The merrow raised both of his clawed hands and bobbed awkwardly on his coiled tail like a kithling's toy. "Do you mind terribly if I just don't go forward? Backing up is not as easy as—"

"Fine," Brigid said, and held the arrow aimed at Sygg as she scooted up the bank with her free foot, keeping her distance from Rhys at the same time—not that Rhys was in any condition to fight. He wondered for a moment if he was to die like a stuck springjack, put down by a kithkin killer.

"Now, Rhys," she said without taking her eyes off of the merrow captain. "You're going to fix my arm, or I'm going to kill your best chance of saving her."

"What?" Rhys said. "How?"

"Don't play stupid," Brigid said. "You already told me you can heal a battlefield injury. Well, I've got a doozy. Heal me."

"But I don't have any—I can't just will it," Rhys objected, which was mostly true. And he certainly couldn't in this case, with such a bad break.

"My belt," the kithkin replied. "The black pouch. What you need is in there. Courtesy of the Gilt Leaf elves and their benevolent oppression of the kithkin people."

"This is political?" Sygg said in disbelief.

"No, it's not political," Brigid said. "No more than anything else. And shut up." She cocked her head toward the elf, and a moment of confusion washed over her features before they hardened again.

"You don't have to—" Rhys began.

"Yes, I'm afraid I do, Rhys." Brigid sighed. "Well? I'm waiting."

The kithkin had him in a corner, and she was right. Ashling would die without Sygg's help, and the elf realized he couldn't allow that. Rhys carefully crawled to the kithkin's side. Slowly, and with exaggerated caution so as not to trigger the arrow's release, he gingerly opened the black pouch. Inside were a few powerful medicinal herbs—expensive ones that were, to Rhys's knowledge, usually only carried by a daen. His own had been lost in the incident at the boggart village, but these were, indeed, exactly what he required to perform an emergency bone-knitting spell. He wondered what else the kithkin carried around for emergencies and if all kithkin were as well-supplied as the traitor.

The elf crumbled the ingredients into both his palms, holding them together as he crouched next to the archer. "This is going to hurt. This is going to hurt a lot. I swear to you, I will do my best, but it's going to hurt so badly I don't trust you with that bow. I'm going to fix your arm, but you've got to trust me and lower your weapon."

"All right," Brigid said, and lowered the arrow so that it was aimed several inches below the utility belt slung around the merrow's thin waist.

"Um," Sygg said, his bulbous eyes growing even wider.

"There. He won't die if I slip," the kithkin said, "which I won't. Now get on with it. Your flaming sweetheart is counting on you."

Rhys stifled a retort, and focused on his training. Every hunter knew the basics, and every daen knew far more than that. In fact, if one chose, most any daen could probably make enough thread to retire for life by spending six months as a healer in any well-off elf community. Not that any daen would ever stoop to do so.

The crushed reagents in his clasped hands grew warm, and he concentrated on that heat. Slowly, so as not to disturb the kithkin's string-finger, Rhys moved his hands, still pressed together, to the black, swollen limb hanging from Brigid's side.

"I'm going to press against your arm on the count of three."

"I'm not going to shoot him unless you fail to fix my arm, but thank you for the warning." She drew in a quick breath and added, "Wait. On 'three,' or—"

"On 'three.' Are you ready?"

"Yes."

"One, two, *three.*"

On the last word Rhys opened his hands palm out and pressed

them against Brigid's shattered arm. Brigid let out a brief yelp, but to her credit—and Sygg's boundless relief—she held her bow steady.

The warmth immediately spread from his hands, seeping in through torn and bruised pores, entering the kithkin's bloodstream, her bones, all the tiny pieces of bone . . . . Rhys closed his eyes. And the real work began. In his mind's eye, a picture formed of the pieces of bone within the blackened flesh. As his focus sharpened, so too did the awareness of how these pieces fit together. He then poured all of his will and some of his own life-force—for such a sacrifice was to be expected of a daen looking after his own hunters—into making the awareness match reality. He could hear the kithkin's labored, agonized breathing, her grinding teeth, and the creak of the bow as she struggled to keep her arrow trained on Sygg.

And still the work was not done. Whoever had broken this arm—and Rhys found himself hoping it was Ashling—had made a very thorough job of it. It took nearly five minutes of feverish concentration and the exhaustion of almost every ounce of energy Rhys possessed to finish the job. But finish it he did, finally releasing the kithkin's arm—during those five minutes his open-palmed press had become a near death-grip—and dropping to his knees, gasping for air. He was drenched in sweat, and feeling an almost overpowering urge to sleep.

"That is better," the kithkin said. She stood and gingerly transferred the bow to the hand at the end of her reconstructed arm. Brigid winced and shot a quick glare at Rhys as she pushed herself to her feet. "It still hurts, elf."

"That arm was in a thousand pieces," Rhys gasped, feeling as if he'd just run from Kinsbaile to Lys Alana and back again. "The bruising will have to heal naturally, but the bones are healed. You want more than that, leave us here and go back to Kinsbaile."

"I wouldn't object," Sygg said, his breathing growing labored. Merrow could only pull oxygen from moist air for short periods before they needed to submerge themselves in water.

With excruciating effort Rhys pulled himself to his feet to look death in the eye as Brigid stepped slowly back from them both, alternately aiming at Rhys, then Sygg again, until she was far enough away that it didn't matter which one she shot first— Sygg and Rhys both knew she'd have time to reload before either could reach her.

"Thank you," Brigid said. "All of you. You too, Captain. I knew I wouldn't slip and kill you."

"What are you talking about?" Rhys demanded.

"You'll see," the kithkin laughed. It was at that moment Rhys realized his mistake in letting Brigid back away—the archer had been able to sidle right over to Ashling's motionless form.

"What's so funny?" Rhys asked, stalling lamely.

"I couldn't possibly have killed him, you know. The merrow."

"I'm right here," Sygg said.

"Why not?" Rhys asked.

"No point," Brigid said, and let fly the arrow directly at Rhys. It struck him in the face, and he experienced the certainty that the next moment he would be dead. But when that next moment came and featured not death, but a small *pop* and an explosion of sticky, fibrous netting that instantly entangled elf and merrow alike, he realized he had completely misunderstood the meaning of the kithkin's words. "Get it?" the kithkin added unnecessarily, but she looked more morose than amused.

The netting clung to both the elf and the merrow, though to the merrow it was a death sentence. Sygg needed water, and he needed it soon. Yet the more they struggled, the tighter the tangled fibers seemed to wrap about them. Rhys could still see, however, and he could still speak.

"Why?"

"Not the time for questions, Rhys," Brigid said as she scooped up Ashling and threw the flamekin over one shoulder, "even if that was the right question. Tell you what, you succeed in breaking free, and maybe I'll tell you someday." The flamekin's toes still rested on the sand, and her knuckles scraped the earth behind the kithkin, but Ashling's weight didn't seem to trouble Brigid in the slightest.

"I don't understand," Sygg gasped. "How do you expect to get anywhere without me?"

Brigid just smiled. She raised her bow overhead with one hand as if she would shoot an arrow into the sun, and then flicked her wrist. The grip twisted the bow around a quarter-turn, locked into place with a click, and then a pair of batlike wings slipped from the elegantly carved and cunningly constructed weapon.

"Are you planning on fanning me to death?" Rhys asked.

"Hardly," Brigid said. "We're done here. I've got what I came for. The only question left is: Will I see you at the tales? I do hope you make it, Rhys. It's going to be a spectacular story."

"Why do you need the flamekin?" Rhys asked.

Brigid's only response was to turn her face to the sky and speak to the bow. "Kinsbaile." A gust of wind materialized from nowhere, blowing cold around Rhys's ears as it filled the bow-wings and launched Brigid and her unconscious cargo into the sky.

By the time Rhys had raised a hand to block out the sun, the kithkin archer, her comatose burden, and her improbable flying machine were only visible for a moment, presenting an almost comical silhouette against the bright orb. Then Brigid veered off to the north and ducked behind a low fogbank.

"I think she . . . wants you to follow her to Kinsbaile," Sygg wheezed wryly. "She concealed it really . . . well, but if we can just get out of this netting, I can . . . do it. Of course, if I don't get out of this netting, I'm . . . going to die. But you know it's a trap, Gilt Leaf. Tell me, what . . . do you owe that flamekin?"

"She's—she's been useful," the elf said, a little lamely. "And if I have to follow her to find out what this is all about. . . ."

"Oh, stop, you're going to make me cry," Sygg gasped.

"We have to find a way to cut ourselves loose."

"Hmm," the merrow managed. "I do not think I can cut anything with . . . words, but if I can reach my belt—"

"Ow! Hey!"

"My . . . apologies," Sygg said, still wheezing. "What I mean to say is, I may not be able to cut . . . the netting, but I think I can dissolve . . . it."

"Cut, dissolve, just get us free, if only to end your wheezing."

" 'Get us free to end your . . . wheezing *please* . . . Sygg,' " Sygg said reprovingly.

"For bog's sake, Sygg—"

"All right, all right. Now this may . . . hurt a little. I have a vial of acid on my belt. I'm going to try to smash the vial against the netting, so you may . . . er . . . get some on you."

"Wait, what?"

"Can you . . . produce your own . . . acid, Gilt Leaf?"

"Look, if this doesn't work, will you do me a favor and kill me?"

* * * * *

Ashling, the flamekin had named her. Like many flamekin names, it came from an ancient word meaning "fire," though the ashling was a special kind of fire: the singular flame that was the last flicker of a larger conflagration. It was a fitting name for a flamekin who might well be the last of her kind ever spawned in the shadow of Mount Tanufel, before they moved to the crags. The flamekin expected amazing things from her. Miraculous things. Some expected her to lead, others to fight and conquer, or to build a true peace at long last with the elves.

She hadn't wanted any of it. The expectations of her kin had driven her to the path. It was a truth she rarely dwelled upon. Every pilgrim had a reason they took that first step, and she didn't think of her journey as more special than any other. It was her village that expected greatness from Ashling, not Ashling herself. And only Ashling among all the flamekin in her village ever entertained the thought she might end up doused and guttered without ever fulfilling her potential.

Unfortunately for the slight sense of vindication that might have offered, Ashling was in no position to boast of her prescience. She had, in fact, no way of knowing what position she was in. If she had, she might have been more than a little surprised to find that it was hanging from the shoulder of a kithkin archer who was in turn suspended some five hundred feet in the air by a thin, membranous flying wing.

But if there was no awareness of the physical, there was still a glimmer of consciousness, of knowing. She knew was going to die. Ashling knew that. In fact she was aware of almost nothing else.

She was going to die. She was frozen. She had returned to the stone. She was encased in the living rock. She was cold and motionless, lifeless without the fire beneath Mount Tanufel, knowing she would never feel it again.

She was going to die. She was encased in ice. She could not move.

She was going to die. She could not feel the unique mountain fire that spawned her. She was trapped. She was cold. She was stone.

She was.

Barely.

But for how long?

* * * * *

"It stings!"

"Of course it stings," Sygg said. "It's acid. Just take a quick dip in the water and quit complaining. We're out, aren't we?" The merrow, who had wasted no time in slipping over the bank to moisten his skin and take a few deep, cleansing breaths of water once the acid had eaten through the kithkin netting, splashed in surprise and squinted at the crest of the small hillock above the beach. "There appears to be someone—Oh, it's Maralen." Sygg waved. "Hello, Maralen. Faeries."

Rhys had hoped his traveling companions would have no more surprises for him, but Maralen's sudden return with the faerie trio trampled that hope underfoot. He was certainly pleased to see that the stranger was unharmed, but this small bit of relief registered about at strongly as a fleabite next to an arrow wound.

Strangely, it did not occur to the elf that he had not remembered the strange traveler's existence, let alone her name, until he had seen her. It was as if she had always been there, even though his memory told him she hadn't fought to help Ashling.

No, of course she hadn't. Maralen had been exploring the area with the faerie clique. Surely she'd mentioned it, though he couldn't remember her specific words. How could he have forgotten? Maybe he did need a dip in the water, too, if only to clear his head.

Maralen strolled out of the forest with her odd, quiet intensity on full display. Her eyes were wide, and her pale cheeks were flushed. The faeries hovered in the air behind her, arranged in a **V** formation with Iliona at the forefront.

"Hello again," the dark-haired woman called casually. She slipped a bit on the muddy banks, and all three faeries lunged forward as if to catch her before she fell. Laughing, Maralen waved them off. "I'm fine, thank you."

"Where have you been?" Rhys said. "And why aren't they babbling?"

"I'm sure I wouldn't know, but I'm not about to complain," Maralen said. To Rhys's surprise, the faeries offered no retort, but maintained their weird silence. Well, he wasn't going to complain about it either. A break from their incessant chatter was welcome, if strange.

"Well you two, climb aboard if you're coming," Sygg replied. "There's not a moment to lose." Rhys turned to the merrow and saw he had called forth a new shapewater ferry, this one smaller and sleeker since it only had to carry a pair of landwalkers.

"You're injured," Maralen said to Rhys, leaving the merrow to grumble about the rudeness of strange travelers. She approached Rhys, shadowed every step of the way by the faerie trio, each of whom eyed her with the steely but bitter attention of an ungrateful servant. What was going on here?

"No, really, I'm fine," Sygg said, "just shot. Oh, and stabbed through the neck. Not so you'd notice, but—Oh, shut up, Sygg."

Maralen looked at Rhys's wounds, from the acid burns on his leg to the bloody knot on his temple, and shook her head with concern. "What happened?" she said. "Where are the others?"

"Brigid attacked Sygg," Rhys said, "and abducted Ashling. After soaking her in the river."

"Why?"

"We have no answers. Only guesses."

Maralen cocked her head and for a moment Rhys saw an

uncharacteristic flash of impatience in the Mornsong's expression. "Guesses?" Maralen asked, and the impatience, if it had been there at all, disappeared.

"None worth mentioning now," Rhys said. "I'm far more interested in what you've been doing."

The strange woman smiled innocently. She glanced up at the faerie siblings overhead and said, "This truly is a magnificent part of the world. I certainly saw nothing of the kithkin or your flamekin. But on the bright side, the trio and I found time to bond, I think."

"Bond?" Rhys said. He turned to the faeries, but continued to address the stranger. "You didn't make any deals, did you? Enter into any kind of long-term arrangements involving spinning a certain amount of gold, or magic seedpods—"

"They took me on a tour," Maralen said. "I've seen relatively little of the Gilt Leaf Wood, and they were eager to rectify that. You'd be amazed how far and how fast they can take you."

"No," Rhys said, "I wouldn't." He took Maralen by the arm and pulled her away from the faeries. "What happened?" Rhys said sternly, his voice a sharp whisper. "What changed? The faeries are clinging to you like bodyguards. I remember them—that is, I remember them agreeing to take you on your little side trip, but—"

"I think they took pity on me. I told you. We bonded." She eyed Iliona. "And now we're thick as thieves, eh?"

"Yes," the faerie replied with uncharacteristic brevity, and to Rhys's surprise neither of her smaller siblings added anything to the sentiment. It was as if they'd had their vocal cords cut.

"That . . . Well, that's impressive. When the four of you left, you didn't seem to be getting along," Rhys said. "Or so I remember."

Do you, Rhys? asked a nagging voice in his head. Wasn't there something about everyone falling . . . falling . . . . Oh, bog it, the nagging voice said in irritation. I can't remember what I was going to say. You're right, they weren't getting along when they left.

"I remember it clearly," he said after a moment. Liar, said a voice inside his head, but he ignored it. There were too many mysteries at once, and all the while Ashling's life hung in the balance. Rhys wasn't even sure he understood why, but he knew in his heart he would never forgive himself if she were extinguished.

"Listen, we—the trio and I—we made a deal, taer," Maralen whispered. "Don't mess it up for me?"

"Deal? What kind of a deal? I told you, don't—"

"They find me interesting because . . . because they've never been to the Mornsong. I'm strange to them, and yes, at first that gave them cause to distrust and dislike me. But we came to an understanding on our little adventure."

"Adventure?" Sygg called from the water, where he was summoning a silvery gangplank for his passengers' convenience. "I thought you didn't see any trouble."

"You will explain the details of this understanding," Rhys said. "Now."

"There's no need to be brusque." Maralen's face settled into a pout. "I'm not too clear on all the details, but it seems that faeries love dreamstuff more than just about anything else. The stuff of my dreams seems to have a flavor and texture the faeries of Gilt Leaf find . . . exotic."

Rhys let this sink in. "You bartered your dreams?"

"In a manner of speaking. Between you and me, I thought I was bargaining for my life at one point—as you said, we weren't getting along, and from that height, I don't mind telling you I was afraid. Perhaps I offered anything and everything I had. They consulted with each other, and with this Oona they're always on about, and then they decided that I was worth more to them alive. Alive and dreaming."

"It's incredibly dangerous to strike bargains with the fae," Rhys said. "Is the Mornsong so remote you don't even know that?"

"I'm a fair hand at bargaining," Maralen said. "I may not be as shrewd as the siblings—or as you, taer—but I know enough not to trade something for nothing." She smiled.

Rhys did not smile back. "Details," he said crisply. "And I'd ask you to stop that."

"Stop what?"

"Calling me by my former status," Rhys said.

"Of course," Maralen said, "Rhys. May I continue?"

"With all haste."

"I agreed to give the siblings full access to my dreamstuff," Maralen said, "all my thoughts and wishes and passing fancies. In exchange, they agreed to attend me and keep me safe from harm. To them I imagine it's much like the relationship between a kithkin farmer and his prized dairy cow. As long as I provide what they want, they make sure I'm well taken care of. I told you I was a traveler, ta—Rhys. They'll let me travel places I'd never thought possible to reach within my lifetime. I'm not like you, my friend. I've had a lot of time to think about it, and I think I'm tired of seeking perfection. I'm ready to seek experiences instead. Maybe there's a little bit of pilgrim in my blood, eh?"

"Where did they take you?" With Maralen answering Rhys's questions, he wanted to know more—much, much more.

"Everywhere. All over," Maralen said. She clasped her hands and said breathlessly, "Oh, you should have seen it. We went as high as the sun and looked down on the Wanderwine, from its source in the mountains all the way down to the southernmost tip of the lowlands."

Rhys shook his head. Elves were far harder to read than kithkin. The faeries had clearly done something to Maralen's mind, changing it in some way to make her more palatable company, because she was talking like no elf he'd ever heard in his life, stranger or no. He eyed the Mornsong closely, looking for any signs of enchantment or glamer, but he could detect no magic on or around Maralen at all. She remained mundane yet mysterious. And the strangest thing was, her story made sense. The faeries were notoriously fickle, but they were also overwhelmingly curious. If they had come to see Maralen as a treat to be savored, they might well pretend to be her servants for a time. Such a game would not end well for Maralen, and Rhys was certain it would end, one way or the other.

"Very well," Rhys said. He had little patience for this particular mystery, and, besides, the faeries were clearly hanging on their every word. If he continued to press Maralen he was sure to weather another storm of twittering from the Vendilion clique.

Rhys glanced over at the faerie trio. This marked the longest period of silence he had heard from them yet, leaving out all the times they were sneaking around and muttering to each other. He had to make one last push for information before giving up.

"Why did you want to make a deal with this one?" Rhys asked, jerking a thumb at Maralen.

"Oh, all kinds of reasons," Iliona said, at last sounding like her old self. "To show her who's boss, for one."

"To find out what makes her special."

"To see if she had any value," Endry said. "Hidden value, that is."

"And once all that was accomplished . . ." Maralen prompted.

"We decided to keep her around. The Great Mother—"

"The Great Mother likes special things," Veesa said, speaking over Endry's explanation.

"So as long as she provides the special, we want to keep harvesting it."

"I'm actually enjoying this a little too much," Maralen whispered. "I know they're just toying with me. I know that they'll eventually strand me in a tree or make me believe I'm a boggart's auntie."

"Eventually," Rhys said. "And much sooner than you think."

"Right now, I'm just happy they've stopped calling me 'fat elf.' " She blinked, then broke into a grin. "Sorry, I'm certain this isn't the most important thing you have to deal with. Aren't we going after Brigid and Ashling?"

"We are," Rhys said, stepping at last onto the reconstituted shapewater craft.

"I would like to come along," Maralen said. "The flamekin saved me a lot of trouble with her magic. I'd like to repay the favor in whatever small way I can."

"We'll come, too," Iliona said.

"We want to help save the pilgrim and punish the nasty archer."

"And to protect our investment."

"Fine," Rhys said. "Sygg!" he called. "We're aboard. Can you get us back to Kinsbaile quickly?"

"Aye," the merrow said. "Though it'll require magic, not muscle. Magic costs more."

"Name any price you like. You'll be paid in full," Rhys said. He was not a wealthy elf, not by the mercantile standards of the merrow, kithkin, and faeries, but he had more than enough set aside in Lys Alana to cover Sygg's costs. Rhys had lost so much more already, of such infinitely higher value, that the thought of quibbling over a few extra threads was almost insulting.

The faeries murmured among themselves, and Maralen called out, "Rhys?"

"Make ready, Sygg. We have a lot of river to cover."

"Indeed 'we' do," the ferryman replied wearily.

"Taer—I'm sorry—Rhys." Maralen's eyes gleamed. "I'd like to make a suggestion. To speed up our transit."

"Then get on with it."

Maralen face remained lively, the rebuke ignored. She smiled patiently.

"What? You have something to contribute?"

"Actually, yes." She looked up at the faeries, and the trio nodded back as one. "I think we do."

CHAPTER 17

Taercenn Nath of the Gilt Leaf packs—the Exquisite alpha who fed and protected the tribe with strength and honor, about whom songs had been sung in Gilt Leaf Hall of glorious Lys Alana, the Guardian of Perfection and the Protector of the Blessed Nation—had begun to daydream like a bored apprentice. But where an apprentice would waste his time dreaming of gold, glory, or perhaps a racy fantasy, Taercenn Nath dreamed of killing kithkin. Sometimes, he imagined scenarios in which the kithkin rose up against the elves, and suffered extermination en masse as a result. If he felt like a meditation upon tactics and strategy, he invariably found himself plotting a siege of Kinsbaile that spread to every rat-infested hovel the barely sentient, little creatures had built along the river Wanderwine.

Most often, he dwelled upon the many ways he would like to eliminate Gaddock Teeg. Dismemberment. Immolation. A long, slow death on a long, dull pike. Skinning alive. Drowning in a vat of vile kithkin wine.

He had begun to entertain yet another method of ending the cenn's life—forcing Teeg to cut himself open and then feeding the fool's intestines to the cuffhounds—when the object of his dark fantasy tromped self-importantly through the open door. Nath did not believe in closed doors. Elves did not lie to their lessers, and had no need to conceal. Nath did, however, like to hear the goings-on outside his new field headquarters, if only to keep track of how many kithkin he would eventually kill when he finally lost control. Teeg was the only kithkin Nath had told personally to knock before entering, and, invariably, the cenn never did.

Perhaps a nice flaying, Nath thought. Two hundred lashes, at least. His men could use the entertainment, and Teeg should die screaming in pain, or shouldn't die at all.

"My taercenn," Teeg said. The kithkin bowed deeply—far too deeply—and promptly—far too promptly—before he rose to face Nath and boldly looked him in the eye.

Far too boldly.

"Teeg," Nath said with a glower, "spit it out."

"Yes, thank you, taer," Teeg scraped pathetically. "I've a message for you, an important message. It's from Daen Gryffid. He reports—"

"He *reports?*" Nath roared, leaping to his feet in fury and snatching the scroll from the kithkin's sweaty hand. "How dare you read an official—"

"As this is operational intelligence, my taercenn, I assumed it was within my purview to offer you my assessment of the information," Teeg said quickly. "But that is not all."

"And who handed this to you? What fool—"

"I do not choose our allies, Taercenn," said the elf who strode into the office at that moment. "But I followed procedure. In the event I should be incapacitated, I sent the message through an adjutant for assessment. This creature was the only one available."

"Creature? Why, I—"

"Quiet," Nath snapped. "Daen Gryffid," he continued, losing none of his menace. "You could certainly have delivered this personally, if you were able to hand it to him."

"Taer, I take responsibility for sending a scout back with that report," Gryffid replied. "A full day ago. I can see now I was in error. When you did not reply, I returned to personally explain, and offer myself up for any punishment you deemed fitting. It was certainly not my intention to allow an animal to peruse my findings."

Nath was genuinely surprised the kithkin had not objected to being called an animal—perhaps he could be trained after all. "And your findings are . . . ?"

"The report read, in essence, that the traitor would be returning soon, and I included a plan of ambush. Unfortunately, circumstances have made most of that report obsolete."

"Out with it, before I have you cleaning the springjack stables!" Nath barked, boiling with impatience.

"The kithkin returns with the flamekin prisoner. She has been extinguished, but there are still a few hours in which—"

"Fine," Nath said, "and the new information?"

"She is returning via wingbow," Gryffid said, "a kithkin contrivance that gives a skilled user the power of flight. However—"

"However," Nath said darkly.

"It appears that Rhys, too, has gained that power. He's headed here with that Mornsong stranger. They're . . . well . . . flying, taer."

"Ridiculous."

"The traitor has been seen in the company of faeries. They are surprisingly strong, for insects, taer."

"Perhaps this is not the problem it seems," the cenn offered. "Archer Baeli knows time is of the essence. She will head directly to the red yew."

"So?" Nath said.

"No, I think I see what he's getting at," Gryffid said and risked offending his taercenn by staying one step ahead. "We could position archers atop the buildings ringing the square. With the way the forest rises over those buildings, we'd be concealed from the kin-slayer until it was too late. We could take them by complete surprise."

"Yes," Nath said. "It could work." He was a trifle annoyed he had not thought of this, but he had not risen to become the taercenn by allowing such annoyances to keep him from taking advantage of an excellent plan. There would be time to discipline Daen Gryffid later. That said, he certainly wasn't about to let his subordinate think he'd solved everything. He strode to the map of Kinsbaile that Teeg kept on the rear wall of the chamber. "If, that is, you position battle druids here, here, here, and here. Don't rely on fire arrows or lucky shots. Do you understand?"

"Yes, my taercenn."

Nath turned to the kithkin. "Leave us," he commanded.

"But—" Teeg began; thought better of it when he saw Nath arch a single eyebrow. He gave a deep bow and shuffled backward through the door.

"My taercenn," Gryffid repeated, but this time it was a polite way of saying, "and . . . ?"

"You have an elf you trust?" Nath asked him.

"I trust him enough to bring Rhys down," Gryffid said. "Aeloch is his name. He's come far in a short time."

"Make sure he's prepared to deal with the druids. They can be prickly," Nath said. "You and I, however, will be elsewhere."

"Taer?"

"This traitor," Nath said, and allowed himself a sigh of exasperation. He produced a scroll from Teeg's desk and, dipping a quill into an inkwell, began to write. "He has escaped death, and he has done it often."

"He has, taer," Gryffid nodded. "Taer, does this have to do with your—"

"Then we must be prepared, mustn't we?" Nath asked pointedly. He finished writing, and handed the scroll to Gryffid. The taercenn nodded, bidding the daen to read the message. It read:

> *The cenn is not to be trusted, though he must be tolerated for now. If he knows of the plan, there's a chance the stranger or the traitor will be able to divine it.*
>
> *Carry through with the rooftop ambush, but keep half your forces back, including your vinebred.* All *of your vinebred. Rendezvous at the following position:*

The remainder of the message described where Gryffid's pack was to lie in wait. Nath was leaving nothing to chance. Gryffid only hoped that when Rhys finally paid for his treachery, he would be there to see his former daen destroyed, whether the battle druids did the job, or Nath, or Gryffid himself. Every hour Rhys continued to exist was an insult to the Gilt Leaf elves and the memories of the noble hunters who had fallen victim to his abominable magic.

Even those elves who concealed their own blight, for the good of the nation. It was a hypocrisy with which Gryffid was slowly coming to terms, and which bothered Nath not in the slightest.

* * * * *

"How many hours have we got now?" Rhys asked. He squinted into the sinking sun and the piercing winds, involuntary tears streaking his face. He would have given a week's thread for a pair of the silver goggles his quarry had pulled down over her eyes once she'd taken to the air.

"It's sure to be inexact," Maralen said, "but if you assume the kithkin told you the truth, and we guess on the low side—that is, about half a day—then the flamekin has perhaps an hour or three left.

"Why can't we catch up to them? She's flying a *bow*."

"Faster!" Iliona cried in a high-pitched, ear-splitting voice that was as close as she could come to a bellow. "You pathetic flock of dung beetles! You can fly faster than this! What are you, flying squirrels? Are you fat, lazy kithkin? Put your *wings* into it!"

"You heard her!" Veesa shouted in support.

"Yeah," Endry added, "flap those wings, you bogging boggarts!"

" 'Boggarts'? Endry, there's no need to insult them," Veesa said.

"I'm just getting into the spirit of it," Endry replied.

"They're volunteers," Veesa said. "Poor blossoms, they can't even talk yet."

"Isn't that a little naïve, Veesa?" Endry asked innocently.

"Bog you."

"Bog you!"

"Will you two focus, for bog's sake?" Iliona hissed.

"Sorry Iliona," the twins replied in unison, but one of them— Rhys could not tell which—added, "Bog you twice."

The trio was positioned at the fore of the flying pair, barking at the two dozen other, much younger faeries hauling Maralen and Rhys. As the clique was only too happy to point out, they could easily have carried Rhys alone, but not as far as he'd wanted to go. It was a nerve-wracking mode of travel for the passengers, but it was efficient. Rhys could not remember when he'd ever been in such an improbably deadly position, but he had to admit they never would have made it back to town in time had they not risked this insane plan. Rhys had to admit privately that he was impressed the trio had been able to call forth so many of their kin to help, but figured the other faeries were merely hoping to be there when the elves hit the ground.

They were moving fast—very fast—and the faeries showed no sign of tiring as yet, but they had lost much valuable time finding the kithkin traitor. They had drawn within a quarter-mile of Brigid's wingbow, but for the last half hour, they'd gotten no closer.

Worse, there was really nothing they could do to stop the kithkin at this distance. Rhys was all too aware that he had no bow, and the few weapons Sygg had provided them weren't any use at this distance. He'd considered sending some of the faerie to harass the kithkin, but that raised the uncomfortable question: Even if he could do so, didn't that put Ashling at risk? Killing Brigid would obviously do the flamekin no good, and a drop from this height would likely break her dying body beyond repair. And if the fall did not kill her, the time lost would do the trick. The hunter's instinct wanted to track this traitor and slaughter her, but his reasoning mind told him the best course of action was to follow her. After all, Rhys had been right about one thing: If Ashling was going to be healed, Kinsbaile was the most likely place, and the kithkin was taking her there anyway. The sensible course was to follow and arrive at the same time, taking Ashling back from the treacherous archer and finding elemental magic that could reignite her dying fires. With any luck, the kithkin would be too busy listening to tales to notice. As for the elves occupying the town . . . that was the another difficult question.

The only answer he had would take him even further down the irredeemable path of the kin-slayer.

"In for a thread, in for a coil," Rhys muttered.

* * * * *

"Gaddock Teeg, you said the elves would be gone by now," Colfenor said softly, or as softly as he could. "All but my apprentice, and he was to have other duties. He was not to return here." The kithkin cenn had taken advantage of Nath's dismissal to consult the yew, and to warn him the time was imminent. But thus far Teeg had heard only criticism. How tired he was of criticism! Yet still the yew went on. "Why do they still hold this town hostage? Where is Rhys of the Gilt Leaf?"

"On his way, though I fear for his life. As to the elves themselves, what can I do, Sage Colfenor?" Teeg asked. It took all of his considerable speaking ability to keep the quaver out of his voice. "They are here. They want in. And if you can't stop them, how can I?"

"You know better than most that the kithkin are not weak," Colfenor said. "So, please, do not insult me, Teeg."

"Of course not, my sage," Teeg stammered. "I merely—"

"It is no matter," the yew rumbled dismissively, turning his eyes to the elves taking positions on the surrounding rooftops. "He has become sentimental about this flamekin, as I predicted he would. He will not risk killing her. I can feel it. He has no idea I can read him so easily at this distance."

"Archer Baeli will bring the flamekin in time, my sage," Teeg interjected. "Every last kithkin in town is willing her to succeed, and the thoughtweft is a powerful thing."

"It is, at that," Colfenor admitted. "But do not overestimate that power. It relies on numbers, and numbers can be reduced."

"Of course, of course," the cenn said distractedly. "But as for the other . . . visitor, we are ready for that, as well."

"I have no doubt," the treefolk replied.

"Your apprentice," Teeg said. "Are you not concerned? The elves—"

"I do not make my choice of students lightly, Teeg," Colfenor said. "Rhys will survive, despite your attempts to eliminate him."

"What? But Sage, I did not—"

"You did, and Brigid Baeli attempted to carry out your order. Do not lie to me. If I'd expected you to succeed, I would never have allowed your moths to escape my sight."

"But—"

"It is done," Colfenor rumbled, "and I have greater concerns than your treachery at the moment. But betray me again, and it will be the last time."

"I . . . yes, Sage Colfenor. I am sorry."

"Sorry, perhaps, that you were caught," Colfenor chided. "But that is beside the point. Regardless, my student has some added protection."

"The Mornsong?" Teeg asked. "That stranger?"

"The one called Maralen. She is a mystery to me. All I can sense is that she is strong, stronger than she has let on. And she is determined to keep Rhys alive."

"You put your faith in this stranger, my sage?"

"She has every reason to ensure Rhys's survival." The red yew said. He took one last look at the hunters and druids lining the rooftops, then turned his wooden face back to the cenn, gazing just over Teeg's head. When he spoke next, it was more loudly, jovial and friendly. "That's enough, Cenn. I believe, as usual, your front-row seat is available."

The yew chuckled, and several dozen kithkin voices laughed in agreement. Teeg took a look around and realized that in the few minutes he'd spent talking to Colfenor, the square had become packed with kithkin gathered to hear the tales. The elves appeared to have fallen still on the rooftops, waiting to spring their trap.

Teeg nodded graciously to the yew, and turned to the towns-folk with the most charming smile he could wring out of the moment. "Thank you all for coming," he said. "It is time for another unforgettable evening of tales—the first evening of this year's Festival of Tales, which I think we can all agree should prove a rousing success!" Teeg waited a few moments for applause that didn't come, and then he drove on. "Let us thank the Sage Colfenor for gracing us with his own tales and, of course, his presence." A smattering of applause rolled through the square this time, including some surprised claps from strag-glers piled up on the fringes of the ever-growing audience.

With that, Teeg bowed, bowed again, and moved to the com-fortable, cushioned seat that was reserved exclusively for him. There was no more applause, but a burgeoning sense of antici-pation spread rapidly through the town. The thoughtweft was strong in Kinsbaile, and had never been stronger when every kithkin in sight was eagerly awaiting the start of the first day of tales, especially those tales that would involve their hero, the one and only Brigid Baeli. And somewhere in the distance, Teeg knew the Hero of Kinsbaile felt the strength of their belief, even if Teeg and Colfenor had twisted that belief to cause the hero to act egregiously out of character.

* * * * *

"We're close to Kinsbaile now," Rhys agreed. "It looks like we're heading straight to the town square. Iliona!"

"Yes taer, Captain Rhys, taer," the faerie responded smartly.

"Don't call me 'Captain,' " Rhys said. "Now, listen. This is going to be tricky. As soon as Brigid and Ashling hit the ground, we have to do the same. We'll then have to convince the kithkin to help us save the flamekin. I doubt they're going to be open to the idea, to say nothing of what the elves are going to try. But we're not here to stay, or to listen to tales."

"I suppose you'll need a ride back then?" piped one of the faeries clinging to his shoulder.

"Quiet, you," Iliona snapped.

Rhys sighed. The closer they got to Kinsbaile, the stronger the sense that Colfenor had betrayed him grew. "We have to find a kithkin who can contact this elemental fire, however it's done."

"And then we all return to the Bosk?" Maralen asked.

"If we make it back to the river." Rhys nodded. "And if Sygg has returned to Kinsbaile."

"You don't trust your own mentor, Rhys," the Mornsong stranger said. "It's written all over your face. Why are you determined to get back to the Bosk? For him?"

"I swore an oath," Rhys said, "one of many. And it's not negotiable on my end, even if Colfenor knew what Brigid was planning. And I'm still not sure he did."

"So what do you want us to do, taer?" Iliona asked.

"Keep us on the kithkin's tail, and do *not* overcome her as she slows—we don't want to knock her out of the sky."

As if on cue, twin blasts of dark green energy slammed into Rhys and Maralen simultaneously, and two dozen young faeries died in an instant, without even time to squeal as the druidic magic dried them to twigs. The energy had only stunned Rhys, but now they were falling, and falling faster than he would have liked. Rhys saw kithkin gathered around a familiar red yew that turned his face upward and locked his eyes with Rhys's own.

Try not to tense up, Colfenor's voice rang in his head.

* * * * *

"Rhys?"

A pair of hands shook him by the shoulders.

"Rhys!" the woman said more urgently. He recognized the voice, but he couldn't remember to whom it belonged. Maralen? Yes, Maralen—that was her name.

Rhys blinked open eyes wet with blood. His own. He gingerly touched a nasty gash that ran between the stumps of his horns from which the blood flowed freely, and instinctively whispered a minor suture spell—one that required no reagents—that closed the wound. Rhys would need to apply real stitches or better healing magic later, but for the moment it would keep the blood out of his eyes and in his head if he was careful.

He blinked again, and the red haze cleared away in an instant. Rhys remembered where he was and how he had gotten there. The faeries—

The faeries that had carried them were no more, and the Vendilion clique was nowhere in sight. Rhys and Maralen lay in a small circle of sponge moss that had miraculously saved them from much more than bruises. Dozens of wide-eyed kithkin surrounded them.

Rhys saw Colfenor, along with Brigid and the motionless form of Ashling. A few of the kithkin had helped the archer to her feet, while others had taken Ashling and were . . . propping her up against Colfenor's trunk?

"Colfenor," Rhys croaked. "Why?"

There was no answer, mental or otherwise, for several seconds. Then, just as Rhys and Maralen had regained their footing, there was an answer of sorts, but not from Colfenor.

"Perhaps a better question," Nath asked as he stepped from the front door of the cenn's office, "is how you ever thought you would leave here alive, kin-slayer."

Rhys ached to the bone. He'd lost more blood than he even

knew he had, and he had yet to recover from the full expenditure of energy he'd used to patch up Brigid's arm—another "good deed" that was going to bring evil returns in the long run. Maralen appeared just as weary.

Defiantly, he turned to his former taercenn. "Call me what you will," he said, "but you're not keeping me from the flamekin. You know me, Nath, and I know you, even if you won't speak my name. Even in this condition, I can beat you in a fair fight."

"You think this is a 'fair fight'?" Nath said, and then he chuckled.

Nath snapped his fingers, and Rhys heard a familiar voice— Gryffid's—issue the order to drop glamers.

The moment he did, Rhys saw that he, and probably Kinsbaile, to say nothing of Maralen or the dying Ashling, were utterly outnumbered.

Elves were everywhere, of course, stepping out from behind their invisibility glamers to aim arrows and swords in his direction. More disconcerting were the vinebred. Vinebred were artful and beautiful, but these had been created with only murder in mind, and that they were revealed to be standing in the middle of Kinsbaile sent a wave of revulsion through Rhys. He'd never particularly cared for the vinebred, though he could appreciate them aesthetically. It was not the appearance, but the very idea of the vinebred that made him so uneasy. He disliked any form of magic that prevented a hunter from being a hunter. With the creation of vinebred, elves became slave masters and borderline necromancers. Rhys counted at least ten, many of whom were stationed outside major buildings bordering the square. True, they were effective, and a way to make even the most useless beings serve a beautiful purpose for the Gilt Leaf nation. Still, it truly bothered Rhys that Nath had obviously chosen to rely on them so heavily.

Finally, Rhys spotted the daen who had issued the order to drop glamers. Gryffid strolled through the wreckage, a silver saber in his hand, clearly intent on challenging Rhys right then and there.

"Well," Rhys said, stooping momentarily to scoop up a loose piece of cobblestone that would serve as a weapon until he could get a better one, "I don't suppose we could discuss this like rational elves."

"I'm going to enjoy watching you die," Gryffid said, "filth." The daen took another step forward, but Nath stopped him in his tracks.

"Daen Gryffid," the taercenn said, "give Rhys your sword."

Rhys could not tell which had shocked his former friend more: that Nath had called Rhys by name, or that the taercenn had ordered Gryffid to give up his weapon.

"Taer," he objected, "the outlaw—"

"Give him your sword, *Daen,*" Nath said. "I have decided to grant this elf a hunter's death."

"He called you an 'elf,' " Maralen whispered. "That's good, isn't it?"

"I suppose," Rhys replied. "And I'd be ecstatic if it weren't for the 'death' part."

CHAPTER 18

Rhys stared coldly at the grip of Gryffid's proffered sword. His former friend marched straight up to him until the weapon was less than an unwavering inch from Rhys's face. Rhys made sure his head remained just as still as the blade, the bridge of his nose and the sword's center fixed in perfect, static balance. His eyes bored into Gryffid's, and Rhys spoke. "Maralen," he said, "get out of here. Do it now."

"I won't leave you here alone," Maralen replied.

"That choice is not yours to make." Nath's deep, smooth voice was for once more snarl than thunder. "Rhys and all who stand with him will answer for his crimes."

"Take the blade, traitor." Gryffid thrust the sword handle forward until it brushed Rhys's nose. "I want to see you bleed."

The main force of elves stood aside as the taercenn swept down the stairs and on through their ranks. The Exquisite stopped twenty feet from Gryffid and Rhys, glorious in his gleaming armor and fearsome in the torchlight. His horns shone like polished steel.

"Daen Gryffid." Nath's voice was clipped and formal. "Take your pack to the gate. If the Mornsong attempts to pass, kill her. If those mewling faeries interfere, kill them as well." Rhys saw the clique now, flying in a circle of mourning overhead, keening on the edge of elf hearing for their lost kin.

"Gladly, taer." Gryffid dropped the silver blade and turned away before it landed on the ground. Rhys did not move. His eyes were fixed on Nath. The taercenn's expression was fierce and hungry, but he stood absolutely still, regal and magnanimous in his patience.

Had he been an onlooker instead of a principal, Rhys would have pitied the scene: a lone, ragged outlaw against the magnificent commander of the Blessed in full martial regalia. He pushed this image aside. His status in the nation had no bearing anymore, especially not here. Nath and Gryffid meant to utterly destroy him. Rank and respect would not save him, nor would the lack of it do him much harm—he would stand or fall solely on his skill, speed, and strength. If Nath and Gryffid truly were superior, then Rhys would die . . . and part of him knew that perhaps he ought to.

By the infernal bog, his life would not end before he solved the riddles that had undone it . . . Nor would he allow Ashling or Maralen to suffer that same fate in his name.

"Maralen," Rhys said, "this is my affair, and I alone must settle it." Rhys broke eye contact with Nath and turned to Maralen. "Don't argue."

"All right," Maralen said. "But we're not through, you and I. I'll find you when this is all over."

Rhys nodded. "Until then."

He heard the faeries' wings buzz and then a rash of excited voices.

"Faeries, away!"

"Twins, we have our orders! Let's get this fat elf on the road!"

* * * * *

Gryffid snarled and sprang past Rhys, his squad moving behind him in perfect formation to follow his orders, even as the faeries boldly made it clear that no one was going through the gate.

Nath marched forward until he stood ten paces from Rhys. "Now, kin-slayer," he said, "pick up the sword."

Rhys glanced down at the silver weapon. He had been torn between two competing disciplines for most of his life: the profound self-reflection of the treefolk sage and the strict military pragmatism of the elf nation. Colfenor's teachings had brought him to this disaster, in a sense, but they had also sustained him through the trials along the way. There was no reason to give up those teachings to resume the role of the warrior. The two paths he'd followed converged within him, and he drew strength from each.

The blighted elf crouched slowly, deliberately, and took hold of the silver sword. Clenching it tight, Rhys stood, hefting the broad blade, testing its weight, and eyeing its keen edge with an appreciative eye. It was a marvelous weapon, worthy of a Faultless daen, maybe even worthy of an Exquisite general.

Rhys slashed the air. He nodded to Nath, and the army of elves and vinebred backed away, forming a circle around the two combatants.

Rhys's mind whirred as he worked through a plan of attack. He was sure he was at least Nath's equal, but there was no way the taercenn would allow himself to be defeated in this arenalike setting. An outlaw like Rhys had no rights, and an Exquisite like Nath owed him no fair consideration. If things went poorly for Nath, his second-in-command would almost certainly step in to preserve the taercenn's honor. Nath might object or even kill the interfering party afterward . . . But Rhys and the others would be just as dead.

There was only one way to ensure Nath would attack alone, one way to establish that Nath and only Nath would strike a lethal blow.

The taercenn drew his own silver sword, one that was even larger and more impressive than Rhys's borrowed blade. "Begin," he said. "I won't sully my sword with the first blow."

Rhys shook his head. "No, taercenn. I will not give you the satisfaction. You promised me a hunter's death."

"Your blasphemy knows no limit," Nath said. "You are nothing. You have no say in what constitutes a hunter's death."

"Nor do you, Nath. You call yourself a hunter? What have you ever run down that wasn't half-tamed and fat from a game-keeper's food trough? You've spent too much time in your palace, Exquisite. Here in the woods, we hunt things that hunt back.

"I don't need to beat you," Rhys said loudly. "I only need to escape you. If you're half the hunter you pretend to be, your victory is assured. Otherwise . . . your pack will see you for the weak, house-bound dullard you are."

"You will be silent!" Nath roared. He raised his sword and took a step forward.

"Here," Rhys shouted. "Let me sound the horn." He drew back Gryffid's sword and slung it forward, putting his entire weight and all of the strength he had into the throw. The glittering blade tumbled end over end, whirring toward Nath's face. The taercenn nimbly stepped aside, letting the sword fly past him. It buried itself in the trunk of a nearby oak, sending a shudder up the tree that shook several leaves free.

Rhys sprang toward the river as soon as the blade left his hand. He reached the edge of the hunters' circle and barreled into the throng of watching elves, knocking several back and clearing a small space where he could maneuver. Insults and blades shot past him as he climbed up onto the shoulders of two vinebred winnowers. He planted his right foot on a vinebred's head, bunched the long muscles in both legs, and sprang high into the air over the heads of Nath's packs.

Rhys landed clear of the throng and rolled to his feet. Voices raged and snarled behind him; swords cleared their scabbards all at once. Rhys saw the river approaching as he ran, and he dived, spearing through the air with his arms extended over his head. He hit the water and sliced through it, working against the current as he stayed under water for as long as possible.

When he surfaced, the sounds of pursuit were louder and angrier than ever. A few torches and arrows splashed around him, but the current and the wind and his own irregular path frustrated his pursuer's aim.

He heard an actual horn peal, the clean, pure sound of an Exquisite lord calling his dogs to heel.

"Coward!" Nath raged. "I will use your remains as mulch in the nettle orchards." There was a pause, and then the horn pealed again. In response, Rhys heard the entire pack surge forward, their feet shaking the ground and cries of bloodlust on their lips.

Rhys redoubled his efforts, pulling his long, lean body across the river. As he splashed up on the opposite bank, he turned back to Kinsbaile. Dozens of the elves were already crossing the river, swimming as Rhys had. Nath himself had mounted his long-legged cervin, and, as Rhys watched, he spurred it into the water. When the river was up to the tall steed's chest, it bounded forward, raising a giant splash every time it launched or landed.

Rhys turned and sprinted into the forest. The hunt is on, he told himself. And I am the prey.

* * * * *

With the lead they had, Iliona and her siblings could have scoured half the forest before Gryffid and his pack caught up. Maralen had other ideas.

They had brought her along without hesitation, without even thinking about it, lifting the stranger with the same magic that they had used before—though this time it was the faeries who were bound and caged by Maralen.

"Here," Maralen said, as if asking for another lump of sugar in her tea, "set us down here."

"They're too close behind," Iliona said.

"I don't see Sygg yet."

"We have to get there first. I made a bet."

"Down," Maralen said. "Here."

The faeries slowed down and gingerly settled over the ground until Maralen's feet touched the soil.

"You know what you are to do," the dark-haired woman said.

"Yes," they answered together.

"Off you go, then. Out of sight. Stand ready for my signal." Maralen smiled slightly, but her voice was sharp and as cold as an icicle. "Don't disappoint me, my dears."

Iliona and her siblings spread out, rising up to the lowest branches of the tree behind Maralen and hiding themselves among the leaves. Nothing the stranger did made any sense to Iliona, but she did not dare disobey. Not yet.

Maralen leaned casually against the bole of the tree and waited. The sounds of vinebred feet shuffling drew near, and Iliona knew that meant the elves in the party were even nearer. Sure enough, moments later Daen Gryffid came out of the shadows, his long dagger ready by his side.

"You there," he called to Maralen, "stand where you are."

"Or what?" the woman replied. "You've already threatened

to kill me no matter what. You don't have a lot of threats left to make."

"Silence. Where are the faeries?"

"You see, you shouldn't order the silence and then ask the question." Maralen laughed. "Makes your meaning a little murky."

"Mornsong, I will kill you, but not before I learn where—"

"You're hopeless. Too bad," Maralen said. "They're gone. Went on ahead to find the merrow. Left me all alone."

"Really," Gryffid said. He waved his free hand and six elf archers stepped up behind him, their bows taut and their arrows trained on Maralen.

"No. Not really," Maralen said. *Now.*

Iliona, Endry, and Veesa flashed past the elves, with their blades drawn, briefly visible streaks of stardust that severed the bowlines of every archer before a single arrow saw flight. The projectiles never reached the ground, but seconds later, three of the six archers fell in perfect sequence, clutching at the arrows transfixing their necks from throat to spine. The faeries plucked three more shafts from the sixth archer's quiver, and a moment later the remaining three elves fell, screaming.

"That old trick," Veesa said. "You need some new material."

"That's a classic," Endry objected.

"What, in one ear and out the other isn't classic?"

Iliona paused, waiting for Maralen to contribute, to confirm or chastise this deviation from her orders. Of late she'd grown to expect whichever of the big folk was nearest would invariably tell her to shut up, or be quiet, or go away. That she could stand. But when nothing but silence came, she found it so unsettling—*especially* after such a brilliant trick—that Iliona ended the discussion before the stranger spoke up. "All right, then," she said with finality. "Classics."

Gryffid spat a curse at the faeries. He brandished his sword at Maralen and said, "They can't save you from this."

"Can too! Can too!"

"Just you watch!"

"Hush now," Maralen said. The faerie fell silent. "He's mine." She walked slowly around Gryffid, staying out of lunging range as she regarded him from head to toe, keeping his focus in motion. She walked in fits and starts to ensure he didn't time out her pace and strike that way. "So, how many more elves do you have, Daen Gryffid? You, personally, under your command? What does Nath allow you? A half dozen? More? I'm not counting you, of course."

"Enough to bury you and your insect familiars."

Maralen chuckled breezily. "I suppose the exact number doesn't matter . . . I just want to know how much it will take to clear you from the field."

Gryffid bristled. With a twitch of his horns, he summoned the rest of his rangers up to the edge of the shadows. His eyes flashed green, and Iliona knew he was calling upon the strength of the forest, on the elf magic that sustained his pack, and using it to make himself stronger, faster, and more formidable. He tensed to pounce, waiting for the next move the stranger or her faeries made so he could cut Maralen to pieces before any more of his elves fell.

"I know all about the Blessed, you see," Maralen said. "You've nothing left to show me."

Iliona felt the force swirling around Gryffid and heard his long muscles tense. She very much wanted to see Maralen run through with the elf's silver blade, but she couldn't allow that.

"Stay out of this for now," Maralen said to the faeries. Iliona forced herself to calm down, urging her siblings to do the same.

"Come on, then," Maralen said to Gryffid. "Let's sort this out, you and I. I don't have much time for you."

All three faeries let out the same small cry as the elf daen rushed forward. He was so fast, so sure, and it seemed like nothing could stop his blade from falling on Maralen's face. And if the daen missed, there were six battle-mad elves right behind him ready to finish the job.

But the stranger clasped her hands and then opened them again, casting them out on each side. Iliona saw a sphere of smoke and fog appear around Maralen, and she heard the rustling of a hundred brittle wings.

Gryffid was the first to reach the sphere, so he was the first to stop short. His pack rushed in around him and likewise became mired, their movements slow and sluggish. Their hooves all dug into the ground as they tried to continue forward, but their faces registered the bewilderment and panic of soldiers being ambushed from all sides.

Maralen laughed again.

"Go away, Daen Gryffid," she said. "I have important things to tend to and no use for you."

Maralen closed her eyes and spread her arms, palm forward. Hazy smoke drifted out from her fingertips and rolled over the elves. The elves cried out as their bodies were snared in the fog and their weapons fell from their hands, only to float in the arcane mists. Then Maralen clapped her hands and the elves disappeared.

Iliona blinked. When she opened her eyes, Maralen was standing alone, without a wisp of smoke in sight.

* * * * *

Rhys sprinted through the outermost edge of the forest that bordered Kinsbaile. He didn't need to spare his legs, and he did need to get as far ahead as he could before Nath and the hunting party caught up to him, so he did not restrain himself. The forest floor blurred below his feet, and sweat streaked across his sharp features.

He was alone and ridiculously outnumbered, but Rhys felt strong and unaccountably confident. He had never been the target of a hunt before, but that only meant no one had ever hunted prey quite like him. He knew how his people hunted, how to exploit their strict adherence to form. If Nath followed the traditional ways as rigidly as he enforced pack discipline, Rhys would have a chance.

As the woods around him grew thicker and his progress slowed, Rhys changed course. He dug his hooves in and turned around, racing back along his own path for twenty paces before springing up into the trees. He methodically scrabbled through the branches, working his steady way around and behind his pursuers. By the time the trackers realized he had doubled back, he would be right where he needed to be: at Nath's throat.

The four-footed tread of the cuffhounds worried him. They were the swiftest and surest of his pursuers, but he had no wish to harm the magnificent beasts. Rhys froze and stopped breathing as the hounds raced through the distant brush twenty yards below. He might have no choice if the hounds found him too far ahead of Nath. He swung out and hurled himself onto a new branch, putting more distance between himself and the dogs.

"There he is!" A chorus of elf voices answered the first, confirming what it saw, calling others to come and see, calling for Nath himself. Rhys's ears flattened, and he gathered his strength. This was not the way he had intended to fight this fight, nor where. The dogs were too close and Nath too far away.

So be it, he thought. He kicked his feet out as he swung by his arms from a stout, thick branch, turning a graceful somersault before landing lightly on his hooves, facing the trackers.

The one who had seen him first sprang forward with his sword extended. Rhys had no blade with which to parry, and he needed his arms undamaged, so he dropped to the ground and lashed out with both hooves. The elf tracker's knee cracked and bent backward, and he fell heavily on top of Rhys. Rhys caught the tracker's sword arm and twisted the long blade free. It fell with its tip in the dirt, and Rhys plucked it free as he rolled away from his stricken foe.

An archer stepped forward. "Bog it," he said, and as he nocked an arrow, four other elves did the same. Without another word, each drew back a bolt and simultaneously let them fly.

Rhys folded his arms tight against his ribs and threw himself to the side. He was quick enough to avoid the first three arrows, but the last two archers corrected their aim enough to follow him across the glade. One of these bolts ripped through his leggings and cut a shallow slash across his calf muscle. The other punched through the meaty part of his thigh, spinning him around so that he landed clumsily on his face.

Rhys instantly reached down with both hands, taking hold of the dripping arrowhead and the leafy plumes. He snapped the shaft off on either side of his leg, emptied his hands, and then he slid the remainder free from the raw muscle. It was quick, but it was not clean, and the searing throb left behind rendered the whole leg nearly useless.

The archers had prepared another volley, but their leader stopped them with a raised hand. Rhys watched the elf's ears twitch and his lips curl into a cruel smile.

"Leave him to the dogs," the elf said. Over the pounding in his ears—that was answered beat for beat by the drum in his leg—Rhys at last heard the sound of the sure-footed cuff-hounds bearing down on him. He struggled to his feet just as the first yellow-brown striped body bounded into view, followed immediately by four of his fellows. Their heads were sleek and triangular, their bodies long and lean and rippling under their silky pelts. They were the true Gilt Leaf hunters, beautiful and strong, disciplined and relentless, faster than lightning and far deadlier.

Rhys crouched as the lead dog came within striking distance. He pressed his palm into the wound on his leg, waited for the cuffhound to leap, and then sprang straight up into the air.

Nath's cuffhounds were exceptionally well trained. Though this was a most unexpected reaction from their prey, the dogs never wavered from their target. Sharp, canine teeth ripped through the flesh on his shins and ankles. They were painful wounds, but not lethal ones, only intended to bring the quarry down. Even the long, graceful muzzles that clamped onto his legs didn't bite hard enough to crack the bones. Rhys hung suspended for a moment, his lower half lost amid a swarm of snarling fur. He fell among the dogs, bitten and trampled as he curled into a ball and cradled his arms against his torso.

The assault continued until a strong, familiar voice called out, "Off." Nath's hounds responded instantly to their master's voice, disengaging from Rhys without doing any more damage. The cuffhounds retreated, growling as they backed away from him. Each hound then sat on its haunches in a semicircle around Rhys and fell silent.

Rhys looked up. Nath's assembled hunting party was spread out among the trees, surrounding the dogs, which in turn surrounded Rhys. The taercenn himself rode into the clearing on his sunrise yellow cervin, his cape sweeping majestically behind him. Nath dismounted ten paces from Rhys, disdainfully turning his back on his prey, and raised his arms in triumph, a ceremonial dagger clenched in his fist.

The pack cheered, and many of them hurled abuse at Rhys's huddled body. He unfolded himself and tried to rise, but his legs barely supported his weight. Grimacing in pain, Rhys settled onto his knees and cupped his elbows in his hands. The ground beneath him was wet and slick. He shuddered.

"You ran, rabbit," Nath said. "But now your race is run." His voice sang out loudly over the clearing. "Once you were an elf, a Faultless of the Gilt Leaf pack, but you deserve to be hunted like the low wretch you are. You will die here, outlaw. I call you traitor and kin-slayer. You will die wallowing in your own blood." He raised his voice in an order to his hunters. "I am the master of this hunt: the kill is mine." Returning to Rhys, he said, "And I swear to you: Once you are dead and we have desecrated your unworthy corpse, we will leave it here for the carrion birds."

Nath charged Rhys with a yell and lashed out with his dagger, aiming for one clean cut across the throat. Rhys slammed his hands into the ground, pushed himself up, and caught Nath's arm midswing, the tip of the dagger scoring the flesh on Rhys's jaw.

Rhys tightened his grip as Nath pressed down. His arms were still strong, however, and the taercenn could not force the blade any closer. When Nath reversed himself and tried to pull back, Rhys clung all the tighter, letting the taercenn haul him bodily off the forest floor.

"Why can't you just die?" Nath spat at him.

Rhys's right hand shot from Nath's arms to the taercenn's throat. Nath grunted and coughed, grasping Rhys's forearm with his free hand, allowing Rhys to settle back to the ground. Rhys prepared to haul himself back up, to force Nath to bear his weight, but the taercenn surprised him. Nath released the arm that was choking him and drove his sharp fist deep into Rhys's belly.

The punch forced all the air from Rhys's lungs, but he

maintained his grip on Nath. The taercenn drew his fist back and rammed it into Rhys's stomach again, and again. Each new blow weakened Rhys's grip. He coughed up a bloody froth, and his vision went red.

Digging his fingers into Nath's windpipe, Rhys let go of the taercenn's dagger arm and pulled himself up to Nath's chest. He wrapped his free arm around the taercenn's shoulder, then relaxed his grip on Nath's throat. He clamped on to Nath's right horn at the base just as the taercenn plunged his dagger into Rhys's lower back.

Rhys hissed in agony, but Nath's reaction was far more violent. With a sudden burst of strength, Nath tossed his head and lunged back, pulling Rhys along with him. Rhys used this momentum to pull himself farther up Nath's body. As the taercenn continued to thrash, Rhys slung himself around behind Nath and grabbed both of the taercenn's horns in an iron grip.

"Get off me! Get off!"

Rhys let his muscles go slack, his whole body hanging from the taercenn's horns. As his weight dragged Nath's head down, Rhys summoned all the strength in his arms and shoulders. When his useless legs hit the dirt, Rhys pivoted at the waist. He gave a short, brutal jerk, and a sickeningly loud crack echoed off the trees.

Nath screamed, as did all of the elves within eyeshot. The taercenn stumbled and flailed, but Rhys held on. There was something heavy and jagged in his hand, but amid the chaos he was unsure of what it was, unsure of his own senses. The furious sounds in the clearing died in his ears as Rhys raised his hand and stared at its contents.

Nath's horn had broken off near the base. It was solid and denser than Rhys expected.

Then Nath's dagger found his ribcage. Rhys felt cold pain spread through his chest. He opened his hand, let Nath's horn fall, and then he clamped it on to the taercenn's jaw.

Nath bit down on Rhys's thumb. It was painful but bearable. A chill, drowsy feeling spread down Rhys's spine, from his brain to his stomach. He tightened his grip on Nath's chin and remaining horn.

"This kill is mine," Rhys said, and then he twisted the taercenn's head until Nath's face glared down over his own shoulder blades.

Taercenn Nath of the Gilt Leaf's body went slack, and he let it fall to the ground. He worked his thumb out of Nath's teeth and rolled clear, scooping up the broken horn as he went.

The lead archer was the first to charge, and he closed on Rhys a full five steps before anyone else. He caught the sharp tip of Nath's broken horn directly in the heart.

Rhys pulled himself up to one knee before the dead elf fell. He felt a dull throbbing in his broken horns. The duel had broken the glamer that had concealed his disfigurement. He wondered if Nath had seen the truth as he died.

Wobbling, still clutching the horn, Rhys stood on his shaky legs and pointed the tip of Nath's pride at the assembled hunters.

"Whoever else wants die on the taercenn's horn should step forward," he said.

The cuffhounds whined, and Rhys silenced them with a withering stare. Their pack leader was dead, blighted and murdered. There were hisses and whispers as the assembly saw the state of Rhys's horns, shorn of glamer. Eyeblight, they said. But it would take a stronger voice than Rhys's to make the cuffhounds attack him, and no such voice was present.

Rhys turned back to Nath's body. He stared at the hard,

withered features, and the cracked, crumbling horns. Rhys's glamer was not the only mask to have slipped during the fight. The glorious and noble Taercenn of the Gilt Leaf stood revealed as a hardened, weathered thing that looked as drawn and tough as a smoke-cured carcass.

Exquisite no longer. Rhys stared at Nath's appalling features, knowing exactly how and why the old man had hidden the signs of his visible decline. It didn't matter that he was as fast and as strong as any he commanded—he was wizened, drawn.

Generals like Nath had drummed into him the concept of Gilt Leaf honor, the notion that hiding behind glamer was beneath a hunter's dignity. Yet here Nath was, mourned despite his imperfection. Perhaps there was a place for Rhys in the Blessed Nation after all.

But not today. Rhys took a single step forward and almost lost his balance, but caught himself. He placed two fingers at the corners of his mouth and whistled. Nath's cervin snorted. "Here," he snapped. The confused animal pawed the ground and tossed its head, but it slowly moved closer to Rhys.

Fighting the urge to run or lunge, Rhys slowly took the two steps that separated him from the cervin. His arms were still strong. It was not difficult to swing himself up onto the cervin's back.

He recited one of the healing rituals, pressing his fingers deep into the arrow wound in his thigh. If his strength held, he would be able to walk again by the time he crossed the river.

"Burn Nath with honor," he said. He raised the taercenn's broken horn high for all to see. "No word of his disgrace need ever reach the nation. Or of his deception. If you value his memory, honor it."

The elf pack stood in mute shock.

"Eyeblight," a lone elf whispered. "Scarblade traitor."

"I am," Rhys agreed, "but I killed my enemy today. You will not have that pleasure."

He spurred the cervin so that it reared, and its flashing legs sent the elves around it scurrying for safety. Rhys guided the steed out of the clearing and back into the dense woods without resistance from the elves. He rode north, away from Kinsbaile in case the hunters did decide to pursue him. He would put some distance between them, and then double back once more for the village on one of the fastest mounts in all of Lorwyn.

CHAPTER 19

Ashling felt warmth within her icy stone prison, and with it a glimmer of something. Feeling anything was a breakthrough. Conscious thought was slow in returning, but it did return.

The glimmer was a thought that became a word. It was . . . hope. Hope in the form of a presence she had despaired on ever feeling again.

The wild elemental was near, the spirit that had first ignited her flames on the day she was born. It was with her here, wherever "here" was. It was close, very close.

I am here, Ashling called. It was a simple sentence, but it took some effort. The effort made her feel warmer.

Yet the elemental did not answer in words. Perhaps it did not have words, or the capacity to form them.

I need help, Ashling called again. *I am trapped somewhere . . . it feels like a block of ice. If you can reach me, free me—even a little of your power. The smallest blessing might be enough.*

The elemental responded with feelings: doubt, but determination. Its strength was faint but its will and its indomitable nature were still strong. It sent more sensations: the last warmth of the setting sun.

Sights and sounds filled Ashling's mind. Among the sights was a horrifying image she could not, at first, comprehend. A large red tree—no, a red *yew*, she realized—was in the center of the image, and propped up in front of its thick trunk was a lump of gray with a familiar shape that she could not place—not at first. Not until she pictured the shape enveloped in living flame, looking back at her from the surface of a calm reflecting pool. Ashling saw herself, and for the first time understood the nature of her imprisonment. The icy cell was her body, and if she could not make physical contact with another flamekin or the wild elemental soon—perhaps in only a few minutes—her fire would go out forever. She would be well and truly guttered.

Help.

Another feeling. One of recognition? Of flamekin, or of Ashling herself?

Help, the elemental called at last. *I can help.*

It might have just been echoing her own words back to her, but perhaps proximity to the flamekin had helped the elemental regain its language.

The elemental seemed to "speak" with great difficulty, as though the elemental were learning Ashling's language on the fly. The flamekin had not had the opportunity to commune with her elemental except in fleeting glimpses of emotion, sensation, and an elusive, indefinable call.

"Her" elemental—how ridiculous and even shameful it seemed, so near to this wondrous goal, to have ever used a word denoting ownership in connection to a being of such mysterious, primal power. The great spirit existed in ways Ashling's mind could only begin to experience as simple shapes, sounds, and colors: as pain, as feelings, as emotions, as tactile sensations. To sharpen her focus, to understand, was beyond her.

A jolt of agony pierced Ashling's consciousness, as if she had been stabbed. It was excruciating and made her rejoice. Physical pain meant physical feeling. She was getting warmer.

Could combustion be far behind?

* * * * *

Gaddock Teeg screamed the scream he had inherited from his paternal grandmother and leaped backwards nearly three feet, leaving a pair of empty sandals where he had previously stood.

"When are you going to tell me what's really going on here?" Brigid asked.

"What do you mean?" Teeg said, his heart leaping into his throat with the strength of a long jumper.

"That's what I'm asking you. Should I ask the yew?" Brigid said.

"Wait, what?"

"Oh yes, the yew's not speaking to anyone. And he's got a flamekin propped up against his trunk, and *you're* letting him lure a damned wild elemental into the middle of Kinsbaile during a festival!"

"That is technically my right as cenn," Teeg objected, "as specified by ordinance—"

"Shut up and listen to me, Gaddock," Brigid said. "What I'm asking you is why? Why did I turn on people who were willing to risk their lives for me? What's in it for . . . well, anybody?"

"Because I asked him to," Colfenor said. "And I too have turned on allies. Friends. And I am going to die."

"Do you hear how you're not answering my question?" Brigid said. *"Why, Colfenor?"*

The yew cocked an eye at the kithkin archer. "Do you know how treefolk are born, Brigid Baeli?"

"What?" the kithkin snapped. "Well, I imagine it has to do with two treefolk who love each other very much—"

"You are arrogant, little archer," Colfenor said. "We begin life as trees. Ordinary trees that choose, after careful consideration and long years of apprenticeship to older masters, whether to take their first steps or leave their roots permanently in the ground."

"You have some kind of awakening," Brigid said. "I know this story."

"Yes. But we are still trees. We still . . . germinate and pollinate. And we produce offspring."

"So you're doing this to impress the kithlings back home?"

"Of course not," the yew rumbled. "I'm doing this to awaken anew. This world . . . the roots and leaves feel elemental changes long before your clumsy kithkin senses. There is a change on Lorwyn's horizon. A new world on the rise. I will be a part of that world. I will awaken again, newly grown and ready to carry the old world into what comes after."

"A new world?" Brigid asked, one eyebrow raised, which for her was the height of incredulity.

"Nothing more, nothing less."

"So you say."

Outside, the Kinsbaile thoughtweft hung in the air like scented smoke. One by one, the inhabitants of the town forgot about the recent strife and returned to the square. The dead were mostly ignored—there would be time for all that after the last tale. The kithkin returned to their various perches and seats around Colfenor. A kithkin matron with three excitable children led them around a particularly grisly display of carnage, triggering questions the woman would be forced to answer until Colfenor spoke.

And he did speak, and the story was the tale of Colfenor's life. The kithkin soaked in every autobiographical word, breathlessly. They delighted in this last tale the red yew granted them, relishing it with even more enthusiasm than they'd greeted the first with.

Brigid was less enthusiastic, though she felt the siren call of her fellow kithkin and the weave of their minds, calling her to join them. Yet she could not, and would not. Hers was another song, the rollicking adventures of the Hero of Kinsbaile.

Even as the last few listeners settled into their seats for the tale of Colfenor's life she felt herself backing away. Her movements drew a few sidelong glances but no more. Kinsbaile was enraptured by hearing how Colfenor had changed the course of the Swiftbend River to prevent a flood that threatened an entire field of birch saplings. And this just in his third season of awakened life!

Brigid had shaken serious qualms about confronting the yew directly, and it had not been easy to do so. But she'd heard Colfenor's reason—insofar as he was telling her the truth—and she could not help but consider it selfish. This "reawakening" the yew had planned implied that he would not otherwise survive this change, whatever it was.

Had she turned on the others, spied on them, and betrayed them, so a single being could cheat death by skirting some undefined catastrophe? And what kind of fate did that leave the rest of them?

As she reached the outer edges of the square and took in the scene, she felt the thoughtweave slip into the back of her mind. She'd spent much of her life relying on it, using the urging of the kithkin who loved, respected, and admired her to guide her decisions and give her strength. Had they all made any effort to keep Brigid there, to pull her into the group consciousness that let the kithkin enjoy the tale as one, she would never have been able to resist, but the more the collective's influence receded, the stronger she felt. It felt strange, because it was her own strength, unaided by anyone's fawning hero worship.

Colfenor held the kithkin of Kinsbaile rapt—all save one, who turned on her heel and departed, unnoticed and unseen, to see if there was any way to undo some of the damage she'd caused.

* * * * *

"*I'm* not being reasonable?" Rhys snarled. "You betrayed us! You hurt Sygg. You *dropped Ashling in the river!*"

"It was my duty," Brigid said. "I've since learned what that meant, and I didn't like it. Don't be an idiot. There's still a chance to save the flamekin, and to prevent your mentor from doing whatever it is he's doing. He thinks the world is going to change without him, and he's taking steps to make sure it doesn't. Hang the rest of us. I'm offering to help. Do you want to rescue Ashling or not?"

"Colfenor wouldn't do this without good reason," Rhys said. "Therefore, he must have a good reason. I just can't believe Colfenor would willingly do what you say he is."

"Believe it," Brigid said. "Told me himself."

"Bog it," Rhys said, and raised Brigid's kithkin dagger. He handed it to the archer and said, "Let's go."

* * * * *

Live.

The sensation flooded Ashling's body, exquisite agony she could feel from the tips of her toes to the top of her head.

She had a body. She had toes. She had skin, legs, and hands.

As yet, she had no sight, and no hearing but the voice of the elemental inside her head. She was not yet alight. But she was alive. If only she could get closer to the elemental. Help it help her.

Can you hear me?

The presence of the elemental drew closer, inch by agonizing inch. With every movement the agony of recombustion flooded Ashling, each time feeding the tiny, self-sustaining fire within her breast.

Quicksilver. She'd been poisoned with quicksilver, and doused in the river. The fires within were burning the poison away. Soon, there would be no stopping the flames within from spreading without. Colfenor would be scarred at the very best, burned alive at the very worst.

Wait, you must stay back.

As she said the last words, Ashling heard the screams. She heard them in her ears, and not just her mind. And then, in a flood of light and color, and an explosion of heat, vision returned. Though blurred, there was no mistaking the shape before her. It was the elemental, and it was running straight for her. The same elemental whose incorporeal form had somehow found her on the river.

"Oh no," Ashling said, and erupted in flame as it passed through her, and on through Colfenor.

* * * * *

"Oh no," said Rhys.

Ashling was not dead, not by far. He arrived just in time to see what appeared to be a gigantic white horse with a mane and hooves of fire run straight through her and Colfenor, igniting both of them. Was this the flamekin's long-sought elemental?

It should have been impossible, but Rhys could not deny what he saw with his own eyes. The spirit was like a horse but more solidly built, with thick, one-toed hooves and a long, handsome face. Its head and spine were wreathed by its own living flames, flames that fed into Ashling's body like liquid down a drain. The flames surged through the flamekin into Colfenor.

"We're going to rescue Ashling," Rhys said. "Everyone who isn't afraid of burning to death, follow me."

Too late, Colfenor said, and for the first time Rhys heard the grate of frenzy in his voice, the touch of madness that accompanied grand triumph and crushing defeat alike. *The seed is planted, the fire cannot be stopped. The change will come. Lorwyn will endure. I will endure.* Something like Colfenor's amiable chuckle rumbled in Rhys's head. *Be seeing you, Rhys.*

"You'd better hope not, old log," Rhys muttered. He dug his heels into the ground and shouted, "Go!"

They charged toward the grand pyre as one; Rhys, Brigid, Maralen, and the faerie. The archer fired arrow after arrow as she advanced, sinking her shafts into the wood that supported Ashling's bonds. The faeries bedeviled Colfenor's face and hands, straying from their tight, circular formation to strike and stab at the flamekin's wrists and ankles, yelping in pain as the flames singed their sharp fingertips.

Rhys threw himself onto Colfenor's burning body, pinning Ashling beneath him. Snarling, he pulled at her unmoving body. She was as heavy as iron, hot as a forge, but he did not waver. The sickening smell of burning flesh reached his nostrils, and he felt his hands splitting, cracking, and blistering away in the flames.

The flamekin's eyes opened. "Rhys," she said groggily.

"Run," Rhys told her. "Get up and run. I can't do it alone."

Still dazed, Ashling struggled to her feet. The flames made Rhys's eyes water and swell. He felt rather than saw Brigid and Maralen alongside him, straining to help her stand.

Ashling's upper body collapsed against Rhys, searing his flesh where she touched it.

He felt a sudden soothing chill fall over his body. The faeries were casting a glamer on him, one that would prevent him from noticing his injuries. It wouldn't keep the fire from consuming him, but it did give him the respite he needed to gather his thoughts and marshal his strength for one final effort. Rhys allowed himself to fall, still cradling Ashling's fiery head against his shoulder, and he shouted, "Her feet! Get her feet!"

The weight and angle of Ashling's body made it easier. Together, Maralen and Brigid lifted Ashling's feet. Rhys toppled back, still clutching Ashling to him despite the fire, and landed heavily on his back.

"Get him out of here," Maralen said. "Get us all out of here."

Swooning, choking, Rhys saw the faeries flutter down and surround his party. Without so much as a gibe or a titter, the trio surrounded them with faerie magic. Rhys felt himself grow weightless, though as the levitation spell took hold the pain-dampening spell failed. Stinging, aching agony crawled across his entire body, and the smell of his own cooking skin filled his head. Rhys let himself float away, and deep, long-needed slumber soon claimed him.

The vision that followed him into his dreams was of Colfenor, tall and proud, unwavering as he burned terrible bright. Wind-driven flames stretched from his boughs to the edges of the kithkin buildings nearby.

The kithkin panicked.

* * * * *

Daen Gryffid found the remainder of the Hemlock Gilt Leaf pack in the woods outside Kinsbaile. He saw trackers and rangers and hunters alike standing about, aimless, undisciplined, and wringing their hands. The daen had two broken ribs, and his left eye was swollen shut, but Gryffid stood proud and straight, his voice strong.

"What is happening here? The kithkin are rioting . . . literally rioting in the streets of Kinsbaile!" He grabbed a stunned hunter by the arm and demanded, "Where is the taercenn?" The hunter was speechless, and Gryffid knocked the fool to the ground.

No one would answer his simple question. He heard whispers, "Outlaw," and "Eyeblight." He repeated his question for the seventh time, and then an unfamiliar elf finally stepped forward. The warrior's eyes were sunken and hooded, and he silently motioned for Gryffid to follow him.

He led the daen to a clearing that was packed tight with kneeling elves. At the far end of the clearing, flat on his back atop a pile of kindling, was Taercenn Nath. Broken, diminished, disgraced . . . and most certainly dead.

The silent elf warrior turned and quit the clearing without a word. Gryffid numbly walked forward alone, his mouth opening and closing as he struggled for words. At last he simply stood at perfect attention, the only way to keep the rage and sorrow fighting for prominence in his proud Gilt Leaf heart from overwhelming him.

"Light the fire," he whispered. "Let no one else see Taercenn Nath like this."

Lit torches approached. They stretched out to the edges of the pyre, but Gryffid stopped them with a single, sharp word.

"Hold," he said. He stepped up onto the pile of sticks and branches. He leaned over Nath, took hold of the taercenn's silver sword, and pulled it from the dead leader's hands.

Flames licked up behind Gryffid as he turned and faced the pack, Nath's sword extended. "This is for the traitor Rhys," he said, "the kin-slayer. The eyeblight. Now many, many times over. We will repay him for every murder, every injury, and we will do it slowly. But know this, my pack: The elf who kills the eyeblight before I do will suffer the same punishment ten times over."

The fire crackled below him and Gryffid leaped down to the forest floor. "I will bury this blade in his heart," the daen said. "And if I have to destroy half of Lorwyn to find him . . . then woe betide half of Lorwyn." Gryffid slammed the point of the blade into the ground. Standing upright, tall and proud, Gryffid cast his arms up and bathed in the fury of his impending vengeance.

"Death to the eyeblight kin-slayer!" he roared.

In the woods outside Kinsbaile, a chorus of voices answered his call.

* * * * *

One day later, Rhys stepped off of Sygg's shapewater ferry onto the muddy ground of the Murmuring Bosk. Ashling, Brigid, and Maralen came after.

There was no shortage of hostile glares and muttered recriminations on this latest journey to the Bosk. Much had passed between the passengers and their captain, and settling each account would take far longer than this trip.

But they were here now. Apart from the black poplars (which had grown to a healthy height of nine feet since he last saw them), the Bosk was still ruined. The fires were all out, but that only meant there was less smoke and were more blackened limbs befouling the once-pastoral scene.

Still, the poplars were an encouraging sign. Rhys didn't trust his own judgment, as he desperately wanted to see new growth in the Bosk, but he had to admit that there were some small signs of improvement. Green shoots and buds were beginning to poke through the layer of carbon and soot, but there was no guarantee they'd survive.

He led the party to the spot where he'd planted Colfenor's seed cone. Sygg had questioned the wisdom of returning, and the others shared his opinion with varying levels of verbosity, but the simple fact was they didn't have any other place to go. At least here they could count on being left alone.

Rhys navigated his way through a lingering cloud of smoke and gazed upon the seed cone's planting bed. The faerie were right to marvel: a full-fledged yew sapling stood in the dirt, reaching over six feet high. It was slender and smooth and healthy, though it only had a few forks and branches.

"Is that normal?" Maralen said.

"No," Rhys said. "But what is anymore?"

Ashling stayed well clear of the sapling, either because she didn't trust Colfenor's offspring to treat her any better than he had, or because she didn't want to risk setting it alight. Either way, Rhys was the only one to walk out onto the bed and kneel before the sapling.

"It's growing fast," he said. "But it will take years, maybe decades, before it becomes conscious. And decades more before it will be able to walk freely through Lorwyn." And, he added privately, decades before it could speak with Colfenor's wisdom, or his arrogance. Perhaps that was for the best. At the moment Rhys could still not reconcile his mentor's betrayal with all the great red yew had been.

"So it's not normal," Maralen said. "But it is a good sign."

"Very good," Rhys said. He stood and peered into the sapling's smooth bark. If he used his imagination, he could almost make out the shape of the new treefolk's face. There were the eyes, and the nose, and the wide, crooked mouth, which would wait for many seasons before they finally sprang to life.

The ground shuddered, pushing Rhys off balance. He inadvertently steadied himself against the sapling.

The sapling promptly opened its eyes several seasons too early. "Ouch," it said. It spoke as if it had a mouthful of grapes.

Rhys shouted in surprise and sprang back. Unsteady on his feet and panting, he stared open-mouthed as the sapling's face moved, feature by feature, until its eyes were open, its nostrils flared, and its lips opened wide, splitting its smooth bark into a crooked smile.

The new yew blinked. It focused its dark, hollow eyes on Rhys. Then the sapling spoke. "Student of my seedfather," it said, "welcome to the Murmuring Bosk."

The treefolk leaned to one side and strained. The thickest of its roots popped free of the loose soil. It dredged itself out of the planting bed and settled onto the hard, ash-covered ground.

"Rhys," Ashling said, but the elf cut off her question before she could ask.

"I don't know," he said.

Rhys turned to Ashling, and to Brigid, but their faces were as lost and confused as his own. Only Maralen's seemed free from shock or awe, and only because it was so full of interest, excitement, and hungry enthusiasm. "Now this," she said, "is worth exploring."

Supple red bark squeaked against new wood as the sapling spread its arms in a wide, welcoming embrace.

LORWYN GLOSSARY

Arbomander: A giant amphibian native to Lorwyn's Wanderwine River. Arbomanders have been known to grow as long as one hundred feet, though tales tell of examples five times that size.

Archer: An elf hunter who specializes in use of the long bow instead of a sword. Kithkin employ their own archers for defense of their towns and villages, organized in a similar hierarchy but without elf caste distinctions.

Arrowgrass: A plentiful, sturdy wild grass of Lorwyn used by elves for arrow shafts.

Blessed Nation: Also "the Blessed." The Blessed Nation comprises all the elf tribes of Lorwyn, ruled by male and female High Perfects with the help of a council of Exquisites and other Perfects. The current monarchs, as well as all High Perfects in living memory, have been of the Gilt Leaf tribe. Non-elves colloquially refer to the High Perfects as the "king and queen."

Cervin: The steed of choice for elves, the cervin resembles a long-legged deer. Certain bloodlines and breeding stock are reserved for high-caste elves; anyone of a lower caste or tribe risks execution for so much as touching one of these rare and beautiful creatures.

Clique: Three or more faeries bonded for life, the members of a clique share an empathic connection that extends to telepathy during times of extreme stress or emotion.

Crannog: A merrow village built to offer access to both the river-dwelling inhabitants and landwalking visitors. Crannogs resemble small floating villages, but beneath the surface they extend all the way to the river bottom. The lower half of a crannog might contain a population of merrow many times larger than is apparent from above.

Cuffhound: Large canines employed by elf hunters as trackers and attack dogs. Cuffhounds can follow a scent for hundreds of miles.

Daen: Commander of an individual pack and the elf who receives directives from high command, decides on their implementation, and issues orders to the hunters under his or her command.

Deathcap: One of the hunting packs of the Gilt Leaf elves.

Dreamstuff: Tangible thoughts and dreams visible only to the fae.

Exquisite: The second-highest caste in the Blessed Nation; includes taercenns, courtiers, artists, and spiritual leaders.

Eyeblight: Any elf who, through disfigurement, physical deformity, or traitorous deed, is judged unworthy of the name "elf." Such creatures are considered to be beneath even boggarts, and their lives are worth nothing to their kin.

Fae: Formal name of Lorwyn's collective faerie population, used in the context of their shared traditions, magic, and identity.

Faultless: The lowest and most populous caste of the Blessed Nation. This status is conferred upon any elf of the minimum threshold of beauty and grace. Equivalent to basic acceptance within elf society.

Gilt Leaf: The strongest and greatest of the Blessed Nation's elf tribes, masters of the Gilt Leaf Wood.

Hemlock: The pack under the command of Daen Rhys, comprised of around a hundred hunters with Gryffid as the daen's second.

Hunter: Trained to bear arms and follow orders, hunters comprise the largest percentage of the Blessed Nation, but are rarely of any caste higher than Faultless. Roughly equivalent to the modern term "soldier," hunters include rangers, archers, and daens.

Immaculate: The third-highest caste in the Blessed Nation. Elves of this caste are seedguides, viziers, diplomats, and other important functionaries. Some daens are also granted this status as a reward for courage and service.

Lanes: Merrow term for the many interconnected rivers of Lorwyn. Also used as an oath, e.g., "By the Lanes!"

Moonglove: A flowering plant with blue-white blossoms that is source of a powerful poison highly prized by Lorwyn elves. Elves use moonglove aggressively in battle and it is the source of their famed and feared "deathtouch." Moonglove is also essential to many important elf rituals and magic.

Mornsong: A lesser tribe of the Blessed Nation, the Mornsong elves are known all over Lorwyn as the finest musicians and vocalists anywhere. The greatest Mornsong singer of the current generation is Peradala, a Perfect.

Nation: See **Blessed Nation**. Also sometimes used colloquially to describe an elf's own tribe as a matter of pride: e.g., the "Gilt Leaf nation."

Pack: A highly mobile and tightly organized squad of hunters commanded by a daen. Packs range in size from a dozen members to several hundred, and are given broad directives by tribal authorities or their taercenn. Most packs operate semi-autonomously with regular but infrequent dispatches to and from their superiors.

Perfect: The highest caste of the Blessed Nation. Perfects are the greatest of the elves, including the most brilliant artists and leaders. The High Perfects are the equivalent of elf monarchs and are chosen by their fellow Perfects to rule for life.

Pilgrim: A flamekin following "the path," a personal and spiritual journey of discovery that entails wandering the highways and byways of Lorwyn to make contact with the higher elemental powers. Most flamekin spend at least some part of their lives as a pilgrim, and pilgrims are often employed as trusted messengers and troubleshooters by other tribes.

Ranger: The lowest rank of elf hunter, armed with sword, dagger, other close-quarters weapons; they can be equipped with spears and pikes. Rangers are trained in woodland combat and tracking. The infantry of the Blessed Nation.

Scarblade: Elves trained in stealthy combat meant to maim and disfigure. The victim of a scarblade suffers a fate worse than death—they become eyeblights. Scarblades are usually employed by high-caste clients to deal with political enemies.

Seedguide: Elf druid-mages who serve as the Blessed Nation's ambassadors to the treefolk tribes.

Seedbody: Also "seedcone." All treefolk begin life as a seed-body, but not all seedbodies become fully animated and sentient. Most become trees, albeit relatively intelligent trees with the potential to become aware and mobile.

Shapewater: Practiced only by the merrow, shapewater magic allows a merrow to manipulate water into solid, sustainable, and mobile shapes. Though these shapes are usually static, the water from which they are formed continues to move and flow through and around the source from which it comes, usually a river. Merrow ferrymen employ shapewater to move landwalkers across and along the many rivers of Lorwyn.

Springjack: A large, horned lagomorph employed primarily by the kithkin as mounts, beasts of burden, and a food source.

Taer: An honorific (originally elvish, but also commonly used by most of Lorwyn's varied tribes) roughly equivalent to the English "sir," it literally means "great." Also a prefix added to ranks and titles to signify the superiority of same (e.g., "taercenn," literally "great master.")

Taercenn: The highest hunter rank, restricted to Exquisite elves alone. An active battlefield general, supreme commander and authority over multiple individual packs. The taercenn usually has some political influence with the High Perfects as well.

Thoughtweft: A form of kithkin magic that relies on shared beliefs, often reinforced with music or poetry. A kithkin can feel and join in strong thoughtweft at a great distance.

Tribe: Generally used to describe the different intelligent species of Lorwyn, e.g., the kithkin tribe or the flamekin tribe. Also used to describe different groups within a species, as in "Gilt Leaf tribe" or "Mornsong tribe."

Vinebred: Living creatures altered and controlled by their elf masters via the parasitic nettlevine. Vinebred are often considered terribly beautiful works of art. The hunting packs of the Blessed Nation sometimes employ them as shock troops, while Perfects often create truly magnificent vinebred to use as guards and servants.

Winnower: Elf hunters charged with and specially trained to hunt down and eliminate eyeblights.

a world of adventure awaits

The FORGOTTEN REALMS® world is the biggest, most detailed, most vibrant, and most beloved of the DUNGEONS & DRAGONS® campaign settings. Created by best-selling fantasy author Ed Greenwood the FORGOTTEN REALMS setting has grown in almost unimaginable ways since the first line was drawn on the now infamous "Ed's Original Maps."

Still the home of many a group of DUNGEONS & DRAGONS players, the FORGOTTEN REALMS world is brought to life in dozens of novels, including hugely popular best sellers by some of the fantasy genre's most exciting authors. FORGOTTEN REALMS novels are fast, furious, action-packed adventure stories in the grand tradition of sword and sorcery fantasy, but that doesn't mean they're all flash and no substance. There's always something to learn and explore in this richly textured world.

To find out more about the Realms go to www.wizards.com and follow the links from Books to FORGOTTEN REALMS. There you'll find a detailed reader's guide that will tell you where to start if you've never read a FORGOTTEN REALMS novel before, or where to go next if you're a long-time fan!

R.A. SALVATORE

The *New York Times* best-selling author and one of
fantasy's most powerful voices.

DRIZZT DO'URDEN

The renegade dark elf who's captured the imagination of a generation.

THE LEGEND OF DRIZZT

Updated editions of the FORGOTTEN REALMS® classics finally in their
proper chronological order.

BOOK I
HOMELAND
Now available in paperback!

BOOK II
EXILE
Now available in paperback!

BOOK III
SOJOURN
Now available in paperback!

BOOK IV
THE CRYSTAL SHARD
Now available in paperback!

BOOK V
STREAMS OF SILVER
Now available in paperback!

BOOK VI
THE HALFLING'S GEM
Coming in paperback, August 2007

BOOK VII
THE LEGACY
Coming in paperback, April 2008

BOOK VIII
STARLESS NIGHT
Now available in deluxe
hardcover edition!

BOOK IX
SIEGE OF DARKNESS
Now available in deluxe
hardcover edition!

BOOK X
PASSAGE TO DAWN
Now available in deluxe
hardcover edition!

BOOK XI
THE SILENT BLADE
Now available in deluxe
hardcover edition!

BOOK XII
THE SPINE OF THE WORLD
Deluxe hardcover, December 2007

BOOK XIII
SEA OF SWORDS
Deluxe hardcover, March 2008

WELCOME TO THE

WORLD

Created by Keith Baker and developed by Bill Slavicsek and James Wyatt, EBERRON® is the latest setting designed for the DUNGEONS & DRAGONS® Roleplaying game, novels, comic books, and electronic games.

ANCIENT, WIDESPREAD MAGIC

Magic pervades the EBERRON world. Artificers create wonders of engineering and architecture. Wizards and sorcerers use their spells in war and peace. Magic also leaves its mark—the coveted dragonmark—on members of a gifted aristocracy. Some use their gifts to rule wisely and well, but too many rule with ruthless greed, seeking only to expand their own dominance.

INTRIGUE AND MYSTERY

A land ravaged by generations of war. Enemy nations that fought each other to a standstill over countless, bloody battlefields now turn to subtler methods of conflict. While nations scheme and merchants bicker, priceless secrets from the past lie buried and lost in the devastation, waiting to be tracked down by intrepid scholars and rediscovered by audacious adventurers.

SWASHBUCKLING ADVENTURE

The EBERRON setting is no place for the timid. Courage, strength, and quick thinking are needed to survive and prosper in this land of peril and high adventure.